THE BROTHERS
Cabal

Also by Jonathan L. Howard

THE BROTHERS

Cabal

JONATHAN L. HOWARD

WITHDRAWN

Thomas Dunne Books
St. Martin's Press
New York

THOMAS DUNNE BOOKS.
An imprint of St. Martin's Press.

THE BROTHERS CABAL. Copyright © 2014 by Jonathan L. Howard. All rights reserved. Printed in the United States of America. For information, address St. Martin's Press, 175 Fifth Avenue, New York, N.Y. 10010.

www.thomasdunnebooks.com
www.stmartins.com

Illustrations by Linda "Snugbat" Smith

The Library of Congress Cataloging-in-Publication Data is available upon request.

ISBN 978-1-250-03754-1 (hardcover)
ISBN 978-1-250-03753-4 (e-book)

St. Martin's Press books may be purchased for educational, business, or promotional use. For information on bulk purchases, please contact Macmillan Corporate and Premium Sales Department at 1-800-221-7945, extension 5442, or write specialmarkets@macmillan.com.

First Edition: October 2014

10 9 8 7 6 5 4 3 2 1

For my brother, Neil, whom I have never sealed in a tomb in
an abandoned cemetery, not even once

Contents

CONTENTS

What strange creatures brothers are!
—Jane Austen, *Mansfield Park*

THE BROTHERS
Cabal

Prologue

IN WHICH WE ARE REINTRODUCED TO A PAIR
OF INDIVIDUALS WITH UNCONVENTIONAL
INTERPRETATIONS OF THE TERM 'DEAD'

Now, let us consider the life of Johannes Cabal, if briefly. He is closing on his thirtieth year and is ageing better than most, although this is a product of a lifestyle where sunlight is shunned rather than the assiduous use of moisturiser. He stands a little over six feet tall. He is blond, blue eyed, and, perforce, pale. These are not unusual characteristics; those are coming.

He has killed himself twice, been resurrected once (the second death was a practical joke of sorts), visited Hell twice, penetrated the Wall of Sleep into the Dreamlands* in corporeal form once—went

---

* For those unfamiliar with the Dreamlands, shame on you. My editor, however, informs me that shame is all very well, but uninformative, and might I actually explain what the Dreamlands are? They are, then, a realised world influenced but not necessarily created by dreams. They are ancient, inhabited by gods and their divine leavings, as well as those who travel there in their dreams or, rarely, in their own bodies. It is also home to zebras. The

as a human, came back as a monster, but the monstrousness has now left him, albeit ill unto death. He has time-travelled in a rambling and undisciplined fashion, but he was a monster at the time, and travelling time was of little import to him except as a means to an end, and as a way to upset the Vatican, which was a perk.

Ill unto death, he returned to his strange little isolated house to recuperate, yet could not enter since his front garden was conspiring to kill and eat him. He saw then that his was to be an ignominious death, to slowly shuffle off the mortal coil while propped against the gatepost of his home, mere yards from salvation. It did not surprise him—it is the lot of a necromancer to die, in all likelihood, an ignominious death, and he could only sigh a small sigh of relief that it didn't involve zombies, because that would have been tiresome. So, necromancer that he was, one of some little infamy yet, he settled down to rattle out his last breath in as much comfort as he could.

There he might have expired, and his bones lay to the inexpressible frustration of the criminally insane and eternally hungry fairies that were contained within his dangerous garden. Yet salvation came, and it came in the form of a taciturn figure who effortlessly lifted Cabal and walked up the garden path with the comatose necromancer carelessly slung over one shoulder. At this new presence, the starving unseelie of the garden scattered in fear, because that which is supernatural and nasty knows supernatural and nastier when it sees it.

The front door was a hefty artefact of English oak and triple locked with a London bar device to resist kicking and battering attacks. The figure kicked it clean out of its frame, and carried Cabal within.

---

curious reader is directed to *The Dream-Quest of Unknown Kadath* by H. P. Lovecraft, or the previous novel in the saga of Cabal, *Johannes Cabal: The Fear Institute*. If the reader only has the time or inclination to read one of these, the author respectfully suggests the latter, both because it appertains directly to the current text, and also because Lovecraft is long dead and doesn't need the royalties.

The synthesis of an antidote for Cabal's overly energetic rehumanisation, slowing it to a rate his constitution could withstand, was managed within an hour or so, and he was saved. The recovery of his health, however, would not be so swift. For a week he wavered in and out of consciousness, rarely awake but for brief periods in the day during which he saw no one else. He was tended to as he slept during the hours of darkness, for his benefactor would not countenance the sun and, again, this was for reasons that had nothing to do with making savings in moisturiser. Cabal was fed and cleaned and he was barely aware of it, and the memory left him quickly with a glance into deep, inhuman eyes and a whisper. 'Not yet, Johannes. When you are stronger.'

As Cabal's strength returned, he grew closer to the waking world and at some deep level he was glad of that, for the dust of the Dreamlands was still on his feet, and there were things he was happy to leave there. On the other hand, his awareness of his surroundings was increasing and, while his perception that he was back in his own home and not, say, swinging from a gibbet was soothing, the nagging gap in his memory between 'dying by the gatepost' and 'comfy under an eiderdown' was beginning to trouble him.

Finally the evening came when he fought his eyes open and looked upon the man who had saved his life, and the man judged he would not take away the memory and let Johannes Cabal sleep again, for time was passing, and it might be that another evening's sleep would lead to the death of the world. The man was not keen for that to happen.

Cabal looked at the man, and he was astonished, and yet so profoundly relieved that when he spoke, the first word was almost a sob. 'You,' he said, his voice thin and weak from illness and disuse. 'It's you.

'But . . . you're dead . . .'

His brother, Horst Cabal, sat upon the edge of the bed and looked at him. He was a man who had lived, died briefly, become undead, become very dead indeed, and yet now seemed to be undead again.

'Hmmm,' he agreed a mite awkwardly, as if being found alive (of sorts) when he was supposed to be profoundly dead was morally equivalent to using the wrong spoon at dinner.

The awkwardness extended into an awkward pause. 'Would you . . .' Horst looked off for a moment, finding something fascinating about the picture rail. He looked back at Cabal. 'Would you like some soup, Johannes?'

The soup—it was chicken—was good, though that was not the unusual thing about it. That it had been prepared by a man who was dead twice over was more notable. As Johannes Cabal—an invalid of some little infamy—sat upright in his bed and slowly sipped the soup, he considered that life was an unpredictable sort of thing. If past events had been different by one single factor, he would probably be a solicitor by this time, he would likely be married, his father would still be alive, his mother would not have disowned him, and his brother would not have died twice and now be making him soup. It was hard to characterise his feelings as to how such things could come to pass; he had to make do with, 'It's a funny old world.'

The wind moaned around the eaves of Cabal's house, a nondescript three-storey structure common in the cantons of the *petit bourgeois* found in most English towns, rendered descript by standing in the splendid isolation of a remote hillside. It had clearly not been built there, but the mechanism by which it had somehow been transplanted complete and without damage remained a mystery to man and civic planner alike. Behind it sat a small back garden with an herbaceous border that needed attention, and a woodshed from which very occasionally movement could be heard. Before it was the small tangled rose garden within which tiny creatures of fey descent, malign intent, and ill manners hid and watched. The garden and the path, which led from one of those waist-high gates intended to mark off a property line rather than represent any serious barrier to the front door of the house, was bordered by a low stone wall that was no more of an impedance than the gate. In truth, there was more to the apparently inconsequential wall and gate than met the eye, a state of affairs that extended to much of the house and its contents.

Cabal regarded the black panes of the window, beyond which the small valley his house overlooked lay in darkness, and he listened to the wind blow. When he felt a light breeze disturb the hairs on his arm, however, he knew it was nothing to do with the weather.

'I am not easily astonished, Horst,' he said, continuing to look at the dark glass. 'But in this you have succeeded.' He turned his head to regard his brother. Horst was standing by the door in his shirtsleeves, looking very much at home. Then again, this *had* once been his home. Cabal noted that the door was closed. 'I didn't even hear the door open and shut. Your abilities have progressed since last we met.'

'Perhaps I didn't open the door, Johannes,' said his brother. Horst still looked like a man in his early twenties even though he was older than Cabal, at least according to the calendar. Being dead suited him very well. He was still abominably virile, and thoughtlessly handsome in the same way that had always made Cabal hate the sight of him. Light brown hair, only a few shades away from blond, and blue eyed, he would look good in a sack. Still, sibling rivalry was a thing for one's youth, and should be put away when one is in a serious profession such as necromancy and one's brother is one of the blood-drinking undead. 'Perhaps I turned into a cloud of vapour and came through the keyhole.'

'And perhaps you transformed yourself into a flood of eyewash and burbled beneath it. Don't patronise me. I have some knowledge of your kind.'

Once, Horst might have risen to a comment like 'your kind'. Now, however, he sat on the side of Cabal's bed and murmured, 'The time has come, the Walrus said.'

Cabal regarded his soup. It was a phrase from their childhood; whenever things got out of hand and the air needed clearing, the moment would be presaged by that little bit of Carroll.

'True enough. There is a great deal to be said. I doubt shoes and ships and sealing wax will be the half of it.' He took the tray from his lap and was just manoeuvring awkwardly to put it on the bedside cabinet when Horst appeared by him. There was no intermediate walking around the bed; he simply appeared with no more fuss than another of those light breezes to mark the transition. He took the tray and walked in a more conventional manner to the sideboard.

'Would you be so kind as to slam that down with enough vigour to make a sharp sound?' called Cabal after him. 'I was intending to do it myself to indicate my state of mind before you turned all Florence Nightingale.'

Horst paused, then put the tray down sharply enough to make the spoon dance in the bowl.

'Thank you,' said Cabal. 'Now. How the hell is it that you are not dead? Properly dead? I saw you die, and you were little more than smoke and ashes by the time the sun had finished with you. Believe me, I know dead, and I don't think I have ever seen anyone quite as thoroughly dead as you.'

His voice had risen as the little colour his recuperation had brought to him had drained from his face.

'It's lovely to see you again, too, Johannes.' Horst walked around the bed to return to his sitting place. 'I can tell you're delighted.'

'I shall doubtless be delighted at some near future date. For the moment, however, I am consumed with a desire to know how it is that my brother, who was dead, and then undead, and then dead again, now manages to once more be merely undead.'

Horst shrugged. 'Perhaps it's a cyclic thing.' It was calculated to irritate, calculated with the finesse that only brothers can attain, and it succeeded like pepper under an eyelid.

'If I had my strength . . . !' began Cabal, but Horst interrupted him with, 'Even if you did, I could still pick you up with one hand and put you back to bed.' He waited until Cabal's wrath subsided to an aggrieved fuming before saying, 'It's a long story, and it will take one night to tell. Then I will sleep and, if you have any sense, you will sleep, too.'

Even Cabal's short temper was a poor match for his curiosity.

'What do you mean?' The curiosity deepened into suspicion. 'Why exactly *are* you here, Horst?'

For once, Horst seemed awkward and unsure how to proceed. Finally, a forced smile appeared on his face, and he slapped his knees and stood to look around the room. 'It's funny being back in the old house again. After all this time. There's still a gap in the terrace to this day, you know. I'm not sure anyone feels confident enough to build there again in case whatever they build vanishes, too. It took a while to find you. Some detective work. I had to ask around. I've heard some interesting things about you, Johannes. But that all took time.' The smile flickered out. 'There's not much time left.'

'You need me for something, that much is evident. It cannot be something minor, as I imagine there are devils in the pit that you would rather deal with than come running to me.'

'Hardly *running* . . .'

'Why me? As extraordinary as I am, it is a big world and there must be alternatives. If it wasn't for me, you wouldn't have died once, never mind twice. You wouldn't have been reborn once, never mind . . . I must admit, the second resurrection confuses me.'

'For what it's worth, I don't hold you responsible for the second time.'

'You're not supposed to come back even once, as a general principle.'

'Nobody was more surprised than I. At least nobody was until your very gratifying reaction when you finally recovered consciousness.'

'I was not . . . !' He thought back and subsided. 'Actually, yes, I was. There is no other way of characterising it. I was surprised. Very surprised.'

'You were gobsmacked. Banjaxed. And any number of similar terms that you obviously don't know.' He laughed drily. 'As for why you—because I know you, and you're good at what you do.'

'You're assuming a lot.'

'You'll want to help once you understand the circumstances of my return and what followed it. Besides, as I say, I heard things about you when I was looking for this place.' Horst closed his eyes for a moment, steeling himself. 'The second time I died . . . I gave up, Johannes. I'd had enough of you. Enough of everything, really. I belonged dead. You were all set to become a bigger monster than I could stand to see. Perhaps . . .' He sighed, not looking at Cabal. 'Perhaps I was a coward. I just couldn't bear to watch. Still, even as dark a cloud as the *Ministerium* had a silver lining.' He raised a finger to hush Cabal. 'You'll hear all about that presently. The important thing is that they undid my mistake.'

'Your mistake?'

'I should have waited. I should have watched. You have done good, Johannes. As a side effect, I know, but there's something in you that wasn't there before. I can only guess that it is your soul.'

There was a silence, marked only by the heavy ticking of the old grandfather clock in the hall below. Then Johannes Cabal said, 'I see. May I vomit now?'

'Be my guest.'

'No, really. I think I drank my soup too quickly.'

As Horst sped to fetch a basin with an alacrity that would make Hermes blink, it would be as well to take a moment before the major part of the tale is set forth. When Cabal was feeling less nauseated, his brother, Horst, recounted to him the tale of his second resurrection, why it occurred, and what happened subsequently. This was all told, naturally, in the first person. Horst, however, did not know every element of the story or the inner worlds of every protagonist. The reader, therefore, is offered the courtesy of Horst's story rendered into the third person, with extra details to which he was not privy. This courtesy comes at no extra charge, but purely from the wholesome glow of the author's good nature.

JLH

Chapter 1

IN WHICH THE DEAD ARE RAISED, BLOOD IS DRUNK,
AND EAVES ARE DROPPED

The party travelled through the flatlands, guided by an unhelpful map. They were a sombre and sober group, ten men and three women, who wore hiking clothes and impressively stacked back-packs. An astute observer would have noted that their clothes and gear were all new, and that several showed signs of blisters due to their boots not being properly worn in, and that none looked happy in a woollen hat. There were no observers, however, for the flatlands are unutterably tedious and usually lacking in things worth the observing.

Their leader paused and consulted the map again. This took the form of a large square of predominantly blank paper upon which the legend and gridlines had consumed far more ink in the printing than any physical features. There were a few paths—even to call them 'lanes' would be an aggrandisement—a few ditches with pretensions towards being streams, and one long earthwork that travelled into the centre of the map and then petered out, as so many things in the flatlands tended to. Drystone walls, interest, lives . . . all fading away.

At least the earthwork had the decency to stick up: a long railway bed for a spur line to nowhere, abandoned decades before. They could see it was heavily overgrown on the steep sides of the artificial ridge, but there were also signs that, relatively recently, much of the heavier undergrowth had been cut back or felled. They clambered up onto its top, past the unhealthy bushes and saplings that grew there, and found themselves on the rail bed itself, still bearing—slightly surprisingly—sleepers and tracks. Even more surprisingly, there was a train there, hidden behind the trees and shrubs.

This discovery certainly surprised the hiking party, and even overawed them. The locomotive, although matte with rust the shade of dried blood, still exuded an air of exultant mechanical malevolence, as if somebody had crammed a black dragon into a giant jelly mould in the form of a steam locomotive and, with the wave of a wand, transformed the creature into the machine. But no; a wand would be insufficient. A magic staff perhaps. Or an enchanted caber. In any event, the iron dragon now slumbered in the sleep of years. Behind it was a train of assorted carriages, flat-beds, and freight cars, all once painted in black with red detailing, the exquisite work now peeling and forlorn. Just readable on the side of one of the cars was the legend *The World Renowned Cabal Bros. Carnival.*

The leader of the group looked at the words for a long moment, and then smirked a very superior smirk of the type that starts at the corner of the mouth and finishes with trouble.

'This is the place,' he said. 'Start the search.'

The search went uncommented upon by passersby because there were no passersby. The flatlands went nowhere in either geographical or metaphorical terms, and no one went into them without the explicit intent to come out again, quickly. It was, in theory, an ideal place for footpads to operate, but the lack of potential victims had always kept its criminal population low, dwindling to none in relatively recent times. So there was nobody to see as twelve hikers, chivvied on by the thirteenth, dutifully dumped their packs, split the area into a search grid, produced strangely wrought weights on lengths of cord from identical pouches each had in their duffel coat pockets, and proceeded to methodically dowse the squares of the grid one by one. As an activity, it combined the mundane with the strange with the clandestine, and thereby rendered itself sinister. This was fair, for their intentions were sinister.

Nor was their apparent efficiency a chimera. Within ten minutes one of the hikers was excitingly calling to their leader. He came over, as did the others, to see the hiker's plumb weight swinging in a manner harsh and angular, showing a brutalist disregard for physics that would have made Galileo enter the priesthood. They watched it twitch in silence, watched it marking out a pentacle in the air.

'Here?' whispered the hiker, aquiver with excitement.

'Here,' said their leader with magisterial certainty.

Again, their activities were efficient yet strange. Quickly they doffed duffel coats and woolly hats and map cases. Quickly they donned robes and then struggled to strip naked beneath them like a charabanc party changing at the beach of a Whitsun weekend. When the undignified hopping and kicking off of trousers was complete, they hastened to create a circle of blue powder about the spot they had detected, and then they gathered around it as the dying sun sank beneath the horizon. It wasn't a happy circle—they were now all barefooted and the area was scattered with chippings from the rail bed—but it was a disciplined one, and they awaited the words of their leader.

When they came, they were incomprehensible.

'*Vateth He'em!*' he cried, excellent projection betraying a thwarted career in the theatre. '*Oomaloth T'y'araskile!*' And so he continued, booming forth an apparently endless litany of dreadful names and imprecations from memory, all bedewed with apostrophes. The hikers-turned-cultists chanted the occasional response, a 'Gilg'ya!' here and a 'Ukriles!' there, and kept their eyes turned to the ground, for the grey skies were darkening and a wind was rising. Something was coming, and none dared to see its arrival.

Around them, the air swirled, centring upon the blue circle. The powder was blown, yet remained in the place, stray motes caught and carried back into it. The breeze was not dispersing the circle; it was concentrating it.

The landscape flickered under silent lightning, and those present scented a change in the air, a mixture of rage and blood that dizzied the mind and turned the stomach. Something wrathful was coming, a creature of death, and their fear was mixed with triumph, for all this was planned. The wind turned and dust was drawn in from their surroundings, drawn in from across the circle to grow in the middle, skittering particles the colour of bone, dancing from their hiding places between stones and from the soil itself. Nearby, a tattered and faded jacket fluttered where it lay at the base of the earthwork.

Then, with a roar that they felt rather than heard, the circle was filled, and they all fell silent in the awful presence, an aching tintinnabulation of the soul sounding a single peal within their hearts that turned their knees weak with dread as it faded.

'Master,' said the leader of the cultists. It came out weakly, his mouth and throat dry. He swallowed and tried again, stumbling over his carefully prepared words. 'Master, you bless us with your baleful . . . personage. We fall in obeisance before you.'

It took a moment before they collectively realised that they'd forgotten to fall, and there were a few seconds of hasty kneeling and sharp intakes of breath as bare knees found jagged gravel.

The leader was belatedly realising that he could have organised the circle a little better before now and he was reduced to hissing urgently, 'The sacrifices! The sacrifices!' until the three women in the group were gathered before the monster in the circle.

'Master,' said the leader, eager to recover face, 'Lord of the Dead.

Please accept these sacrifices we humbly offer you, that you may feed and gain strength after your long and dreamless sleep.' He lowered his head and hoped that three would be enough. Even among their fanatical ranks, it had proved difficult to find three who would willingly sacrifice themselves for the greater good.

Then the Lord of the Dead spoke.

And he said, 'I won't say I'm not a bit peckish. Famished, in fact. But not nearly as much as I'm surprised. And naked. I don't suppose anyone thought to bring along a spare pair of trousers, did they? There are ladies present, and I was raised to believe that being naked in front of strange ladies is something reserved for special occasions.'

They had not, in fact, remembered to bring along any clothes for the Lord of the Dead, indicating another failure in planning that would later result in some sharply worded memos. One of the cultists was, however, about the same size as the Lord of the Dead, and was pleased to give him a change of clothes from his pack. The Lord of the Dead thanked him and promised that he would give them back, freshly laundered, as soon as he was able. The cultist said it was fine, really. The Lord of the Dead insisted, and also said that everybody should stop calling him 'Master' and the 'Lord of the Dead', and just call him 'Horst' instead, because that was his name.

'My Lord Horst,' said the leader, who was slightly scandalised that any puissant supernatural force of darkness and destruction should want to be on first-name terms so early in their acquaintance, 'you *must* feed.'

It was true; Horst did not look well after his period as dust. His eyes were sunken deep within their sockets and bone showed beneath the parchment of his skin. He looked like a corpse in the mid-stages of mummification, and his borrowed trousers would not stay up without assistance.

The three women who knelt at his bony feet were quickly running through personal variants of 'It is a far, far better thing that I do, than I have ever done', and drew back their cowls and exposed their jugulars to him.

'No,' said Horst, shaking his head slowly, the best speed his desiccated neck could manage. 'No, no, no. That's not enough.'

'Not . . . enough?' The leader looked around the circle of his acolytes and saw faces as worried as his own. 'How many will you require?'

'Well, if I just feed from these three . . . Hello, ladies . . . I'll kill them, and that's not very polite. If I take a little from all of you, nobody has to die. I'm sure everybody would be happier with that, don't you think?'

The leader was slightly baffled. 'But, master . . .'

'Horst.'

'My Lord Horst, you are the embodiment of Death. You live without breath or vital spark in the umbral shadows, you are the wolf that preys upon we mortal cattle, you are . . .' The leader's voice was no longer very magisterial, just petty and wheedling. 'Well, you're a *vampire*, damn it. We brought these three here specially.'

'I'm sure their mothers . . . Hello, ladies . . . didn't raise them to be all-you-can-eat buffets. As for me, I've beaten up a few people in my time, but I've never killed anyone. Never felt the need to. I'm not saying I'm incapable of it, but it's not something I've ever really aspired to, yes?'

'But you're the Lord of the Dead!'

'No,' said the monster in the loose clothes. 'I'm Horst Cabal, and I don't murder for the sake of a snack. Now, as you pointed out, I need to feed. I shall only take what each of you can spare.'

The leader was feeling peevish that the sacrifice that he had so selflessly ordered others to make was being snubbed. 'We dragged those three all the way out here for nothing,' he muttered furiously under his breath. Unhappily for him, inhumanly sharp senses are common amongst vampiric folk.

'I think,' said Horst, regarding the leader with a wolfish expression, 'we'll start with you, shall we? Leading from the front, and all that.'

'Me?' The leader was certainly intending to protest in the

strongest terms, but then he made the mistake of looking at Horst's eyes and whatever he had been intending was lost in a sudden simplification of his mind's working.

Horst flicked back the leader's cowl with an offhand gesture, took hold of his hair, and pulled his head back to expose his throat. 'Yes. You.' Horst's lips parted and unusually long canine teeth showed as he leaned in. He paused and said to the silent onlookers, 'The rest of you, form an orderly queue.'

About halfway through the ad hoc transfusion session, Horst noticed that those that had already donated were clearly envied by those that hadn't, and those that hadn't were being patronised by those that had. He wondered vaguely if, in the time he had been away, vampirism had become fashionable. How long *had* he been away, exactly?

He was feeling sated before he had finished with the ninth. Not completely revivified, he knew, but he was conscious of taking too much too quickly. He had been careful the first time he had drunk blood, and that had proved wise. It would prove equally wise to stop now, but then he looked at the faces of Victims 10–13 and felt he couldn't let them down. Sighing inwardly, he finished with 9 and wearily gestured over 10. It would just be a nip, but at least duty would be honoured. His situation was not improved by 13, the third of the women, who insisted on making orgasmic noises at the first graze of his fangs. Under the circumstances, it seemed ungentlemanly to be perfunctory, and so he soldiered on until she'd run out of expressions of passion. He straightened up, feeling replete, reborn, and generally resanguinated, but also irked that performance anxiety should pursue a fellow beyond the grave.

'So,' he said as the cultists—practically, if unromantically—passed around a box of sticking plasters, 'now what?'

'We must take you to the castle with all dispatch, my lord,' said the leader, who it transpired was called Encausse.

'The castle. Of course. Should have known there would be a castle involved. Which particular castle would that be?'

Encausse looked uncomfortable, and Horst guessed he was wrestling between a conspirator's natural desire for secrecy and a conspirator's equally natural desire to tell everyone how brilliant the conspiracy is. 'I am not permitted to say, my lord.'

Horst considered softening his mind a little until the concept of 'permission' became more malleable, but reined in the impulse. After all, that was the sort of thing real monsters did, and Horst didn't care for it.

'Well, is it far?'

'Yes, my lord. It will take several days to transport you there. I am sorry.'

'For what?'

'The inconvenience.'

Horst looked down at his newly reconstituted hands, and rubbed them in the manner of one getting down to brass tacks. 'The inconvenience . . . Well, don't be too hard on yourself. You've resurrected me, which was decent of you. We'll just consider ourselves even between that and the inconvenience.'

Horst was finding all manner of things not to like about the situation, and nestling high upon the parapets of his misgivings was why such a band of well-equipped and well-informed eccentrics had gone to all this trouble in the first place. For the first time he felt a small pang in his slowly beating heart. He hoped Johannes was still alive somewhere and he wished he could be here. All this occult malarkey was much more his brother's meat and drink. Johannes would have identified the group concerned, insulted everyone, and probably settled into a spirited gunfight by this juncture. The pang troubled Horst again; to his profound surprise, he was missing his brother.

He looked at Encausse and saw the man was nervous. Horst guessed he'd got it into his head that vampires kill people willy-nilly for every little disappointment. Perhaps they usually did. How would he know? Nobody had ever given him an induction lecture or even a pamphlet on the subject. He spoke to defuse the tension as much as anything. 'And how do you intend to get me to this castle? I think my passport has probably run out by now and, anyway, wouldn't being dead invalidate it?'

Encausse waved away the point, his relief at not being summarily murdered clear. 'All is in preparation, my lord. The means to transport you are at hand.'

Horst looked around. They didn't seem to be *that* at hand. He looked quizzically back at Encausse, who smiled awkwardly. 'Not exactly here, that is. But there is a small port a mile or two away to the west. There, the means to transport you *are* at hand.'

At least, thought Horst, the man hadn't added '. . . honest' at the end of the sentence, and thereby undermined all credibility.

As it turned out, however, planning was clearly a strong suit with whatever organisation had decided to, for reasons that currently remained obscure, locate the place of Horst's second death by means that remained obscure, resurrect him by means that also remained obscure, and then blithely offer him three lives. Three *volunteered* lives at that. As the lid of his beautifully appointed coffin closed upon him, Horst wondered if he was doing the right thing going along with them. Escaping his honour guard would have been simple, yet it would have left him with no answers, and he had a feeling that answers might be important, and not only to him.

They had a castle, for heaven's sake. A *castle*. From his conversations with Johannes, Horst had received the impression that most occult groups might stretch to hiring the local Scouts' hut monthly for their meetings under the pretence of being philatelists or something. A castle made things seem very well funded. Also, Encausse had dropped enough hints to confirm to Horst's satisfaction that the thirteen cultists were by no means the entire strength of this particular organisation. Between all this and their single-minded desire to avail themselves of a 'Lord of the Dead', he was sure their aims were not at all philanthropic and that they deserved whatever scrutiny he might bring to bear upon them. Being a vampire didn't mean he couldn't be socially responsible. If things turned unfriendly, he was confident he could light out of the proceedings before the unfriendliness manifested in the form of a stake through the heart, he would find some way to report the affair to the forces of law and order, and his curiosity and conscience would be assuaged.

This was his plan, simple to the point of barely being a plan at all. Still, as he reassured himself, it wasn't as if he was busy doing something else.

His coffin was loaded aboard a train at the head of the flatland's spur line; the track there not having been certified as safe for some time, the points at the junction were locked against it. They travelled through the night in a secure baggage van, and Horst was able to stretch his legs in the company of Encausse and some of his entourage. The thirteenth donor sat on some mail bags and regarded Horst silently the whole night, biting her lip now and then. Horst returned wan smiles and felt more awkward about the situation than a Lord of the Dead probably ought. He was relieved when dawn approached and he was able to return politely to his coffin with expressions of regret that he in no way felt.

Encausse had told him that they were heading to the port before embarkation for the rest of the trip. Horst had naturally assumed he would awaken at the next dusk aboard a ship. Ideally not one called the *Demeter*; it never pays to tempt fate. He was therefore, astonished, delighted, and yet slightly disturbed to find himself aboard an aeroship, the *Catullus*, a relatively small but well-appointed pleasure yacht apparently donated or lent to the cult by one of its supporters. Horst was astonished because he had naturally understood the port they were making for to be a coastal one, not an aeroport, delighted because he had never been aboard such a vessel despite years of yearning, and disturbed because, once again, his benefactors seemed to have very deep pockets indeed.

Benefactors. No, that was looking very unlikely in itself. Presumably the bill for all this largesse would be presented on arrival at the castle.

The journey was eastwards; that much at least was apparent, and they had crossed the Channel onto the Continent as he slept the first day. Encausse was still evasive about details, and—for the moment at least—Horst was still reluctant to use methods of persuasion more supernatural than gentle nagging. For the moment at least.

Only Encausse's two lieutenants had joined them aboard, leaving Horst's admirer behind. This relieved him greatly. It would only have been a matter of time before he would have awoken one evening to find her fluttering around his stateroom in a peignoir, draping herself over the furniture here and there like a particularly available moth, and his life was complicated enough as it was.

The crew was small, and taciturn to a man. They wore black uniforms without any insignia at all, only the design of the clothes serving to designate rank and role. Horst, who had an eye for such things, noted the paramilitary styling of the uniforms and the distinctly Teutonic aesthetic informing them, and wondered if he was bound for the Germanys. He imagined the coincidence if they were to set down in Hesse, his homeland. He could drop in on his mother. And probably put her in her grave with shock. No, perhaps that wasn't the best idea. His former life was gone, twice over. *That* Horst Cabal only lived on in memoriam and legal declarations of death in absence of a body.

So he sat silently in the yacht's small but extravagantly appointed salon, watched the clouds go by, and accepted that he wasn't really Horst Cabal at all, but just an echo of a slamming crypt door. He was aware of being observed at such times by Encausse and his people, and observed approvingly. The more laconic he became, it seemed, the more seriously he was taken. Certainly his brown studies were far more in keeping with the image of a saturnine Lord of the Dead, so he maintained them even when his spirits rose.

Instead of engaging his keepers in conversation, he amused himself by practising the abilities that had replaced such trivial things as being able to walk in direct sunlight without messily combusting. He did not care to practice the placing of the human will into neutral—it was too addictive a sensation—but he had always taken some pleasure in the remarkable bouts of speed of which he was now capable. They were short, a matter of seconds, but for those few seconds he could travel with such speed as to become momentarily invisible. This he tried and was pleased to discover he still did easily. Indeed, there was a distinct impression of improvement, which perplexed him. Where before he had found it necessary to apply himself carefully to navigating around obstacles, now it seemed so instinctive as to be reflexive. He hypothesised two possible reasons. Firstly, in his first bout of being vampirically inclined, he had been nervous about taking too much from any single donor in case he seriously weakened or, heavens forfend, killed them. His current experience, he realised, was the first time he had ever been truly replete. It made him feel powerful. It made him feel very good indeed.

The other theory was that, in conversation with his brother, Johannes had made reference to a steady increase of puissance throughout a vampire's existence. Did that existence include periods as dust? Perhaps so. In any event, he found it child's play to be out of his chair and into the corridor behind the sidekick of Encausse who had been surreptitiously watching him.

Horst saw the man start, heard him gasp, and smelled the adrenaline suddenly flush his system. The man reflexively turned to scan the corridor behind him and looked straight at Horst. Another little gift of the vampiric unlife was that of psychic invisibility. Horst pushed himself out of the man's perception and the man accepted him as something of no interest. Indeed, with an irritated grunt, the man leaned to one side, looking past Horst as he looked for Horst. 'Where the hell has that bastard leech gone?' he muttered, proving that eavesdroppers seldom hear well of themselves.

As the man scurried into the salon to search behind the bar, under chairs, and beneath the cushions, Horst strolled forward at a more human speed, but still repressing his presence.

He heard voices and found them coming from the ventral observation room, a small chamber protruding slightly from the yacht's belly, glass walled and floored but for a solid section on which were arranged a cluster of armchairs. The intention presumably was for the owner and his or her guests to gather here to look down on the world below, literally and figuratively. At night, however, the view was unengaging even to Horst's sharp eyes. Occasionally the lights of a town might go by below, but otherwise the nocturnal landscape was disappointing.

Encausse and his other lieutenant were sitting there and watching the darkness, a half-empty bottle and a pair of wine glasses sitting on the table between them. '. . . set up for a fall,' Encausse was saying. 'I've got a couple of people who'd love to see me look a fool.'

'Von Ziegler,' offered the lieutenant, a surly man called Donner.

'Von Ziegler for one, arse licker that he is. I can't see how they can blame me, though. The mission's a success. We have the vampire, alive and . . . Well, you know what I mean. Up and around. Not what I was expecting, though.'

'Not what any of us were expecting.'

'Did you hear what he said? He's never killed anyone. What kind of vampire's never killed anyone? I don't understand why he was chosen. There *must* be others, mustn't there? Even if they're dust, we can still raise them. Vlad Ţepeş. Lord Varney. And we end up getting Count Form-an-Orderly-Queue.'

He touched the side of his neck and winced at the memory. 'Ours may not be to reason why, but I cannot help but wonder if the *Ministerium* hasn't made a mistake.'

Horst raised an eyebrow. The *Ministerium*? Interesting. Very interesting. He had no idea what it meant, but that didn't stop it being interesting.

'I thought the order didn't come from them?' said Donner.

'What?' Encausse was taken aback. 'Of course the order came from them.'

'Well, maybe *via* them,' conceded Donner. 'I thought Her Majesty insisted.'

There was a definite sneer in Donner's voice, and Horst wasn't sure if the honorific was meant sarcastically or not. But then Encausse replied, 'The queen wanted him?' He sank back in his chair and took a draft of wine that was an indecent use of a good vintage. 'I didn't know. I didn't know. I just thought . . . We fulfilled our orders to the letter. It's not our fault the "Lord of the Dead" is a namby-pamby, is it?'

Donner shook his head. 'We did as we were told. She was the one who did the choosing. She picked him, he's her problem.'

Encausse seemed reassured by this line of reasoning. 'Yes, true enough. We didn't choose him. I'd have gone for a proper *nosferatu* if it had been left to me, not that bloody fop.' Horst raised both eyebrows; spying was turning out to be quite hurtful to one's feelings. 'But what the queen wants, she gets, and she can't blame anyone else if that's a bad choice.' A pause, and he added a little shakily, 'Can she?' He took another gulp of wine.

'Wouldn't worry about it. She's hardly there most of the time. By the time she turns up again, his nibs will be the *Ministerium*'s problem. How he got from where he was to where he is won't matter anymore.'

Further reassuring noises from Donner were interrupted by the arrival of the other lieutenant, Bolam. 'He's gone! He was in the salon and he just vanished! Poof! I was looking right at him! I can't find him anywhere!'

The ensuing search was short and confusing for Bolam, as the missing Horst was found to be exactly where he was supposed to be, in the salon, watching the darkness through the aft windows.

'Is there a problem, gentlemen?' he asked as the three men burst through the door.

As dawn approached, he was escorted to his coffin perhaps more assiduously and with far more narrow-eyed suspicion than previously. To these unfriendly airs he seemed blithe and friendly, but he was markedly aware of them all the same and wondered how the night's events might have altered their perception of him. Momentarily, he remembered standing behind the astonished Bolam, and the thought of how easily he might have reached out and snapped the man's neck flittered across his mind. Before he could quell it, there was the flickering beginning of the next idea to follow on, a spectral carriage in a ghost train of thought. He saw Bolam's exposed neck, saw the blood in him. How easy to drain, kill, and fling the corpse from the aeroship.

Horst paused by the coffin in the small, windowless freight hold as Bolam and Donner lifted the lid off. Encausse saw his face tighten and watched with concern as Horst swayed a little.

'My lord? Did we leave it too close to daylight? Are you well?'

Horst swung his head sideways to look at Encausse. There was something dreadful burning in Horst's eyes that made Encausse take a sudden breath in surprise and even fear, a sullen, dark fire that had no place in the face of anything human.

'When we arrive,' said Horst, and his voice was grating and unfamiliar even to him, 'I will require blood.'

'Yes.' Encausse blinked quickly. He had a growing sense of danger of a sort that was alien and terrible to him. 'Yes, my lord. It will be arranged.'

Horst shifted his gaze forward, and Encausse felt he could breathe more easily again. Horst stepped quickly into the coffin on its low bier, settled onto his back, and, for the first time Encausse had seen in their short acquaintance, crossed his arms across his heart. Scowling, Horst closed his eyes very positively, dismissing them with contempt by the action. Bolam and Donner were very happy to replace the coffin's lid, and the three of them left the hold with haste.

They closed the hatch behind them and, without thinking, Encausse locked it—another first. He looked at his lieutenants in silence for a moment and saw that they were as pale as he felt.

'Well,' he said at last, unsurprised and unashamed by the waver in his voice. 'Perhaps the Red Queen knows her business after all.'

An Interlude

'Would you be so kind as to fetch me a notebook, Horst?' said Johannes Cabal from his sickbed. 'I keep a supply in the writing bureau there. Also, please charge my fountain pen and bring it with you. Yes, the black ink. It's in the upper part, right-hand drawer.'

When he was supplied with these essentials, he settled down to fill the first few pages of the virgin notebook with a series of curious symbols, a coded shorthand of his own invention. Horst knew better than to interrupt.

Finally, Cabal looked up at Horst and asked, 'Do you have any idea whatsoever as to how they resurrected you?'

Horst shook his head. 'I was dead for much of it. All I saw were some people in robes. There was a bit of chanting going on as I recovered my wits, but that dried up pretty rapidly.'

'Do you recall the language in which this chant was couched?'

Horst tilted his head and gave Cabal a wry look. Cabal pursed his lips and made another note.

'*Subject unable to identify even the language of the ritual due to lollygagging around in his youth instead of applying himself,*' Cabal recited as he wrote. He looked back at Horst to check his brother was suitably chastised, but only found him smiling and nodding.

'I did apply myself, Johannes. Very enthusiastically. Just not on anything you'd find interesting.' He leaned forward and said in a confidential tone, 'My lollygagging was of a very high standard.'

'Get away from me, you vile sewer,' said Cabal coldly.

Horst's smile widened. 'You really have missed me.'

'I . . .' Cabal wavered. He closed his eyes and said, 'Yes, I really have.' He reopened his eyes and was relieved to find Horst looking somewhat surprised rather than smirking. 'I bear a soul now, Horst. A wretched nuisance much of the time. Much of the time.' He waved his pen impatiently at the momentarily befuddled vampire. 'Carry on. What happened when you arrived at your destination?'

Horst took a moment to gather his wits, and returned to his tale.

24

Chapter 2

IN WHICH HORST MAKES THE ACQUAINTANCE
OF HORRID PEOPLE

The arrival at the castle had been carefully timed to occur shortly after dusk, that the Lord of the Dead would be up and about and able to appreciate the power and the glory of the grand scheme to which he was being introduced. Encausse had spoken to the yacht's captain to perhaps hurry things along a little so their undead cargo might be decanted while it still slumbered, but the captain said they were already at full speed just to stay on schedule and that they would arrive as planned, the only other option being to tarry a little and arrive late. Would that please M. Encausse? The thought of being cooped up in a small space like the *Catullus* with something like Horst Cabal was suddenly less bearable to M. Encausse after the events of the previous night, and so, no, M. Encausse would not be pleased by any delay. The captain had clicked his heels and returned to his post, and the yacht had sped on through the lightening skies.

Now, hours later and the darkness deepening her lines, the *Catullus* angled her approach and swept down towards the landing area prepared on the top of a wide circular tower, part of the great castle's central keep.

The castle, a great looming monstrosity of clashing styles from both eastern and western Europe, stood above a small city that had certainly seen better days. Parts of it were in ruin, burnt to the ground during riots, while others were armed camps. It was a dying metropolis in a decaying country, and the castle rose above it all, haughty and unconcerned. It was a place for evil to fester, because none would or could stand against it. The castle was an abscess of corrupt ambitions in a place the world deemed unimportant and so, within it, wickedness fermented unseen and unchecked.

Horst was a friendlier creature when they opened his box; he didn't mention that he had heard them lock the door previously and knew full well their attitudes to him had changed. Even without smelling the fear that swelled from their pores, the tension was clear in their faces, and this he sought to defuse with a smile and a weak joke about travelling cargo class. He also made a point not to mention that he had been conscious for some minutes already and could have unboxed himself quite happily before they arrived. Better to give them an illusion of at least that much control over him, he thought. The return of the silly fop persona did much to settle their nerves, although he could still almost see a little extra adrenaline pulsing around their weak, mortal bodies, to give them a head start on a fight-or-flight response should he suddenly decide that they were of more use to him as nourishment than companions. *For all the good it would do you*, he caught himself thinking, and crushed it down into a dark place in his mind that he did not recall being there previously.

'We have arrived, my Lord Horst,' said Encausse.

'At this castle of yours?'

'Not *my* castle,' said Encausse, and laughed just awkwardly enough to obscure whether he was joking—as if *he* would have a castle—or truly thought Horst had believed that.

Horst was unsurprised that they were at their destination; he had known by the tilt of the yacht as it manoeuvred that it was no longer cruising and the timing fitted with what he had been told about the length of the trip. Oddly, he no longer felt very interested in exactly where they were. Such concerns—borders, territories, flags, and nations—seemed very artificial and trifling. When he imagined the world now, it wasn't as the political jigsaw of countries he had studied on maps as a schoolboy, but rather a living, physical world of mountain and forest, river and coast.

'I have little luggage,' said Horst, indicating the coffin and a small trunk containing several changes of clothes that had been waiting for him when he boarded. Remarkably, they were excellent fits. Less remarkably, he didn't much care for the cut and choice of colours. They were very restrained, and black dominated throughout, with a little scarlet and imperial purple to lift affairs. But for these small peacock flashes, Horst thought they may as well have been chosen by his brother, a man for whom black and white would do until something less gaudy was devised.

'That will all be attended to, my lord,' said Encausse, and gave a sideways nod at the coffin while looking at Bolam to tell him that this was now his concern, thereby satisfying Encausse's personal definition of 'attended to'. Bolam shambled off to talk to the captain about it, thereby satisfying his.

'It's raining,' said Horst suddenly.

Encausse looked at him with surprise. 'Well . . . yes. How did you know?'

'I can hear it,' said Horst, and he could. He could smell it, too, along with a faint scent of wet stone, but this he kept to himself. He already made them nervous enough.

The rain was not heavy, but it was persistent and it swept in waves across the castle rooves. The *Catullus* had not set down—there was not quite enough room to do that safely—but instead had dropped off anchor lines fore and aft that were gathered up and run through heavy iron rings deeply emplaced in the stout stone parapets.

Drawn tight by the gentle ascent of a few feet, she was held in position, barely moving even in the gusting wind that came in from the east. It was clearly a well-practised routine, and was carried out with familiarity and competence.

The yacht's forward gangway lowered smoothly on its cables until the leading edge touched down with a reassuring steadiness. In the rain, a welcoming committee of sorts—the sort that isn't very welcoming—waited beneath umbrellas. They were lean and ascetic people, all men, and they dressed as if in permanent mourning. The appearance of a corpse proceeding down the ramp followed shortly by his coffin borne by Bolam, Donner, and two members of the yacht's crew did nothing to alter this impression.

The group of waiting men looked no more excited by Horst's arrival than if he'd been a London omnibus arriving exactly on schedule, so he did not entirely take the words of the first of the men who stepped forward to greet him at face value. 'My Lord Horst,' said the man. His tones were dry, educated, and perhaps a little arch under the circumstances. 'It is a delight to meet you.'

'The pleasure is all mine,' replied Horst with equal sincerity.

'I am Velasco de Osma.' A strong brow and nose were betrayed by a weak chin on an otherwise noble countenance. It was the sort of face that would have looked at home over a polished chest plate while busily engaged in the infection of South American natives with Catholicism and smallpox, while all the time robbing them blind of every grain of gold they might have. 'And these are my associates.' He turned to the two men who stood by, and indicated them one at a time.

'Ewald von Ziegler.' A small man bowed and attempted to smile graciously, but the effort made his neck retract into his collar slightly and the smile slipped up one side of his face as if trying to escape before admitting failure and settling into a weak beatific smirk. The outmoded 'wipers' of hair in the middle of his cheeks did little to improve matters.

'And Burton Collingwood.' The third man was tall, perhaps three inches over the six-foot mark, and broad shouldered. He was sleek with the effects of wealth, but it lay upon him like a silk scarf on a wolf. He regarded Horst with calculating eyes for a moment before speaking. 'My Lord Horst,' he said, 'Lord' sounding as false on his tongue as titles always did with every American. 'It is surely good to have you with us.' Horst detected no mendacity in his tone, but nor did he find any friendliness. He realised Collingwood was only pleased to see him as one might be for an expected package.

'It's kind of you to say so,' he replied. 'Such a pleasant reception. Thank you, gentlemen.'

He was directed through the double doors of a tile-roofed shelter to descend via a broad curving stone stair that followed the tower's outer wall. Behind him processed the coffin bearers, and behind them von Ziegler, de Osma, and Collingwood. Horst noted a possible significance of the order—if the coffin were to be dropped, it would careen down the stairs causing all sorts of alarums and excursions en route. His welcoming committee would likely end up battered and broken, a very sensible reason for their following rather than preceding it. He, however, would have to deal with the situation himself. He was confident of his ability to do so—at the very least he could evade an errant coffin with ease or, if the whim took him, he could stop it providing he could find enough traction. Was, therefore, the order of the descent a test? Would the coffin be 'accidentally' dropped? He hoped not. It was a nice coffin, well finished and very comfortable, and he would hate to see its corners dashed and its surfaces scratched by a short career in stair tobogganing.

His hosts, however, had decided on nothing so cheaply dramatic, and the landing below was reached with all due decorum.

Horst's welcoming committee inveigled him to walk with them, while his coffin was conveyed off in another direction. 'It is being taken to your chambers, my Lord Horst,' de Osma explained.

'My chambers?' Horst wasn't really used to the concept of 'chambers' since his change in subspecies. A cellar or especially spacious cupboard would certainly have sufficed. Indeed, his last habitual resting place during the daylight hours had been a chest of the type used for storing out-of-season clothes or blankets. He halted for a moment, unexpectedly nostalgic for the cosy darkness and scent of camphor.

Misinterpreting the hesitation for displeasure, Ziegler interjected, 'The windows have all been bricked up, my lord. All but one of a northerly aspect, that is, through which the sun never shines.'

The men stood and regarded Horst—an implacable expression on de Osma's face that might even have been hiding boredom, and all the time Collingwood watched Horst as a man might watch a snake at feeding time in a terrarium, his distant coolness a mask over an expectation of sensation. As for von Ziegler himself, the apparent eagerness to please overlaid an evident lack of surety, and Horst realised that this was a man unused to making accommodations for others in either the material or immaterial sense.

'That is very thoughtful of you,' was all Horst could think to reply, to his own disappointment. Everything he said, however, seemed to carry a subtext for the men. They nodded sagely before moving on again. Horst followed, deciding as he did so to say as little as possible to them in future. He wasn't sure whether to be pleased or irked that they believed him to be more intelligent, or wiser, or perhaps both, than he actually was. In any event, it was certainly wiser to keep them believing that, and he appreciated ruefully that there would be no quicker way of disabusing them of those notions than opening his mouth.

As they processed—and Horst could not help feeling that they were in a procession without an audience—he heard the hollow beats of a dinner gong sounding some way ahead of him.

'Ah, just in time for dinner!' said von Ziegler. It was a lie; they had passed a low table upon which a French bracket clock had been sitting and Horst had noted the time in passing. Unless it was customary to keep remarkably eccentric mealtimes in whatever part of the world they had brought him to, then the gong had been sounded specifically for their convenience.

They arrived at what was apparently the dining room, double doors closed and, beside it, a well-Macassar-oiled butler of the shimmering sort waited with the implacability of an Easter Island sculpture. On their approach, he opened the doors and moved smoothly through ahead of them as if it were a dance step in a particularly graceful waltz.

'Graf von Ziegler, Vizconde de Osma, Mr Burton Collingwood, and,' he announced, pausing a beat before continuing, 'Horst Cabal.' Another beat, and then he added in an odd, rapid diminuendo like an English vicar finishing the parish announcements, 'Lord of the Dead.'

Even while part of Horst's mind was wondering what Debrett might make of that idiosyncratic use of titles, the rest of his attention was taken up by what greeted him within the room. The room was vast and high vaulted, certainly more likely to have once been an audience chamber for some ancient king given to grandiose gestures than anything as cosy as a dinner room. Feasts for hundreds of revellers that involved a lot of throwing chicken legs around and the harassment of serving staff, perhaps, but an intimate *tête-à-tête*, never.

Within the great echoing stone void of a hall, a dining table that would have looked impressive in almost any other setting stood a little beyond the centre of the room from the entrance, and aligned along its long axis towards it. Despite the bulk and grandeur of the table—some twenty-five feet in length—it was still like having a picnic blanket in the concourse of a major metropolitan railway station, the place of commuters taken by the staff who stood around, white towels over livery sleeves, even their practised *savoir faire* seeming insufficient for the setting. On the left-hand side of the table, a man and a woman stood talking, and they turned at the announcement to face the newcomers.

A servant appeared unbidden beside de Osma and his colleagues, and Horst was very nearly startled by the appearance of another at his own elbow. His senses far surpassed those he had enjoyed when merely mortal, and so he was not at all used to people sidling up to him undetected, demonstrating that a good butlers' school can teach stealth skills that would put the ninja of Japan to shame, as well as how to fold a napkin, starch a collar, and other abilities generally more useful to the world than throwing *shuriken* around.

He was conducted to the left side of the table, the woman being seated by another of the ubiquitous servants as he approached. As was his wont, honed over years of hot-blooded hormonal exhortation and still ingrained despite his changed nature, he cast an evaluative eye upon her as he approached. Her hair and eyes were dark, what he would have said was a Mediterranean type but for her deadly paleness. She was thin, too, and the suspicion of illness rose in his mind. He gauged her to be in her mid- to late twenties, though the simple black dress she wore would not have looked out of place on his grandmother, down to the choker and locket at her throat.

Belatedly, he shifted his attention to her companion, and discovered himself under at least as much attention from that quarter as he had lavished upon the woman. Horst's hackles rose; he immediately disliked this man, and not simply because he was smiling arrogantly at Horst, having caught him in the act of assessing his companion.

In Horst's earlier days when he had enjoyed such simple pastimes as routinely breathing and not bursting into flames in daylight, he had excelled in what he termed 'seeking companionship' and what his parents had called 'womanising', his mother with pursed lips, his father with a stern brow during the lecture and a wink at the end of it. He disliked the term himself; it sounded predatory when all he was doing was being friendly, usually very friendly, and frequently extraordinarily friendly. He liked women and, he was relieved to discover, they liked him.

In his joyous odyssey through the massed ranks of womanhood, he did, however, often happen across other men who fitted the epithet *womaniser* rather too well. They did not tend to be nice men, which was why Horst cavilled so strongly against the term being attached to himself. They used, often abused, and discarded. Rudeness was one thing—indeed, Horst excelled in applied rudeness when that application involved himself in limited engagements with an audience of one, occasionally two, and on a particularly memorable occasion, twelve (a women's lacrosse team had won a famous victory, the players were looking to celebrate, and Horst was looking lonely in the tavern where they discovered him. The progression of subsequent events seemed almost inevitable in hindsight). To repeat, rudeness was one thing, but these *womanisers* stooped to impoliteness, and that was unconscionable to Horst. These men broke hearts, and when they noticed at all, it made them laugh or, at the very least, smirk. It was a distinctive sort of smirk and one of the few things in the world that could move the usually equitable and equanimous Horst to feel murder flicker in his breast.

The man was smirking that very class of smirk, and Horst knew there and then they would never be friends.

The head of the table was occupied only by a high-backed chair, no more decorative than any of the other chairs, but its height gave it the air of a throne. Horst remembered the whispered references to the 'Red Queen' and decided to ignore the chair until such time as it was occupied. On the tall chair's right hand sat the unknown man to whom Horst had developed such an easy and swift animosity. His clothes were expensive enough that the slovenly manner in which he wore them only served to add to his undeniable charisma by advertising his nonchalance. He was wearing a jacket of maroon velvet that Horst found himself coveting somewhat, a black waistcoat, a soft white linen shirt, and a black cravat. The cravat was partially untied and the shirt's top button undone. It was a statement of style that Horst had used many times in the past and it galled him to see this man using such similar devices. He became very aware of his own impeccable turnout and wondered at what point he had turned into his brother. He would have to study some periodicals and find out exactly what had been going on between the period of his second death and his second resurrection. News and events he would get to certainly, but he would turn to the fashion pages first.

As for the man himself, his lean and hungry look would leave Cassius seeming bloated and soporific. His face was well shaped and, it pained Horst enormously to admit to himself, undeniably handsome in a shallow, matinee-idol sort of way, should you happen to like that sort of thing. He wore his hair long, in a flowing mane of gentle waves that ran from a sharp widow's peak to comfortably below his collar. Horst, unused to envy, found words like 'gigolo' and 'widow-chaser' slithering around inside his head, hissing and dripping venom.

Fortunately, he didn't have to sit next to the man, for the pale woman sat between them. As the welcoming committee arranged themselves on the other side of the table, Horst noticed that the place to his right was also left empty. 'Are we expecting anyone else?' he asked de Osma, who had taken the seat directly opposite to him.

'Not quite yet,' said the Spaniard as he smoothed an errant raindrop into the cloth of his jacket's biceps. 'When he has been recovered, he shall join us.' He looked up and straight into Horst's eyes, a brave or foolish thing for a mortal man to do. His expression was sleekly satisfied. 'Just as you were.'

Horst looked down at his dinner setting while he considered his next words. Part of him noted that it seemed very simple in comparison with those of the other diners, but he did not give that so very much consideration. He looked up again and said, 'And just who are we? Gentlemen, I am grateful for your efforts in bringing me here, but your reasons . . . what *are* your reasons?'

'We shall dine first,' said de Osma. 'Discussion can wait until afterwards.'

Horst glared at de Osma and he felt that strange and all-too-atavistic sensation flex within him again. It would be simplicity itself to transfix the irritating little human and make him . . .

Human.

Horst bit down his emotions with difficulty. He had always been an even-tempered man, a man to whom anger was a rare and unwelcome visitor. He didn't like the way that somehow it had gained a latchkey. He liked even less how he had started to take a shine to its visits.

And 'human'? What had possessed him to think in such terms?

Something flexed inside his heart again and he felt both fear and pleasure at its presence. So distracted was he that he hardly noticed the waiter—again—until the man was at his side, filling his wine glass.

'No,' said Horst, angry at himself, angry at these men, confused, uncertain. 'I do not drink . . . wine . . . ?'

For now he saw it in his glass, red and opaque, and he smelled it, warm and tinged with iron.

His first impulse was one of disgust, yet even as he tried to find words to express it, his hand closed unbidden around the stem of the glass and it was rising towards his mouth. He was conscious of the eyes upon him, and closed his own that they might not see the fear there as his lips parted, his upper canines extending in a small smooth tensing of muscle that was a small ecstasy in itself, the tiny *tchink* as one grazed the brim of the glass, his slow inhalation that drew the scent into his mouth where it stained his tongue with need, and finally the slightest inclination to start the warm, fresh blood trickling into his mouth. For the first time in his life and his unlife, Horst Cabal was truly terrified, and it was of himself.

The glass was empty. Somehow it was empty. He opened his eyes and saw the redness thin against the glass, the drops pooling inside. It took a small effort not to lick them out. Instead he carefully placed it back on the table, rested his hands on the tablecloth, and looked at de Osma.

De Osma hardly noticed him; servants were fussing around, placing plates of food and restocking wine glasses with, in the cases of all the other diners, wine. Horst sat and glared, fighting down a tempest of violent emotion while these men who had raised him from dust and brought him here laughed and fluttered napkins and ignored him when he could have killed every one of them where they sat and before the supercilious smugness of their expressions had had time to fade. He felt like a bomb on the edge of detonation, a ferocious animal on a fraying leash. Didn't they know who he was? Didn't they know *what* he was?

'No,' Horst said. The repressed violence sounded in his voice like the warning creaks of thin ice underfoot. 'We will not discuss it later. We will discuss it now.'

The table grew suddenly quiet. Von Ziegler shot de Osma a nervous glance. For his part, de Osma seemed momentarily startled, but he guarded that moment well and looked at Horst seriously though with a small hint of reproachful acquiescence. 'As you wish, my Lord Horst.'

'Horst?' It was the man two places to Horst's left. He spoke with an English accent, the Thames Estuary evident in even that single syllable. 'You're never called "Horst", are you?' Then to the woman between them he said, 'Once knew a German girl and her uncle was called that. She said it was an old man's name.'

Horst's head swung to face the man as smoothly and as threateningly as a gun turret. Their eyes met over the woman's head and, despite the violent animosity bubbling inside him, the man met his glance easily and arrogantly.

'Who,' said Horst, the tight grip on his emotions making his voice toneless and mechanical, 'the fuck are you?'

Where repressed violence charging the air so strongly it stank of psychic ozone had failed to make much of an impression on the man, a single expletive succeeded. The woman squeaked, but whether with outrage, amusement, or amused outrage, it was impossible to tell, although whatever it was, it caused her to drop her fork. The man—surprised first by Horst's words, and then by the sharp tinkle of silverware on china—quite lost his aura of sangfroid for a moment. When he recovered it, it was no longer pure; now it was streaked with wariness and hostility.

It was Collingwood who stepped in as peacemaker. 'Gentlemen, please. We're all friends at this table, all with a common goal. Perhaps'—he looked to de Osma as he spoke—'we should go along with my Lord Horst's suggestion that we, ah, fill him in on what this is all about.'

'That would be lovely,' said Horst, forcing a smile onto his face. 'Thanks.'

De Osma looked at his dinner, sighed, and put down his knife and fork, apparently not a man who could eat and talk business at the same time. 'Very well. Perhaps you're right. We shall start with introductions. My Lord Horst, may I introduce you to my Lady Misericorde, Lady of the Risen, and my Lord Devlin, Lord of the Transfigured. My lord, my lady, Lord Horst, Lord of the Dead.'

'The Risen?' Horst looked closely at Lady Misericorde. The paleness brought on by long hours away from the sun, the intense gaze of a driven personality and a keen intellect, the chemical burns on her fingers. It all seemed very familiar somehow. Then he understood, and almost laughed. 'You're a necromancer.'

She frowned slightly at his tone. 'I am, my lord. That amuses you?'

'Not in itself, no. Just a coinci . . . Oh, it doesn't matter. I'm pleased to meet you,' he said, silently adding *I think*. He leaned over and looked at Devlin. 'Transfigured. Meaning what?'

Predictably, Devlin took the opportunity to behave in a superior fashion. 'What? You're saying you can't work it out?'

Horst wasn't entirely listening. He was looking at the enormous steak on Devlin's plate, and detecting a scent that was not entirely human. More canine, but somehow moderated. He made the obvious guess based on it. 'You're either a lycanthrope, or you need to stop sleeping with dogs,' he said. 'You stink of mutt.'

There was an awkward silence. Then Devlin laughed drily. 'Right first time.' He returned his attention to his steak. 'You were right the first time.'

Misericorde, who appeared to have been bracing herself for a confrontation, looked in some wonderment at Devlin, then at Horst with a slight smile albeit one still topped with a frown of curiosity. She returned to eating her own dinner of chicken and green vegetables.

If she was tacitly congratulating him on his muscular approach to diplomacy, Horst knew it was ill deserved. Devlin was not backing down; he was biding his time. Still, trouble piled up in the future may conceivably be avoided, a luxury unavailable when trouble is toe-to-toe and breathing heavily in one's face. He would deal with Devlin when the time arose, by which he meant he would avoid Devlin, or buy him a beer and let bygones be bygones, or perhaps simply tear his head from his shoulders and drink deep from the fountain of arterial blood rising from the fool's still-beating heart.

Horst blinked. Where had that come from? Furthermore, why did his mouth water at the prospect?

He could smell blood, and he could hear the sound of one of the servants approaching, hear the weave of the cloth of the servant's trousers brushing so near absolutely silently as to make almost, *almost* no difference. But he could hear it, hear the tiny creak of joints in the man's ankles, hear the slop of liquid in a bowl.

Then it was in front of him, a red circle of blood in a gleaming white circle of the soup bowl against the matte whiteness of the tablecloth. His silverware sparkled so brightly, the orange light of the wall sconces and the great fire in the fireplace in the wall behind him, and how had he not noticed it before, when it *stank* of smoke and dry wood and coal? His silverware sparkled *so* brightly, the pale yellow light, so close to white, reflected there, falling from the great chandelier now refitted with electric light bulbs, a nod to modernity or perhaps an embracing of it, and yet Horst was aware of it all, the sound of Devlin's knife as he sawed through his steak with an anger he thought he was hiding and the sound of Misericorde's throat as she swallowed her food, her fine white throat. And Horst's mind ravened and whirled within his head—there was too much, too much world to deal with sanely, too many sensations and thoughts, his mind was losing its grip. But that was fine. That was good.

There was a new way of thinking just waiting to be accepted. All he had to do was let it go, all that detritus he'd carried around with him, those inefficient ways of thinking, what his brother would have called *thought processes*. Cloying, filled with muck that just *hurt* as he tried to think through it, how did he, how did they, how had he ever put up with this garbage, this filth blocking his mind?

He looked at the red circle, and his head drooped a little towards it. He inhaled and the smell of death filled his senses. His hand shifted across the tablecloth until the tips of his fingers touched the tip of the soupspoon's handle. Some of the filthy mess in his mind suggested perhaps he might like croutons with that? What did that even mean? How did that do anything but waste time and effort that might be more profitably used?

Distracted by the clash of thoughts, somehow the words slipped out.

'I think I'd like croutons with this.'

The three men across from him looked at him with expressions varying from bemusement to mild amusement. The Lady Misericorde, however, laughed. A quiet laugh, true, and one that was as much a release of tension after the scene with Devlin as much as anything else. It was still a laugh, however—an honest, unforced laugh, and it reminded Horst suddenly exactly what the point of saying such things is.

The mess in his mind became familiar instead of alien, and the clarity of thought that had abhorred it so withdrew into the shadows where it had lain for such a long time. With a careful, gentle impetus delivered through the thumbs and forefingers of both hands, Horst pushed the bowl away from him.

'I will not feed like this,' he said. He glared across the table at these men, these rich, powerful men who had gone to so much trouble to bring him here because of something they desired so much they could not easily express it. 'Blood in a wine glass. Blood in a soup bowl. Are you mocking me?'

Without waiting for a reply, he rose and walked out, the abruptness of his action catching the servants by surprise such that when he reached the door, nobody was in place to open it for him. He opened it himself and enjoyed doing it, leaving the diners staring at an ajar door since he could not even concern himself enough to slam it behind him.

Chapter 3

IN WHICH HORST MEETS THE HELP AND
THERE IS MILD SAUCINESS

Horst located his chambers by the simple expedient of finding a passing servant and demanding to be led to them. Although Horst had never seen the man before, the footman seemed very aware of who Horst was, taking him there with marked swiftness and courtesy. Horst could smell the fear on the man, and it took a conscious effort not to predate on him to make up for his interrupted dinner. *Oh, yes,* he told himself, *because feeding on the help shows so much more panache than lapping blood from a soup plate.* He wasn't sure if it was the thought of drinking blood, or how it was taken, or from whom it was taken, but whatever it was, it disgusted him and the footman was allowed to scuttle away with whatever decorum he could summon the moment the door of Horst's rooms was opened.

As a boy Horst had read far too many lurid romances full of sword fights, towering castles, inscrutable Orientals, luxuriant potentates, evil uncles, poisons unknown to science, and some kissing. Despite the broadening and heightening such material had provided his imagination, his chambers still caused him a moment of astonishment as he stepped inside. There was an antechamber, which was something of a surprise in itself, as he wasn't used to bedrooms having architectural overtures in this fashion. There was a maid reading on a *chaise longue* on the right as he entered. Ruffled by his unexpected appearance, she threw the book under a cushion and leapt to her feet, smoothing down her skirt as she did so.

'Who are you?' demanded Horst, his own surprise manifesting as curtness.

'Alisha, mein Herr. My lord,' she said, the correction following the error without hesitation. 'I am part of your staff.'

'Are you? Well, that's . . .' He stopped to consider whether he had heard aright. 'Staff? I have staff?'

'Yes, my lord. Myself and Herman.' Horst could almost see the train of thoughts as she expressed inner irritation with a slight tautening of her brow, followed by grudging *esprit de corps* by a wry drawing back of one side of her mouth, and then finally re-engaging him with frank eye contact. 'We weren't expecting you quite so soon. I apologise for both of us, my lord.'

For his answer, Horst walked past her and recovered her book from its hiding place. '*The Art of War*?' He looked at her quizzically. 'I'll be honest. I wasn't expecting this. I expected a novel with . . .' He quickly ran through the usual activities practised within novels in his experience, discarding most of the subject matters as he went. '. . . kissing, primarily. I don't suppose Sun Tzu has much to say about kissing. Does he? I don't know. I've never read it.'

'I'm sorry, my lord. I'm not supposed to read on duty.'

'No?' He wafted the slim volume at her. 'Funny sort of book for a maid to be reading.'

Again the eye contact, and there was a flicker of anger there. 'I'm trying to improve myself,' she said. The anger guttered out. 'Please don't report me, my lord.'

'Very well. I shan't, on one condition and for one reason. The condition is that when those stuffed suits aren't around to be outraged, you call me "Horst".'

'Of course, my Lord Horst.'

'Don't be awkward. *Just* Horst. And the reason is'—he smiled, feeling a lot more human in himself—'you share my mother's name, Alisha.'* He tossed the book to her. She caught it easily. 'Best hide that a bit better in future. Don't want them thinking you're getting ideas above your station or anything seditious like that.'

'Thank you, my . . .' She saw his eyebrow rise and stopped herself. 'Thank you . . . *Horst*.'

'There. That wasn't so hard, was it? Right.' He walked to the antechamber's inner door and rested his fingers on the handle. 'Let's see what this lot thinks is suitable lodgings for a dead man.' His smile slipped. 'You do *know* I'm dead, don't you? Technically, anyway.'

Alisha nodded. 'We were told what . . . you are.'

Horst sighed. 'Good. Much as I love surprises, some things shouldn't be, you know? Looking after one of the undead— effortlessly charismatic and supernaturally charming, I grant you, but nevertheless, a dead bloke—it's not something that should just be foisted upon you. That doesn't really make for a good work experience, does it?'

'I'm enjoying it so far.'

Horst dropped his hand to his side and turned to regard her. 'Are you? Really?'

She shrugged. 'You're not at all what I was expecting.'

He laughed, a little bark of a laugh that made her jump. 'I don't think I'm at all what your employers were expecting, either.' He swung the door open and walked in.

---

* Johannes Cabal interrupted the narrative at this point. 'What is this nonsense? Mother's name is "Liese".' To this Horst said nothing, except to smile the smile of a freelance lounge lizard. Cabal grimaced, and muttered, 'You are disgusting.'

Somebody had been reading too many novels of the sort Horst had once favoured, and then topped them off with a course in interior decorating. The walls were papered in a deep maroon pattern detailed in crimson, and it took a moment of *déjà vu* involving memories of several mid-market restaurants before he realised that the colours were those of venous and arterial blood respectively, at least by intent. The overall effect was of trying rather too hard.

He smiled ruefully. He was no lord, no matter what people kept telling him. A real lord would probably have harsh things to say about such decor. '*Déclassé,*' he muttered quietly to himself. Not quite quietly enough as it turned out, as Alisha appeared beside him.

'Hmmm,' she said, looking around and nodding. 'It is dead classy, isn't it?'

Horst laughed. 'It's just as well I've given you leave to be familiar, because some people would be kicking you around the room by now for your damned impudence. I gather you're new to the whole business of being in service?'

Alisha looked a little crestfallen. 'I'm sorry. I'm not doing a very good job of it, am I?'

Horst was only half listening. The large room he was in was some sort of reception room or possibly a lounge, full of candle stands, overstuffed sofas, and low tables. He looked around and saw a door standing open. This, he gathered, was the bedroom, although the bed itself was no longer in evidence. Instead, his coffin stood on an impressive bier of red and black silk, each corner guarded by a tall floor-standing candelabra, each bearing three black candles.

'Oh, good heavens,' he said to Alisha. 'Will you look at that? It's all very pretty and everything, but how's a chap supposed to get in there?' He took a couple of steps closer, craning his head to see further into the room. 'Is there a footstool or anything handy? All those candles are a dreadful fire hazard, too. You'd think they'd have electrical lighting in here, all the money that's washing around, wouldn't you?'

He received no answer, and turning to Alisha, found her wearing an expression that contained elements of amusement and puzzlement. 'Have I said something funny?' he asked.

'No, my . . . No, Horst. Just . . . well, it's just that you're *really* not what I was expecting.'

'Oh?' Horst noticed the one remaining window in the chambers—arched double French windows opening onto a semicircular balcony. He could guess from the proportions of the room where other windows might have been, but for all their failures in the choosing of colours, whoever had prepared the chamber had done an exemplary job of filling and covering the old openings for there was no trace of them at all. 'And what were you expecting? This faces north, then?'

'Just something . . . somebody more . . . yes, that's north . . . somebody a bit more . . .'

Horst reached the balcony and leaned on the stone balustrade. Looking over the edge, he could see the sheer curved wall of the castle's corner tower extend into the gloom, to its foundations within a narrow grass-covered bank, beyond which a moderately sized river crept sluggishly by, protecting the castle within its natural meander. 'The part?' he asked.

'A bit more scary,' admitted Alisha.

For a moment Horst felt a sort of dizziness, but it was nothing to do with vertigo induced by the view, or even any sense of instability—physical or psychic—that he had ever experienced before. He felt divorced from everything for a moment, more invulnerable than the great castle, and with a sense that he would outlive it. Everything seemed so small, so ephemeral, so insignificant. Everything but he himself. He looked at his hands resting upon the cold ancient stone of the balustrade rail, pitted by time, and imagined himself holding the world in them, imagined himself crushing it. It felt easy. He looked over his shoulder at Alisha. She recoiled a little at his expression, the distance in his eyes. 'My dear, *dear* Alisha,' he said. 'I *can* be a great deal more scary.'

He looked back out into the night again, but his eyes were

closed. Inside the mansion of his mind, he was putting snakes back into boxes.

'I'm sorry,' he said eventually. 'I've been given a role, and I keep finding myself playing it instead of myself.' Alisha did not answer and, when he turned to look at her, he found her gone. 'Nicely done,' he said out loud to the empty room. 'Wonderful that a year's contact with Johannes ended up with his social skills rubbing off on me and not vice versa. That worked out well.'

Or maybe it was mutual, he mused. Perhaps right that moment Johannes was in a tavern somewhere, employing a warm eye, an easy smile, and an insouciant line in chat to add new recruits to his coterie of adoring women. Horst smiled at the image, until it faltered at the memory of why Johannes would never do such a thing, would never betray the one woman he'd sacrificed so much for. Then the smile vanished altogether. Of course. Silly of him. His brother was dead and in Hell. How had he forgotten that, he wondered. After all, Horst had put Johannes there himself.

He looked at the clock, suddenly eager to be back in his coffin and insensible. Things usually seemed better when he was incapable of thought. The hour was late, but only to the diurnal. He realised he wasn't even sure of the time of year. There was a nip in the air and he had a feeling it was early autumn even if the leaves hadn't started falling yet. Still, it could be early spring. Nobody had even told him what year it was. Perhaps that was because he hadn't asked anyone. It had all seemed so stupendously irrelevant in the days immediately after his re-rebirth when it had all seemed a little dreamlike. But now he was up to his knees in rich men not explaining things to him, and lady necromancers, and men whom he disliked for reasons that he appreciated weren't just to do with how they wore their cravat. Now he realised he would have to start being more methodical, not really for reasons of self-preservation nearly so much as curiosity. He'd been dead twice now, and was beginning to understand why it had concerned Johannes so little.

There had been nothingness.

Horst frowned. Why hadn't he gone to Heaven or Hell? Johannes had been very vocal about his scorn for the former and personal animosity for the latter. Shouldn't Horst have found himself in one place or the other? It was a peculiar sort of theological question and not the sort that was best suited for answering by a priest, should one be handy within the castle, and that seemed remarkably unlikely. Again, Horst found himself wishing Johannes was about. It was a shame about the whole sending-his-brother-to-Hell thing. It had seemed like a good and moral thing to do, but now it was turning out to be a bloody nuisance. Where was he supposed to find a necromancer at that time of night?

There was a gentle, perhaps nervous tap at his door. Before he could say anything, the door opened and Lady Misericorde leaned around the edge. 'I hope I'm not intruding, my lord,' she said, despite the very obvious fact that she was. 'There was nobody around so I just . . .' She stepped inside and closed the door behind her.

'Ah,' said Horst regretfully. 'I appear to have frightened away my maid. I hope she comes back.'

'I doubt she has any choice,' said Misericorde, smiling a little wanly. 'The castle is very secure. She can't just walk out.'

'That sounds like the voice of experience.' He waved vaguely at one of the ludicrously over-appointed ottoman sofas, dripping with cushions and decadence. 'I'm forgetting my manners. Please, sit.'

She looked at the sofa and shook her head. 'I dislike seats without backs. I'll forget myself, lean back, and fall over, and where shall my dignity be then? I shall stand.'

Horst half smiled. He regarded her shrewdly. 'That accent of yours. Not quite German and not quite French. Are you from the Alsace?'

'Very good.' She favoured him with her own half a smile. 'And you were brought up in Hesse, although there's provincial English in your vowels.'

Horst's eyebrows rose. Although technically true, nobody enjoys the slight pejorative taint inherent in *provincial*. 'Yes,' he said a little sharply to cover his discomfort. 'I have had a chequered sort of life so far.'

'Life. Perhaps not the perfect technical term for it,' she said. 'But it will have to do.'

Horst gave her a hard look. According to his upbringing, there were certain subjects that it was ill-mannered to raise in conversation with a new acquaintance. With the likes of politics, religion, fatness, and house prices, it seemed reasonable to assume that 'being dead' was likely to be somewhere on the list.

'So,' he said when it became apparent that his hard look was not doing all it might in humbling her, 'you're a necromancer.'

'So,' she replied, 'you're a vampire.'

An awkward silence followed, as if they had just met through the offices of a cryptic dating agency.

'I believe I shall sit, after all,' said Misericorde. There followed a few moments of silent reorganisation. A good number of cushions ended on the floor, from where she did not trouble to recover them. Finally, she arranged herself with a little difficulty but with decorum intact. Half reclining, she looked up at where he stood across the room from her. 'I can hardly believe that you've come along with this so far and have no idea what it's all about, my lord.'

He considered asking her to call him by his name rather than the very new and, to his ear, very false title, just as he had done with Alisha. But, he considered, he liked Alisha, so he would let Misericorde continue to wrestle with the title for a while. 'It was hardly my choice. I was just lying around, minding my own business, when some of *their*'—here, he gestured sideways with a jerk of his thumb in the general direction of the dining room—'hirelings turned up.'

'You didn't have to come.'

'It seemed rude not to. So . . . what *is* it all about?'

She smiled, or—as her very next action was to avoid answering the question—possibly smirked. 'I don't have much experience of vampires,' she confided. 'There aren't that many of them around these days.'

'You probably know more about that than I do. Now, this little group we find . . .'

'No, there aren't. People keep hunting and killing them. Which is to say, hunting and killing you. Still, that's what you get for trying to predate upon humanity. We don't take it very well.'

'This little group into which we find ourselves recruited . . . this conspiracy, it seems . . .'

'Our little cabal. Yes?'

The woman really was infuriating, Horst was finding. Now that she was ready to talk about the subject, she threw that needless little roadblock in the way. 'Not the term I'd use, for obvious reasons.' She looked off to one side, digesting his words, and Horst saw that she was honestly confused. 'My name,' he explained. She held out her hands and shrugged, still unilluminated. He sighed. 'It's nothing important, just that you said "our little cabal", and that's my name. "Cabal", that is. Not the whole thing. I'm not called "Horst Our Little Cabal".' He grunted, exasperated at himself. 'I'm rambling.'

It hardly mattered. Misericorde had sat up at the revelation, eyes wide. 'You're a Cabal?' she said in astonishment. 'Does the name "Johannes Cabal" mean—'

'My brother,' Horst interrupted. 'Yes, the name definitely means something to me. He was my brother.'

A modicum of a new expression was colouring her surprise and Horst, who was bracing himself for the usual hatred and name-calling, had to remind himself that he was not in normal company when he saw that the expression was pleasure. 'This is such a surprise,' she said. 'I had no idea. Cabal . . . your brother, that is, he has a remarkable reputation.'

'Infamy,' he corrected her. 'Not especially widespread, but . . .'

Misericorde waved the comment aside. 'Most people can't even explain electricity. Their opinion is worthless.'

Horst laughed, though slightly troubled. 'You sound just like him.'

'That,' she said with emphasis, 'is a compliment.'

'It is?' It all seemed a long way from the usual reaction his brother's name provoked. Then again, this was a very different parish. 'I didn't realise he was so well regarded in your community.'

'My community?' Again that frown of real incomprehension. Her expression cleared. 'Oh, of course. You wouldn't know. You've been . . . incommunicado for a while, haven't you?'

'I don't know,' he admitted. 'That clock over there tells me the time, but that's all I've been furnished with. I don't know the day, or the month, or the year. I'm beginning to think that might be useful data to know. A desk calendar would have been nice.' He looked around the otherwise exhaustively furnished room. 'A desk would have been nice.'

Lady Misericorde was pleased to bring light to his temporal darkness, although if she had been expecting an Olympian detachment to the flight of time, she was to be disappointed.

'Dear God,' he said, and perched on the end of her ottoman sofa. He put both hands over his mouth and gazed fixedly off, reconciling what he knew to the current date. After almost a minute, he lowered his hands and looked at her with disbelief. 'That's over two years. Over two years. It hurt, but not for long. When the end came, what I *thought* was the end came, the world just turned off. Over two years. Oh, my God.' He looked away, still battling to take it in, relieving her of the stress of his regard. But it was only for a moment before he turned back and demanded, 'I wouldn't know what? Surely Johannes is dead?' He licked his lips and anguish flickered across his face for a moment. 'Dead and damned.'

'I don't know if he's dead,' Lady Misericorde replied in slow, careful tones. Sharing an ottoman with a distracted and upset vampire seemed to be a new experience to her, but—interesting as it was—she probably had no desire that it should be her last. 'I only know he wasn't a year or so ago.' Horst did not respond, still caught in a web of memory and regret. 'He saved us all.'

That got Horst's attention.

His head snapped around to bear on her as if she had just shot a spitball in his ear. 'He saved who?' he demanded. 'All the necro-mancers?'

'No.' She smiled as she shook her head. She had read animos-ity in his reactions to mentions of brother Johannes earlier, but she saw a very human concern beneath that now. 'No. He saved *everyone*.'

And then, to Horst's increasing astonishment, she told him a tale learned at second, third, and fourth hands, from a lover's in-discretion in speaking of the goings-on in a London gentlemen's club, to the researches of an occult investigator seeking the truth behind an historical mystery of the Ugol hordes and of fatal red snow that fell from a cloudless sky, to an outraged exchange of let-ters between an archbishop and the chief of police for some little border town somewhere.

'That's an exaggeration, isn't it?' he asked finally. 'That's not doomsday?'

Misericorde shrugged. 'Perhaps not. But if even half of what I have learned is true, then your brother saved the world from a horror that would have left nations in chains, and a hundred bat-tlefields piled with the corpses of those who tried to resist.'

Horst's mouth opened and closed several times in the manner popularised by goldfish as he tried to absorb this difficult intelli-gence. It was not the scale of the averted disaster that troubled him, but that his brother had been the one to deal with it. This was, for him, far more difficult to comprehend than any number of eldritch horrors from ancient centuries or inconvenienced arch-bishops.

'Wow,' he said eventually.

'Has your little brother made you proud?' she said, sowing mischief.

But to her apparent mild yet pleasant surprise, the mischief failed to take root. Instead, the Lord of the Dead, bane of human-ity and master of evil eternal, smiled a huge beaming smile. 'Proud? Yes. Yes! You have no idea how happy this makes me!' Then, with sudden emphasis, he added, 'You are *sure* he isn't dead?'

'I have no idea if he's alive or not at the moment, but he was alive a year ago.'

'Then he wormed his way out of trouble somehow,' Horst said quietly to himself. He brightened up again. 'He'd got into a situation, you see. He was going to die. No possible way out of it, one would have thought. Still, if anyone could do it, he could, slippery swine that he is!' He rose to his feet and started pacing. 'Just as well. There to save . . . or probably save . . . or at least save quite a bit of the world. There when it mattered. My brother.'

He halted and looked down at her. 'Oh, yes. I'm proud of him.' He was smiling and, Misericorde saw, there was a little extra glimmer of light in his eyes. Horst blinked fiercely, distractedly, and the glimmer vanished.

'So . . .' He looked seriously at her, the joy of a moment before evaporating as he re-ordered priorities and re-sorted the factors that made up his current circumstances. One large factor was still notably absent, and priorities could not be arranged without it. 'Why are we here?' He held up his hands, fingers spread, a gesture that—combined with a suspicious twitch of his eyes to take in the left-hand wall, ceiling, right-hand wall—indicated that he was talking about the castle rather than in any larger philosophical sense. 'What is the business of those men?'

'They call themselves,' said Misericorde, leaning back into her nest of cushions to regard him, 'the *Ministerium Tenebrae*.'

'Do they? Do they indeed?' He thought for a moment. 'That's not very good Latin, is it? Is it?'

'It's fine.'

Horst considered further. 'Something to do with shadows, isn't it?'

'That would be *umbras*, I think.'

'Oh, of course.' He scratched his head and laughed self-consciously. 'Johannes was always the one for languages. And sciences. And most things like that.'

'The Ministry of Darkness,' she supplied. 'Although *Tenebrarum* might have been better.'

'Yes, it might have,' said Horst, nodding for no good reason. Certainly not from an informed opinion. 'So . . . they sound . . . a bit . . .' He seesawed his head as he thought, trying to find the *bon mot*. 'Evil.'

'That's a very absolutist term, don't you think?' she said. 'Do you feel as if you're evil?'

'Well, no. But I never really wanted to be like this.'

'Nobody necessarily wants to be what they end up being. You seem very nice, my lord. A very nice man.'

'I've always tried to be good. Decently good, anyway. Not sort of St Francis of Assisi good necessarily, but . . .'

'But most decently good people in the world would call you a monster, and the Dee Society would kill you on sight.'

'The who?'

Misericorde waved the question aside. 'Unimportant. It doesn't matter how you define yourself, the point is that you have *been* defined. You are a leech that walks like a man, a parasite, an unnatural aberration, an abomination in the sight of man and God, a vile mockery of—'

'All right, all right,' said Horst, his tone offended. He walked up and down while the wound to his feelings knitted a little.

'Yet *you* know you are a thinking, rational individual. It is unjust how you are treated.'

In reality, Horst had no experience of being chased betwixt pillar and post by aspiring Van Helsings. He had spent the majority of his vampirehood locked in a crypt, amusing himself down the long years with spider races, followed by a sumptuous feast of mainly spiders. On his release he had largely enjoyed a year as a showman in partnership with his brother, Johannes, who had largely hated it. They had travelled constantly, and Horst had been discreet and careful as and when he fed. Thus, he had never encountered stern-faced men with sharpened stakes and strong moral imperatives.

The year had finished with a bit of a falling-out with his brother, and Horst had condemned Johannes to death and eternal damnation, and himself to brief agony then endless insensate and thoughtless dark.

Except now it transpired that Johannes was not only not dead and not damned, but was actually doing things that, for lack of a better description, would have to be characterised as 'good'. He himself, Horst, was also no longer dust, but thoroughly thoughtful and sensate. For example, Lady Misericorde's throat looked very tempting. He was vaguely conscious of his eye teeth slowly extending in the same way an adolescent boy is vaguely conscious of a pleasing tumescence when contemplating a pretty girl. The similarity extended to the sudden embarrassment when it is realised that the effect has been observed and noted by the female in question.

Horst turned away, putting his hand to his mouth in a pathetically chivalrous manner. Misericorde compounded his humiliation with a light laugh. 'You see? You're thirsty. It's not your fault, and you don't even need so much blood to survive, do you? If people understood you, vampires and humans could co-exist. But there is no desire for compromise. Sooner or later you will finish with a stake through your heart, and the mouth of your severed head stuffed with garlic flowers.'

'Actually,' he offered, as if it would somehow mitigate such a fate, 'I still quite like garlic.'

'Really? Well, I'm sure the garlic flowers will more than make up for the whole impalement-and-decapitation business,' she replied. She let a silence form before saying, 'The thing is, the day doesn't understand the night, and the creatures of the day outnumber the creatures of the night. We are discriminated against—hated, hunted, destroyed.'

'You're not a creature of the night, though,' said Horst. 'You can go down the shops and buy yourself a loaf and a newspaper and no one will think anything of it.'

'True, but you can say that of Devlin and his ilk, too. We are not defined by our ability to purchase a baguette and a copy of *Le Figaro*. If I stood in a town square on market day and identified myself as a necromancer, I doubt I would leave that square alive.'

Horst thought of his brother's travails and did not argue. 'It's always been that way, though,' he said. 'You just have to keep a low profile.'

'Do generals keep a low profile? They send tens, hundreds of thousands of men to their deaths, killing more in a day than we might be responsible for in a century. Do the politicians who create those wars keep a low profile?' Her gaze became intense, her words evangelical. 'Don't you understand? *We are not the monsters.* They call us that because they have the numbers and the power, and all we can do against them is run and hide and "keep a low profile".' She said it with a pent-up disgust that Horst had seen his brother express, albeit with different emphasis. To his brother, the denizens of the day and of the night were all equally obstructive to his researches and he gave them all short shrift—greengrocer to gorgon, showgirl to succubus, they had all been put on the Earth to get in his *verdammten* way.

She continued, 'So, we have had enough. We shall marshal our forces and make a stand against them. We shall carve out an empire of the night for ourselves and defend it against them. We shall force them to negotiate and to compromise with us.'

Horst regarded her with astonishment. While the *Ministerium* was clearly organised, well funded, and capable, he had assumed its aims would be relatively small and focussed, albeit achieved by supernatural agency. The titles assigned to him and the others suddenly made a dreadful sense to him. They were not simply exercises in sycophancy—the intention was that they would indeed become nobles in this new nation of shadows. And to achieve that, they would first be . . .

'Generals. That's what we're supposed to be, is it?' he demanded of her. 'We're to raise armies?'

'Very literally in our cases. Yes. Now you understand, my Lord of the Dead. I shall raise dry bones and revenants. Devlin already has a regiment of shapechangers at his back. Not just wolves but bears from Scandinavia, tigers from India, foxes from Japan, hyenas and lions from Africa. You will create more of your line to become commanders and elite troops, and—when the Lord of Powers is brought to us—he or she will summon outsiders to fight for our cause and forge nature herself into a weapon. The mundane world will have no defences sufficient to resist our army. They will negotiate a settlement or every night will bring new suffering to them.'

She was breathing hard, her passion for the cause evident in her heat and the vigorous pulse at her throat. Horst found he couldn't look away from it.

He wanted to say that their plan was abominable. He wanted to say that the forces they commanded were by their very nature difficult to control, and that many innocent lives would be lost in the chaos of such a war. He wanted to say that he wanted no part of such madness. But all he could do was watch the blood throb beneath her pale, pale skin and say, 'What part in all this do the *Ministerium* themselves play? They all seem mundane. What do they do? How do they help us?'

'They are rich, and they are ambitious. De Osma is an occultist, as well as landed gentry. I think he was the one who formed the *Ministerium* in the first place. Collingwood is a businessman; von Ziegler is some minor noble seeking to re-establish his family's estates by gambling everything on this.'

'Investors. This is just about money and power to them.'

'De Osma has a scholarly interest in drawing together the darkness into one place where it can be more easily studied and classified. But yes. When were those worthy people who live in the light ever interested in anything more than money and power?'

Horst was raging, furious that these men were rallying forces that they must know would cause untold death and terror, yet there was not a tremor of that fury on his face. Horst seemed to be sinking away from control of his own body. There were other impetuses that were rising in importance, and none of them required rage for expression. Only cold, rational thought, so cold it lay like ice upon the surface of his reason. He saw how the ranks of those he would turn stood before him in his imagination, subordinate, obedient, and his. He felt how individually powerful they would be, and how all that power ultimately belonged to him. He saw the day running from him, the solar terminator fleeing like a routed army, and the world turning to eternal night in its wake. He saw Lady Misericorde removing the locket and choker from her throat and running the tip of her finger down the line of her jugular vein as she looked him in the eye.

'That glass wasn't enough, was it, Horst?' she said. 'You must be so very thirsty.'

He was astride her before he knew it himself. She gasped in surprise at the suddenness of his actions, but then laughed the delighted girlish laugh of getting a long-sought pony for her birthday. He was hardly aware of it; the coldness in his mind was turning to a single icy need and he no longer knew how to control it.

'So eager, aren't you? So needy . . .' She turned her head to expose the vein, coquettishly veiled in skin. 'Just a little, darling. Just a goblet's worth. We both need to be ready for tomorrow night.'

She sighed as the fangs penetrated, and held his head as he drank. She lay, complacent and aware as Horst fed. Beyond the obvious, even an astute onlooker would have been hard put to decide exactly who was taking what from whom.

Certainly, watching through a small gap where the door to the antechamber had been left ajar, it wasn't at all clear to Alisha.

An Interlude

Johannes Cabal lightly touched the side of his neck. A close examination in good light might have revealed two small scars as from punctures, fractionally paler than the already pale surrounding skin. The gesture was unconscious, but Horst pulled a sour face when he noticed it.

'Once,' he said. 'I did that once. And, to be fair, it was at least in part because you were being such an arse.'

'As I recall, I was running away,' said Cabal, lowering his hand to join the other on the counterpane. 'In what way does that fit your recollection?'

'You were running away like an arse.' Horst maintained an aggrieved face for some seconds before giggling.

'You are the least suitable "Lord of the Dead" I can imagine,' said his brother. 'Still, this "*Ministerium Tenebrae*" of yours . . .'

'Very distinctly *not* of mine . . .'

'This conspiracy of darkness, I don't suppose I should be surprised. They tend to pop up every few centuries when the not-entirely-human of the world finally have enough of being chased around by ubiquitous mobs, all equipped with burning torches and pitchforks as if there's a retail chain somewhere that supplies all their lynching needs. God knows I've had to put up with enough incidents like that in my time. I can almost sympathise with this *Ministerium*.'

Horst looked at him askance. 'Almost?'

'Of course. Except they do a poor job of learning from history. Every time somebody tries to do something like this, it ends in early victories quickly followed by a mass extermination of the supernatural rebels. It's like that statistical cycle they teach in schools about foxes and rabbits. It serves to shove them back into the misty coils of myth so the nice people can pretend such things never existed.' He ruminated for a moment. 'Although this is different. I don't recall it being backed by human agencies right from its onset, helping the legions of darkness as an investment opportunity. Still, free market capitalism and elemental evil have so much in common, I suppose the marvel is that it's never happened before. The other interesting detail is that the intention is to make limited gains. To create a new state and defend it instead of just galloping along as a horde, trying to take over the world. That shows foresight and a lot of common sense.'

Horst's look grew ever more askance. 'Does it?'

'Surely a regulated nation of assorted vampires, werewolves, necromancers, warlocks, witches, and the usual bump-in-the-night suspects is better than the alternative? A bogey man who's a citizen of Teratolia is . . .'

'A citizen of where?'

'"The Land of Monsters". You really are weak at classical languages, aren't you? As I was saying, a monstrous citizen of that shrouded land is, by definition, not under one's bed. He's at home, reading the paper, because he *has* a home. I imagine many governments, specifically the ones far away who wouldn't be losing any territory, would find that a very equitable solution.'

Horst shook his head. 'There's more to it than I've told you so far.'

'I thought there would be.' Cabal tilted his head back and breathed through his nose as he changed trains of thought at Cognition Junction. 'Misericorde. Never heard of her. While as a profession, we're not friendly with one another, we are wary, and that means we tend to be aware of one another's existences at least. A female necromancer—necromantrix?—is a rare creature indeed. In fact, with the exception of the dead yet delightful Miss Smith, I can think of none who are currently practising. Even she's more of a witch these days.'

Horst, however, had caught on to something else in Johannes's words that attracted his attention. 'The delightful Miss Smith?' he asked with a roguish smile. 'Does my little brother have a crush?'

Cabal started to deny it, but then instead blushed a little, and a small, perhaps even shy smile appeared on his own face. He leaned towards Horst and said in a lowered voice, 'She told me where to find the fifth volume of Darian's *Opusculus*.'

'Did she now?' Horst straightened up, his smile broadening. 'You old dog, you. Sharing occult books is like a dirty weekend to necromancers, isn't it?' He looked at the clock on Cabal's bedside and his amusement abated. 'I'd better crack on. I still have a lot to tell you, and dawn won't wait.'

Chapter 4

IN WHICH THE DEAD WALK AND THE LIVING FALL

Horst awoke with a feeling familiar from his mortal life, a feeling that he had done something the previous night that he would regret in the morning. That he awoke in the early evening of the following day did nothing to diminish that sense. He lay for several minutes within the darkness of his coffin, putting off the moment when he would have to lift the lid, climb down onto the step stool he had found tucked away in an alcove, and face up to the consequences of his weakness with Lady Misericorde. He wasn't sure whose morals he might have outraged in doing what he did, but he was confident that he had managed it nevertheless.

He pushed back the lid and rose to a vertical position as if his feet were attached to some ghastly hinge. It was a trick he'd learned some time before and, while he had no idea why vampires should be able to do such a thing, he was glad they did. Getting vertical without it would have involved a lot of half rolling and hanging a leg over the side, and the silly silk bow would likely have fallen off the bier, and it would all be terribly undignified.

As it was, it transpired he had an audience of the slow-clapping variety.

'Devlin,' he said, jumping lightly down. 'How boring to see you. You know, watching somebody sleeping could be construed as a bit creepy.'

Devlin leaned against the wall and crossed his arms, years of practise at playing the bad boy evident in his every move. 'We got off on the wrong foot, you and I. We're on the same side, after all.'

Horst wasn't sure they were. Lady Misericorde's succulent neck and divine blood aside, there was little he found to commend about his recent experiences. There was a belief inherent throughout the *Ministerium*'s thinking that all the creatures like him would eagerly embrace the concept of a land of the differently alive, but he, for one, just wanted to be left alone. The part of the plan assigned to him, for example, began perforce with the need to raise an elite cadre of vampires, 'raise' here used in a more ghoulish sense than most recruiters would be familiar with. He had never, ever infected anyone else with his condition and, given how unpleasant he found it, he was loathe to do so. The very idea of spreading vampirism, when he would happily have cast it off in a second if the means were provided, disgusted him. Yet, here he was, taken on as a human plague rat.

Feeding was pleasant enough—and here he was briefly distracted by memories of Misericorde's skin, the taste and scent of her, the effortless breaking of her skin and the smooth slide of his fangs into her flesh, the first spray of hot life onto his tongue before he fastened tight to her alabaster throat and . . .

Horst blinked, trying to recover the thread of his thoughts. Oh, yes.

Feeding was pleasant enough, as was the speed, the strength, and the ability to cloud minds. But they were balanced against being a monster, and that had never once been a feature in any of his planned careers. He missed the sun. He missed daylight and blue skies. He missed not being a target for vampire slayers.

He missed not having to talk to snotty werewolves.

'Yes, perhaps we did,' Horst lied, confident that the wrong foot was exactly the right place to be with the likes of 'Lord' Devlin. 'You seem very at home,' he added, letting *especially when uninvited in other people's rooms* float around unsaid. 'How long have you been here, in the castle?'

'I was the second to arrive. That was about a month ago. Lady Muck was here first. Got her legs well under the table, that one. Had laboratories set up and everything. They even provided her with staff, scientists and whatnot.'

Horst could not hide his surprise. 'How much money have these people got?'

Devlin shrugged, pleased at the impact the news had. 'Who knows? I think they more or less own this country, run-down little shithole that it is.'

'You've been out of the castle?'

'Ways and means, old man. Ways and means.' His smile turned to a grimace. 'It really is a dump, though. You're not missing much.'

'Even so, I'd like to sample the nightlife. So . . .'

Devlin looked at him, slightly amused, but thoughtful. 'Soon enough. Soon enough.' Without another word, he turned abruptly and walked out.

Horst was disinclined to pursue him. Instead he waited until he was sure Devlin had sufficient time to be thoroughly gone before venturing out into the main room. Alisha was there as was a bullet-headed man who snapped to attention and maintained a steely eyes-forward even when Horst deliberately crossed his line of sight and peered into his face as one might look down the barrel of a decommissioned cannon on a seafront promenade.

'You would be Herman, yes?' he asked.

'Yes, *sah!*' snapped the man. Then there was a near-audible crunch inside his head as one set of protocols attempted to override another. 'I mean, yes, m'Lud Horst. *Sah!*'

Horst regarded him with repressed amusement. 'You wouldn't happen to be ex-military, would you?'

For the first time, the little dark-brown eyes lurking beneath a ridged brow of similar aspect to a coastal artillery emplacement (to continue the heavy gun theme) swivelled away from the forward position. 'Yes, m'lud.' He spoke slowly and with obvious suspicion.

'It's in your bearing,' explained Horst, settling on the most flattering lie with the acuity of the practised wastrel. 'Shoulders, chest, you can tell a trained military man a mile away.' This seemed to placate Herman, for his eyes slid back to stare ahead.

Horst turned to smile at Alisha, but as he did, he noted that the ottoman sofa on which Lady Misericorde and he had, in their own ways, enjoyed a meal, was now neatly arranged once more. When he finally faced Alisha, her expression was prim to the point of hostility.

'Alisha,' he acknowledged her.

'My Lord Horst,' she replied, her politeness so perfectly insulting that she might have been to an English finishing school. He wasn't sure how she managed it, but the last time he'd felt so ashamed of himself was the time he discovered that his mother had discovered his discovery of onanism.

'You may return to your duties,' he said, and waved his hand in dismissal, hoping to cover his embarrassment. That both Alisha and Herman stayed exactly where they were did not help matters. 'You *must* have something to be getting on with,' he said, a little desperately.

'We are your staff, m'lud,' said Herman, impassive as a bollard yet slightly less attractive. 'Our duties are here.'

'Well, you don't both have to be here, do you? I can always call if I need both of you for something.'

Herman's thick brow thickened a little further. 'Like what, m'lud?'

'Oh, I don't know. I'm just talking eventualities.' He looked from one to the other with an emotion that sidled between exasperation and desperation. 'I'm sure you don't both need to be here every minute of the day. Night,' he added, old habits proving remarkably tenacious.

Alisha looked around. 'I suppose I could tidy up, my lord. Again.'

'I,' said Herman, fervour growing in his eye, 'shall polish your shoes, m'lud.'

Horst started to protest that he hadn't really had much of a chance to dirty them yet, but Herman was already collecting Horst's pristine shoes from his dressing room to go off and make them more pristine still, if such a thing were possible. Moments later and a peremptory door slam later, Horst was alone with Alisha.

'Look,' he began awkwardly. 'I detect some distinct hostility that wasn't there the last time we spoke. By a process of deduction, I'm assuming it's something to do with last night . . .'

'None of my business, my lord,' she said. She went to a low door in the bathroom and recovered cleaning supplies from it.

Horst watched her as she made herself busy with a can of metal polish, a soft cloth, and the fittings. He felt unhappy and uncertain why he felt so. She was right, after all—it *was* absolutely none of her business. Yet she was the closest thing to a normal person he had met since his unexpected return to the world of the near-as-damn-it living and he missed the moment of friendly intimacy he'd had with her the previous night, when she had been a nice lady called Alisha, and he had been a nice enough gentleman called Horst. Now he was the Lord of the Dead again and she was somehow aloof of him for all the apparent imbalance of power between them.

He sank into an armchair and watched her work for five silent minutes. Then he said, 'I don't want to be the Lord of the Dead, you know.'

She paused in polishing a candelabra, then continued without any further response.

He tried again. 'I'm just Horst Cabal. I never asked to be . . . this. I never asked to be risen from dust by the *Ministerium*. I never asked to be here. Where is *here*, anyway? Nobody tells me anything.' He rose to his feet. 'Apart from you. You're the only one who's spoken to me at all like a person speaks to another person. I'd appreciate it if you could talk to me like that again.' The polishing never faltered. 'I'd really appreciate it. Please.'

Alisha finished with the candelabra and started with its twin. Defeated, Horst sank back into the chair.

'I didn't realise it was such an obsession with people in this castle. Look, if you're envious about Lady Misericorde, you don't have to be. We could . . . you know . . .'

Alisha turned to face him across the room. 'We could *what*, exactly, my lord?'

'I could . . .' Horst had a feeling that he was no longer on thin ice but had already fallen through it. Now his every action was tantamount to flailing uselessly and making things worse, but you can't ask a drowning man to stop his flailing and just quietly slip into the freezing depths. 'You and I.' He lifted his upper lip and tapped a fang. 'You know.'

The hand holding the soft cloth was white-knuckled. 'Don't you dare touch me,' she said. 'You think that's why I'm angry? Because you haven't deigned to use me like cattle?'

'To be honest, I'm not sure,' he began. 'It's hard to understand what—'

'I'm not angry with you because you didn't fasten onto me like a great leech, you idiot.' She was becoming quite wonderfully angry, and Horst found himself liking her more and more. If he'd really been the monster the *Ministerium* had been hoping for, she'd probably be dead around now, but he wasn't, and so she wasn't. Instead, he sat and took it as this marvellous person tore into him as if he were some office Lothario trying his luck with the secretarial pool.

'I'm angry because you're letting that woman get her claws into you. You're right—you shouldn't be here. You're a monster and all, but you're better than them.' She dismissed her employers with a disdainful toss of the head.

'You.' He raised an accusing finger to point over her head. His mother had always taught him that you only pointed at men if they were in a lineup or you were looking for a fight, and you never pointed directly at women *at all*. He might have been the Lord of the Dead, but that didn't mean he had to be rude. 'You are going to get into trouble, talking like that in this place.'

'But you're not going to report me, are you, Horst?' She said it with certainty and he was so pleased with the sudden return of first-name terms, he didn't think to argue.

'I'm not, no. But walls have ears. You should be careful. I'm not sure the *Ministerium* dismisses staff like most employers. If they let you go, it'll be off the battlements.'

'I know.'

He leaned back, hand behind his head, and looked at her seriously. It felt strange, this slipping into a conspiracy within a conspiracy, but he had to say he preferred the company in this one. 'You're taking a lot on trust. I could be as bad as them.'

She shook her head. 'You've only drunk from people who have willingly given you that privilege.'

'Not quite true,' he corrected her. 'I didn't give wotsisname much choice. Encausse. Him.'

Alisha wrinkled her nose. 'Encausse is an arse,' she said, and they both giggled childishly.

'Don't call him an arse,' Horst chided her. 'I don't like the thought of drinking from one.' To which Alisha pulled a face and then they giggled again, mainly at her reaction.

Alisha sobered first. 'That won't happen again, though. You know that? They won't give up any more of their precious blood for you. In their new order, there'll be other people to provide it.'

Horst thought back to the sacrificial victims that Encausse had offered him when he was newly risen, and grew serious, too. 'There were some people who seemed to be willing enough.'

'How many?'

'Three. Encausse had three lined up for me to drain. I refused; it would have killed them.'

Alisha shook her head. 'No. You'd have risen them. Three women, was it?'

Horst started to nod and suddenly realised the significance of their sex and number. 'Are you seriously trying to tell me that they were to be "The Brides of Cabal"?'

'I'm perfectly serious. They want Vlad Țepeș, and they're using Bram Stoker for their research. They thought three brides was the necessary number because that's what it said in the *Vampire Instruction Book*. In any case, apart from carefully chosen candidates for you to convert, your general care and feeding will not involve members of the *Ministerium*.' She crossed her arms and looked at him critically. 'How do you think Alsager and his cronies feed?'

Horst looked at her uncomprehendingly.

'Devlin Alsager,' she explained patiently. 'He was in here just now. The Lord of the Transfigured.' This last she said with ironic disgust, as if the words tasted vile on her tongue.

'What does he eat?' said Horst, uncertain of why she had raised such a question and unhappy about the way it was likely to go. 'He had steak the other night.'

'He might settle for that when his pelt is on the inside, but do you really imagine a werewolf handling a steak knife? Now, Alsager, he really is a monster. Even if he had never transformed in his life, he would be a monster. He loves changing. He enjoys being physically powerful and dangerous. He likes the violence and the terror he causes. Then the *Ministerium* comes along and offers him political power to go along with all that. He's not having doubts. Not like you are.'

'What makes you think I'm having doubts?' he asked. He couldn't fathom her at all. She worked for the *Ministerium* yet took every opportunity to deride them and undermine any loyalty he might have felt to them for bringing him back from the dead. The possibility that she was an *agent provocateur* sent to test that loyalty continued to trouble him.

She didn't answer him directly, but said, 'It's a mystery why they chose you. The ritual to raise you was expensive to prepare—travel to the middle of nowhere to find you, transport back—it's a lot of trouble when there are active vampires closer at hand.'

'There are?' Horst abruptly felt a lot less special.

Alisha wrinkled her nose. '*Nosferatu*. Little more than rats in human form, but they're not all stupid. It would have been pretty easy to find one with enough brains and no morals to take the job.' She looked critically at Horst. 'Maybe they just wanted something prettier for their general of the dead.' Before he could say anything about his dismay at being chosen for the purposes of good public relations—presumably with the intention of putting him on recruiting posters at some point—she said, 'In any case, Alsager leads his pack out once or twice a month, out there.' She indicated the city below with a nod of her head. 'When they are sure you're the right . . . man for what they want, when they think they can trust you, they'll let you do the same.'

'Do what, exactly?' asked Horst with a growing sickness in his heart.

'Leave the castle. Go down into the city and find your own food.'

'Why would . . .'

'That's what a Lord of the Dead does, isn't it? You can go down there and feed, and start making new vampires.'

'I've never . . . I *would* never . . .'

'Where did you think the blood for your meal came from last night? Willing donors? It was taken.'

Horst thought of the bowl full of blood, he thought of the glass. He remembered a piquant scent to it, that he had known even then that it had all come from a single source, had known he could smell terror in it, all the chemicals a human body dumps into the bloodstream when it wants to fight or fly. This body had been able to do neither, just lie helpless while a needle was inserted and a meal for the newcomer was drained. Over a pint of blood drawn. He thought of the empty glass, how good it had made him feel as he savoured the blood and the taint of fear that came with it.

Horst put the back of his hand to his mouth and stood aghast, his gaze flicking from one section of floor to another but all unheeding of anything he saw. He looked at Alisha. 'Who are you? And don't say "a friend".'

'I'm not your friend,' she replied, meeting his gaze unflinchingly. 'But you're really not what we expected. I'm not so very sure that I'm your enemy either, after all.'

'What? What does that mean?' Horst was confused and the confusion was making him angry. He was starting to get the very distinct sense that when Alisha spoke of *we*, she was not talking about the *Ministerium Tenebrae* at all. 'That you *were?*'

Alisha started to reply, but never got that far. The muffled sound of a shot stopped the words in her throat. She looked at the window. 'Sometimes there's shooting in the city,' she said. 'There's almost no law down there.'

'No.' Horst was heading towards the door. 'That came from inside the castle.'

He flung open the door to the antechamber, crossed it in a few long strides, and opened the door out into the corridor more circumspectly, Alisha a few steps behind him. If he was concerned about his exit being overheard, it was all for naught as pandemonium was breaking out in the castle, shouts and the clatter of footsteps echoing from the stone walls. Then there was another shot and a cry of mortal agony.

Horst gained the walkway around one of the castle's sundry halls, this one being an impressive entrance from the inner courtyard. Some twenty feet from the door to the courtyard was Herman, a revolver in his hand, and a naked man some small distance from him, writhing prone in a widening pool of dark blood. The man was hirsute to a freakish extent, but as Horst watched and the death throes weakened, the dense hair on the man's back thinned away as if melting into his flesh. With a blink of amazement, Horst realised he was watching the death of a werewolf.

Herman backed away towards the door, his revolver swinging from side to side, a warning to anyone else who might be foolish enough to try to stop him. Horst watched events playing out, utterly confused. Why had the werewolf attacked Herman? Weren't they all on the same side? One big happy family of conspirators ushering in a shiny new age of monsters' rights?

Then the door swung open and Herman turned to face this new threat. For a moment there was nothing visible outside. Then something moved slowly, walking steadily and implacably towards Herman. From somewhere Lady Misericorde's voice rang out. 'Keep your . . . people away from him, Lord Devlin! No more need die. I shall deal with this.'

A moment later the reason for her confidence became apparent. Why risk the living when the dead are available? The shape in the door resolved itself into a walking corpse, appallingly thin, its clothes hanging as loosely upon it as its own skin. Without hesitation Herman shot it in the head and it fell without a sound but for the faint crump of dropped laundry. Already there were three more behind it, and beyond them in the darkness of the courtyard that terrible, ponderous rhythm like a deathly pendulum marked by the walk of the dead.

Belatedly, Horst was beginning to realise that perhaps Herman did not hold the *Ministerium* in very high regard.

'Oh, no.' Alisha was at Horst's side at the railing above, an audience for an impromptu Grand Guignol performance. Her voice was barely above a whisper, quavering with emotion. 'Herman . . .'

It was impossible that he could have heard her. Yet, he looked up and saw them there. He did not waver or show the slightest expression of manifest fear. He only spoke, not shouted, a single word, and it came to them as if he had been standing a pace away.

'Run.'

Then he turned, dropped two more of the revenants with perfectly placed bullets to the head, and then without hesitation placed the gun barrel in his mouth angled up towards the centre of his palate, and fired the last round in his revolver.

As he fell, a red mist in the air above him, Horst turned away. He wanted to think it was in horror, and in a sense, it was. But it was an inner horror that, if he watched Herman collapse, his blood spraying across the blue marbled floor, Horst might find his dismay was rooted in the arrant waste of that sustaining, precious blood.

Turning away did, however, have the advantage of distracting him. Alisha was gone. Perturbed by her stealthiness as much as by her absence, Horst re-entered the anteroom.

Entering the room beyond, he surprised her at the cupboard where the cleaning supplies were kept. He was in the process of being impressed by her devotion to duty being such that she wanted to clean up the mess while Herman's heart had barely stopped beating, when she pulled from the cupboard a coil of ochre-coloured rope with one hand and a semi-automatic pistol sporting a very businesslike silencer with the other. This latter she then shot him with, twice, once through each lung.

'Ow!' he cried, at least as much with indignation as pain. The pain, he had to admit, was not as great as he would have expected from two probably fatal wounds. 'What . . . ?' It was, however, also suddenly much harder to speak, as the air wheezed out of the bullet holes like a poorly maintained harmonium. A moist, slightly bubbly harmonium.

He staggered a little, unsure whether he should drop to one knee because he'd been shot or because it was the dramatically correct thing to do. He did so anyway, to give himself something to do while he thought about it.

Alisha, in contrast, required no thinking time at all. She had shoved the gun into the loop of her maid's apron and opened the French windows and was now on the balcony, tying the end of the rope off around two of the stone balustrades. When she was done—and it took only seconds—she gave it a few fierce tugs to check its security before heaving the coiled bulk of the rope over the rail and into the darkness. It had not even had the chance to become taut under its own weight before she was pulling a simple looped harness over her head and shoulders to rest in her armpits, snapping its carabiner onto the rope, and curling a length around her body. She climbed over the rail and leapt without hesitation into the void.

She got perhaps a yard into her spectacular escape when it all came to an abrupt halt. Her first thought was that a tangle in the rope had jammed the carabiner, producing the sudden shock, but then she looked up and saw Horst standing on the balcony, his feet braced against the bases of two alternate balusters, one hand upon the rail, and the other holding—she realised with a sharp flame of terror in her guts—the free end of the rope, slightly frayed where he had apparently snapped it atwain as a child might a thread. He looked down at her, and by his expression, she took him to be greatly irked.

'I want you to remember this,' he said. Blood, black in the half light, glistened from the bullet wounds, pulsing slowly like crude oil from a punctured drum.

She swallowed, forced down her fear. 'If you're going to kill me, just do it, monster. Don't gloat. It's unseemly.'

Horst's expression darkened still further. 'How are you supposed to remember anything if I just drop you?' he demanded. 'You're a member of this Dee Society they mentioned earlier, aren't you?'

'I'm telling you nothing.'

Horst almost spat with frustration. 'They are going to be here any minute to find you. Dee Society . . . yes or no?'

She said nothing but looked defiantly up at him, and then gave a quick glance below. Horst was sure she was gauging how far she could rappel before he let go and whether it would make any difference to her chances. The quickness of the glance and the fact that she didn't then try to go any further assured him that she had arrived at the conclusion that the only difference conceivable was a fractional one in the depth of the crater she would make on impact with the riverbank below.

'I'll take that as a "yes". You're opposed to the *Ministerium*?' He didn't even wait for an answer this time. 'Good. I can't say I like them, either. Go. I'll tell them I threw you in the river. But you and I, we are having a serious conversation soon. I will look for you.' Alisha looked at him somewhat dumbfounded and he found he had to waggle the rope a little and repeat, 'Go!' to motivate her. 'I'm strong, but I'm not Atlas. I can't hold you up forever.'

Demonstrating the admirably pragmatic and rapid decision making with which he and his lungs were already acquainted, she slipped away without another word, making swift progress towards the earth below where, Horst had no doubt, the next part of her pre-planned escape route waited. Perhaps a dehydrated bicycle or a folding horse; he could put nothing beyond her. Such fancies kept him occupied for the next minute as he gathered the remains of his failing strength and concentrated on not inadvertently killing an ally.

Probably an ally, he corrected himself. There was still much to learn in this mysterious castle of the Red Queen before he could be reasonably sure where lay the battle lines.

Devlin Alsager crashed through the door some twenty seconds later. He was a good eighteen inches taller than he had been last time Horst saw him and a great deal hairier, but he still bore the very distinctive swagger and poor choice in cologne.

The werewolf stopped abruptly when it saw him, forcing a little backpedalling as his claws skittered on the polished stone of the floor. Still, he did it with an agility and, it had to be admitted, a *soupçon* of panache that rendered the performance quite stylish rather than ridiculous, and for that, Horst disliked him all the more. Devlin made an attractive werewolf; all rippling musculature beneath a pale grey pelt of beautiful fur that curled and ran in waves as if part of the metamorphosis involved a small army of cosmetologists and a gallon of hairspray. 'Where is the bitch?' he roared in a voice that would have shredded the larynx of a stevedore.

'Bitch?' said Horst mildly. He arranged himself in an armchair with elaborate nonchalance. 'Why, were you planning on mating with her?' He found himself unexpectedly unimpressed by the presence of a werewolf. He had, after all, spent a year with a travelling carnival and had thus spent plenty of time with freaks, monstrosities, and other members of the public. A massive, powerful man-wolf hybrid, a creature of primal myth was, therefore, disappointingly underwhelming, all the more when you understood that its human form was a scoundrel, a *poseur*, and an awful dick.

'Where *is* she?' demanded the wolf-cum-boor. He took a few steps closer and finally seemed to notice the blood on Horst's chest. 'She shot you!' His tone implied Horst had allowed himself to be tagged in a playground game and therefore ended up kissing a girl or something else equally horrid. There was certainly an air of the class bully in the way he said it that made it through the wolf's vocal cords of rusty piano strings.

'She certainly did,' agreed Horst. He grimaced slightly, a man finding a strawberry pip stuck between his teeth. He coughed once, then again more violently, and spat into his hand. He held his expectorate up between thumb and forefinger—more solid than one might expect, and slightly shiny. 'Ah. A souvenir. A .32-calibre, I think. The other did me the decency of going straight through. So, yes. She shot me, and you can see the good it did her.'

'Where is she?' repeated Devlin, low and threatening.

Horst tutted, a first-class passenger who has just discovered some ruffian in his train carriage. 'I threw her out of the window. I heard a splash after a few seconds.' He rocked his head while he recollected the moment. 'Quite a few seconds. You don't realise how high we are here until you throw somebody out of the window.'

And here he paused, and looked significantly at Devlin.

'She still managed to shoot you.' Devlin's wolfishness was slightly in abeyance, the muzzle shortened, the hair less flowing. Horst hoped he wasn't going to change all the way back, since he was naked, and Horst had endured enough unpleasantness for one evening.

'I was distracted by the commotion in the hall,' explained

Horst, keeping his tone light and bantering enough to be profoundly insulting without being obviously so.

Horst was also playing for time a little. He was concentrating on regenerating the torn and friction-burnt skin of his hand where the rope had been wrapped around it, and where the length secured around the balustrades had argued with him for a second as he snapped it off. These tattered shreds of expensive silken climbing rope now lay under him on the chair. He hoped Alisha had shown enough aplomb under pressure to dump the bulk of the rope into the river, or he might find himself faced with some difficult questions as to its provenance. 'That man Herman. Your travelling dog show seemed to come off second best there. Just as well m'Lady Misericorde was to hand with her shambling entourage or I might have had to deal with him, too.'

This barb landed, and Devlin's still very lupine ears folded back with anger. 'He had silver bullets!'

Horst held up the bullet again, scratched at its side with his thumbnail, and showed the resulting gleam to Devlin. 'So did my former maid. It didn't slow me down greatly.' He smiled complacently and, he gauged, infuriatingly. 'I really must crack on and create some new vampires as we're obviously going to need them. Not too quickly, though. I'll be careful about who I choose for the honour. Don't want to let just anyone in, do we?'

This, at last, was too much for Devlin, who turned on his heel and stamped out all of a dudgeon. Horst was displeased that such was the state of his metamorphosis by this point that Devlin was showing very little tail and far too much buttock cleavage. 'Don't forget to shut the door!' he called after the retreating werewolf. 'I am temporarily without staff.'

The door slammed, and Horst—perhaps forgivably, perhaps not—laughed.

Chapter 5

IN WHICH HORST CLIMBS A WALL AND
DISCOMFORTS A WEREWOLF

It took perhaps twenty minutes before it occurred to anyone that it might be a good idea to see if there was any trace of Alisha beneath Horst's window and, when they did, they neglected to bring along any of Devlin's gang of shapechangers who might have been able to find a scent. There was no body and no rope in evidence, and they accepted Horst's story without demur, two bullet wounds and a scowling vampire lord being sufficient to close that avenue of inquiry.

Horst changed his shirt and, his hand having already healed, he applied his will to knitting the chest wounds shut. It proved tiring and, although he was able to close them, they were a long way short of healed. He obviously needed more blood.

He made do with some gauze and surgical tape he found in a first aid box. The front wounds were easy enough, but the exit wound through his right lung proved awkward to get at and he spent a frustrating quarter of an hour puppeteering a dressing into position using far too much tape and the bathroom mirror. Not for the first time, he was relieved that the tale about vampires casting no reflection was—for his brand of bloodsucker at least—not true.

For the first time Horst was beginning to see that the true weakness of a vampire is not all the business with bursting into flame in direct sunlight, inconvenient though it may be. Nor was it a vulnerability to stakes through the heart as, when one pauses to really think about it, that's rather a vulnerability of all animals. Astonishing yet true. Running water did not hinder him, nor did holy water or garlic cause him any great dismay beyond 'Oh, I'm wet' and 'Oh, that's quite smelly'. In short, being a vampire was not nearly as unpleasant as it might have been but for the one great weakness that was the reliance on human blood.

Horst had experimented with the blood of other animals, but quite apart from the inconvenience of stalking a sleeping horse or cow and the difficulty of penetrating horsehair or cowhide with fangs that aren't all that long really, the result did not warrant the trouble. Their blood was foul, and offered little sustenance. Human vampires had evolved or been created—depending on which authority one listened to—to predate on humans only. It was a nuisance, but there it was. A very great nuisance.

He had been able to work around it in his previous existence. The life of a travelling vaudevillian with a carnival moving around the countryside had been ideal. He had taken a little here, a little there, gently erasing memories of his semi-willing donors, women all, leaving just a pleasant and pleasurable reminiscence of some feverish canoodling with a tall, handsome man in the shadows behind the Ghost Train. Not having a carnival to hand, he was at a loss as to how to refill his veins without resorting to the kindnesses of the *Ministerium Tenebrae*. To do so would exacerbate the vulnerability that already troubled him. They would smile and bow and fetch him some blood from somewhere. From someone. Who knew what horrors they were perfectly delighted to commit on his behalf in the castle dungeons? However they did it, he would ultimately be responsible.

Possible alternatives, however, seemed little better. He could haunt the corridors and take, as was his wont, a little here and a little there, endangering no one. Yet this was not a regimen he could practise for long before he was leaving everyone around the place looking terribly anaemic. Another alternative . . .

He finished dressing and went out of his apartments. His path took him by the hall in which Herman had mounted his last stand and Horst paused to look down at the site of the little battle. It was predictably and, Horst found, dispiritingly clean. No sign of Herman's blood and brains, nor the blood of the werewolf whom he had slain, nor of grave mould from Lady Misericorde's platoon of walking dead. The cleaning staff here were clearly efficient, thorough, and unsurprised by such things.

Thinking of the shambling, implacable horde of revenants put him once again in mind of his brother, Johannes, and the acidic disdain in which he held such things. Apparently it was relatively easy to create zombies of that ilk, but they were so mindless and divorced from the truly living that Johannes regarded them as a frippery, a silly trick to impress the peasantry. It was plain that Lady Misericorde held no such foibles. She was an impure creature in so many ways.

Horst found his breathing had deepened and shook himself from a reverie that was loitering on the outskirts of luridness.

He pushed himself away from the railing and wandered off with no great intention of going anywhere especially. The corridors were not anonymous, littered with distinctive bric-a-brac that made navigation easy. A suit of armour with a helmet visored with a bear's likeness here, an occasional table decorated with a vase of only slightly dusty silk flowers there. He wandered past them all, unconsciously noting them, but otherwise steeped in thought and a growing hunger.

After some ten minutes, the unending artificiality of his surroundings began to wear on him and he sought the open air. This he gained through a door into an unoccupied suite of rooms less imposing yet more impressive than his own. Here the ceiling was at a slightly more human height although still high, with delicate renderings in blue and white set into the plaster. It all seemed very grandiose and, given the number of visitors of one hue or another that the castle was currently enjoying, a little odd that it was vacant. He walked silently amid the furniture, all of it bulky and anonymous beneath dust sheets. Still, it had what he most desired at that moment, a wide set of windows opening onto a balcony three times the size of the one in his chambers.

The doors out onto the balcony were unlocked and the handles moved easily beneath his hands as he opened them and stepped out into the coolness of the night air. He looked up at first, at the almost clear sky, the harshly glittering stars only occasionally occluded by dashing rags of high cloud. A gibbous moon hung over the scene, soaking the world in an unhealthy blue-white glow. Then Horst looked down and was surprised to find the city below spread out before him. The river ran narrow here—no more than thirty feet across—and was crossed a little to his left by a covered stone bridge that finished in a drawbridge. This, he noted, was up. Beyond it lay a great square that must have been impressive when occupied by a crowd, or a market, or even when empty. Now, however, it was home to a shantytown of sorts. He looked down at the few figures wandering hither and yon, and the fires that glowed in front of some of the lean-tos and caravans that made up this temporary addition to the permanent fibre of the city.

Not *that* permanent, Horst had to admit to himself as he looked at the buildings that bordered that square on three sides. Several seemed to have been abandoned to squatters and looters, holes poked in the rooves by ridge-walking thieves and the actions of unmitigated weather. It was a sad sight. When it was all in repair it would have been as pretty as a picture on a box of reasonably expensive biscuits, he was sure. To see it dying, the ribs poking through the skin, was horrible. Those poor people down there, living hand to mouth in the ruins of their lives.

He watched a young woman carrying a bucket to the municipal pump. That, at least, was still working. She hung the bucket over the nozzle and started pushing down hard on the pump handle. He could hear the water rushing in short, energetic bursts into the waiting steel. Those poor people. He could see her back curve in the moonlight as she put her weight into it. Those poor, poor people. He could almost hear her heart rate increasing, could almost hear how her pulse hammered. Those poor, poor, vulnerable people . . .

Horst closed his eyes and carefully released his grip on the balcony rail. The words Alisha had spoken to him barely an hour before echoed in his head. When the *Ministerium* were sure that they could trust him, they'd let him loose on the town to feed, and to recruit. It wasn't that they could think such a thing appalled him now. Not nearly so much as how reasonable it all sounded to him at that hungry moment.

He clenched the rail again until he could feel flakes of paint crackling from it. A marred coat of paint seemed a small price to pay for a moment's stillness inside him.

Across the night air, he could hear distant cries from the city, laughter, even some music, and this calmed him. Human durability, the knack of being able to make merry amid the ruins, was heartening and, although he didn't realise it then, reminded him that these were not herd animals to be hunted. Once, he had not been so very different from them.

He could hear an argument going on, too, and in his meditative state he did not understand immediately that it was not wafting up from the fragrant stews of the city below, but rather from the castle above. He leaned out a little and looked upwards. Across the castle's frontage, some fifty yards away and a floor further up, a window stood open, and through it he could make out the voices of the *Ministerium Tenebrae*. They did not sound angry nearly so much as worried, perhaps even a shade panicked. It was not the image they had gone to such lengths to portray earlier, as efficient, emotionless, and rational. Surely a couple of spies in their midst had not caused such disarray, he wondered. Especially given that, to their imperfect knowledge, both were dead. So, why the raised voices?

He closed his eyes and focussed his senses, but the light wind blew their words away but for the occasional snatch of speech. 'Inconceivable,' he heard. 'Loyalties lie.' 'Procedures.' It was provocative to his curiosity, and for once his curiosity and his self-interest were perfectly aligned.

The castle was the best maintained of all the buildings he could see, but it was old and the stonework was rendered imperfect by the actions of time and climate. A human with the privilege of walking in daylight without igniting like a perambulatory Roman candle would rightly have regarded the ascent and traverse of such a distance without climbing gear as a ridiculously dangerous undertaking. Horst, by contrast, had his shoes, socks, and jacket off in a twinkling and was already making a slow but steady assault on the wall. While he might not be able to transform into a bat or a large black dog, Horst thought to himself as he made a diagonal beeline across the curtain wall, he at least had the remarkable climbing ability ascribed to some vampires. This was a revelation to him, as he had never previously known cause requiring him to impersonate a great gecko. Now that the talent was revealed, it was actually rather fun. Possibly not as much fun as turning into a bat, but one takes amusement where one finds it.

He crept under the edge of the open window and grew still, listening while marvelling how little effort the feat of sticking to the stone like a limpet was costing him.

'. . . a covey of ill-organised, inconsequential romantics.' That was de Osma. 'Their spies were detected and dealt with in good order. And, mark you, by our generals.'

'You're being pretty relaxed about a breach in security,' replied the dry, slow tones of the American, Collingwood.

'I did not say I was *happy* about tonight's events . . .'

'That they were dealt with is really not what concerns me,' Collingwood said over him. 'It's that they got in here in the first place. Hell, how did those nutjobs even find out about us?'

'Yes!' von Ziegler piped up. 'That worries me, too. We've gone to so much trouble to keep this secret until the time is right. How did they know?'

'And how much did they report?' added Collingwood.

'The former we don't yet know,' said de Osma, ever the leader. 'The latter we know a little of. Herman, the spy who killed himself rather than be taken, was detected in the act of preparing a messenger pigeon to fly from a loft of sorts he'd established in a disused tower.'

'Pigeons?' Von Ziegler was shrill. 'How did he get pigeons in here undetected?'

'That is the least of our concerns,' said de Osma. Horst could almost hear the shrug in his voice. 'Conjurors conceal birds easily. Smuggling in a few pigeons was probably a more trivial task than you think. No, how many messages he had managed to send before we stopped him, *that* is of concern to us.'

'I would've guessed Lady Misericorde might be able to get something out of him,' said Collingwood. 'Can't she—I don't know—use some of that necromancer hoodoo and make him talk?'

'Apparently not,' said de Osma. 'She tells me that the bullet destroyed the brain, so she has nothing to work with. Might even be the reason why he did it.'

'The fact remains that they are small in number and widespread,' said Collingwood. 'How great a threat do they represent?'

There was a pause marked by light footsteps on a carpeted floor and the *chink* of glassware as de Osma poured himself a drink. The ghost of a gulp, then: 'If you had asked me that a week ago I would have said no substantial threat at all. Now . . . I am not nearly so certain. There was money and organisation involved behind this infiltration. I think the Dee Society may be more capable than we had previously believed.'

'We've been so careful,' said von Ziegler, returning to his previous theme. 'Everybody vetted. Everybody observed. How is this possible?'

'We had done everything possible,' agreed Collingwood, but after an ironically measured pause he added, 'everything *humanly* possible.'

'You suspect one of the generals?' said de Osma in a peremptory tone. 'Impossible. They have as much to gain by our plans as we do.'

'That Cabal fella doesn't seem convinced,' said Collingwood.

'Oh . . . No. No, we have some way to go with him yet. But the spies had entered our employ before he was even resurrected. I doubt his powers extend quite that far.'

There was a grumble of reluctant agreement from Collingwood. 'That leaves us with Misericorde and Alsager,' he said. 'And, no, they don't make sense, either.'

'What about Alsager's mob?' suggested von Ziegler. 'He gathered them very quickly, in a matter of months. How do we know he didn't sweep up somebody who doesn't agree with our aims?'

'Because even Alsager doesn't trust them,' said de Osma. 'He keeps a close eye on them, believe me. Gentlemen, we are going in circles. Worse, we are falling into the trap of doubting ourselves. If this evening's business has any utility to us at all, it is to make us realise that we are not unobserved, and that time is of the essence. We must move ahead. Immediately. This very night.'

There was some consternation at this.

'But we're not ready,' rumbled Collingwood. 'You admitted that our "Lord of the Dead" may not be all we had hoped for, and the Lord of Powers is still not with us. That means we only have two generals to count upon.'

'But they are the two who can provide numbers,' said de Osma. 'In military terms, we have infantry—or at least we shall when we have raided enough mortuaries and graveyards—and we have cavalry. We shall just have to forgo vampiric elite troops until Cabal either toes the line or is replaced, and the occult artillery the Lord of Powers will supply when he is finally brought here. He is overdue, I admit, but should be here shortly. The field agents' reports have been reassuring on that front—we shall have our thunder and lightning soon enough.'

De Osma started to speak, but he was interrupted by raised voices beyond the room's door, which was suddenly flung open.

'Alsag . . . My Lord Devlin!' said von Ziegler. 'What is the meaning of this?'

Horst suddenly had a very bad feeling. He crept in a tight circle and started making his way as quickly as he dared back to the balcony from which he had sortied. It did him little good. There was a clatter of the window being opened more widely and Alsager's triumphant cry: 'There!' Horst stopped and performed a clockwise half turn so he could look back. Alsager was leaning out of the window, pointing at Horst for the benefit of the *Ministerium*, who were crammed behind him in the window, as if they might need assistance in noting a man clinging to a sheer wall not twenty feet away.

'Lord Horst! What is the meaning of this?' cried de Osma, astonishment losing ground to an outrage so acute that he was reduced to shouting people's names and demanding what the meaning of this was.

'Oh, you know,' said Horst noncommittally. They evidently didn't know, so he clarified. 'Just getting some air. Such a nice evening I just thought I'd just . . . have a bit of a scuttle.' He left it there, hoping that they'd accept this as perfectly normal behaviour for vampires.

'I think we need to have a talk,' said de Osma. 'Please join us here. And use the stairs.' He and his colleagues disappeared back into the room, but it did not require the acute hearing of a vampire to know that they were muttering suspiciously among themselves the instant that they were out of view. Only Devlin Alsager was left, and he took the opportunity to smirk like the class snitch who has successfully contrived to get somebody into trouble with the teacher.

'I can't wait to hear what you come out with to explain spying on them,' he said. Then his eyes flicked away and the smile faltered, dimmed by surprise and curiosity. 'What's going on down there?'

Horst followed his gaze off onto a large area of scrubland beyond the river that might have been a common at some point. A few tents clustered in the corner closest to the town, but otherwise it was tangled and wild with brambles and thistles. Rising from its far side was a thin vaporous trail of pale smoke that caught the moonlight strongly as it drifted slowly in the slight breeze. Horst followed the track into the sky to its end just in time for it to suddenly erupt into a brilliant green light that floated slowly back to earth, illuminating the broken land beneath in a stuttering, eerie glow that threw long, shifting shadows. Horst's first thought was somebody had shot off a firework, but he immediately corrected that. It was a signal flare. How odd, he mused. Who might they be signalling, and why?

He was answered in the next moment by a high-pitched *chink* as stone above him cracked and flaked away, accompanied by a momentary whine like an angry hornet flying by to cause mischief elsewhere. Such was his surprise at all these entertainingly unusual events occurring so closely together that he was, by his own later admission to himself, ashamed that he did not immediately divine what was happening.

That took Alsager's cry of anger as he ducked away from the window in the same instant that another passing hornet dealt the glass a shattering impact.

Oh, thought Horst with all the calmness of the utterly surprised. *Those are bullets.*

He looked around and saw flashes down amidst the shanties of the town square and spread around the common. Distant cracks of rifles firing floated to him, sounding so unthreatening as to be almost pleasant. A bullet ricocheting from the wall close enough to his head to make him wince disabused him of that notion and he started to scuttle as quickly as a vampire might horizontally. When he was over the balcony, he allowed his grip to fail and fell some twenty feet onto the hard stone, a landing he achieved gracefully. He snatched up his jacket and shoes from where he had left them and was about to dash into the safety of the abandoned apartment when he saw a flash on the common that illuminated what seemed to be ripples spreading from its centre, as if from a pebble tossed into a pond. His curiosity was such that it did not occur to him that this might presage a bad thing, until said bad thing turned out to be a mortar shell striking the castle wall. Then the window behind him shattered from the blast and he was thrown onto his back, stone chippings peppering his clothes and skin.

It could only be the Dee Society, he was sure. So much for the tiny gathering of concerned academics that the *Ministerium* had posited. Any society that could field upwards of fifty armed souls with supporting light field pieces was not a very polite society.

He felt the thud of a distant concussion travel through the land, through the castle walls, and into his back with a swiftness that the airborne sound lacked, and was thus warned of another incoming shell while it was still in transit. He rolled onto his front and thence to his feet in a blur of accelerated motion that left stone chippings that had been lying on his chest still in the air by the time he attained the safety of the room.

The detonation was closer this time, and he didn't feel quite so happy with said attained safety as the gorgeous plasterwork cracked and rained down on his head and shoulders. Hoping to attain somewhere that actually *was* safe, he dashed for the door and so out into the hallway.

There he was, jacketed and lacing his second shoe, when his most recently attained safety was rendered anything but, although not on this occasion by a kilogramme of explosive but by the appearance of the far too ubiquitous Lord Devlin Alsager. He appeared at the base of a flight of steps to Horst's right in a flurry of collarless linen and frills, Byronic and uncalled-for. He fixed Horst with a furious glare, and cried, 'You!'

'Obviously,' said Horst, concluding the business of tying his shoelace.

'You didn't kill her, did you?'

Horst straightened up. He had a distinct sense that things were going to get very unfriendly in the next few minutes. When he was rested and fed, he was literally faster than the human eye could follow, could force himself from the perception of mundane folk, and had the strength of ten. Unhappily, he was neither rested nor fed, and he had consumed much of his reserves in repairing assorted pieces of damage he had suffered that night—rope burns, bullet holes, et al.

He looked at Devlin Alsager, a man better suited to propping up hotel bars in search of lonely divorcees, yet given the rank of general, the title of lord, and *carte blanche* to feed—quite literally—upon a population who looked to have enough problems without being further victimised by a twat.

It didn't seem right to Horst, it didn't seem fair, and he was a man who had a problem turning his back on things that were neither right nor fair. No more duplicity, he decided. No more going along with this charade.

'By "her", I assume you mean Alisha?'

'First-name terms, eh?' sneered Alsager, a man whose upper lip looked bereft without a sneer, a smirk, or a curl to disfigure it.

'Of course first-name terms. She was a maid. It's traditional.' The strange alien part of Horst was playing around with ways of killing Alsager in the most exquisite of agonies amid a concerto of cracking bones and snapping sinews. For once, Horst let such fancies run.

'Yes, of *course* it is,' said Alsager, giving the impression that he was making a noble concession in admitting the point. 'Yes, the maid. You didn't kill her, did you?'

'The maid who shot me? Twice, that is. Once through each lung. That maid? Just trying to be sure. Wouldn't want to end up talking about a different one.' Horst could feel his patience with the preening idiot slipping. The cold part of his mind was wondering if he could keep Alsager alive long enough to make him eat his own spleen, having first pulled it directly from the abdomen before driving it down that yakking mouth and sealing the gullet. *Possibly*, thought Horst. *Why don't we give it a go?*

Alsager looked as if he'd just about done with the dance before the big event, too. 'Of course her. You let her go, didn't you?'

And there Horst was, his last chance to dissemble before him. He simply could not be bothered.

'Yes,' he said clearly. 'I let her go. This whole thing, this conspiracy, it sickens me. Alisha and poor Herman, God rest him, there's more to admire in them, more bravery in their little fingers than in this whole debased fiasco.' His words were punctuated by another shell striking the castle ramparts. 'Yes, I let her go. Now, what do you propose to do about it, you mutt?'

Alsager advanced a step, his posture arcing forward a little as he did. Horst could hear bone and cartilage creaking and re-forming as Alsager began his metamorphosis. It sounded injurious to health if practised frequently, and Horst could only assume old werewolves resorted to walking sticks. It also sounded painful. As he watched Alsager sweat and grunt and tear at his clothes, he sincerely hoped so.

'You think you're so much better than me, don't you?' said Alsager, more in a snarl than a human voice.

Horst shrugged while he wondered if he should run or fight. 'Oh, I wouldn't say that. It would be rude to actually *say* it.'

Alsager was finished with talking, however, both temperamentally and physiologically thanks to his larynx becoming rather too lupine for easy chatter. He took another step, and this time fell forward onto all fours. Clawed fingers scratched at the floor as he sought purchase for a headlong charge at Horst.

Horst, for his part, was wearing shoes with sensible rubber soles, and had no such problems. This he demonstrated by running at the wall with sufficient rapidity to run up it to head height, along until he was behind Alsager, whereupon he landed lightly, swivelled, and kicked the werewolf forcefully up his hairy arse.

His foot landed upon the wolfish perineum on the upstroke with sufficient force to loft Alsager's hindquarters over his head in the manner of an airborne forward roll that lacked sufficient height to complete successfully. Instead Alsager landed on his back with his head pointing towards Horst. From this perspective, he saw Horst smile, wave, and hare off down the corridor at an impressive sprint. Alsager, while grateful that at least his testicles hadn't been crushed in the encounter, was nevertheless furious at this outrage to his dignity. He rolled onto his feet, or paws, or claws, and sped off in murderous pursuit.

Horst had no clear idea where he was going, but anything in the 180-degree arc that did not include an angry lycanthrope seemed to have its charms. He was well past the stairs from which Alsager had emerged when he heard voices he recognised raised in anger from that same direction. It seemed he had blotted his copybook with the *Ministerium Tenebrae* to an irredeemable degree. Ah, well.

Horst broke left and headed in the direction he fondly believed must contain the main entry. As a child, he and his brother had been trooped around a fine selection of English castles by their parents in an attempt to inculcate them in the perplexing ways of their new home. In these he had taken a romantic interest, and could trace the evolutionary path from an Iron Age hill fort, through a motte and bailey, up to the concentric castle—his favourite—and onward to the star redoubts of the Napoleonic Wars. This place, however, confused him. While undoubtedly of great defensive worth, it seemed relatively modern, certainly no more than a couple of centuries old. It was full of halls and great chambers, but not a single courtyard he had yet seen. It was as if some terrifyingly rich individual had taken a fancy to some site, probably that of an older and more practical castle, and extended it so ruthlessly in his preferred style that the former building now only lurked here and there in the endless corridors that enwrapped the place.

He burst through a door and found himself overlooking the entry hall. Any pleasure at a successful piece of intuitive navigation, however, was swiftly muted on discovering it blocked, shoulder to shoulder, by a great crowd of dead men. As one, they looked up and watched him with no curiosity at all, merely seeking out movement. He glanced across their ranks and saw at their rear Lady Misericorde. She gave him an indecipherable look that disquieted him far more than the dead-eyed stares of her zombie army. Then the main castle door was opened ahead of them and the dead stumbled out into the night, to hunt and kill the attackers. The doorway was hopelessly congested, he could see; there was no swift exit to be had there. Alsager appeared at the door he had come through himself only seconds before, the werewolf's claws clattering against the doorframe as he thrust himself through in pursuit. Horst had already gone, seeking out an alternative exit.

Horst dashed down a servants' staircase and along a narrow gallery that brushed both his shoulders as he ran. Ducking through a low door, and running across an unused kitchen, he found one remnant of the original castle and the imposing newcomer that sat in its lap as he plunged down a spiral staircase and the new stone turned to old amidst scar tissue of cement. His first thought on realising that he was entering the dungeons was pleasure. After all, a visit to the dungeons was the highlight of any trip to a castle, exceeding even the delights of a cream tea and the gift shop. His second thought was more prosaic. *Dead end.*

The sound of Alsager on his trail grew.

The first chamber of the dungeons was a guardroom: rough benches, a table, a stove with a metal flue that vanished into the ancient brickwork. There was a mirror hung in the corner over an outcrop of stone that the original builders had apparently decided was too much difficulty to remove and would, in any case, lend itself to the general air of entombment that they wanted to project to future inmates. On the outcrop was an old enamel basin, a jug, and a cut-throat razor. Hanging by this little still life from a steel spike driven into the wall was a leather strop. Horst momentarily considered taking the razor as a weapon, but it would put him in a corner, and there was no time. He ran from the grimy little room into a corridor that appeared to have been excavated by dwarves with a minimal sense of job satisfaction; all narrow and low, and with bits of stonework sticking out of the walls and ceilings.

Horst negotiated it sideways and so he was looking straight onto it when he found himself facing a barred window in the wall. For a moment, he was unmoved—it was nothing, just some silly grotesquery put on for the tourists, like that dummy beneath a bladed pendulum he'd seen with his family that time during a fort-night in Wales. Then he remembered that this castle was most cer-tainly not open to tourists, that there were no cream teas, no gift shop, and that the corpse in the cell was most assuredly real.

It was hard to be sure, but the woman had probably been in her thirties. Her clothes were not badly soiled and Horst felt sure she had simply been taken from the town and died the same night. Her executioners had propped a table lengthways up against the far wall, tied her by her ankles to the upper edge, and then they had cut her throat.

There was little blood on the floor, but Horst knew there wouldn't be. All he could think of was a wine glass, and a soup bowl, a solid red circle bounded in white china.

'Found dinner, have you?' Alsager was at the end of the cor-ridor. Horst risked a glance the other way and saw it ended in a heavy door of tarred wood, bound in iron straps. In the full ex-pression of his strength, he *might* have been able to tear it from its hinges, but he doubted it. He looked at the dead woman again, hoping to find enough anger to fight, but it wasn't in him. All he could do was feel sickened soul-deep, and grieve for her. He was too tired and sorely dismayed to do aught else.

'They wanted to feed her to me and mine after she'd been emp-tied for you, you ungrateful bastard,' said Alsager as he moved slowly closer. His great bulk filled the narrow way. 'I told them no. Give it to Misericorde to add to her collection. We prefer to kill what we eat.' Alsager had won, and they both knew it. He could smell Horst's indecision and weakness as surely as he could blood. 'Course, you're not really alive, are you? Never mind. In a minute you'll just be properly dead.'

Horst pressed his back to the wall behind him, only to dis-cover that there *wasn't* a wall behind him. Alsager dashed forward but was too late to grab Horst before, with an 'Oh!' of honest as-tonishment, he flipped over the low wall of the well and fell into darkness.

An Interlude

'I have some small acquaintance with castle dungeons,' said Johannes Cabal in ruminative tones.

Horst paused in his narrative to say, 'I'd be surprised . . . in fact, I'd be *amazed* if you didn't. They seem very "you" environments.' His gaze wandered, and his mood darkened as it did. 'That poor woman. What a horrible thing they did.'

Cabal nodded slightly. 'There seems to be an incipient sadism lurking beneath this enterprise. It's odd. The *Ministerium* are clearly in it for money and power, the business of it all. It doesn't seem in their style.'

'The Red Queen,' suggested Horst. 'The dry sticks in the suits are the money and the executive expertise, but the grand sweep of the scheme . . . it seems a bit outré for them. It's the mark of the Red Queen, I'm sure of it.'

'*The Mark of the Red Queen*,' repeated Cabal slowly. 'Your speech sounds like it's stitched together from the titles of yellow novels, as it ever was.'

'Life's an adventure. Well, mine is. Yours, too.'

'Not by choice.' Cabal was adding marginalia to his notes. 'If the knowledge I seek was readily available, and if society wasn't so protective of its corpses, few of the travails I needs must undergo would be at all necessary.'

Horst shrugged and rolled his eyes in mock sympathy. 'People and the mortal remains of their loved ones, eh? So unreasonable.' Then he remembered something and grew serious. 'But be fair, Johannes,' he said, his voice slow and deliberate. 'How would you feel if, say, Father's grave was desecrated and his body despoiled?'

Cabal's pen stopped abruptly. He stared at the page without reading a single character for several long seconds. Then he looked up slowly to meet Horst's gaze. 'Desecration,' he said, just as tonelessly. 'Despoiled. Very emotive terms you choose, brother. Let me answer your . . . hypothetical question with one of my own. If Father was still alive, and one of us was in danger, terrible mortal danger, and the only way he could save us was at the cost of his own life, what do you think he would do?'

'That's not a fair question, Johannes.'

'Nor was yours.'

There was silence, but for the ticking of the clock. Johannes Cabal turned his attention back to his notebook. He gestured impatiently at it with his pen. 'Continue.'

Chapter 6

IN WHICH SCUTTLING AND VIOLENCE OCCUR

When most people look at a stream tumbling down from the mountain heights—fed by melt water and bubbling springs, jogging merrily down past rock and tuffet, glistening and giggling, finally arriving with a hastily acquired sobering air of maturity to disembogue into the river in the valley below on the inner side of a meander—they pause a moment and sigh with appreciation at a beautiful and natural spectacle.

Some people, however, think, *Oh, happy day. What an ideal location for a military construction. And that delightful stream can serve both to provide water and to carry away corpses and shit. Oh, happy, happy day.*

This was the fate of the stream that—its gambolling days long behind it—now sluiced its way down a covered culvert from the mountains backing the castle and ran through rigidly defined parameters beneath the structure providing water first in a well in the kitchens, then in the dungeons, and finally received the outpourings of the soil pipes. The tunnel ran without airspaces down to the concavity of that pretty meander of yesteryear, now forced into the role of moat, and ejaculated its filth and leavings via a grating that was cleared of bones and bodies once a year, or biannually if the dungeons had seen unusual numbers of traitors, dissidents, and other expendable types.

Recent years had seen a collapse in such protocols, however, and the grating had not been cleared. Then again, it had not been maintained, and the press of rags and disposable humans against it had created a partial dam some weeks previously. The rising levels of water in the wells had gone unremarked, as had their sudden lowering in the early hours of one morning a fortnight before. Thus, no one was aware that the uncared-for bars of the grating had broken and it now hung partially ajar, letting the castle's leavings flow directly into the river without hindrance. In terms of living souls, this was moot. Prisoners tended to be in poor condition and often already dead before being dumped down the dungeon well in its part-time role as a cadaveric waste disposal. Even those who had not breathed their last always found that breath to come soon after the fall, the length of submergence in the subterranean stream being challenging even to a practised pearl fisher. The arrangement worked to almost everybody's satisfaction, with the exception of those making the trip, and if their opinions had mattered so very much, then they wouldn't have found themselves diving down the dungeon well's gloomy throat in the first place, obviously.

Thus was the case with living souls and dead bodies, but as the exception proves the rule, so the undead found said case wanting and this was much to his relief.

Horst's moment of surprise was just that—a brief moment—before he reacted autonomously with shock, and time slowed as his reactions accelerated. By the time he hit the water, the wait was boring him. His arms were already leading him and he broke the surface of the dark, turbulent water with his fingertips, slipping into the cold embrace of the imprisoned stream with ne'er a splash.

The cold helped him focus, to shuffle away his confusion and uncertainties about recent events and concentrate on the business of not drowning. Although he wasn't as heavy a user of air as had once been the case, he still needed it. He also entertained a suspicion that drowning was far too mundane an exit for a vampire to make and he would somehow be letting down the side by doing so. Still, he was going to need the energy to survive from somewhere and, all unbidden, his body's altered metabolism was burning the blood in his guts to do it.

The coldness without was coupled with the cancerous cold in his mind; he blinked once in the torrent and then his senses swept out to show him the curving tunnel ahead. The flow was fast, but not fast enough. As easily as if he were considering a game of chess in a warm and quiet study, he analysed his situation both immediate and pending. Of the two, the former was simpler; he would follow the tunnel to its exit, which must surely be into the river. There he would breathe again and stop consuming his limited inner resources with such speed. What might be waiting for him, however, was of concern. Ahead of him was the Dee Society, who likely wanted him destroyed. Behind him was the *Ministerium Tenebrae* and its soldiers, all of whom definitely wanted him destroyed. Of the two factions, the former was probably the lesser threat, which was handy as it allowed him to press forward rather than falling back. He would gain the town and lose himself in its back alleys and abandoned houses. From there he would . . .

The next thought looked a little like 'feed', but Horst couldn't allow it to be so and quickly slammed it behind a mental door labelled 'To Be Attended To'. It might not have been 'feed', he told himself. It might have been 'feel'. Or 'feet'. Certainly, swimming in shoes was no fun. 'Feet'. It was definitely 'feet'. Nothing vampiric at all.

The grating loomed up in front of him a few seconds later, and he was glad to be necessarily distracted from the necessity of distracting himself. In the submerged gloom afforded him through the few lunar rays penetrating the water and the agency of his inhuman senses, he could see the bars, slimy with ancient filth, some scraps of cloth caught at the welds and wafting mournfully in the flow like the battle standards of a defeated army, and—jammed against one of the frame struts—what looked a lot like a human femur. More important for his immediate needs, the hasp by which it was normally locked had broken free and the whole assembly was swaying slightly on its simple pin hinges. One good shove was enough to open the gap wide enough for him to pass, and he did so, sliding into the more sluggish flow of the river and freedom, or at least a greater freedom by a few small degrees.

He rolled over onto his back and sculled slowly a few inches beneath the surface. Above him, he could make out the outline of the covered bridge, its roof aflame. Through the medium of the water, he was still aware of the muffled concussions as the castle walls were struck again and again by shells, but it was a wasted effort, he knew. The thinnest part of the castle walls would still be far too deep for the mortars to do more than scar them. This Dee Society had acted with haste, presumably fearing that the discovery of its spies would provoke the *Ministerium* into precipitate action. In this they were perfectly correct, but that had not made their own assault any more effective. Horst wondered what carnage Misericorde's walking dead and Alsager's petting zoo of doom was currently wreaking in the ranks of the Society.

He rolled back over and swam for the far bank of the river. Here he emerged against the dank stone of the riverside wall and gratefully took his first breath in almost three minutes. As he inhaled, he felt the surge of strange energy settle back with the air of a panther returning to its lair. It did not go entirely willingly.

Horst quickly analysed his situation; Alsager would be back up from the dungeons by now and Horst doubted that even the posturing wolfman would be so foolish as to believe that being dunked in a well was a certain end for a vampire. Once he had discovered where the stream emerged, he and his—for lack of a better word—minions would be combing the far riverbank at just about the point where he was indeed to be found. Horst decided not to be there by the time they got themselves so organised. Swimming against the current was more than he cared to do, but Alsager would expect him to travel downstream. Luckily, Horst's recent discoveries in vertical travel might stand him in good stead, he hoped. Removing his shoes, knotting the laces together, and stringing them around his neck, Horst rose from the cold, black water like a primeval amphibian with aspirations towards dapperness assaying a first journey onto land to spread the word about good tailoring. That his current ensemble had not suffered the indignities of mortar attack and submergence unscathed had not escaped him.

Once clear of the river surface, Horst turned himself to the horizontal and crept into the shadows beneath the bridge. Above him he could hear the crackle and crash of burning wood as the bridge's palisade was consumed, and some exasperated moaning from zombies that found themselves afire. The stone part of the bridge was still standing firm, but the heavy timbers were starting to smoke and char even beneath. Anything that slowed Alsager was a bonus, Horst concluded, and kept creeping.

He was almost clear when he glanced back and noticed, in the gloom beneath one of the stone piles supporting the castle end of the bridge, a small flickering light. At first he thought it was a match, but there was a vivaciousness in the way it flickered and danced that suddenly tickled a happy memory back to life from the depths of his lost life.

All of a sudden he was a boy again, it was November the fifth, and he was in the back garden of their home. He had a sparkler in his hand and was waving it back and forth, taking pleasure in the afterimage it burnt into the air while his father marshalled the other invited children away from the bonfire and his mother nervously doled out treacle toffee to the guests, unsure if she had got the recipe *just so*. It was a peculiarly British celebration, this Guy Fawkes Night, and *die Familie* Cabal had adopted it with enthusiasm in an attempt to become more British. Horst loved it. Not just for the fire and the fireworks, the treacle toffee and baked potatoes, although he adored those, too, but for the odd sense of paganism about it. Guy Fawkes had died (horribly) back in the time of James I, and had died (horribly) in a multitude of effigies ever since, yet the ritual felt much, much older than the era of the Stuarts. It felt ancient, primal, atavistic, and there was toffee. Horst recalled the taste of it, the smell of the bonfire and the smell of gunpowder, the stony expression on his brother's face ('It seems ridiculous to me that the British should celebrate a failure,' Johannes had said, thereby demonstrating a basic lack of understanding for their new home), and the white star of his sparkler as he waved it before him against the backdrop of an autumn night.

Somebody appeared to have attached a sparkler to the underside of the bridge, a rum sort of conceit. The misapprehension only lasted a moment before Horst was scuttling away along the wall like a startled spider. He had barely progressed fifty feet before the explosives planted beneath the bridge detonated.

Once again Horst found himself in the river, the blast wave having overwhelmed his grip on the greasy stonework. It took a few seconds to re-orientate himself, a few more to clear the ringing from his ears and the flash from his eyes, and by then the river's flow had taken him back beneath the bridge. Frustration as much as mild concussion kept him in the river; it seemed Fate had no desire for him to work his way upriver and he had grown exasperated with trying. Instead he allowed himself to slip back beneath the surface and be carried towards the heath from which the mortar shells rose. There he could simply crawl ashore up the shallow bank instead of having to contend with more filthy, slippery stone.

He burned a little more of his valuable reserves to remain submerged for the next five minutes, although as he wasn't exerting himself but was allowing the river to do all the exhausting 'escaping' business, it was a small price and well worth it. Indeed, he had almost forgotten that there was a battle in progress when he washed up on the shallow sand and clay beach of the open common. He lay there for an interval, and then sighed. It was no good; all the shooting was too distracting.

Inwardly disappointed that he had once again to become more active in the whole procedure of fleeing, and seeing that this was as good a place to come ashore as any rather than be taken further downstream and perhaps be caught out by the rising sun, he gained his feet and ran for cover in a crouch. By the shade of a rowan bush, he emptied his shoes of water, wrestled for a few minutes with the sodden knot with which the laces were joined, inwardly decried the state of his clothes and the loss of his socks now bound seaward within the triumphant river, and finally wondered just how he might proceed hence.

There he lay, conscious of the slow turn of the world and the sun creeping gently around the eastern horizon to say, 'Peep-bo! I incinerate you!' and no plans of action occurred to him.

A zombie walked by at one point and, on seeing him, paused. Horst told it to do something that would have involved a novel new take on necrophilia; the zombie took the hint and moved on, bearing with it an ineffable air of hurt that made Horst feel a little guilty. Presently it returned, an arm and half its skull missing. Hopelessly disorientated, it walked into the river, and was shortly borne away by the waters, demonstrating that merely being dead does not preclude having bad days.

Horst looked in the direction from which the unfortunate corpse had first come and saw it was a forerunner. Or forewalker. Or foreshambler. A force of perhaps forty more, obviously deployed before the destruction of the bridge, were heading roughly in his direction en route to engage the attackers, and he wondered if they would be as astute in telling living from undead as their scout had been. He decided that the night had been fraught enough without having to battle better than three dozen zombies in a case of mistaken mortality, and broke cover, heading off at an angle to try to reach the riverbank on the far side of the next meander about half a mile away. The ground was broken and cluttered with undergrowth so, given the nocturnal limitations of human senses and the perennial limitations of zombies in all senses, he calculated he would probably make it without interference.

His calculations were wrong. It transpired that even his enhanced sight could still be fooled by an artful piece of camouflage right up until he fell through it and found himself in a dugout shelter surrounded by very tense people with guns.

'It's not a revenant!' a male voice cried to one side. 'It's a man, not undead!'

Horst was just beginning to feel relieved when a gun barrel was applied with unseemly force to his temple. He was wondering if he had sufficient strength to be up and out before they could react, when the bearer of the gun said, 'No. He's both.'

Horst managed a weak smile. 'Oh. Hello, Alisha.'

'Hello, my Lord Horst. Of the Dead.'

'Oh, God,' said another man, younger than the first. 'That's one of them?'

'It is.' The pressure of the muzzle against his skull increased a little, and then it was gone. 'He's the one who helped me escape.'

'After you shot me,' said Horst. 'Twice. Which I think was very patient of me.' He eyed the circle ranged around him, more than one gun still bearing on him. 'May I get up, or will that get me shot again? I'd prefer not to be shot again. It's been a rough evening.'

Alisha gestured peremptorily with her pistol, a military .38 rather than the discreet semi-automatic she had punctured his lungs with earlier. 'Get up.'

Horst clambered to his feet rather more slowly than he had to, but thought that seeming slow might be a good ruse. That said, in mid-clamber he began to realise that it was not such a charade after all; his reserves were perilously low. He recalled how he had spent the first years of his vampiric existence trapped and with only the footling life forces of insects, spiders, and the very occasional small rodent to survive upon. It had been a hellish time and his humanity had suffered. He had no desire to see what another enforced blood fast might do to him.

On his feet, he looked at the faces ranged around him, some grim, some frightened. In all of them he could hear the hearts beat. In all of them he could sense the blood pulse. In any of them he could take what he needed and kill or maim the others so they could not prevent him. 'I need blood,' he muttered under his breath.

'Yes, you're a vampire. I think we know that,' said a third man, a hard-faced creature with a military bearing. His pistol hand was down, but the arm was tensed to bring it to bear again quickly.

Not quickly enough, thought Horst. He could see the man's Adam's apple over his collar and wondered how good it would feel to punch it hard enough to crumple the cartilage of his windpipe. *Step aside, step forward, punch the throat, break this circle, attack from without.*

He gasped, surprised at the coherence of the idea, the vividity of it, the casual horror of it. He didn't like these thoughts. He didn't like that they were expressed in his own inner voice. Sometimes they were hard to tell apart from his own thoughts. Hard to tell apart, and becoming harder.

'Is he all right?' It was the older man, the one who had spoken first after Horst's unexpected entrance through the ceiling. He was bespectacled, bearded, and could not have been more obviously an academic if his trench coat had borne elbow patches.

Further conversation was interrupted by a man appearing at the entrance to the dugout, dishevelled, bloody, and near hysterical with fear. 'The mortars have been overrun!' he sobbed. 'They're dead! They're all dead! We have to run!'

The hard-faced man swore under his breath. 'It's a washout,' he said. 'We're done here. Maybe done for good.'

'We're running?' said the young man.

'We're making a fighting retreat. It's that or a pointless death in this hellhole. Come on.'

He made to move towards where the messenger stood shaking, but had not even taken a step when the attack reached them. In a flicker of motion, something furry inside and out took down the messenger in a mass of limbs and screams. The Society members stopped and stared as they tried to assimilate what had just happened, but for Horst, the moment was already old and he was already responding. He did not consciously decide to burn the last dregs of Lady Misericorde's blood that remained to him; the situation had decided it for him, and he felt them flame inside his body as he accelerated hard past the startled mortals, angled his torso forward, and hit the lycanthrope hard in the ribs, producing a satisfying *cr-crack* nearby his ear as a couple of them snapped in his target's chest.

The two of them rolled away from the lycanthrope's stricken victim—and he *was* most definitely stricken. Horst could smell the blood, could taste arterial spray in the air, and his hunger flared up in tongues of ice that froze his beleaguered soul. Happily, the subject of his violence seemed to deserve it. As their tumble ended in them rolling apart, both combatants were on their feet in a moment, facing one another and ready to fight.

'Oh, you're kidding me,' said Horst, taken aback and a little underwhelmed. It was hard not to be dismissive. 'A bloody *werebadger*? Really?' While he appreciated that the European badger is a short-tempered creature and not to be trifled with, encountering a stripy-faced renegade from a brutalist interpretation of *The Wind in the Willows* somehow failed to communicate the supernatural menace a werewolf, werebear, or even a were–cocker spaniel might have brought to the occasion.*

'Die!' growled the creature in a strangulated croak that did nothing to raise its stock. 'Die in the name of Lord Devlin!' It rushed Horst, but he danced aside easily.

'How does anyone even get to be a werebadger?' he inquired with the most polite curiosity. 'Did your father have some sort of romantic interlude with a very pretty lady badger one night?' The badger's eyes widened with fury as it turned to face him again. 'He did? What a card. I can only imagine how romantic a sett is by moonlight.' The creature charged again, this time making an asthmatic sort of roar as it passed by Horst, who once again dodged. 'Now, now. No need to be like that. I'm just trying to understand how you ended up being so ridiculous.'

The first two failed passes had made Horst overconfident,

---

* 'You're aware that, by strict definition, a lycanthrope is specifically a werewolf, aren't you?' asked Johannes Cabal of his brother. Horst muttered something about the magnificent mutability of language, popular usages replacing dry old meanings, and anyway, 'by strict definition,' weren't necromancers only supposed to be fortune-tellers? Johannes conceded the point, and Horst continued.

however, and it transpired that being cocky with a werebadger is a tactical error. The badger stopped short and swung hard, one heavy claw looming up and out of the shadows so quickly that it caught Horst before he was even aware of it. It cracked into the side of his skull, and he was knocked from his feet by the vast violence of the blow, spinning along the length of his body in a graceless pirouette before crashing to the ground by the dying messenger.

Horst had felt his cheekbone break under the impact. Where once upon a time, his first thought would have been 'Not the face!' now a need for vengeance arose in him as urgent as hunger. No half human was going to get the better of him like this. No mongrel thing would crow and swagger over his defeat. Especially not a bastard demi-badger.

Before him was the messenger, staring up into the night sky, his throat lying open and awareness leaving his eyes. Already deep in shock, it was obvious he would be dead in a minute or so. Horst watched blood arc in a small fountain from the damaged but not severed carotid artery, and felt his fangs extend. No time for that, however. He glanced over the dying man's body and noted the ex-military webbing belt, laden with pouches, knife scabbard, and an empty holster. Behind him, he heard the badger lumbering forward. Horst sucked down the pain—not nearly as agonising as it should have been—of his shattered cheek, and moved.

He left the ground feetfirst, thrust back by his arms, a moment in the air, and then his feet set down, and he whirled to face his foe, staying low and balanced, his arms outstretched. They scythed through the air, passing close by the werebadger's face. It started to shy away, but then flinched and stopped moving altogether as Horst settled into a combative crouch. Then the badger stepped back, gripping its throat. Horst held up his right hand. It contained the broad-bladed fighting knife he had found in the messenger's belt. There was blood across the first three inches of it, the same blood that was pulsing thickly over the badger's claws.

'I think you're about done for,' said Horst. His voice was harsh and dangerous, and he barely recognised it himself.

The badger turned, made to stagger away, but Horst was on it in a second. He drove it to the ground, pushed its arms aside, and, jaws agape, fastened himself onto the creature's opened throat. As the Dee Society members watched in varying degrees of horror and relief, Horst fed on the dying lycanthrope until its heart faltered and failed.

When he was finished, he rose and faced the mortals. He could see the fear and the loathing in their faces, except for Alisha's. She was unreadable. When she said, 'Well. That was efficient,' he had no idea whether it was a compliment or an irony.

Efficient? He looked back at the creature, but it was a monster no longer. The corpse of a man lay there, minding Horst of a young farmer with dark hair cut short and ill-advised sideburns. 'I've never killed before,' he said.

'What?' It was the brusque tones of the military man. 'Never? I thought you were supposed to be the Lord of the Dead?'

Horst turned on him, rage billowing in his chest. 'I have never killed before!' he snarled into the man's face. He was aware his face was covered in blood, he could see his reflection in the man's eyes. It made him feel good in that moment, because that was what he was—a bloodthirsty monster—and these little people had better start understanding that. 'They didn't discuss the job title with me.' Horst stepped back, collaring the rage and putting it away for when it might do some good. He was breathing heavily, with anger, with exertion, with the glorious feeling of new blood to burn. He said it once more, quietly.

'I have never killed before.'

The older man edged past him and knelt by the messenger. He didn't need to check for life; the wounded carotid was no longer pulsing out blood. 'Poor Redmond's had it, I'm afraid.'

The military man muttered a heartfelt oath, then said, 'Deny him.'

In response, the older man fumbled at the webbing belt that seemed to be the one piece of standard equipment among their force, and withdrew a small test tube from a pouch. Horst was irresistibly reminded of his brother's proclivity for carrying elements of his laboratory around with him as he watched the man remove the tube's cork and sprinkle the contents over the body of the hapless Redmond. It was a crystalline powder, but certainly a mixture as Horst could see harsh metallic glints within it.

'What's that in aid of?' asked Horst. The man didn't answer but rose and stepped back as the powder combusted, quietly and unspectacularly, like a diffident flambé in a shy restaurant. Horst opened his mouth, then closed it again as he didn't know what to say about this. He especially didn't know what to say about how Redmond burned away almost silently in strange, cold, golden flames.

'Poor Redmond,' said the older man, putting away the empty tube.

'At least we've made sure he rests,' answered the military man grimly. He looked at Horst a little suspiciously. 'You don't have many friends, do you?'

'Not around here,' Horst admitted. 'My social skills seem to have suffered.'

He noticed the man's eyes were regarding the corpse of the demi-badger. 'We seem to be in this together,' he said. 'We'll worry about your motivations later. Come on.' He hefted his pistol up to a ready position and headed out into the night. They filed out past Horst, the younger man avoiding looking at him. The last out was Alisha.

'Sorry about the thing with the lungs,' she said, and then she was gone into the night.

Horst was suddenly very aware of the poor state of his attire, the blood on his face, the crushed cheekbone. At least he could do something about the latter. With an effort of concentration and through the agency of the werebadger's blood, he re-formed the bone, knitting together the splinters and resetting it amid a muffled series of clicks and pops. Wincing slightly at the mild soreness with which it left him, he followed the others.

It seemed that the badger had been the furthest end of a picket line following a stagger or lurch or whatever the collective noun is for a group of zombies. Certainly, the action appeared to have passed them by, and was now close to the far side of the common away from the riverbank. There was some desultory gunfire from that direction that died away as Horst and his group headed away, parallel to the riverbank where Horst had come ashore. They would meet the river again, he knew, as it turned away from the mountains, and he hoped that the Dee Society people had a plan that didn't involve swimming.

They seemed to. The military man, who did indeed turn out to be a major, or a former major, led them in Indian file through the dense undergrowth along a path that he had blazed earlier. From the far side of the common, the shooting had died out altogether. After a silence of almost a minute, there was a single shot. The young man paused to look back as if anything would be visible to him beyond the walls of briars and the darkness, but Alisha pushed him on impatiently.

When they reached the edge of the overgrown field, they found themselves facing a swathe of open land some fifty yards wide with a dirt track running alongside the river. 'They'll be clearing the common now,' said the major, terse and direct. 'The changers will play bloodhound. They'll find our dugout, and then they'll find our path. We have perhaps ten minutes before they catch us.' Horst started to comment that this wasn't much of a plan, but the major held up a hand. 'We shall be beyond their reach in five. Follow me.'

He did not make for the path, but instead skirted the edge of the overgrown common, until they saw ahead of them where the dirt path joined a road that led to a wooden bridge. On the far side was what looked to be a derelict farm. Abandoning the cover of the bushes, the major led them in a run across the open swathe in a direct line for the bridge. They were still some yards from it when behind them, a howl of pure animalistic rage split the night. In seconds it was joined by others.

'They've found their striped friend,' said the major. 'And there I was thinking ten minutes was pessimistic. Run! Run for your lives!'

Chapter 7

IN WHICH THERE ARE EXPLOSIVES AND ACID

The boards amplified their running footsteps up to a rumbling thunder so loud that, to their ears, it might as well be a public address announcement that this was their escape route and that any otherwise unengaged werewolves or zombies should make their way to the bridge, where they would find an opportunity to rend and tear mortal flesh.

Unhappily, in this they were essentially correct. The running Dee Society members and Horst—who was running at a determinedly human speed to demonstrate solidarity—were barely halfway across the bridge when the first of the lycanthropes broke cover from the undergrowth and headed straight for them.

Alisha skidded to a halt, unslinging the satchel from her shoulder. 'Keep going!' she shouted at the others, and they did. Not Horst, however, who, being the Lord of the Dead and not a dues-paying member of the society, considered himself a free agent.

He watched as she took a knee right in the middle of the bridge, opened the satchel's flap, and fussed with its contents. Horst thought it an odd sort of time to go rummaging through her handbag, but kept his counsel, which was wise as he would have looked a terrible idiot if he'd said as much. Alisha looked quickly through a handful of odd metallic pencil-shaped objects, dismissed them as redundant, and dropped them into her jacket pocket. 'Too slow,' he heard her mutter.

The wolf had almost reached the end of the bridge. Horst was just wondering if he should dash over and have a word with it when there was a loud percussion next to him. The wolf went down screaming. Alisha carefully placed her still-smoking pistol, doubtless loaded with silver bullets, within easy reach and carried on tinkering with the inside of the bag. Horst gave its innards a curious glance and noted that it seemed to be filled with blocks that reminded him of how tea arrived from the grocers back in the halcyon days when he drank tea. Alisha had stuck some sort of device into the side of one of the blocks and what they actually were occurred to him at about the same time she pulled on a cord and a fuse spluttered into coruscating life. She snatched up her pistol and headed off at full pelt after her companions. Horst let her go, watching the fuse crackle angrily as the sparks crept towards the detonator. It was November the fifth all over again, again. Whether her cry of 'Well? Run, you idiot!' was entirely necessary was another thing. In any event, Horst was running easily alongside her in a moment.

'That's quite a short fuse, isn't it?' he asked. Behind them, a mixed mass of undead and lycanthropic ill intent was surging onto the bridge. 'Pardon me.'

And so saying, he picked her up, slung her over his shoulder, and accelerated as hard as he dared with a living passenger. He was still a good twenty feet from the far bank when he felt the boards of the bridge beneath his feet ripple and, knowing what it forewarned, threw himself forward. The blast wave rolled across them and seemed to carry them along on its raging front like flotsam on the surf. He was surprised intellectually but not viscerally when they landed on the rough earth of the farmer's track at the far end of the bridge. They tumbled head over heels as the bridge was torn to pieces by the angry impact of four blocks of plastic explosive turning largely to gas in a ball of heat and fury. The night sky glowed as the wood of the bridge spontaneously combusted beneath the violence of chemistry.

As for Horst, he was reliving yet again how it feels to be hit in the head by an irate badgerman. This time at least, no bones were broken, but he was terribly disorientated, and could only think of bonfires and toffee and clung to the belief that there had been an accident with a Roman candle. A face appeared over him and he said, 'Vati?' even though part of him was saying that this was a question that would never receive the answer 'Ja' ever again.

'Afraid not, son,' said the major. He looked away, towards the bridge. 'How is she?'

'She's—' began the young man's voice, but was interrupted by an impatient 'Get off me! I'm fine!' Alisha appeared in Horst's eyeline a moment later, beating out areas of her jacket that were smoking.

'Smoking jacket,' said Horst, and laughed weakly.

Alisha looked down at him, and wiped away blood trailing from her nose with the back of her hand. 'Thank you,' she said. 'Again. You were right; that was a very short fuse.'

Horst struggled upright. His head spun, and his back felt as if he'd been given a playful whack with an oak tree. He flexed his shoulders and there was a visceral crack that sounded serious. He could sense warmth there as his injuries rapidly healed in the offhand way they did these days. He had a feeling that if he wasn't undead, he'd be very thoroughly dead by now. For lack of any other conversational gambits, he said, 'Did you blow up the other bridge, too?'

Alisha frowned. 'What other bridge?'

Somewhere nearby, Horst heard an engine turn over. He clambered to his feet with the catlike grace of a drunken orang-utan to witness an ageing open-bed lorry drive out from the farm buildings and wait, engine idling. The older man of academic mien threw open the door and called at them, 'Could we get a move on, please? They're coming across!'

A quick glance showed the truth of it; while the bridge was destroyed across two of its three pilings, the lycanthropes were massing to make their way along the surviving lengths of shattered wood to jump the gaps, while the zombies—with a forgivable air of long-suffering—were attempting to cross the river in the manner of army ants. By sheer numbers and the bloody-mindedness of those who are past the point of having anything to live for by dint of being dead, they were walking into the river and clinging to one another in an effort to form a bridge that, if not living, was at least animate. There were those that were carried away by the flow, and did so slowly thrashing the water and pedalling their legs as if demonstrating how to drown. Some, semi-skeletal and holed below any waterline one cared to draw, sank from sight to walk the riverbed as if it were the surface of the moon. Unhappily, having poor navigational skills, this availed them little and they were as likely to walk to the sea as anything else. Others at least slightly bloated with the gases of putrescence bobbed on the surface like inflatable beach toys intended for children whom one wishes to traumatise. Examples of these who failed to join the bridge were to be seen floating off with expressions of dull-witted embarrassment, while those who *had* been incorporated into the bridge found themselves used as pontoons, which was scarcely better. However inefficient their efforts, it was clear that the barrier offered by the river would be breached in a matter of minutes.

Quickly, therefore, Horst and the Dee Society members gained the lorry and departed that hellish scene in a dense cloud of exhaust fumes that coincidentally made them all think 'carburettor' without actually saying it.

Horst rode in the back with the young man, whose name turned out to be Richard. 'Well,' said Horst as they bounced around in the flatbed, ricocheting from the metal sides, 'this is travelling in style.' Indeed, the lorry was making along with a vigorous enthusiasm to be away from the environs of the castle, and the ridged farm track did much to amplify this vigour into vertical motion as they bumped their way towards putative safety.

'Do you think we'll be all right now?' said Richard, apparently already blasé to the joint threat of being in a badly driven vehicle with a vampire.

'Frankly?' said Horst. 'I have no idea. I wouldn't put anything past the *Ministerium*.' He glanced back at the castle and what he saw did little to undermine his misgivings. '*Mein Gott!* What are they doing?'

The castle was aglow. Not simply the windows, but the walls around the upper reaches of the structure, the towers and battlements, and even some way into the night sky throbbed with a violet glow that was just short of invisible, flickering at the edges of perception. It was a strangely vivacious effect, as if the light was in some sense alive and aware, and the suspicion grew in the mind of the observer that the glow was not so much emanating from the castle as squatting upon it like a ghastly, ghostly toad.

Richard pounded on the glass in the back of the lorry's cab. 'Professor! Professor! Oh, stop! Look!'

The professor obligingly stopped by stamping on the brake and clutch pedals simultaneously, sending Horst and Richard up against the back of the cab with uncomfortable momentum. While they were untangling themselves, he flung open the driver's-side door and leaned out to look back at the castle.

'Madness!' he said. 'They've rushed into some work of great power, and trebled the danger in so doing!'

'What sort of thing?' asked the major as he leaned out of his side. Alisha, in the middle of the bench seat, looked back through the glass.

The professor shook his head as much in disbelief as in answer. 'Truly, I cannot say. They are dabbling in rituals that have not been practised in centuries or even millennia. No living eye has seen them, and no reliable accounts of them survive. But all I can say is, just *look* at that bugger. It bodes ill, can't you feel it in the very marrow of your bones?'

'You know,' said Horst in a conversational tone, 'they might not have done it if you hadn't provoked them.'

'Oh, good point,' conceded the professor. 'You're right, of course. We should have just left them to conquer the region and cast its mortal inhabitants into slavery and worse. Why didn't we think of that? So much easier. Thank you for pointing that out, my lord.'

'Sarcasm,' said Horst.

'Yes,' said the professor.

'Thought so,' said Horst. 'My brother employs it often. I've grown rather good at spotting it.'

The unearthly glow was shuddering in waves across the parapets, and even the most insensitive of them could feel some terrible inchoate energy upon the air, and somewhere within it, a definable emotion.

'It feels . . . joy,' said Richard. 'Some sort of horrible joy.'

'Exultation, I was about to say,' said the major. 'I think we've lost this round.' He climbed out and walked around to the driver's side. 'Shove over, Professor. I'll drive.'

Grumbling a little, the professor complied. As the major climbed in behind the wheel, Horst felt sharp pains in the pads of his thumbs that made him gasp where, for example, being pasted across the face by a werebadger had not. On each thumb, drops of blood stood out in sharp contrast to his pale skin. The pain faded quickly to be replaced by a deadening numbness and the left thumb started twitching spastically. He regarded them with disbelief, then heard an oath muttered with feeling behind him. He looked over his shoulder to find the professor looking at the drops of blood on Horst's thumbs, too, but where Horst was bemused, the professor was horrified.

'Drive, man! Drive!' he snapped at the major. 'Something wicked this way comes!' He looked at Horst. 'You didn't think Shakespeare was being anything less than literal, did you, my lad?'

The major slammed the lorry into gear and pulled away almost as violently as the professor had braked. Over the sound of the engine, Richard shouted to Horst, 'Do you know what they're doing?' and jerked his head at the castle. Horst shook his head, but he had suspicions. Perhaps the Lord of Powers had been closer at hand than even the *Ministerium* had guessed. Certainly from his knowledge of necromancy gleaned from Johannes, this seemed too gross a manifestation of arcane energies by several magnitudes for a necromancer's liking. Lady Misericorde's little army of the unwilling dead was impressive enough, but there was a personal touch to it; every one of them had been raised with personal attention from the necromantrix herself. The great lowering cloud of malevolent violet light, however, was the very embodiment of impersonal potency, as unconcerned of the individual as a naval bombardment. Horst knew the professor had been right to say it boded ill, as had the major when he said they'd lost this round. Whatever the *Ministerium* had conjured, it moved on their agenda in no uncertain fashion.

As the major drove them away, Horst and Richard had little else to do but hold on tight and watch the castle diminish into the distance, a black excrescence upon a midnight-blue field, detailed with flickering yellow from the burning drawbridge. As they watched, however, an uncomfortable realisation slowly dawned upon them. 'I say,' said Richard. 'Is it my eyes, or is that glow staying the same size?'

Horst himself had been watching how the glow had failed to grow distant along with the castle and had been looking for reference points in the landscape to mark scale. What they showed him was not comforting. 'It's getting bigger.' He turned and found Alisha and the professor looking through the cab's rear window at the glow, too. 'It's following us!' Horst shouted through the glass.

The lorry was off the farm track and onto a narrow country road, lined with tall, dense *bocage* on either side blocking the view. Richard unslung the Winchester action carbine he was carrying and checked the load. 'If you've got any hoodoo to throw around

in times of trouble, this would be one ⟨
Horst.

'Hoodoo? To be quite honest I might we⟨
what it is or how to use it. I only found ⟨
climbing and going without breath tonight. ⟨
practised at the whole "Woo, I'm a vampire" j⟨

Richard looked at him curiously. 'You're act⟨
whelming for a Lord of the Dead, y'know.'

Horst shrugged. 'What can you expect from ⟨
heart was never in it. Oh, here we go.' For the glow⟨
over the top of the hedgerows in their wake. Horst fro⟨
something up there. In the glow . . .' The view was mo⟨
off by an area of woodland, but the glow filtered throu⟨
mist, implacably closing the distance upon them.

Richard brought the carbine to his shoulder and wo⟨
action, loading the chamber. He squinted at the strang⟨
which illuminated the branches and trunks yet seemed to h⟨
central source of light within itself. 'It's in the trees!' he warn⟨

Through the glass, Horst saw the professor's lips move sou⟨
lessly.

It's coming.

The aberrant light closed steadily on them despite the major'⟨
repeated protestations to the professor that the old lorry was already in its highest gear and his foot had the accelerator clamped
down to the floor. It was perhaps just as well that they could go no
faster in that narrow, twisting lane, the hedgerows and embank-
ments looming at them in the headlights at every turn. 'God help
us if we meet anyone coming the other way,' said the major.

Horst thought this was all rather unfair of Fate. He had quite
liked the idea of becoming an architect perhaps, or an engineer. At
no point had his career plans involved becoming a vampire and
ending up pursued by something horrible while in the company of
very strange strangers. This was a Johannes sort of job, he felt, and
sorely wished his brother were there with him or, better yet, instead of him. Johannes would have identified the glow by now,

pithily dismissive about it, pulled some useful sort
of his Gladstone bag, and dealt with it, probably
something else pithy. All Horst could do was sit
wait a thus far undefined sort of awfulness while un-
ng his companions with his poor monster skills.

wasn't an entirely undefined awfulness, he realised. The
uldn't seem to see it, but the glow had a sense of being
ce of something that broke the usual laws of physics, per-
and even perspective. He had a real sense that there was
ing—some*things*—just beyond that surface that wanted to
through. He could see the light bulge in a manner that he
never have described to his satisfaction even given a moun-
of dictionaries and thesauruses. It wasn't that his vocabulary
ed the words; it was that the words didn't exist.

'They're coming through,' he said out loud. The glow was chang-
g shade in places, extra-dimensional stresses pushing the violet
rough black and into colours that one would hunt for in vain upon
he electromagnetic spectrum.

'What?' said Richard, squinting at the glow. 'Who's coming
through? What d'you mean?'

He plainly couldn't see the stresses in the colours, Horst realised.
The others couldn't see how the colours, glimmering darker than
dark, were so close to bursting, like the meniscus of a soap bubble.

And then they did. The glow vanished abruptly, paradoxically
making the night lighter, but this only served to allow them to see
what had burst through in greater, horrifying detail.

The creatures had no right to . . . no right to anything at all.
They had no right to fly, lacking wings. They had no right to breathe,
lacking mouths or nostrils or even spiracles. They had no right to
see, lacking eyes. They had no right to exist, yet they did, and they
came on rapidly towards the fleeing lorry, flying without wings,
screaming without mouths, seeing their prey without eyes. Off-
cuts from failed species, cancers given autonomous life, wriggling,
writhing entanglements of animate offal, they descended towards
the lorry, dripping acid and hunger as they came.

Richard responded admirably under the circumstances. He paled, his eyes widened, he mouthed, *Oh, sweet Jesus*, and then he opened fire.

The silver long rounds tore through the closest of the oncoming creatures. Its screams rose to an ululating shriek, but it was a scream of fury rather than agony. The fleshy arms, or legs, or tentacles that jutted asymmetrically out from the crooked core of the thing flexed and writhed, but it barely slowed its pursuit. 'Keep firing!' ordered Horst, feeling desperately useless.

'Get your heads down!' shouted Alisha through the glass, and gave them very nearly a second's grace before shattering the pane with the butt of her pistol. Throwing sacking from the cab floor over the glass fragments jutting up from the frame, she and the professor levelled their guns at the creatures and joined the fusillade.

The closest of the abominable creatures was receiving almost all the fire. Chunks of writhing flesh were blown from it to land, hissing and fuming, in their wake. Its enraged screaming continued unabated until, with no warning, it dropped from the air and fell heavily into the road like a haphazardly sewn giant squid toy that had been mistakenly stuffed with bowling balls.

'What . . . what happened?' said Richard, lowering his carbine.

'Reload!' Horst ordered him. As Richard started thumbing fresh rounds into the breach, Horst turned to the professor and said, 'What happened? You weren't hurting it, and it suddenly died.'

The professor had broken open his revolver and was slotting in fresh ammunition as he spoke. 'Perhaps a vital spot was hit although . . . I don't know. Those things seem to be made in very general terms, almost as if they are single organs with no specialisation at all.'

'Is that possible?' asked Alisha as she finished replacing the magazine in her pistol and worked the slide.

'On Earth, only as single-celled creatures like amoebae. But . . . well, they're plainly not from around these parts. As for how it died, I don't think it has any vulnerable points. I think we just filled it with too many holes for it to carry on living, and it was too stupid to know how badly wounded it was until it died.'

'There *are* another five of them,' Horst pointed out. 'Hypotheses later, shooting now? Perhaps?'

'Quite, my boy,' said the professor complacently, and opened fire.

It didn't seem to be how many times the creatures were hit that turned the trick nearly so much as how ragged the storm of bullets had left them. Between loud concussions, Alisha bemoaned their lack of a shotgun; it would have worked nicely against the creatures. But they didn't have one, nor did they have infinite ammunition. It took approximately a full load from all three weapons to bring down a single pursuer; when the field was thinned to three, the ammunition gave out.

The hammer of the professor's pistol clacked down on an empty casing. 'Well,' he said, regarding the useless weapon as one might a fountain pen that had run dry, 'that's a blessed nuisance.'

'I'm out,' said Richard, patting his pockets in a vain bid to find any stray rounds.

'Me, too,' said Alisha. She slammed the empty pistol into her shoulder holster with an angry grimace. 'So, I suppose we're done for now?'

The surviving aberrations grew closer, a drooling chittering growing under their screams as they scented their prey so near. 'I fear so, my dear,' admitted the professor.

'Damn it!' shouted the major. 'Railway ahead, we'll have to turn parallel. They'll have us for sure! No! Wait!' When he spoke again, there was a small spark of hope. 'There's a train down there, taking on water! Could we outrun them in a train?'

'No idea, but we won't lose them in this wreck,' said Alisha. 'Try for it, Major. What kind of train is that, anyway? A carnival?'

Horst had been having a hard time taking his eyes off the creatures, but this comment made him spin violently to look forward.

The hedgerows and trees had cleared to reveal a shallow valley stretching out before them under the moonlight. A meadow lay on their left and beyond that a road and a railway on a raised earth-work. Where the road forked with one arm disappearing into a short tunnel under the rail bed, there was a concrete base up by the rails upon which stood a water tower in a siding alongside the through line. There, by it, was indeed a train.

It was not a long composition, consisting of an inelegant but practical tender locomotive, three freight cars that bore something like the fanciful lettering style Horst remembered so well from the Cabal Bros. Carnival, a sleeper car, and finally a passenger brake van in the British style. It had come to a halt in the siding beneath the water tower, and it was just possible to discern the figures of the driver and his mate working by the light of paraffin lanterns. Horst's keen eyesight could make out some other movement in the near shadows cast by the moon across the train, but beyond being able to see the dancing glow of a couple of cigarette tips—one moving energetically while its smoker presumably waved it around expressively as they talked—it was too dark even for him to read the painted legends on the freight cars, although he was prepared to make a confident guess that the last word was 'Circus'. A very small circus if that was all their gear and personnel, he thought.

'Hold on!' called the major. 'Shortcut!'

They all braced themselves; there was only one conceivable shortcut and it would involve ramming the two-bar wooden fence that separated the road from the meadow.

The major looked for a stretch that angled slightly towards the road in an effort to make the impact as perpendicular to the bars as possible, swerved away from the fence to the right, and then turned hard to the left. The unexpected right-hand swerve caught Richard unaware and he lost his grip on a welded stanchion in the lorry's side. As the vehicle ran up the small bank, smashed through the fence, and flicked its tail up as the rear wheels leapt over the top of the bank, he went rolling aftward and was then sent flying over the tailgate by the sudden bounce. He disappeared from view with a despairing cry.

'Stop!' bellowed Horst. 'Stop this damn thing!' He was already on his feet and running back as he spoke. He accelerated his reactions as he approached the tailgate, knowing the rough ground would make the vehicle move unpredictably and appreciating this would be a very bad time to fall over. It was a wise decision; as he jumped to place one foot on top of the metal gate, the lorry's rear wheels fell into a rut and the gate moved away from his descending foot. Seeing it all move so slowly before him, as sedate as an over-cranked movie, it was easy to lower his foot just that little bit faster, using the tailgate as a jumping-off point and leaping down from the moving lorry. He hit the ground hard, rolled, and came up sprinting. The green swathe hadn't done much for his clothes, a smear of chlorophyll staining one shoulder, but his vanity had long since given them up as a lost cause anyway.

He couldn't see Richard—the embankment was in the way—but he could hear him. He was screaming. For a moment, Horst thought Richard must have been injured in his fall, but as he crested the top of the bank, he saw the true reason. One of the creatures had got ahead of its fellows and was on Richard. It couldn't really be called an attack, exactly, as the creature was making little effort to hurt him. It was simply digesting him where he lay, pinned beneath it. Horst could see its surface was slick with an oily, iridescent sheen as if it were salivating. Rivulets of the substance were drizzling onto Richard and, where they fell, he burned. He was screaming, and the creature was screaming, but where his were in agony and terror, there was an alien exultation in the cries of the monster.

Horst hit the creature in a hard rugby tackle just above the untidy nexus of its variform limbs. His shirt immediately grew wet with the thing's slick coating, and then he felt his skin start to burn. The part of his mind—no, the growing part of his personality—that regarded human life as a convenient way of carrying around fresh blood for it sneered at the pain. *There is no use for that*, it commented tartly, and the pain receded to something unpleasant but distant, like an unpaid invoice from a patient creditor.

The creature was thrashing beneath him as they rolled into the road. Horst knew it was a living thing, but even without the alterations in his outlook, he couldn't regard it as deserving of life. It was a virus made massive, a bacterium made greater than man-size. Its life was only infinitesimally more natural than a clockwork mouse, and well-bred clockwork mice did not try to dissolve and digest young men. Horst wasn't having it. Not only was the creature not of this Earth, vicious, violent, deadly, and disgusting, it was also really getting on his nerves.

Horst dug his fingers into its flesh, made sure they were firmly anchored, and then tore a limb off. The creature didn't take kindly to this, making the same ululating cry as its brethren emitted when injured. The stench of his own burning skin choked Horst as he thrust his hand into the open wound in the closest analogue the aberration had to a body and groped around for something vital to crush. There didn't seem to be anything; just a greasy inner flesh with the colour of old newsprint and the feel of firmly packed scrambled egg. Could the professor be right and these things were no more complex than amoebae? *But even an amoeba has a nucleus*, he reminded himself, and as he thought it, his hand found something saggy and liquid-filled buried deep inside and he tore it open without hesitation.

The creature didn't die immediately, but it did die, its screams becoming attenuated as the poor parody of life that gave it its animus leaked away.

Horst threw the carcass from him and went to Richard. He was lying on his back, sorely injured, mercifully unconscious, but moaning through it. Horst looked at his own hand, the hand he had used to kill the creature. The flesh had run, and he could see bone breaking the surface here and there. Fumes rose from the destroyed muscles, skin, and fibres. There was no point trying to heal himself for the moment, he realised, not with the acid still upon him. He would let it react away, or evaporate—the great mercy of acids, he remembered from school, being that, unlike alkalis, they were volatile—or, better yet, wash the foul stuff off him.

Wiping what he could off his arms with strips of his shirt, he lifted Richard and carried him up the embankment with a fast walk. On the other side, he almost ran into Alisha, the professor a few steps behind her. She looked at him and then Richard, and raised the back of her hand to her mouth, the first time Horst had ever seen her register a strong emotion other than anger.

'Oh,' she said quietly, lowering her hand. 'Poor Richard.'

The professor reached them and saw the state of matters. 'Oh, Lord,' he said. 'They did this?' Horst nodded. The professor shook his head at the wonder and the horror of it. Then he started ambling back to the lorry, gesturing Horst and Alisha to follow. 'Come along, come along. The other things will be here soon.' He sounded sick at heart. 'We must reach the train. It's our only hope.'

An Interlude

'If,' said Johannes Cabal, one finger raised in temporisational style, 'I might momentarily distract you from your lurid and occasionally believable narrative, you mentioned something that intrigued me.'

'Something?' said Horst. 'All of that and it's "something" in the singular?'

'Yes. You mentioned the destruction of the castle's drawbridge, and this woman Alisha's offhand implication that she, despite a predilection to blowing up bridges, was not responsible.'

'I've wondered about that, too. She had no reason to lie.'

'So, who did it?'

Horst shrugged.

Cabal looked at him a little dispiritedly. 'It never crossed your mind to ask later—and I'm sure there was a later or else your presence here is impressive—it never crossed your mind to make inquiries?'

'How acid. As it happens, I did raise the subject, but no joy. It's a bit of a mystery.'

Cabal took up the mug of warm drink Horst had prepared for him from the bedside cabinet and nestled it in both hands. 'I detest mysteries.' He took a sip and the focus of his attention shifted quickly to it. 'How is that my tea tastes of cow?'

'It's beef tea, Johannes.'

Cabal regarded the mug with, if not greater acceptance, at least an understanding. 'Ah,' he said.

Chapter 8

IN WHICH WE ENCOUNTER LADIES
WEARING TROUSERS

The lorry arrived at the base of the rail berm in a spray of gravel as the major jerked the wheel sideways and they skidded to a halt. The two cigarette smokers Horst had spotted on the approach looked down at them in not so much astonishment as suspicion. Horst was slightly surprised himself to discover both were women, although not nearly as surprised as the major was at a telling detail that had escaped Horst.

'Good Lord,' said the major as he jumped down from the driver's position to land with a crunch on the gravel track. 'Ladies in trousers!'

They were indeed, and shamefully, wearing trousers. Both were in their mid-twenties, and both would not have been suitable for polite society. Wanton smoking aside, they were dressed in what appeared to be male work clothes, one in dungarees and the other in farming trousers of denim cloth and wearing a short, brown leather jacket of the type worn by pilots. Beneath it were visible a checked shirt and a neckerchief. Neither of the pair were wearing nice shoes, either, instead seeking to compound their crimes against femininity by wearing work boots in one case and what looked shockingly like army boots in the other.

'They're *lesbians*,' said the major in a ghastly whisper. He looked back up the meadow, searching for their pursuers; he was plainly unsure which fate was worse.

While the major agonised over whether death by otherworldly creature or associating with ladies in sensible shoes would be more injurious, Alisha called up to them, 'We have a wounded man and . . .' She looked back at an exclamation from the major. The two remaining creatures were rising above the embankment by the shattered section of fence across the meadow, clearly visible in the moonlight. Alisha looked desperately up at the women. 'Please! We're all in danger!'

The woman in the flying jacket squinted across the meadow and then, demonstrating the depths of her sapphic depravity by not swooning on the spot, threw her cigarette stub to the floor and snapped to her fellow, 'Tell the driver to get this thing rolling *now*!' As the dungareed woman ran along towards the locomotive, the leather-jacketed woman ran back a few windows along the sleeper car before pounding fiercely on its side. After a brief moment, the narrow ventilator window popped open.

'What the hell is it, Boom?' demanded a female voice. This one had an American accent, convincing the major that it *was* possible for things to get worse, after all.

The woman in the leather jacket—Boom—never took her eyes off the creatures, already a quarter of the way across the meadow and closing. 'We have company, Boss.'

'What kind of company?'

'Bad company. The worst.'

The window's roller shutter shot up to reveal a woman in her mid-thirties, dishevelled and pulling on a dressing gown over pyjamas. She leaned close to the open window and looked up the meadow. 'God *damn* it,' she snarled, sounding more peeved than affrighted. 'What in creation are those?'

'Really dangerous!' shouted Alisha. 'Please, we need help!'

'Boss' looked down, noticing them for the first time. She quickly took in Horst and the Dee Society survivors, and the slight wince when she saw Richard carried in Horst's arms showed she knew a man at the edge of death when she saw one, and that it was not a new experience to her.

'Get 'em aboard! Wake everyone and tell 'em to be ready.' She vanished into the gloom beyond the glass.

'Come on!' shouted Boom at Horst and the others. 'Don't you wanna live?'

They stumbled up the embankment onto the earthwork to where Boom was waiting by an open door where, as they arrived, another woman was coming out. She, too, appeared to have been in slumber and she, too, was unconventionally dressed in a pair of denim trousers, hastily pulled-on work boots, their laces flailing, and a pyjama top over which she wore a navy surplus peacoat. She was also sporting a pump-action shotgun. As she jumped down beside them, the major was horrified to note that, not only was she yet another member of what was clearly some dreadful hive of perversity, but that she wasn't even a Caucasian pervert. Between the short hair, shotgun, and the epicanthic folds of the inscrutable Oriental, he was quite at a loss.

'What the hell are those?' she demanded, and she demanded it in an American accent.

'Weird stuff, Mink,' answered Boom. The abominations were still closing, now only a hundred yards away. 'Dangerous weird stuff.'

'Interesting,' said Mink, and pumped a shell into the chamber. 'I'll let 'em get a bit closer. Choke's open on this thing.'

Alisha looked at the shotgun, and then the 9mm semi-automatic that had appeared in Boom's hand, apparently stowed in a shoulder holster. 'You've all got guns?'

Boom had climbed into the train, but Mink remained, watching the abominations with a clear eye. 'Oh, yeah. This is bandit country, all 'round these parts,' she said. 'You're a fool if you don't plan for trouble.'

'We have weapons, but no ammunition left,' explained the professor. 'If we could reload . . .'

Mink jerked her head back towards the train, never once looking away from the approaching enemy. 'Follow Boom.'

Aboard the train, the corridor ran down the side away from the meadow. The carriage had certainly seen better days; the carpet was worn down to the boards in several places, the woodwork was scuffed and scratched, and half the light fittings were devoid of bulbs. Whatever kind of circus this was, 'lucrative' seemed unlikely to be its crowning adjective. As the group led by Alisha—the major having passed the role of pathfinder to her in case they should run into any other women in their night attire—moved forward, there were shouts and responses coming fore and aft. All, the major noted inwardly with a sense of moral defeat, were female.

A door opened inward to their left and the woman Boom had called 'Boss' stepped out. She was in the latter stages of buttoning up some sort of one-piece boiler suit, but the simplicity of its design was offset by the cloth being of a striking crimson and the cut allowing for a double-breasted front. She left the flap of cloth across her upper chest loose and shrugged into the shoulder holster she'd had hanging from one elbow while attending to the buttons.

'Who are you people?' she demanded. 'And what are those things?'

The sound of a shotgun firing, slow and considered shots two seconds apart, stopped the dialogue before it had even begun. The woman gave them a wary glance, then turned her back on them, drawing her handgun and working the slide as she went.

'It's an . . . *odd* sort of circus, isn't it?' said the professor.

'I've seen odder,' replied Horst. The woman had left the door of her compartment swinging, and he shoved it open with his foot before carrying in Richard.

'You can't just go into a lady's bedroom!' said the major, still

127

finding some deep reserves of propriety that had not yet been scandalised in the last few minutes.

The room was not an obvious lady's boudoir, it had to be admitted. The impression it engendered was somewhere between the dressing room of an actress and a light engineering workshop. A clothes rack of the type usually found in secondhand shops—bare, grey steel tubes arranged upon castors—was in one corner, burdened with a mixture of fluffy fripperies, work clothes that would not have gone amiss on an oil rig, and a collection of pseudo-military stylings rendered upon a variety of one-piece boiler suits. The scents of jasmine and lavender mixed with that of fine machine oil, a not displeasing combination.

'She's not in it and Richard needs medical attention,' said Horst. He laid Richard out on the bed, wincing inwardly at the mess the blood and filth were going to leave on the bedding, and stepped back. 'I can't help him,' he said, and pushed past the Dee Society members gathered around the door. 'But I can help defend the train.'

Horst reached the still-open carriage door to find things were going very badly, at least for the otherworldly creatures. From positions on the rail bed, an open door at the other end of the sleeper carriage, from the windows, three guns were blazing at the unhappy unearthly invaders, blowing chunks of steaming supernatural flesh from them as they advanced through the hail.

The nearer of the two had inevitably drawn most of the fire, and it finally gave up whatever it used for a ghost by the abandoned lorry, flopping to the ground and expiring with a scream that spoke of distant stars, strange angles, and the sheer bloody unfairness of being dragged to Earth just to be chopped to shribbons by gunfire.

The second creature becoming the only surviving creature coincided with a pause in the shooting. In the same way that sometimes all the conversations in a crowded room can simultaneously reach natural pauses that, in their synchronisation, seem very unnatural, so may the reservoirs of ammunition in a variety of firearms all run dry at the same time. The crack of guns was replaced by the frantic clickings of shells being slipped into chambers, and the silken swish and clatter of box magazines being withdrawn and discarded. The creature, in its non-Euclidean way, seemed to regard the cessation of fire as a declaration of unconditional surrender and desire to be butchered on the part of the defenders. Perhaps that was how such things were signalled in its home dimension. In any event, it responded by screaming more gleefully yet, and swooping towards the train, hurdling the lorry as it came on.

That it was then introduced to the concept of full automatic fire at this juncture was unkind but salutary. From the roof of the carriage came the perfunctory bark of large-calibre rounds being fired with the mechanical disinterest of a sewing machine making a hem. The creature slowed as the bullets tore through it, its scream sounding a mite less self-assured. That momentary slowing was all the time required for the other gunners to complete reloading and within a second, four guns were blazing hell and damnation at a monstrosity that had previously considered itself very much at home to both. The scream choked, returned more weakly, ululated into a flutter, and then the creature fell onto the embankment, before rolling nervelessly back down to lie dead at its base.

Horst jumped down and walked past Mink to look up onto the carriage roof. On it stood Boom, bracing a very serious-looking piece of combative machinery against her hip while she checked its action.

'Is that a *machine gun*?' he called up to her.

'It's a *sub*-machine gun,' she corrected him. 'A Thompson. Fifty rounds of .45 ACP in the drum. Well, there were.' She lowered the weapon and nodded at the corpse of the last creature. 'Most of them are in that now. That was fun. Coming down,' she said as she started to turn towards the open roof hatch through which she had gained the roof in the first place. She paused, looking back up the meadow to the road. 'Oh, what is it now?'

A small convoy of four lorries were emerging from behind the bank on the far side of the meadow as they processed down towards the bend that would bring the road parallel to the track. Horst saw the passengers—dull-eyed and long-suffering—in the back of the first and knew the danger was far from over.

'We have to get moving!' he shouted up at Boom. 'How long does it take to get this thing under way?'

Boom gave the approaching vehicles a last glance of such profound suspicion that Horst could almost hear her hackles rising. She looked forward and was unhappily surprised to find the woman she'd sent to the locomotive nowhere near it, absent-mindedly slotting fresh shells into her revolver as she watched the approaching lorries. 'Daisy! What the hell? I told you to tell the driver to get us out of here!'

'Helmut's gone,' said Daisy, as if this were a piece of news of incidental interest. 'Him and Tomas lit out when they saw the flying leggy things. They're probably a mile away by now.'

The Boss lady appeared at the far carriage door. 'And you waited until *now* to tell us?'

For the first time, Daisy seemed to realise that 'moving the train' was of more than incidental importance. 'Sorry, Ginny,' she said, all contrite.

She had already fallen from Ginny's attention; there were more pressing matters to deal with. 'Becky!' A woman in a flat cap, her red hair hastily crammed under it, looked up. 'Can you drive the train?'

'They wouldn't let me play with it, but I've watched them. I reckon so.'

'I've driven a train,' said Horst, which was true.

Travelling between towns aboard a carnival train had not been without its pleasures, and one such had been the realisation of a childhood dream to ride the footplate of a locomotive. The crew had not complained, partially because he was one of the bosses, and partially because they were dead. Originally a pair of breathtakingly incompetent highway robbers, they had encountered his brother, Johannes, who had shot them more for the crime of irking him than any other. He had raised them in a spirit of 'waste not,

want not', and they had found service driving the brothers' dia-
bolical carnival for a year. Being dead seemed to suit them, by all
accounts. They were certainly friendlier if no brighter than when
they were alive, and it would have been an ideal state of affairs but
for the decomposition. Still, they had been happy enough to share
their footplate on a good few nights in that strange year, and had
demonstrated to Horst the esoteric art of throttle and brake, sand-
box and condenser.

'Then get to it!' snapped Ginny. 'The rest of you, all aboard!'

Horst burnt a little blood to blur ahead and reach the locomotive as quickly as he could. He was already checking the valves when
Becky climbed up. 'What?' she said on finding him there. 'How did
you get ahead of me?'

'I'm very quick when I want to be.' He tapped the pressure gauge.
'There's barely a head of steam. We need more heat.' He opened
the firebox door, took up the coal spade, and started shovelling fuel
into the hole.

Becky was watching this performance with thin-lipped distrust. 'And how did you open a hot firebox door without burning
your hand?' she said slowly.

Horst hesitated, then looked at her. He noted her hand was on
the butt of her pistol, and smiled apologetically. 'Look,' he said.
'It's turning out to be an unusual sort of night for you, I know. And
I won't lie to you; one of those unusual things is me. But I just want
us to get out of here alive, while the unusual things in those lorries
really want to kill everybody here. So . . . can we discuss this later?'

She considered for a moment, then went to the cab side to look
back along the track. She plainly didn't like what she saw as she
slipped her gun out of its holster. 'We'll do that. Right now, keep
stoking!' She sighted and fired at the newcomers while he shovelled in coal as quickly as he could without sending it flying in all
directions. 'Jesus Christ,' he heard her mutter. 'Now it's zombies. I
hate this stupid country.'

Horst shovelled until he feared the fresh coal was starting to
choke the fire. Slamming the firebox door shut—making a point of

using the spade for the operation this time—he checked the pressure. It was starting to build, but was still a good way from allowing the train to reach top speed. Then again, he reasoned, how fast does a train have to go to outrun a bunch of shambling undead? He released the brakes and slowly started to open the throttle.

The train shuddered forward a little, then halted. Slowly, it started to move again, slowly, and remaining slow.

'Can't we go any faster?' demanded Becky as she reloaded. Horst was quietly impressed to note that, unlike the Dee Society, these people carried around enough ammunition to last them through any situation short of a protracted land war.

'Not enough steam. But moving slowly's better than not moving at all.'

Becky watched as a zombie that had been trying to board the rearmost car fell on its face between the rails. It did not attempt to rise, but lay there facedown, gloomily aware that the Afterlife was proving just as frustrating as Life.

'I think you're right,' she conceded. 'Looks like we might just . . . Oh, now. What's this?'

Horst leaned out behind her to see what new developments were apparent. While the walking dead were shambling as quickly as they could, a gap was growing between their ranks and the train as it sped away from them at a heady five miles an hour. The last lorry had pulled up, however, and it was disgorging its passengers with far greater quickness. These leapt and sprinted now on two legs, now on four, and they were past the zombies already.

'Lycanthropes.'

'Lycan who?'

'Werewolves. And foxes. And tigers. Maybe some bears. I think they only had one badger, and I killed him.'

One of the shapechangers—a jackal or a hyena—was hit by a shotgun blast from a window and fell, rolling down the embankment. Before it had even reached the bottom, however, it was fighting to regain its feet. In another moment, it was up and running once more.

Becky turned to Horst and said in disbelieving tones, 'Are we going to need *silver bullets*?'

Belatedly, Horst realised why the Society's ammunition supply had been so slight compared with the circus'. 'Ideally. Yes.'

Becky shook her head and re-holstered her pistol. She went to the controls and studied them. 'Well, shocking news, mate. We don't have any. All we can do is keep knocking 'em over until we can outrun them. Ah, look, you're venting pressure here, see?' She closed a valve and, despite Horst's mumbled claim that he was doing nothing of the sort, the pressure started to build more rapidly. Satisfied that they were finally getting some decent acceleration, she looked back along the side of the train again. 'They're on the train! I can see one on the roof!'

On the roof, Boom had just finished emptying the Thompson into the oncoming werewolf. It had staggered under the leaden hosing-down she had given it, but now the sub-machine gun was empty and she had no more loaded drums ready. She swung it into the small of her back on its sling, and drew her pistol. The wolfman grinned, the slavering lips raising to expose the long fangs, and advanced upon her in a bestial crouch.

Deciding that discretion was the better part of not being torn limb from limb by an atavistic monstrosity, Boom backed away towards the open roof hatch, firing steadily as she went. The .32 bullets did little more than make the creature flinch as it moved forward, matching her step for step, all the while its tongue lolling from the side of its mouth, waggling obscenely in the growing slipstream of the train's passage while drops of saliva flecked onto its fur. Step for step they moved, she retreating into the direction of travel, it advancing, each step punctuated by a shot, until the pistol's slide stopped in the back position, showing both antagonists that the last shot had been fired. Boom risked a quick look behind her to see if she might risk a dive for the hatch and, at that very moment, the werewolf leapt at her.

That it didn't reach her was surprising to them both, neither having allowed for the possibility of a vampire—moving at inhuman speed—intercepting the wolf in midair and the two of them crashing to the carriage roof in a tangle of fur, fangs, limbs, and aggression. The sudden change in matters caused Boom to freeze for a moment, but only a moment. Then she busied herself reloading, never taking her eyes off the fight.

It had immediately become apparent to Horst that the fundamental difference between werewolves and werebadgers were that the former were so much more *bitey*. Where the badger had led with his heavy claws (although he might have got around to biting later if he had lived that long; after all, new werebadgers have to come from somewhere), the wolf's tactics were all based around biting, grappling and biting, slashing and biting, and biting as an overture to more biting. Horst wasn't having any of that, however; he had no idea if it was possible for a vampire to contract lycanthropism, but—diverting as the concept was—he had no intention of allowing werewolf saliva into his veins to find out. Besides, he'd already drunk werebadger blood that night, so, if anything, he'd end up striped, fanged, and with claws very useful for grubbing up worms and insects. He could hardly wait. Still, what if it were possible to be infected by more than one kind of lycanthropy? By the light of a full moon, he would turn into a vampiric weremenagerie, and that would just be confusing.

Thus, he dodged and blocked the snapping jaws while ignoring the claws slashing his sadly abused clothing. He could always heal the wounds after all, and his clothes were already in such a state that a rag and bone merchant would turn his nose up at them.

He was also eager to avoid falling from the train, a fate that the roof's camber, the peripatetic nature of the fight, and the growing rocking motion as the train gathered speed were all starting to make a concern. The wolf was on him with its claws at his throat when, in an effort to re-centre the confrontation, he raised his hands between its arms and forced them apart, breaking its grip before punching it hard. As it reared back, momentarily stunned, he backhanded it, sending it stumbling backwards to fall supine along the raised centre ridge of the roof. Horst was on his feet in rather less than a second and positioning himself for the kill when he hesitated. The werewolf was possessed of dugs.

It says something about Horst that the hesitation was provoked by two considerations. Firstly, that while this was certainly a ravening monster from the realms of phantasmagoria, it was a *lady* monster from the realms of phantasmagoria, and he had been raised to find it hard even to manage impoliteness to ladies, never mind killing them in hand-to-hand combat. Also, it must be admitted, he was wondering how two managed to manifest as six during the transformation and what it must look like as they shifted from chest to midriff, and back again when wolf-time was over. Alas, it was this second thought that occupied much of his concentration at the critical—indeed, *fatal*—moment, although there are probably worse things to be thinking while one is gutted by a werewolf.

That it was not his last thought was entirely out of his hands. As the werewolf rolled to its hind feet and crouched to leap at the vampire, distracted terribly by inappropriate musings, a well-placed bullet entered its skull from behind, neatly between its laidback ears, the strange charm that usually protected the were-folk from such mundane deaths failing to protect it at all.

Horst looked forward, slightly stunned and caught in a mist of werewolf fluids. Boom was crouching by the hatch up through which had appeared the upper body of Alisha, her pistol still levelled in a two-handed grip, stabilised by laying her upper arms on the hatch's frame. She raised the gun while reaching into her jacket with her off hand, and brought it out again with a few metallic objects rolling in her palm. 'Found some more silver bullets in my other pocket,' she called. 'I'd forgotten all about them.'

Horst looked down at the werewolf's body. It . . . *she* was already beginning to transform back into a human. Standing over the carcass, the miracle of wandering breasts no longer seemed so fascinating to Horst. He knelt down and rolled the body off the roof while she was still monstrous, inhuman, and easier for him to deal with on the balance sheet of his conscience.

'There may be others,' he shouted, distracted by an inner voice that was just pointing out that it was the wolfwoman or him who had to die, so obviously better it was the woman. If he would just put all these weak emotions in a box and burn them on a bonfire of ambitions now made possible by his elevated status, he would find things so much simpler and less painful. He ran aft to see if there were, indeed, others attackers to be dealt with. The precipitate decision surely had nothing to do with covering his confusion, oh no.

There was sporadic fire from the rear car as the train pulled away from its pursuers. The shooting had settled down into a game of 'Knock Down the Werewhatever' after it had become apparent that the creatures were thoroughly resistant to lead. The vanguard of the pursuers were of the more fleet-of-foot varieties—wolves, mainly, along with a couple of great cats—and both they and the train's defenders had discovered that things went badly for them if they were knocked off their feet by a shot. While the bullet itself was a small inconvenience, the great werebull—a magnificent minotaur possessed of vast slabs of muscle and little brain—that was following up the rear would likely run over them. The lycanthropes' resistance to harm seemed very specific; bullets were nothing, but more immediate physical damage such as that caused by knives and the hooves of a clumsy werecow could cause great injury. Those knocked over by a flying bullet, therefore, prioritised getting out of the way rather than regaining their feet. That the minotaur was relatively slow, despite his enraged and protracted charge in pursuit of the train, meant that while he stood no chance of catching them, he was inadvertently aiding the cause of the fugitives. Finally, however, even he realised that if you're running after something and yet it continues to grow smaller, then the chances are it's getting away from you. He slowed to a halt, clouds of vapour rushing from his muzzle in gouts, and bellowed his frustration at the diminishing train.

Horst waved at him, which didn't help.

* * *

Finally, the time for formal introductions had arrived. The venue was a rarely used spur line leading up to a worked-out tin mine in a festering of small, heavily wooded hills between which the main line snaked. The practised manner in which switches were thrown, the metal stop sign mounted in the middle of the track was lifted and replaced after the train had moved by, and then all traces of its passage erased indicated that this was a bolthole they had had cause to retire to on several occasions.

In the penultimate carriage of the train, Ginny the Boss was holding court; whether it was a court of the royal variety or the judicial sort was open to interpretation. She sat behind a desk at one end of a large compartment that seemed to double as an office and a common room, regarding them with a jaundiced and suspicious eye, while her four colleagues sat or stood around her. Before them were Horst, Alisha, the major, and the professor. All were subdued; outside just by the tree line was a fresh grave. Richard had not survived his injuries, dying quietly while the fight had raged outside. The burial was preceded by a grim little piece of post-mortem surgery to 'deny' him to the enemy, the professor having no more of his strange chemical mixture left to affect a convenient cremation.

Ginny regarded them one at a time, taking her time as her gaze swept along the line of her new passengers. Finally, she said, 'That's not the kind of way I like to be woken.'

'Apologies, madam,' said the major, bravely taking the onerous task of communicating with these unnatural women. 'The situation was not of our choosing.'

'Yeah. I figured that. So, since you've cost me so much time and trouble, maybe you could explain the zombies, the werethings, and'—she pointed at Horst—'*him*.'

The major looked at Horst uncertainly. 'While I can assay an attempt to explain all else, ma'am, to be frank I'd have a few problems explaining Herr Cabal myself.' He turned back to Ginny. 'I am Major Haskins, late of the Guards . . .'

Ginny held up a hand. 'What guards? Train guards? The Coldstream Guards?'

'The Grenadiers, madam!' said Haskins, plainly more affronted by the second suggestion than the first. 'As I was saying, late of the Guards. These days, however, I fight in a different sort of war. I should introduce my colleagues. This is Professor Stone'—the professor bowed, then made subsidiary side-bows to the other women of the circus—'an antiquary and anthropologist.'

'*Amateur* anthropologist,' the professor quickly interpolated.

'He's too modest to say so, but he's quite the polymath. And this is Miss Alisha Bartos.' Alisha showed no inclination to bow or, heaven forbid, curtsey. Instead she simply nodded. 'She's . . .' The major foundered, at a loss to explain succinctly what she was. 'She's . . . well.'

Ginny looked at her. 'What do *you* call yourself?'

Alisha considered for a few seconds; it appeared summing up her career briefly was not something she'd had to do before. Certainly, her *curriculum vitae* seemed to be of an involved sort, given her evident concentration.

Then her brow cleared and she smiled very slightly. 'I'm a spy.'

Ginny leaned back, her old round-backed office chair creaking. 'Poor kind of spy who admits to it.'

Alisha shrugged slightly. 'An ex-spy.'

'Who for?'

'Prussian Intelligence.' There was an amused snort from Mink at that, earning her a cold scowl from Alisha. 'Which is *not* a contradiction in terms.'

Ginny shook her head slightly and looked at their faces one by one. 'So. We have us a soldier, an academic, and an *ex*-spy.' Amid more creaking she leaned forward and rested an elbow on her desk and her chin in her palm as she looked at Horst standing there in the wreck of his outfit. 'I can barely wait to hear what you are.'

'Oh, I'm a vampire,' said Horst. 'Speaking of which, do you think we might rattle on a bit more quickly with this? The sun will be up soon, and we don't really get on very well.'

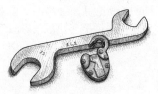

Chapter 9

IN WHICH ACQUAINTANCES ARE MADE
AND MEASURES TAKEN

Horst slept that day in an arms locker, which was a novel experience. As they were currently in dangerous country dense with
bandits, outlaws, and—as it turned out—zombies, shapechangers,
and sundry forces of darkness, the weapons were not to be found
in there at the moment. This left them with a welded steel safe
box, perhaps a yard square, guarding some cleaning kits, empty
packages, and the petty cash. These were spirited out, and Horst
invited somewhat tersely to take up residence. He was disappointed but not surprised to hear the box's heavy padlock put
into place and clicked shut once he was uncomfortably curled up
within. Another confined space, another padlock; how history repeated itself.

Although he could not see it, he was aware of the sun rising
outside and of its purifying rays driving away all evil from the
hemisphere, with the exception of bankers. A few minutes later, a

great weariness settled upon him and he fell rapidly into torpor. There was little air within the box, but that didn't matter; he wouldn't be using any of it.

Some events occurred during the day, as events are wont to do, but Horst was unaware of these and all else.

The sun moved on. It was a pleasant enough sort of day for those who were not in deadly danger, but the passengers of the train regarded the slow arc of the sun as a slowly creeping indicator of growing menace. The night would shoo away the bankers, but all other evils would be unleashed.

Horst awoke in the reverse of how he slept. As the sun slipped beneath the unseen western horizon, animation returned to him, and he stirred in an unnatural sleep. Through the long minutes of dusk, he slept as he had once slept when his blood was warmer and his hours diurnal until as the last glimmer passed from the sky, his eyes opened.

He was still in a box, and the blasted thing was still locked.

After some minutes of gentle pounding on the box's side with the occasional polite cry of, 'Hello! Excuse me, hello?' he heard approaching footsteps. The lock rattled in its hasp, and the lid was flung up. He uncurled himself, cramp fortunately being a mortal failing, and raised his head slowly to look out.

One of the circus women, presumably whoever had just re-leased him, was returning to a firing line centred around Ginny. They looked at him from above gun barrels and their intent to shoot him if necessary was perfectly evident. Horst found some-thing to lament in that this wasn't even the worst wake-up call he'd ever experienced.

'Good evening, ladies,' he said quietly, so as not to provoke. The carriage was swaying slightly; he wondered how long they had been under way. 'Two things worth considering. Firstly, you could have destroyed me easily during the day. But you didn't. Many thanks for that. Secondly, you must appreciate that your guns are next to useless against me. I could probably pop out of here and . . .'

Hunger, said the nagging little voice that wasn't him yet spoke with his voice. *Kill them and feed.*

'Pop out of here and . . .' *Kill.* '. . . defeat you.' Knuckles whitened as trigger fingers grew taut. 'But . . . I'm not going to do that.' They continued to stare at him *from behind their ridiculous, useless weapons*. 'Because'—he smiled, fighting the urge to let his fangs extend—'I want us to be friends.'

'He's right,' said Alisha. Horst hadn't consciously noticed her; she'd been standing alongside the box the whole time. 'The guns are a waste of time. Believe me, I know.'

Horst nodded, hands on the edge of the box, head barely exposed. 'She shot me.'

'I shot him,' Alisha confirmed. 'Twice. I knew they wouldn't kill him. I just needed to slow him down a little.'

'Unnecessarily.'

'I didn't know that at the time,' she said, with the tiniest hint of apology in her voice.

Ginny sighed and returned her revolver to its hip holster. 'Put 'em away, girls,' she ordered. Hammers were thumbed down, safety catches engaged, barrels lowered, holsters filled. Ginny was obeyed without question, perhaps, but with evident reluctance. Even given the ineffectuality of firearms against a vampire, there would still have been some satisfaction in punching a few holes in him if things had become physically unfriendly. Ginny Montgomery sat on a crate and regarded both Horst and Alisha with the same air of mild hostility. 'Waifs and strays I can deal with, but this is a new one on me. Monsters and monster hunters, and one of the hunters is a monster himself. This is just great,' she said, although whether she really thought it was great was disputable.

'Life's strange, isn't it?' said Horst. He had decided that to take offence at the term 'monster' would be undiplomatic. In any case, it was true. 'May I get out of the box, please? I feel like half of a ventriloquist act in here.' Nobody said he couldn't (although nobody said he could). As he climbed out, he asked, 'So, anything interesting happen while I was sleeping?'

'Miss Montgomery here,' said Alisha, nodding at Ginny, 'has agreed to take us to the next town. Then we're on our own again.'

'*Town* is putting it strongly,' said Mink. When Alisha looked questioningly at her, she expanded with, 'It's a farming centre. Calls itself a town, but really it's just a place for the farmers to come in to buy supplies. Maybe a couple of hundred people there.'

This was not the sort of news Alisha was hoping for. 'There'll be a telegraph office, though? Other trains coming through?'

Mink shrugged.

Alisha raised her hands in frustration, her tension apparent. 'You've seen what's going on around here,' she remonstrated. 'They know their security's compromised, they're moving ahead more rapidly already. Unless we stop them, this whole region will become a living nightmare.' She examined her words and shook her head with a slight disbelieving smile. 'That's not even a fanciful way of describing it. That is exactly what it will be like.'

'Tell it to the Marines,' said Miss Virginia 'Ginny' Montgomery wearily. Nobody seemed to have had much sleep. 'It's not like we're kicking you off the train at Hicksberg or whatever it's called when we get there. We're doing three days of shows there, maybe some agricultural work if we can find it.'

Agricultural work? mouthed Horst, but nobody minded him.

'It's our job. We don't fight bogey men 'less somebody brings 'em to our door,' Miss Montgomery said pointedly. 'There are authorities, aren't there? Tell them. It's their country after all. Their country, their problem.'

Alisha took a step forward, her anger growing. 'The authorities? For this place? Don't you understand? They're in the *Ministerium*'s pocket. We'd have to go to the neighbouring states. By the time we've convinced them of the threat . . .'

'If you ever do,' said Horst quietly.

Alisha shot him a glance. 'We can be very persuasive. We have connections you know nothing about. You think private citizens can just lay hands on field mortars and shells if they get a sudden urge to siege a castle? Do you?' She turned her attention back to Miss Montgomery. 'By the time we can convince them and they mobilise, it will be far, far too late.'

'What were you planning on doing by yourself, then? There's the four of you.' Miss Montgomery rose from her crate and walked over to where Alisha stood, almost palpably fuming with angry frustration. 'Look, darlin', I have no idea if this is all you say it is. I'll be honest with you—this whole place is in such a state of disarray that I don't know if the citizens will even notice if they're being ruled by vampires and goblins and the Lord only knows what. The bottom line of the account reads that there's not a thing you can do by yourself. No matter what, your best chance is to persuade the neighbours to get involved. Yes, yes, I heard you. That'll be too late to nip this thing in the bud. Maybe so, but it's the only game in town. The place we're going to, we organised where we're going to be putting on the show by wire, so you can rest assured they've got a telegraph office there. Get your message out. That's all you can do, so you better get comfortable with the idea.'

Alisha could *not* get comfortable with this, but she relayed the intelligence to Major Haskins and Professor Stone and, after a very short discussion—because really, what alternative was there?—they committed to do what little they could. 'There comes a point where you can charge around all you like, but there's nothing to be done about it. It's the nature of war,' said the major, shrewd though disconsolate. 'We shall call it in and wait.'

Alisha paced around. She had called herself a 'spy', but this had only been marginally true. She had been mainly involved as an agent of sabotage and assassination during her eventful time with Prussian military intelligence, but she wasn't about to communicate that willy-nilly. The whole 'blowing things up and doing people in' milieu would only upset people. Thus, patience in the face of the enemy was not one of her fortes. She would much rather have been off putting silver rifle rounds through lycanthropic heads and putting enough gelignite in the cellars of the Red Queen's castle to put the whole sorry bunch of them beyond the orbit of the moon. You knew where you were with gelignite; ideally, running away from it while the fuse burned down. All this not-blowing-things-up-or-shooting-people palaver, however, was wearing thin for her. 'And what if we're needed?'

'They also serve,' said the professor, 'who only stand and wait. I'm afraid the major is right, Alisha. We can do more good relaying what we know and awaiting the call to action that will surely follow.'

The train reached its destination in the early hours. Everybody but Becky on the footplate and Horst, who went to assist her, were sleeping as they approached an unassuming little conglomeration of clapboard buildings in the middle of a broad river valley, situated by a broad and shallow river that ran over a rocky bed. There were no curious onlookers, and the only greeting they received was from an official at the wooden box of a station, who wandered out in his nightshirt, made a note of the locomotive's number, was singularly uninterested to see that one of the crew was a woman, and told them to put the train 'over there' while indicating a field into which ran five sidings, all overgrown. It was clear that the settlement must have seen a lot of rail traffic at some time to make such a facility necessary, and now it was equally clear that those days were long since gone.

His duty discharged, the stationmaster turned his back on them and shuffled back across rough boards in slippered feet to return to his rest. The impression received was that he got a lot of that.

The train's stopping and starting, and its slow entry onto one of the sidings accompanied by the unavoidable clanks and bangs of a train manoeuvring without benefit of somebody in the guard's van helping with the brakes awoke some aboard, and they woke the others. By the time the train was fully off the through line and the points closed behind it, Miss Montgomery and the rest of her party were up, dressed, and ready to work.

Horst, who had previously travelled up and down the train by corridor where possible and across rooves where it was not, was still vague about the nature of Miss Montgomery's circus, beyond the fact that there was sufficient machinery involved for them to include a dedicated mechanic among their number and a small workshop in the guard's van. Nor had the subject really had a chance to come up in conversation, what with all the chat about Forces of Darkness and the End of Civilisation having taken up so much time.

Now he had the luxury of jumping down from the locomotive and walking back to take in the hoardings mounted on the sides of the two mysterious freight carriages.

MISS VIRGINIA MONTGOMERY'S
FLYING CIRCUS

. . . he read there. 'Oh,' he said. 'Oh, my.'

The troupe had lost almost eight hours with their unexpected layover at the forgotten mine workings, and were eager to make up time. The hoardings were taken down, Horst good-naturedly lending a hand where he was able and permitted in an effort to recompense them for the inconvenience, revealing one car to be bearing three entomopter fuselages in cargo frames and its neighbour one larger fuselage, several crates of spares, and a substantial fuel reservoir.

Horst had never seen an entomopter close to, and had to be shooed away from them as a hand-cranked crane mounted at the end of the car bearing three close by its neighbour was brought into play. Here, at least, his help was welcomed, and he enthusiastically wound the first of the aircraft up, across, and thence down onto the loading track that ran alongside the spur.

As the machine's carrying frame was unlocked and removed, Becky joined Horst. He had seen photographs and drawings of the small, agile aircraft, usually illustrating exciting tales of firm-chinned pilots who flew their dragonfly-like steeds into tricky situations on a weekly basis. Seeing one close up—all rivets and sheet steel and linkages—was so much more . . . *mechanical*. 'I thought they had bigger wings than that,' he said, trying to make an intelligent comment.

Becky laughed, indicating that it wasn't so intelligent after all. 'Those are just the wing stems. The wings are dismounted for travel. We have to put them on.' She checked her wristwatch, a sturdy man's model that she wore face turned inwards. 'And you've got to do it properly. Don't want to lose one in flight.' She looked seriously at him. 'That would be *bad*.' And she smiled.

As each entomopter was disembarked from the train and its frame removed, it was manually rolled out of the way on its landing gear so the next could follow. Each was painted differently, each customised to its pilot's show persona. Horst attempted to match them to what he knew of the women with moderate success. He had a free start with Miss Virginia Montgomery's aircraft—he had learned not to call her 'Ginny' already—as hers was the first off the train and the first he examined closely, so noting her name painted in flowing copperplate by the cockpit edge. Miss Mink Choi's was easy; the world over, there is nothing more guaranteed to appeal to the common man than to accentuate the uncommon and the exotic. In that bucolic European setting where most had never even seen a face that wasn't Caucasian, it was a sure bet that her Eastern roots would be played up to the hilt. Thus, her entomopter was as generically Oriental as could be managed, with Chinese dragons running along each side, crossed Japanese swords upon the rudder, and an exhortation in what, to Horst's limited linguistic skills, looked to be Siamese running in a vertical column down the upper surface of the nose. Beneath each dragon was written in faux–Chinese style *Striking Dragon*.

As he helped hold up a wing while it was slotted, locked, and bolted into position by Mink, he asked her, 'Might I ask where you're from, originally?'

'New York,' she said, not looking up from her work.

'No, I more sort of meant your ancestry.'

'Korea. Why the interest?' She noticed his line of sight to the entomopter's fuselage. 'Oh, that. Ignore that. That's just for the rubes.'

Horst smiled. *Rubes.* 'Haven't heard that word for a while,' he said, skipping over the period of that time when he'd been very dead even by undead standards. 'I helped run a carnival for a while.'

She looked up again. 'It's a pretty American word,' she said. 'Where was the carnival?'

'England, but on the strength we had an . . .' He paused while he considered how to explain that the 'American' from whom he'd learned the word was actually a demonic construct raised from the blood of Lucifer. It seemed like a lot of work and would likely cause whatever goodwill he was earning with Mink and her comrades to evaporate. He contented himself with saying, 'an American,' and left it at that.

By a trifling coincidence, trifling due to the clear national majority within the women, the next machine he looked at was clearly an American's aircraft, judging from the screaming bald eagles on either side, the red, the white, the blue, the stars, and the stripes that occupied every square inch of the fuselage. Beneath the eagles was the aircraft's name rendered in urgent, forward-leaning capitals: *Spirit of '76.* This had been the first aircraft Horst had seen unloaded, and he knew it to be Miss Virginia Montgomery's.

The next machine also used an American theme, equally dramatic but more sober; on a field of blue skies, white clouds, and tan desert sands, the profile of an American Indian chief of indeterminate nation, arrayed in full headdress, looked forward on either side of the entomopter's nose above the legend *Queen of the Desert.* The tail sported crossed six-shooters, and they reminded him of the Colt he'd seen Miss Daisy Hewlett firing with evident satisfaction into the face of a zombie on the night of their first acquaintance. She was, on reflection, almost the archetypal cowgirl: tall, rangy, with sandy blond hair and what he now took to be the verbal drawl he had read about in so many cheap Western novels he had read in his youth, much to the exasperation of his father and disdain of his brother. Perhaps, he mused, she really was an actual cowgirl. She certainly looked very at home in her jeans. He mused on this for some further moments until belatedly recalling that he was dead these days and really shouldn't think along those sorts of lines anymore.

He did not have such an easy time with the next entomopter he examined, however. This one was decorated with sparse harshly angular patterns of long lines in different colours against a white background. The only part of its paintwork that was at all figurative was a curious logotype painted on either side of the rudder: an image of a falling bomb of the modern type, cylindrical and finned. Riding it in its descent, however, with an expression of great determination, was *another* bomb, this time of the old spherical grenade form, much beloved of anarchists if one is to believe the cartoonists. This bomb was anthropomorphised to the extent of having stubby arms and legs, like a character from a comic strip, the former gripping the bomb with its little gloved hands, the latter straddling it. The anarchist bomb's round eyes were squinted in concentration. The entomopter's name was written at the usual location in a very modernistic, brutalist style: *Buzzbomb*.

By a process of elimination, this must belong to the engagingly named Dutch woman, Dea Boom. He had already inquired as to why, of her four companions, Miss Virginia Montgomery only ever referred to Dea Boom by her surname. This, Becky informed him, was because the alternative made it sound as if Miss Virginia Montgomery was using an affectionate term usually associated with married couples, and Miss Virginia Montgomery did not care for such familiarity. When time was not pressing, she might refer to Dea Boom as 'Miss Boom', but time always seemed to be pressing.

Though Daisy might have fancied herself the 'Queen of the Desert', Becky was undeniably 'Queen of the Entomopters'. No major process in their reassembly and preparation went without her close attention and, even when everything was in place, she still went over each with a clipboard in one hand and a stoic determination that there would be no mechanical failures on *her* watch written upon her countenance. She was also drinking a vast amount of black coffee, and Horst calculated that she must be running on nigh a full twenty-four hours of demanding activity without even a nap. His sole attempt to get her to rest ran onto the rocks immediately when she snapped, 'We're running late. No time for rest,' and gulped down a large mug of glutinous coffee, one bright and feverish eye resting askance in his direction like that of a peevish wolverine that just wants you to take one step closer.

Horst was wise enough not to take that step, but instead induced short, covert periods of rest upon her utilising the ancient and honoured technique of gossip. Specifically, he brokered his real interest in entomopters and his equally real ignorance of their finer points into opportunities for her to stop what she was doing and lecture him briefly.

All the entomopters were, with one exception, surplus Senzan Royal Aeroforce CI-650 Giaguaro interceptors, long since superseded by the CI-880 Ghepardo.

'The Eight-Eighty's a nice bird,' she confided, 'but the Six-Fifty was no slouch in her day, either.' Apparently the CI-650 had greater pretensions towards being a strike aircraft than its successor and allowed more of its weight towards payload. This turned out to be unnecessary as militarily it was more used in controlling its own national airspace, so the CI-880 was made faster. 'That worked out well for us, though. We don't just fly displays—there isn't enough loose money floating around in this part of the world for that. We do a lot of general flying work, too. Pleasure jaunts, light cargo, surveying, crop-dusting, that sort of thing.'

Horst looked at the proudly painted former war machines with raised eyebrows. 'Crop-dusting?'

'It pays the bills,' Becky said a little shortly, so he changed the subject.

'So three are Six-Fifties? What kind is that, then?' He nodded at

Spirit of '76. It was not as lean a machine as its fellows, but sleek for all that, with fairings that seemed perhaps a little larger than they needed to be if only to project a sense of power. It was also the only one to have two seats, arranged one aft of the other.

Becky shot the entomopter a cynical look, her lips slightly pursed. 'More trouble than she's worth. Yankee machine, J-55 Copperhead. Can't get spares for her, so I spend half my waking hours bent over a lathe making 'em myself.'

Horst nodded sympathetically. 'Looks good, though.'

Indeed it did, the artful exaggerations in the design making the entomopter look muscular and purposeful.

'Flies like a 'bus,' said Becky unsympathetically. 'Lousy engine in her, underpowered. Put a Rolls-Royce Hyperion in her, like the USAAF eventually did after all their pilots told 'em she flew like a 'bus, and she's a decent bird. Can't afford one, though, so we're left with the lowest-bidder piece of rubbish that she came with. Fly better if I put in a sewing-machine motor.' She looked gloomily at it. 'Or a piece of wound-up elastic. Anything.'

'But . . . I don't understand this. Isn't Miss Montgomery the star of the show? Shouldn't she have the best 'mopter?'

Becky shook her head as she took up her spanner once more. 'Nah. It's a circus and she's the ringmistress. She just has to look flash and stand out from the others. Don't get me wrong—she's a decent flyer. But she's no barnstormer. She keeps this show on the road, and that is plenty, believe you me.'

Horst had no experience of keeping a show on the road; he had avoided the bookkeeping end of things in the Cabal Bros. Carnival, leaving that in the capable hands of his terribly detail-orientated brother. Horst had been more than content to simply swan around in a variety of expensive suits, safe in the knowledge that a carnival that operates with next to no overheads and is underwritten by the Devil himself is never going to run into financial problems. At some level he had blithely assumed that this was only a small advantage and that normal carnivals made only slightly less money. Looking at the state of affairs with Miss Montgomery's

Flying Circus, however—the battered rolling stock that probably would not pass muster for moving condemned cows, the way everyone did what needed to be done regardless of their usual roles, the constant battle to keep the entomopters airworthy and the smiles bright—he could see that he had been naive.

Changing the subject slightly, he asked, 'What happened to the military gear that was on the 'mopters when you bought them?'

Becky didn't look up from the engine mounting she was checking. 'You mean the guns? Stripped out before we ever saw them. Had to plate over where the barrel louvres were. You can see the patches under the paintwork. They left the mounting hardpoints on, though. We use them to mount the spraying gear and I knocked together some external cargo pods that can sit on them. There were a bunch of specialist tools for the weapons these birds used to carry, too, and we've got those. Priming levers, tensioning grips, that kind of thing. No use to us, but they were in the kits.'

'Do you fly?'

'I can, but I don't very much. Fuel's too expensive for pleasure jaunts. I used . . .' She stopped her work and glanced at him, looking for a reaction. 'I used to be in the Royal Aeroforce, you know?'

She was rewarded with raised eyebrows. 'I didn't know the RAF took female pilots.'

She grinned, pleased, and returned to disciplining an awkward bolt. 'They won't let women fight, but 'mopters have to be ferried around, so that was my job.'

'Fun?'

She rocked her head to indicate it had its moments. 'Got a lot of air hours. Not fancy flying, but good bread-and-butter stuff. Certified for night flying, which puts me one up on a couple of the girls. They might be able to barrel roll a 'mopter under a bridge, but they can't navigate to save their lives once the sun goes down.'

Horst smiled. 'I'm sure you don't remind them about that much.'

'No, that'd be rude,' she agreed. 'I keep it down to no more than a couple of times a day.'

* * *

The hours wound on until Horst felt the turn of the Earth bring the killing sun around again. He made his apologies and headed for his locker, telling them he'd be fine, no need to tuck him in. No need to padlock the lid, either. In the carriage, he found Alisha, Major Haskins, and Professor Stone, all clearly recently awakened.

'This is nice,' said Horst on seeing them. 'Is somebody going to read me a bedtime story?'

'Mr Cabal,' said the major. 'We need to know where you stand.'

'Mr Cabal,' Horst echoed. He went to the locker, opened the lid, and started rearranging the dusty old blanket he had been given as an afterthought the night before. He would have preferred to have stripped before getting in to avoid creasing the clothes Miss Virginia had found (which is to say stolen, although she character-ised it as 'commandeering') among the belongings of the errant train crew. It seemed unlikely that they would have got far with a tide of zombies and frustrated werecreatures stalking the area af-ter the train's escape, she had explained. Horst found her logic irrefutable, if ethically questionable. Still, as his clothes had been torn, soaked, muddied, burnt, and corroded to a state where it took a brave man to call them clothes at all, he had decided that practical-ity and modesty were of greater moment than the property rights of the two men, missing, presumed eaten.

'"Mr Cabal" was my father. These days he's my younger brother, assuming he's still alive. I'm just Horst.' He looked at them, but they seemed in no great hurry to leave. It seemed likely that he was going to be wandering around in crumpled clothes the following night. 'Where I stand is next to my box. It's not as nice as my old box, but you have to make do, don't you? The sun will be up soon, so if this is going to be an involved conversation, can it wait until the evening?'

'What we would like to know, Horst,' said the professor, 'is if we can count upon you as an ally in the coming war?'

'War?' Horst slouched against the box. 'Look, I know the *Min-isterium* is made up of bad people, but do you really see a war happening here? As a country, this place is already dead. Did you see the locals get involved the other night? They just locked their doors and let it happen. Monsters running loose all over the place and nobody even tried to stop them. There'll be no war here.' He lofted a leg over the side of the box and started to climb in. 'There's no elegant way of doing this,' he said with a slightly embarrassed smile.

None of the others seemed to care so very much about the deportment of vampires. 'Mr Cabal,' said the major, 'is that honestly what you think is all the *Ministerium* have in mind? A safe haven for poor, hapless monsters to escape the prejudices of humans?'

Horst was now inside the box, both hands on its edge as he faced them. He felt like a defendant in court. 'Yes?' he said, a little uncertainly.

'The country is in a state of collapse and anarchy,' said the professor. 'It is useless in all respects to the needs of the *Ministerium Tenebrae*. All but one.'

'They'll kill everyone, Horst,' said Alisha. 'They'll make them into new monsters. Everybody.'

Horst could not reply. Dawn was so close now. He wanted to rest, to sleep. He did not want to reply.

'So,' said the major. 'Where do you stand?'

An Interlude

'I note,' said Johannes Cabal, while making notes, 'that there is a certain warmth in your tone when you refer to Fräulein Bartos.'

'No, there isn't,' said Horst a little too abruptly.

'There is. Even when you recounted how she shot you in the lungs, it was described in much the same mode one would expect if she'd sent you a poem of poor scansion and cloying sentimentality such as the ones that Greta Thorndike used to send you.'

Horst looked offended. 'You read Greta's poems?'

'You used to read them to yourself, sigh happily, and leave them littering the place like dandruff. Of course I read them. You obviously intended them to be read, so I indulged your ego by doing so.'

'I'm sure I intended no such thing,' protested Horst, not at all sure he intended no such thing.

'Execrable poetry aside—the one likening you to a robin redbreast and herself to a turtledove in particular still causes me to flinch involuntarily when it comes to mind, not least because of the biological unlikelihood of it all—that aside, you have a mooncalf air about you at such times. I see elements of it when Alisha Bartos is mentioned.'

'Honestly, Johannes, you really say . . .'

'Don't,' said Cabal peremptorily. 'Simply don't.'

Horst rocked his head in indecision between moral outrage and gleeful agreement, and gave in to the inevitable at speed. He smiled. No. He grinned.

'She is a bit wonderful,' he said.

'She's a trained killer, practised dissimulator, and a sworn enemy of necromancers.'

'I know, and she's really pretty, too!' He looked at Cabal with uncharacteristic nervousness. 'I say, Johannes. You don't think . . . you know . . . a fellow like me, and a lady like that might somehow . . .'

'A monster and a killer of monsters. Oh, yes, Horst. Romance is certainly on the cards.'

Horst's enthusiasm waned a little. 'You think that might be a problem?'

'Honestly? Yes, I think it might put a few brass tacks in your path.'

'Oh,' said Horst. His shoulders sank. 'Oh.'

Cabal looked at Horst and sighed. 'Do you recall the offer I made you when I first liberated you from the crypt?'

'The crypt you locked me in for eight years?'

'The same,' said Cabal, unperturbed. 'Eight years and thirty-seven days, as I recall. Do you remember the offer?'

'That you'd try to cure me.'

'It still stands.'

Horst crossed his arms. 'Why should I believe you?'

'Why shouldn't you? You did then . . .'

'I wouldn't put it that strongly.'

'. . . and you have far more reason to do so now. Horst . . .' He lowered his voice, ashamed. 'I've done things since then. Things you don't know about.' The confession almost choked him, but somehow he forced the words out. 'I've done *good* things.'

Horst feigned astonishment. 'Good Lord.'

Cabal was distracted, lost in terrible memories of altruism. 'Awful, selfless things. Sometimes I commit sensible, rational acts and I get a pain in my chest. And then *undoing* what I've done makes me feel better. Sometimes it even makes me feel good.

'Horst, I think I may have a conscience.'

His brother bursting into laughter did not help Cabal's metaphysical suffering in the slightest.

Chapter 10

IN WHICH BIRDS FLY AND DEATH COMES TO TOWN

As dawn arrived and Horst slipped into a deep sleep from which only the next night would rouse him, the small community awoke to find Miss Virginia Montgomery's Flying Circus among them.

The locals were moderately excited by this development, and a great milling throng of perhaps eight people gathered at a respectful distance from the train and the row of gaudy entomopters that stood before it along the access road, gleaming and so out of place in the determinedly bucolic setting that they may as well have just set down after a long migration from Mars.

Miss Virginia herself approached the worthies and spoke to them of aerial thrills, adventures, excitement, and very good crop-dusting rates. This last raised most interest and, along with a few courier requests to carry reasonable loads for reasonable distances, represented the first part of the Circus's trade for the day. The afternoon would feature a display, providing the media blitz represented by a foolscap-sized poster placed within the covered town notice board a fortnight before proved sufficient to provide a viable audience. The town, for all its profound failure to whelm, was still the centre of a substantial farming area and should, according to Miss Virginia's calculations, provide enough financial reasons to linger for three days. She had been wrong before, though.

Deals were made between the exotic visitors and the locals. All seemed workable enough, but for one request to send a spiced ham to an émigré family in Chicago and another to transport a prize heifer sixty miles. After brief explanations of just exactly how far away Chicago was, and how unhappy a heifer would be strapped to the underside of an entomopter as it gamely hopped hedgerows and rivers for sixty miles because there was no way it could hope to fly with that much weight, business was concluded and jobs assigned. Three of the entomopters would be carrying packages distances of up to a hundred miles, while Miss Virginia's own *Spirit of '76* with its relatively capacious cargo capability would be sporting spray wings and flying the stars and stripes over several fields of cabbage threatened by caterpillars, leaving a vapour trail of DDT in its wake.

The major had seen plenty of entomopter flights in his time so, while Alisha and the professor watched the aircraft lift and depart on their sundry missions, he busied himself with encoding a detailed message and then standing over the telegraph operator at the station as it was sent. He rejoined his colleagues and said, 'Well, it's out of our hands now.'

'How many of the others do you think survived the assault?' asked Professor Stone.

'I'm reasonably optimistic about that,' replied the major. 'The enemy focussed their efforts upon us, and we were the smaller part of the force. I think the mortars may have antagonised them somewhat. In any case, I didn't see them attempt to attack any of our people in the square. It would have meant rousting out all the poor wretches in the shanties, and we were far more obvious. Unless the *Ministerium* and its minions performed some sort of follow-up action of which we are unaware, then our people should have had ample opportunity to fade into the night. We'll know within a few hours in any case. They should have fallen back to the rendezvous points and reported in to London as I've just done. When the committee sends their reply, we should have a better idea how things stand.'

'Did you mention Horst Cabal to them?' asked Alisha, her indifference a little too studious to be convincing. The major looked at her oddly.

'Of course I did. How could I fail to mention that the Lord of the Dead has come over to our side?'

'What do you think they will say?'

'That it's a bloody good thing, I would expect.'

'You're sure of his sincerity?'

'As sure as I can be. Look, Miss Bartos, there is always the chance that this is all some sort of devilishly clever plot to make us deliver the rest of our forces into a cunningly laid trap. I've racked my mind over it, though, and I can't see how such a plan could have been created in the time they had. Unless Mr Cabal is entirely committed to their cause and is busking his way towards betraying us, I cannot believe there is such a plan.'

'What,' asked the professor, 'if that is exactly what he is doing?'

'Then we're doomed,' said the major. 'Obviously.' He nodded to where they could make out the distant shape of Miss Virginia's Copperhead performing tight turns and swoops as it rained a fine mist of insecticide across cabbages and dismayed caterpillars. 'She's good in that thing, isn't she? It looks about as manoeuvrable as a coal barge, but it's actually quite nippy.'

Midday brought the return of the couriers, Daisy with a story of having to fight off the advances of a station agent at her destination who apparently harboured a secret lust for cowgirls, inspired by cheap novels bearing ridiculously romanticised renderings of Calamity Jane and Annie Oakley upon their covers. 'He kept saying, "I lof der cowgirls". I was telling him that was all very flattering, but would he just sign for the damn package? Then he got grabby, so I drew on him.'

'You *drew* on him?' asked the professor, imagining something involving pen and ink, and having difficulty seeing how this was an appropriate response.

'Sure,' she said, laughing, and tapped a finger to the grip of her revolver where it showed in the shoulder holsters all the women wore, presumably because it was easier to reach the weapons there when in a cockpit.

'Oh,' said the professor, both relieved by the explanation and embarrassed by his slowness.

'I bet that quieted him down,' said Dea Boom of the explosive name that, disappointingly, only meant 'tree' in Dutch.

'You'd have thought so, wouldn't you? But, no. Having a cowgirl draw down on him was about the most exciting thing that had happened to him since his voice broke.'

'So what happened then?'

'He signed. Thanked me, signed, thanked me again, proposed, took it like a trouper when I said no, and waved when I went.'

'He proposed?' interrupted the professor. 'On a first meeting? He actually proposed marriage?'

Daisy grinned at him. 'Marriage? Heck, no, Prof. He didn't propose *marriage*.'

And she and her colleagues left the professor in his slowly deepening scandalisation to go and ready their aircraft for the afternoon's show.

A decent little crowd of perhaps fifty had gathered at two o'clock. The major, however, regarded them with an air of concerned disappointment. 'This can't possibly be economically practical for Miss Montgomery and her girls,' he said, pronouncing it 'ghels'.

'It can't be cheap running an operation like this,' agreed Professor Stone. 'How much do you expect to make from this?' he asked Becky, who was standing nearby with a collection box.

'This? Drinking money and a few washers. The idea is we do a couple of small shows to get people talking and spread the word. Then we do the big one on market day and that should see us through until we reach the next place.'

Stone looked at the size of the crowd and asked, 'This last big show; how many people would you anticipate turning up?'

'More or less everyone in the area. There's not much entertainment around here, so people grab what they can while they can. I'd say'—she pulled an estimative face—'perhaps two thousand or so.'

Haskins and Stone were visibly surprised. 'That many?' asked the former.

'It's true. Happens just about every time. They'll come in from all over, bringing their families. We'll have a good crowd.'

The crowd they had was therefore small, but appreciative. The 'show' was informal to say the least, but no great buildup was necessary as the onlookers were already eager for diversion. Necks craned this way and that as they searched the cool blue sky for the entomopters, distantly audible but hidden from view.

Becky leaned closer to Haskins and Stone. 'Hold on to your hats,' she said quietly.

Even as they were drawing breath to inquire why that might be necessary, their hats were blown off by the shockingly low passage of Mink's and Dea Boom's entomopters appearing from behind the train. They must have been approaching rapidly, close abeam, their craft almost brushing the grass beyond the line of carriages to have made such a stealthy approach, before opening their throttles and hopping over the roof of the carriage by which the professor, the major, and Becky were standing. This also brought them up behind the crowd, who, collectively bamboozled by the engine tones more easily audible ahead of them, had assumed that this would be the direction of approach.

Alisha arrived with a bag full of supplies she had just bought at the general store in time to see her colleagues chasing their headwear. She put down the bag by the fence alongside the access road and leaned against it to watch as Mink and Dea broke in opposite directions and into the area of open sky framed by their craft, two oncoming entomopters appeared, rising from behind a stand of trees. Miss Virginia Montgomery's *Spirit of '76* was plainly in the lead, its silhouette rounded and luxuriant, a lioness flanked by a jaguar. The crowd were still laughing in delighted surprise from the first approach when they realised that the two newcomers were also heading dead towards them. To their credit, they limited their nervousness at this development with some more nervous laughter and perhaps a surreptitious communal crouch that only knocked an inch or so from their individual heights, but served to make them feel a little bit safer.

They had nothing to fear, however. Miss Virginia shot over their heads with a clearance of a good ten feet, while Daisy broke right at the same moment, moving off to re-form with Dea while Mink fell in line astern to *Spirit of '76*.

Although Becky claimed that the display had been cobbled together only a few hours beforehand based on the lay of the land, it remained terrifically impressive. It was true that the ringmistress was there primarily to top and tail each sequence of barnstorming, powering through a scattering formation to punctuate rather than participate, but she was clearly no mean pilot if not nearly as impressive as those she led. They had the advantage of leaner, more agile aircraft, too, and while the Copperhead might not have been quite the flying version of a No. 24 to Pimlico that Becky had suggested, it could not hope to compete in anything but cargo capacity, and that attribute was not usually considered much of a crowd pleaser.

A small piece of genius that both Alisha and Haskins noted was the way by which the display hinted that the entomopters were capable of doing far more. They would bank so hard that it seemed likely that they would roll, but they did not. They would climb so steeply and dive so precipitously that there was always the hint that continued pressure on the yoke would finish in a loop, either upwards or in a bunted inverse finish. Yet they never quite followed through on these, but only stall turned, or pulled out. It was a tease; a great beckoning finger drawn across the sky to lure the punters on to the big show in two days' time, and to make them excited enough to talk about it. The flying display that afternoon did not last long—only perhaps fifteen minutes—but that was just long enough to whet appetites for more without overstaying their welcome.

'Masterful,' murmured Professor Stone as the four aircraft performed a last flyby in line astern, the pilots waving to their small but highly appreciative audience as they passed before curling off towards the distance, then returning and performing simultaneous vertical landings in a neat line along the length of the field they had hired as their showground. Becky was already ahead of the crowd, collecting coins and washers while simultaneously keeping them a healthy distance from the blurred wings of the insectlike aircraft as the engines wound down, for it is a truth universally acknowledged that knocking an arm off a local will put a dampener on subsequent relations.

It had its effect, too. The next day (after a night in which Horst was told of the skills of Miss Virginia Montgomery's Flying Circus and spent the rest of his waking hours in a mild sulk because he would never see them at firsthand), the crowd was somewhat larger, numbering perhaps eighty, of whom the great majority of the previous day's audience constituted a part in addition to those excited enough by word of mouth to skip tasks and chores to spend a few minutes watching the flying wonderment of it all.

Nor were they disappointed, this show being different enough from the first display to excite the old hands along with the new. When they performed their flyby and synchronised landing this time, the applause was louder and there were fewer washers to be found in the collection box subsequently.

The major, professor, and Alisha were not on hand for it this time, however. They had been sitting around the telegraph office since shortly after noon, awaiting a reply from London. As the day wore on, however, they accepted one by one that it was unlikely that there would be a telegram arriving for them and returned to the train in various states of dudgeon.

The major was used to waiting (and waiting, and waiting for something to happen, for that is the lot of a soldier), and as long as he was ready when the call came, he was content. To this end, he had bought a set of silver teaspoons from one of the farmers he had met at the general store and, after the professor had assayed the metal as being of sufficient purity, had with a cold efficiency that would have saddened the heart of the farmer who had sold him the heirloom proceeded to cut the spoons into small pieces. These he melted in the small furnace in Becky's workshop and then poured into bullet moulds. He could not produce rounds of sufficient precision to be used in the semi-automatic weapons, nor did he have enough metal to make many, but at least it represented a full load for each of their revolvers, Alisha having found a snub-nosed .32 lying forgotten in a drawer of the Circus's office and thus liberated it for the good of mankind.

Of Horst, there is little enough to say at this juncture, except for one small oddity. Since his original death and re-birth as the result of a contretemps with a vampire (in which he prevailed) and his subsequent contamination with the curse by dint of eating bits of it,* Horst had lost the ability to dream. His sleep was as abrupt and featureless as general anaesthetic: a blink with a duration of hours. He had missed it at first, but as his year with the Cabal Bros. Carnival had wound on, his memories of dreaming had faded as phantasmagorically as do the memories of dreams. Now, very unexpectedly, they were back, and yet he could never quite remember them. All he could recall on waking was a faint sense of watching trouble unfold for someone else. He felt a grudging sympathy for the hapless protagonist of the dreams, not least because he was

---

* By necessity rather than any culinary desire. The story by which this occurred is too involved for a footnote such as this, but the uninformed reader is directed to the first novel dealing with the life and times of Johannes Cabal the necromancer. Indeed, if the reader finds themselves here *without* having read the previous tales, they are brave indeed, and should brace themselves for further incomprehension.

aware that he was not the only observer and this unseen other watcher's emotions were unreadable beyond a stark malevolence that flowed and ticked with machinations and methodicalities like a clockwork anthill.

This was almost the limit of his recollection, but for a new tendency to awaken with a blurted exclamation. On the dusk of their day of arrival, it had been 'Cats!' On the evening after the first show it was 'Crabs!' He had no clear idea why he said these things, only that there was a fading impression of lazy malignancy with the first awakening, and of a vicious stupidity with the second. It was a mystery, and not one that he felt comfortable discussing with anyone else.

On the evening after the second display, he awoke with the words 'You little *bastard!*' on his lips, and this time he felt something familiar about the venom with which they were spoken, as if somebody was expressing their animosity through him, somebody he knew. His first thought was his brother, but he failed to see how Johannes could or would do such a thing. Cat, crabs, and little bastards were an unlikely triumvirate for casual conversation or urgent messages. Why would his brother go to all the trouble of creating some sort of psychic link if only to communicate such disparate trivialities? It was ridiculous, but he appreciated that did not make it impossible.

The day of the Great Flying Circus Aeroshow arrived. 'Great' is a very relative term, but it would certainly be the first time any kind of real aeroshow had been held in the area, unless one counted that time five years ago when a trainee pilot flew into the windmill. That had been a very short sort of show, and memorable for only the worst of reasons. Thus, based on available metrics, Miss Virginia Montgomery's Flying Circus was set to put on the greatest aeroshow the area had ever seen.

It was a beautiful day for a disaster. The skies had remained cool blue throughout the circus's stay and today was no exception. A breeze strong enough to be refreshing without being strong enough to trouble the entomopters had appeared at dawn blowing in from the east, bringing with it high scudding clouds formed over a distant sea. It was a market day, so the breeze started blowing in farmers and their families almost as soon as the sun was up, and they had spent the morning discussing prices and selling between themselves and the traders who had hired freight cars in the trains that now occupied two of the remaining sidings next to the circus train. There was some grumbling that it had the siding by the access road, meaning some creative use of boards and cargo pallets was necessary to get goods to and from the newcomers, but the promise of an unusually large gathering for the show ameliorated such complaints. The possibility of extra custom is always a balm to the heart of even the most curmudgeonly of traders.

The show was set for two o'clock, the idea being that this would give people a chance to eat and, ideally, drink in the odd, thrown-together building that passed for a tavern in what passed for a town. A slightly drunk spectator was likely to be a slightly more generous one, and slightly drunk male spectators are more likely still to be generous when the collection boxes are wielded by presentable young women in close-fitting flight suits. This was part of the wisdom of Miss Virginia Montgomery's Flying Circus, and it had always proved true.

While Horst slumbered in a deathlike sleep that was less dreamless than he was used to, the three Dee Society members kept themselves out of the way of the aeroshow's preparation. A response had finally arrived to the major's report, a lengthy telegram that must have set the Society back a few pounds to transmit. The tavern no longer being the nest of quiet corners it had previously been for them, the three retired to the compartment aboard the train that doubled as a common room and waited impatiently as Major Haskins slowly teased the meaning from the enciphered phrases with frequent reference to the code book he carried, a small leather-bound volume printed on very flammable, very edible rice paper.

After some time during which the professor closed his eyes and waited in silent meditation while Alisha looked out of the window and fought down the urge to sigh, grunt, and possibly scream with frustration, the major laid down his pencil and took up the finished message in clear text.

'Good news first,' he said. 'Almost all of our people in the town escaped. We lost two who were acting as sniper and spotter from a rooftop close by the front of the square. I would think it's possible they simply missed the withdrawal signal, and may still be alive. Anyway, that's the state of affairs there.'

'Is that all the good news?' asked the professor, his eyes still closed.

'No. The Society has taken its findings and placed them before our sister organisations. There is to be a general mobilisation.'

'You call that good news? We can handle this,' said Alisha. 'We don't need anyone else coming in and . . .'

'Yes, we do, Alisha,' chided the professor quietly. 'We rather shot our bolt at the attack on the castle, and they sent us packing. This is more than the Society can deal with.'

'We're putting ourselves in the debt of a bunch of lunatics.'

'Hardly,' said the major. 'There are no debts being called in here, no favours asked. The threat the *Ministerium Tenebrae* represents is too great for point scoring. "An unassociated organisation", it says here, is joining the effort.'

The professor's eyes blinked open. 'The Templars?'

'I would guess so. It's the usual formula for them.'

Alisha's mood was not improving. 'But we've *fought* the Templars. How can we work with them?'

'"My enemy's enemy", Alisha,' replied the major. 'Approaching apocalypses make for strange bedfellows. We may have had our disagreements in the past, but they're a very moral bunch and very committed to their principles. One of those principles is the hunting and killing of monsters, although they have a rather more biblical way of saying it.'

'Quite,' agreed the professor. 'Given the choice of continuing the silly feud between us or joining us to prevent the creation of a teratarchy, they will and, by the sound of it, *have* opted for the latter.'

'What's a teratarchy?' asked Major Haskins.

'Government by monsters,' said the professor complacently. 'A neologism, freshly minted. I think the Greek works.'

'We've been given a rendezvous point,' said the major, reading further down the decoded message. 'We're to make best time there and join the rest of our people from the initial attack.'

'What,' said Alisha slowly, 'what if this attack fails, too?'

'Then it's out of our hands altogether. Sympathetic contacts within local states have been briefed and, I hope and pray, are already mobilising. If we can't nip the *Ministerium*'s grand scheme in the bud, it will turn into a war. Our strength is we respond a great deal faster than any army can hope to. The business with those flying monstrosities the other night proves they have their "Lord of Powers" already. They miscalculated with our Mr Cabal, but he was only ever intended to provide small numbers of specialised troops anyway. Between the shapechangers, the mindless undead, and whatever party tricks the new recruit brings with him- or herself, no neighbouring country is safe. Even with their armies standing ready, they have never trained to deal with this manner of threat.'

It was a view he'd aired before, but previously without the possibility of them re-entering the fray. Then it had been about hopes that the conventional would be ready and capable of defeating the unconventional, with an underlying fear that it would not. Now they were in the unenviable position of being the first line of defence, civilians who would face death in an unusually literal sense so that soldiers might be spared the horrors of this new war. It was ironic, certainly, but not in any pleasurable way.

There was no point in staying with Miss Virginia and her crew; they would be travelling in the wrong direction for the needs of the three Dee Society agents. One of the market trains, however, would take them back to the city from which they had so recently fled, and so they made arrangements to bed down amid fruit barrels in one of its freight cars.

In the meantime, however, they would sample whatever delights market day had to offer, and enjoy the show.

*   *   *

At ten minutes past two—the carefully calculated tardiness being both to allow some anticipation to rise and also to give the slow crowd from the tavern time to show up—the aeroshow began. Unlike the *in medias res* openings of the previous two, this began with a single entomopter sitting in the middle of the field, Miss Virginia's very own *Spirit of '76*. It had been the object of intense observation for the forty minutes the crowd had been building, it being the closest almost all had ever been to such a machine. They admired its striking paintwork, commented upon the four thin wings, and speculated on the function of assorted struts, intakes, and flanges.

The many conversations gave way to applause as Miss Virginia Montgomery walked onto the field and, with practised insouciance, stood by the nose of her aircraft. Here the mechanic, Becky Whitten, arrayed in her cleanest, least-frayed overalls, awaited her with an electric megaphone. Virginia took it with a polite nod, and addressed the crowd in good German, made exotic to the listeners by a discernible American accent beneath it that hinted at the moon in June and mint juleps. She thanked them for their presence, she thanked them for their patience, she told them a little of her circus's history, and she promised them a show they would never forget.

In the light of subsequent events, it was an unfortunate promise; not because it was unfulfilled, but because it was fulfilled all too well.

At the conclusion of the little speech, timed to a nicety based on past experiences of slightly inebriated farmers, Miss Virginia returned the megaphone to Becky, exchanging it for a British Army surplus Very pistol. This she made a show of loading with a flare cartridge before raising it high and firing the white star shell into the heavens. Even as the parachute flare was still rising, she'd handed the pistol back and was climbing into the cockpit of the big American two-seater. The canopy slammed shut and Miss Virginia fired the engine before even strapping herself in, the preflight checks having been completed by Becky just before Miss

Virginia made her grand entrance. Strictly, this was against protocol; the pilot should make their own pre-flight checks as it's their life on the line and ultimately their responsibility. That, however, would have undermined the drama of the moment, and in the open spaces travelled by a wandering circus, protocols are sometimes revised. Besides, Miss Virginia and the rest of the Flying Circus routinely put their lives in Becky's hands, and she had proved time and again that their faith was well founded.

As the engine, still warm from a short readying session earlier, wound up, the entomopter's four insectile wings started to sweep in their complex figure-of-eight patterns, slowly as the clutch was only in its initiator setting. Miss Virginia finished strapping herself in, pulled the cinches until they were just the right side of comfortable, and gave Becky a thumbs-up signal. Becky quickly returned the signal before raising the reloaded pistol and firing a second flare. This one exploded into a flickering green light in the clear sky, floating away on its parachute borne by a light breeze. The sense of growing immediacy conveyed to the crowd by these actions was no mere stagecraft; two miles away in either direction, entomopters waited in distant fields. On sighting the first flare, they fired their engines and stood by to lift. On the second, they rose vertically, their wings whirling. Up to a height of fifty feet they climbed, nosed down to allow the wings to provide more forward motion, and accelerated hard towards the showground. As their airspeed increased, they started to develop transitional lift, allowing them to bring the nose down still further, turning more and more of the wings' blur into a headlong hurtle.

In their wakes, grass bowed and boughs shook violently. On and on they came, Mink and Daisy from the northwest, Dea Boom from the southeast, flying hard and sharp, the nap of the earth flashing below them reflected in the gleaming gloss finishes of their fuselages, smooth now the landing gears had all been retracted within seconds of launch. Ahead of them they could see the showground growing so large, so quickly, the green flare still falling off to the west beyond the crowd's left flank. There would be no place for any 'seat of the pants' flying here; their lives depended on everyone staying exactly to the plan. No extemporisation and no showboating while a sister pilot was in the same arena.

Every entomopter had its reflector sight up and active, all the better to focus the pilot on their craft's heading. The sights—angled panes of glass onto which a targeting reticle was projected via the offices of an optical collimator, beam splitter, and a little engineering ingenuity, thereby allowing a true sighting without parallax problems—were artefacts of the CI-650's operational past but, being slightly superseded by the CI-880's model, they had not been stripped out when the entomopters were decommissioned. It almost felt like a kindness for the old warhorses.

Now, where once bandit entomopters would have filled the sights' graticulated fields, now they centred on an ally, in this case Miss Virginia, that they might better avoid her at the last moment.

Avoid her they did, to screams of shock and horror from the crowd who only saw the closing aircraft at the last moment and barely had time to fear a four-way collision before the moment had passed and the fright was washed away by relief and laughter and applause.

The three members of the Dee Society had some of the best seats in the house, having climbed onto the roof of the train's sleeper carriage to watch. The rhythmic tightening of fearful anticipation followed by the release of the tension as stunt after stunt was performed with the almost supernatural panache of the highly practised professional also served to take some of the Society members' own tensions, and they found themselves able to forget the *Ministerium Tenebrae* for a little while at least.

'Just as well they started when they did,' noted the major. 'The weather's closing in. Probably start raining in an hour or two.'

'Is it?' said Professor Stone. He looked into the slight breeze, but all he could see were a few high clouds. 'Looks clear to me.'

'You're looking the wrong way, professor,' laughed the major. 'Over there.' And he pointed to the west.

The professor looked, and then climbed to his feet. 'How extraordinary,' he said under his breath.

There did seem to be a storm coming after all. An angry thunderhead, so dense it appeared almost black, was rolling in from the west. It was vast, yet still seemed dwarfed by the even greater extent of clear sky around it. As they watched, a curious effect could be discerned around its edges; a violet miasma seemed to follow the cloud yet not necessarily be part of it, as if there was an afterimage around it, or the cloud was overlaid upon a slightly larger coloured version of itself.

'That,' said Professor Stone with certainty, 'is not natural.'

'Good Lord,' said Major Haskins as he and Alisha joined the professor on their feet, 'it's moving against the wind. Look at the other clouds.' He was right; the other strands of cumulus, too reedy to suggest rain, were at a similar altitude to the storm head, yet they were running dead against its direction of travel. Indeed, the storm head seemed to be bringing its own winds with it; they watched as one of the pale natural clouds ran close by the dark mass and was progressively torn into nothing by violent yet thoroughly localised turbulence.

Over the showground, Dea and Mink were engaged in a mock dogfight while their two comrades flew in a wide circle around the conflict. Dea had just performed a textbook rolling-scissors manoeuvre to come in on Mink's tail while Becky bellowed out a commentary through the megaphone for the benefit of anyone who wasn't just staring, eyes wide and jaw loose, at the display. Dea was intended to trigger a pyrotechnic roughly equivalent to a string of very large firecrackers in a trick box attached to her fuselage at this point to suggest the rattle of mini-cannon, to which Mink would respond by firing a smoke cartridge clipped to the tail boom to represent damage, after which she would limp pathetically from the field *hors de combat* before setting up her approach for the next set piece.

Instead, Dea Boom performed a split-S manoeuvre to disengage. Unable to hear if the firecrackers had gone off or not over the roar of her engine, Mink triggered her smoke cartridge anyway, and performed her aerial version of 'The Dying Swan' despite her attacker having passed up the chance to fire. Instead, Dea headed west. Becky paused her narration of the life-and-death struggle in mid-sentence. Dropping the megaphone, she took up the Very pistol at her feet, shoved in a new flare, and fired it into the sky. This one was red, indicating the display had gone awry and all pilots were to scramble for clear air before regrouping. As the other aircraft separated and staged north of the showground, Becky took up the megaphone and said, with not a sign that this was all anything but planned, 'And there we see Miss Dea Boom in *Buzzbomb* perform a perfect split-S disengagement, allowing Miss Mink to escape with her dignity intact.' She added in an electrically boosted *sotto voce*, 'Although perhaps not her tail plane.' She pointed at the smoke trail, and the crowd laughed, even while they tried to figure out the joke.

In the air, Miss Virginia was furious. The show had gone beautifully so far, and to have one of the real crowd-pleasers fall apart like that was madly frustrating. She did not, however, hold Dea Boom responsible, at least not without proof of wrongdoing. Her first thought was a mechanical failure, and Dea had broken off from the staged combat for safety's sake. That still didn't explain what was so fascinating about the western horizon, though. In any case, they couldn't progress without *Buzzbomb* rejoining the formation, so Miss Virginia testily signalled to Daisy to form up into a staggered V and to pass the message. It was hardly necessary; they had flown so long together that they could almost foretell one another's thoughts. As soon as the *Queen of the Desert* was in position on the *Spirit of '76*'s starboard aft quarter, *Striking Dragon* was taking position in the port aft, still trailing the last of the smoke from its canister.

Dea Boom was behaving oddly, simply flying back and forth, northeast to southwest and back again as they approached. Perhaps a mile beyond, the landscape grew dark under the shadow of the thunderhead. They had all noticed it in the air, but had all discounted it as being too far to be a problem during the display. It seemed to have come on towards the town with strange rapidity, they now realised.

Miss Virginia signalled to her wingwomen to fall back as she flew on alone to parallel Dea. At a range of perhaps ten feet between their respective wingtips, a short conversation in mime took place.

Miss Virginia pulled an exaggeratedly mystified face and mouthed, *What?*

Dea pointed down and replied, *Look!*

Miss Virginia opened some space, dropped back, and lost a little height before winging over enough to see the ground. All she could see were fields, probably with cabbages in the majority. She'd seen a lot of those over the previous two days. Cabbage fields with scarecrows and nothing else.

She was just realising that she didn't remember seeing any scarecrows at all on her crop-spraying jobs—and did they really need this many?—when she saw one stumble on the rough open ground and fall. It got back to its feet slowly, watched her circling entomopter with a slow, almost mechanical turn of the head, then continued walking towards the town, the showground, and the train.

Zombies. Hundreds of them, arranged in a ragged line a mile wide.

'Oh, God,' said Miss Virginia Montgomery. 'My dear God.'

The shadow of the cloud swept across her then, across all the entomopters, but it was less an occlusion of light and more a spreading of dark. Where it fell, the air itself held a tint of a horrible thin shade of violet that has no place in any world upon which one might want to bring up children. It was alien and unwholesome, smelling of dread and tasting of madness. It bloomed across the town, the showground, and the train.

At 14:35, with the sun up and storming down rays of purifying light that pitter-pattered hopelessly upon the darkness, the vampire Horst Cabal awoke. He awoke in fear and mourning for a death too close, and with tears filling his eyes. He awoke with the name of his brother, Johannes, on his lips.

Chapter 11

It was daytime. It was impossible. Dark, overcast in some way he couldn't quite understand, but it was daytime. Horst threw open the door and leaned heavily on the jamb as he tried to take in what was happening in the confused world outside.

The first thing that didn't happen was that he didn't burst into flames. Sunlight was falling on him, but its purifying power to remove spiritual aberrations like him from the world in a fount of dust and agony was gone but for a slight, unpleasant prickling. It was as if the sun's ferocity had been somehow drained away, and this was all it could do to discomfort him, like receiving impolite personal comments in the post from a great white shark. He could almost feel the frustration in it.

The sun was up, but it looked the wrong colour; not how he remembered it at all. But *everything* looked wrong. The grass and trees looked diseased, the people at the showground were washing around making a dull roar, the sky seemed strange and alien, dominated by a great cloud that, he noted with the disinterest of the otherwise distressed, was moving against the wind.

Somebody said 'Horst?' and for a moment he thought the voice was in his own head, a filament of the confusion that swirled there, but then he heard it again, and looked up. Alisha was standing directly over him, looking down from the carriage roof, astonishment written in her expression.

'How are you awake?' she demanded. 'It's only mid-afternoon!'

He tried to speak, but there were too many things going on inside his head, an inability to talk to somebody whose head appeared upside-down from his current position being too much to process in his disrupted intellect at that moment. He jumped down, took a couple of steps, and turned. Yes, that was much better. Now she was the right way up and had a body, standing on the train carriage roof, and so helped him anchor down his sanity a little in the high wind that was blowing through his mind.

'I don't know. Something's wrong.' The prickling of the ineffectual sun made his shoulders twitch at the formication. 'Everything's wrong. What's happening? What's happening to me? Johannes . . . he's going to die.' He swung drunkenly about to face the showground, thoughts boiling in cascades of irrelevance in his head. He could see one of the entomopters was landing—the *Spirit of '76*, he could identify it by its silhouette—while the others milled in a stack. He couldn't see what was happening through the mass of the crowd for the next few seconds, but his grasp on time was reduced to events rather than progressions, and he knew only that it took as long for the next thing to happen as it took him to crouch on the gravel, close his eyes, and try to squeeze the pandemonium from his thoughts.

Then he heard Miss Virginia Montgomery's electrically amplified voice crackle out over the lowing of the crowd, and he raised his head to listen, but kept his eyes shut. This refracted version of reality, he had discovered, was less upsetting when one didn't have to look at it.

'Ladies and gentlemen,' came her voice, distant and echoed, 'please disperse from this area as quickly as you safely can. Do *not* go to the west. I'm sorry . . .' The crowd were suddenly if understandably restive. 'I'm sorry, there is no time for explanations, but the town is in danger and must be abandoned immediately.'

Still nothing happened; the crowd did not disperse, nor panic, nor do anything of import but mutter, and wonder aloud amongst itself whether this was all part of the show. The lack of action was obviously clear to Miss Virginia, too, judging by her uncompromising tone when the megaphone clicked back into life.

'Zombies. Okay? Zombies. There are several hundred zombies closing on the town from the west. You think that cloud overhead is natural? You think a little travelling aeroshow like ours can do a thing like that? Get your asses out of town and just make sure you're heading east, northeast, or southeast. Just so long as it's got *east* in it, you should be okay. They're not fast, but they're not nice, and they will be here in maybe quarter of an hour. So . . . move!'

Becky came running up, heading for the locomotive. When she saw Horst, she stopped and gawped at him. 'You're out! In the day . . . I thought . . . Somebody said you were . . .'

'He is,' Alisha called down to her. 'We've seen something like that cloud before. This one's fifty times the size, though. Do you need help getting the engine going?'

'The firebox is lit,' said Becky. 'We were planning on leaving as soon as the show was over. It'll take a while to get us moving, though.'

'How long to load up the entomopters?'

Becky shook her head. 'They're flying on. We'll meet up with them up the line. Yes, I could use your help.' Without waiting for a reply, she carried on running for the locomotive, Alisha heading there, too, along the carriage tops.

'Mr Cabal,' said the major as he stepped off the roof access ladder and dropped onto the tracks. 'We may need to defend the train, both against these creatures when they get here and, before that, from people wishing to leave the town.'

Horst forced his thoughts into some sort of order and rose painfully to his feet, the weight of the light bearing down upon him. 'We can take a good few,' he said, feeling and sounding sick and weary. 'Room on the freight cars. If we can, we should.'

The major looked off at the crowd, who finally seemed to have been motivated by the possibility of being chewed upon by the recently dead. Unhappily, Miss Virginia's motivational technique had also generated a degree of panic. However, her bellowed commands to 'Walk! Just walk! They're zombies, for crying out loud! If you start walking now, you'll outpace them. You do *not* need to run!' seemed to take the wind out of any putative hysteria.

Haskins nodded. 'You're right, of course, old chap. We should take everyone we can. The whole point of the Dee Society is to protect the commonplace world against supernatural threats. Just not very used to doing it quite so publicly.'

He and the professor set off to winnow out those from the crowd, now belatedly heading eastwards in a great confused flock, who could not make good time. There was no panic, just a lot of confused people who were given to understand that going that way was preferable to going the other way. They had heard the words 'several', 'hundred', and 'zombies', all of which were individually comprehensible. Even country folk had heard about zombies. They might call them by other, local names, but when the newspapers spoke of a necromancer being strung up somewhere or another for crimes against humanity, God, and nature, the usual generally acknowledged term for the frightful monstrosities that the criminal had raised from the slumber of cold clay was 'zombie'. They tended to be individual, however. An undead servitor shuffling around an isolated house, or a mute killer created for the express purpose of revenge, or—in one infamous case—a children's entertainer. The idea that anyone would have the resources and the will to raise not one or two, or a dozen, or a hundred, but hundreds of zombies was beyond the ken of the common mind. Thus, they were unable to entirely digest the threat at anything beyond a superficial level. The situation was dreamlike, the response *faux* somnambulistic. As the walking dead shambled in from the west, so the walking living shambled out to the east.

Horst pushed his way through the crowd to reach the showground as quickly as he dared, the discomfort of the daylight threatening to distract him from the limits of human resilience; it would be far too easy to inadvertently elbow somebody's sternum through to their spine in a moment of absent-mindedness. By the time he reached the ground's railing, he was more worried about doing it advertently. They *were* a flock, he saw now. Stupid sheep on two legs with vacant expressions, stinking of sweat and beer, and the only good thing about them beating in their arteries. Three days he had gone without blood. Three long days, and here he was surrounded by ambulatory bags of the stuff. He clenched his jaws and tried not to listen to the voice that was quietly but insistently pointing out that what with all this chaos and a wave of undead killers closing in, a sheep or two could go missing from this flock and none would put the blame anywhere but with the zombies.

It was tempting. It was sorely tempting.

He leapt the rail easily and ran for Miss Virginia. She was just climbing back into the cockpit as he reached her, burning a little more of his strength away to blur through the distance. When he appeared by the entomopter, she started with surprise. 'Dear God, boy, but you can move,' she snapped to cover her startlement as much as to air the obvious.

'How far away are they?'

'Less than a mile now.' She frowned. 'Ain't you supposed to burst into flames or something?'

He looked up at the cloud. 'I did last time I was caught out in the sun,' he agreed. 'That thing, however, is changing the rules.'

'In a good way?'

'I think waking me up is just a side effect. Last time we saw a cloud like that, flying, acid-dripping limb-things came out and tried to kill us.'

Miss Virginia glanced apprehensively at the cloud; she remembered the encounter with the creatures that attacked the train a few nights previously all too well. The thought of being under a swarm of things that dripped acid was unappealing. 'I have to get airborne,' she said abruptly, and finished climbing into the cockpit.

As she strapped herself in, she said, 'You'd better get going, too. Once Becky gets a head of steam up, she won't be hanging around.'

Horst didn't answer; he was watching a tatterdemalion of a figure walking across a field not even a quarter of a mile away. The vanguard of the dead was almost upon them. 'I'm going to try and give her the time she needs,' he said, and then he was gone.

As he sped, conserving his strength so that he merely travelled at an impressive sprint rather than an impossible blur, he was already asking himself questions about what was about to happen. Was he right in thinking that zombies would provide less of a challenge than werebadgers and acid-dripping weird things? He certainly hoped so, as there were an awful lot of them coming. Was the cloud there as some sort of enabling mechanism for the approaching horde, or was it going to be spitting out further examples of otherworldly fauna before long? From his perspective, the former was certainly the more preferable, but he didn't really believe it for a moment. And finally, were the zombies so far gone that he couldn't drink from them? Whether the answer to that one was *yes* or *no*, he couldn't tell yet, but he was sure that whatever the answer, he wouldn't like it.

He leapt at the fence at the end of the showground closest to the town while still some twenty feet distant, landed on the uppermost bar with both feet, and powered himself into a broad jump with enough impetus that the wood was breaking as he left it. He sailed in a graceful arc that ended less gracefully in the lead zombie's chest. They went down in a shower of fetid viscera that assured Horst that zombies would not make good blood donors, and that he was going to have to find yet another change of clothing shortly.

He stood for a moment, up to his shins in complaining revenant, and wondered how he should proceed. He could see the untidy picket line of zombies now only a couple of hundred yards away, their wide spacing narrowing as they converged to close on the showground and the town, and confined by the strictures of the terrain. At the moment they were too far apart to offer immediate aid to one another if one were attacked . . . no, that was saying too much for their motivations. They would not come to one another's aid, but they would move to attack anybody they saw, and if that somebody happened to be fighting another zombie at the time, the effect would be much the same. While he might be able to take on one, two, or several simultaneously, he didn't fancy his chances if he ended up layered in them.

Speed, then, was of the essence, but speed cost him blood, and his reserves were low. He looked at the retreating crowd, now draining down the highways and byways to the east of the town like the dregs of a popular uprising after the militia show up. There were stragglers, he saw. Nobody would notice the loss of one. Then he saw that the stragglers were in fact being shepherded and directed to the Flying Circus's train, and he felt ashamed. Alisha, Major Haskins, and Professor Stone were helping those who could not escape quickly enough by reason of age or handicap, usually attended by desperate family, while Horst had been wondering who would make a suitable meal. He saw Haskins lift an old woman and run as fast as he could to take her to the relative safety of the train while the zombies grew ever closer. There was steam rising from the locomotive already; Becky had managed to build pressure quickly, and the locomotive probably had enough to get under way. Yet it waited while the Dee Society agents did their work. It was selfless and heroic, and Horst felt more angry with himself than he had ever felt before.

Out, he said to the wheedling voice within. The voice of predation and depravity whose tone he had at first had trouble telling from his own. Now he could taste the inhumanness of it on his tongue, and it made him want to spit with revulsion. *Out. I am done with you. You are what the* Ministerium Tenebrae *believed me to be. You are what I am not. Out. Be quiet. I am done with you.*

And, as if to underline the intensity of his feelings and the sincerity of his intent, he blurred out of vision, reappeared beside a zombie some hundred yards away, and punched its jaw into the next field. Presently, the rest of the skull followed.

Alisha paused in her efforts to get as many as possible aboard the train. She had feared Becky working alone wouldn't be able to get the train ready quickly enough, but the crew of one of the other trains in the sidings were helping in return for passage away from the oncoming army. Alisha was just wondering if it was time to break out the heavy guns to deal with the first wave of attack when she saw zombies starting to explode without the aid of explosives. For a moment she thought that the gases of putrefaction were overwhelming them in some sort of chain reaction whose mechanism evaded her yet gave the satisfying sight of zombies blowing apart as if it were an open day in a piñata test facility.

Then she saw Horst, besmirched in gore, magically appear beside a couple of the attackers and divest one of its head and a quantity of spinal cord, which he then used to belabour its partner into a ruin of pulped flesh and pulverised bone in a few furious blows. Assured neither were likely to be getting up again, he flickered from sight once more.

'I'm very glad he's on our side,' said the professor, pausing by her side. 'You did a good job persuading him to come over to the side of virtue.'

'Persuade him?' She laughed. 'I shot him a couple of times, and he forgave me. He never needed any persuasion. Ouch.' This last as she observed a zombie thrown into the trunk of a proud old elm hard enough to leave an imprint in the bark.

Horst stopped to rest, leaning against a toolshed at the side of a wheat field. It wasn't much of a rest; he didn't need a pause nearly so much as he needed to drink. He couldn't understand why the *Ministerium* hadn't sent any of their shapechangers. Their blood was entirely acceptable, and their ethics so abominable that he only experienced the smallest regret when feeding on them. Perhaps that was why they hadn't sent any; to deny him of sustenance. So Lady Misericorde had dispatched her army (and he was aware of the awful possibility that this was not the entirety of it), and it seemed they had their precious 'Lord of Powers' with his unusual cloud formations.* This one hadn't performed its party trick yet, whatever that happened to be, assuming that it was ever intended to do anything but fly against the wind and glower. He considered the possibility that it was simply a way of corralling the zombies around; where the cloud went, they followed. That would certainly make sense given the available evidence. Perhaps, he hoped, that was the limit of the cloud's threat.

He was just about to re-embark on his zombie-splashing exploits when something fell from the cloud. It thudded to Earth some fifty feet from him at the edge of the wheat, throwing soil in a halo around it.

Horst wasn't sure what it was meant to be. At first glance, it was as if a lover of classical art had struck a blow by pushing a modern sculpture over the railing from a passing aeroship. It stood comfortably over two yards high on three supports, and seemed to be made of metal, and as a result was really quite heavy. He looked at the sculpture, all organic curves and enigmatic holes where it stood at the edge of the field, an impromptu installation by a guerrilla sculptor. Apparently the *Ministerium Tenebrae* had decided to conquer the region using the unusual twin-pronged attack of zombies and avant-garde artwork. Then the piece of sculpture lifted itself up on its three supports and shook itself in a remarkably

---

* '*Cumulonemesis*,' said Johannes Cabal. 'It's called *cumulonemesis*. There are a surprising number of supernatural weather conditions.' This was no more than the truth, he himself having personally encountered the Bone Wind as well as an ill-starred meeting with the monstrous genius who created the flesh-dissolving, soul-devouring Red Snow.

doglike action, scattering off the clods of damp earth thrown up on impact that had stuck to its skin. Horst realised with both wonder and horror that the sculpture was nothing of the sort. It was a machine, yet it was living. Some sort of evolved device from some alternate plane or strange dimension where people had been altogether too indulgent of their toasters, and the consumer durables had inherited their Earth.

As if it knew it was being watched, the machine stumped around on—he could no longer think of them as supports—its three legs and regarded him somehow, for there were no obvious eyes. There was an intelligence in that regard that Horst did not care for, and he was aware of a great hatred, as if he had just said something derogatory about Henry Moore while standing by one of his works, and it had taken umbrage. For his part, Horst did not like the look of the thing, either. Not so much on an aesthetic level (he was actually quite fond of the modern art), but with respect to the resilience necessary to survive a drop from a couple of hundred feet, the hardness of skin to disregard the impact, the mass to make three small craters where the supports—the *legs*—had come down, and the likelihood that, should the creature (for creature it surely was, of some sort) have anything analogous to veins and arteries beneath that skin, it would likely be at best machine oil, and at worst mercury. Neither represented a decent meal for Horst, should he manage to vanquish it.

The thing moved a little closer with the careful step of a bird-eating spider. Horst slid down the side of the shed away from it, never taking his eyes from it as he moved. The thing took another step, a step that was cautious only in the way a predator not wishing to alarm its prey is. Horst backed away still further; it was like being stalked by an obelisk and he did not care for the sensation at all.

A part of him—not the cynical, monstrous part; that seemed to have gone, or perhaps was only waiting for an opportunity to return when his defences were down, or alternatively was off in a corner of his psyche somewhere, sulking after being harshly spoken to—wondered just how a man like him ends up in a situation like this. He had always imagined himself becoming something that doesn't involve too much work, like a poet or a speculator, being endlessly fascinating to an endless stream of delightful girls. Eventually, he would have become a 'silver fox' sort of gentleman *roué*, and so ended his days chasing nurses. It wasn't the most evolved or ambitious of careers, but it had the undoubted advantage of a great deal of female company. Yet here he was, a vampire, a long way from home, being menaced in a field by statuary. How could such a thing come to pass? How could he have missed his mark in life so very, very thoroughly?

Then he remembered his brother, and all became immediately clear. He didn't think of his brother's miraculous ability to turn everything on its head with rancour; that would be like railing against the wind for blowing or water for being so very wet. He simply accepted it with an inner nod, and a philosophical 'Oh. *That's* why.'

He also realised what he had known at some psychic level for the past few days of restless sleep; that somehow his brother was still alive, although possibly in some hue of peril. This surprised him only rationally; emotionally he had found it easy to accept. Johannes should have been suffering eternal torment in Hell by this point (even if he had dodged the particular damnation Horst had anticipated at the close of the Cabal Bros. Carnival, according to Lady Misericorde), yet it seemed he wasn't if Horst's curious deathly dreams were to be believed. And he did believe them; there were some things he'd come to accept about being a creature from a nightmare, and one of them was that when he experienced odd things like this, he should pay them credence. He still had humanly hunches, just as he ever had, but he knew those might lead him astray, just as they ever had. These more supernatural senses, however, he had come to trust.

All very interesting, he told himself, and something to ponder on sometime after he had managed to escape the attentions of a large metallic thing, which might be alive in some sense. A couple of hundred yards away, something else large, dense, and distinctly not of the Earth fell in the middle of the wheat field with a re-sounding *thud* that Horst felt through his feet before the sound reached him. Further local seismic activity told him that shortly he would be surrounded by enough of the things to fill a notably dangerous gallery of very challenging artwork.

The statue-thing, perhaps startled into activity by the arrival of its colleagues, leapt at Horst, a manoeuvre that in terms of being unexpected was on par with being pounced upon by a smallish stately home. A human would probably have ended as puree beneath the massive form, but Horst was not as human as he used to be, and while the thing's legs shoved several inches into the ground as the impetus grew to launch it, he was already reacting. By the time it landed, it was to find that Horst was no longer there. One of its legs tore a long splintered scar through the wall of the shed and, as being slightly in the way was apparently regarded as an unforgivable crime in whichever dimension the creature had been summoned from, it spent the next half a minute smashing the rest of the shed into matchwood using a strange dance of destruction that positively reeked of petulance.

Horst, meanwhile, was making himself a scarce resource in that part of the field. He ran slower than was his wont, because he didn't wish his last memories to be of cutting a new furrow with his mouth after a high-speed fall, immediately followed by something that looked like it had been spawned by Stonehenge jumping on his back. It was one thing to be humiliated, another to die horribly, but he was damned if he'd do both simultaneously.

He tore to a halt in a shower of earth and wheat ears somewhere in the middle of the field. Before him lay something like a solid wheel, but as if taken from a huge toy automobile. It was black, sleek, and shiny, fat and rounded, a regular transverse ridge pattern making him think of a tyre's tread. It was also large; wider than a man was tall, and chest high to him. His first thought was that perhaps it was an abandoned wheel from some farm vehicle of the sort that he'd heard of before he became a vampire. That was years ago, now; perhaps they were common these days, and much bigger than he'd anticipated. That these poor farmers were able to afford such a machine seemed unlikely, however, which troubled him, as did the shininess of it, betokening newness. When the tyre started to uncurl itself, he realised that the 'tread' was actually the ridges between body segments, and that he was watching an unreasonably large woodlouse in action. It found the soil with its multitude of legs, arranged itself for movement, and swung its front end around to face Horst as if scenting him. Its face was far less insectlike than he was expecting; two very mammalian eyes mounted in a skull-like head but for the complex mouthparts that juddered spastically vertically, horizontally, and on the diagonals regarded him with an expression of concentrated malevolence. That didn't mean it actually *was* malevolent, he reminded himself. It wasn't the creature's fault that it looked like that, after all. Perhaps it was actually just being friendly. Then he noticed it was starting to drool, and—with the best will in the world—decided that he was being optimistic.

The giant woodlouse reared up on a multitude of legs, waving another multitude in the air and champing its mouthparts together like a topographically challenged horse. By the time it struck, Horst was already moving out of the way. Not nearly as quickly as he would have liked, however; his reserves were finally dry.

His attempt to run away and not stop until he had passed through at least three international borders finished less than ten feet away with him wallowing weakly in a furrow. The great woodlouse reared again, spitting soil from its mouth with far less concern and far greater ability than Horst could manage, re-acquired him as a target, and prepared to strike again. Horst floundered his way behind a row of wheat, in the desperate hope that the stalks might interfere with its vision. It was a thin sort of hope, but he was suddenly so enervated, he wasn't even sure he could stand unaided. The weakness was terrifying in itself, but the timing of it didn't help affairs. He remembered suffering from flu back when such things bothered him, and being left so weak that he had to crawl across the room. This was worse. There was none of the sense of his muscles trying to do the job they usually did so easily yet failing. Instead, there was nothing to call upon at all. His arms felt boneless, afterthoughts stapled on at the shoulders by a slipshod creator. His legs flopped behind him, scrabbling slowly across the soil.

The great louse was looking dead at him, those narrow, moist eyes clear and focussed upon him, unperturbed by the intervening line of wheat. This, Horst concluded, was going to be a stupid and inglorious death. Hardly an uncommon state of affairs to humanity, but one he'd been hoping to avoid. If he had to go, something more noble than this. He'd done a decent job of dying the last time, but it seemed his encore would be perfunctory and nasty.

Above, the strange cloud rolled and shuddered as it dispatched more unearthly monstrosities to destroy the town and, incidentally, those it had been sent to kill. To his eye, it seemed to Horst that the cloud was no longer as large or as dense as it had been previously. He remembered how the much-smaller cloud they had first encountered had vanished altogether after disgorging six monsters; perhaps the same was happening here but with a proportionately greater number. At some point the cloud would be too thin to exert its curious ability to shield him from the usual effects of daytime and light upon him, which is to say, coma and combustion. Not that he'd be alive (in the vampiric sense) long enough to experience that. The great louse loomed, and Horst braced himself for the lightning-fast strike that would take him.

And it came. Not, however, from the louse. Unseen and unsuspected, the giant woodlouse had been stalked by the prowling sculpture. Now, in a flail of great rounded shapes with aesthetically placed holes here and there, it pounced upon its prey. The great louse went down in a jumble of art and arthropod.

Horst crawled from the fight, trying to find his way back to the edge of the field. Somewhere off to the other side of him there was an odd sound like a very large pair of scissors closing. Seconds later half a zombie—bisected from crotch to crown—landed in a wet wave in front of him in much the same way a slice of bacon might be laid in the pan. It seemed to Horst that whatever the Lord of Powers had summoned were many and varied, and poorly briefed as to what they were supposed to be attacking. If any further proof were needed, another zombie walked by Horst a few seconds later, head down and furious of expression, death failing to mediate its displeasure at being covered in a pulsating slime, transparent and animate, that was visibly dissolving the flesh of the walking corpse.

Horst dragged himself through the field, the sound of argumentative monsters filling the air as the attack on the town devolved rapidly into a free-for-all among the summoned and the raised. Staying low actually seemed to be the wisest thing to do, as well as the necessary thing to do thanks to his legs feeling like overcooked noodles. Thus, he crawled slowly and painfully through a battlefield of the dreadful, the fights between summoned, and the attacks of the summoned upon the zombies. For the zombies never seemed to retaliate, this being outside their orders. Instead they confined themselves to trying to struggle on despite eviscerations, amputations, and other nuisances. They did, however, look very cross by dead people standards while doing it, as if regarding the actions of their extra-dimensional tormentors as highly unprofessional.

In this, Horst had to concede that they might have had a point. Whatever control the summoned creatures were under seemed either loose, or perhaps their orders had been careless.

Abruptly the wheat thinned away and he was at the edge of the field. He had managed to navigate in the right direction—before him lay a country lane, the town off to his left, and dead ahead was the showground. Beyond it lay the train and sanctuary. Using the fence as a support, he pulled himself to his feet and awkwardly between the bars. Now all he had to do was travel a quarter of a mile across open country with legs that weren't as reliable as he was used to.

Then he saw the steam and smoke rising from the locomotive start to puff rhythmically and he knew it was moving. His unrequited need for blood was dimming his sight, his senses dulling as they starved, but even through the growing attenuation of his hearing, he could hear the *chuff* of the engine as it headed for the main line.

Despairing, he took a step and immediately fell. He tried to shout, but his voice was nothing but a croaking gasp in his throat. Behind him, he could hear things—what things they were he had no idea—moving closer. He started to crawl, but knew he couldn't outrun a hogtied terrapin in his current state. He was abandoned, he was helpless, and he was doomed.

An Interlude

It should be pointed out that Horst's recollection of events necessarily skipped over some facts that he did not know or was unaware of—as mentioned at the beginning of this narrative—but also things that he decided not to mention both for reasons of brevity, or because he simply did not wish to talk about them. Into this latter category fell the inner conflict he had felt with his inhuman side. Johannes Cabal, however, was very at home to his own inhuman side; indeed, he was less welcoming to his human side. This gave him a certain understanding of the sensibilities of the unconventionally moralled, and he had scented his brother's evasions throughout the telling.

'Tell me, Horst,' he said with studied nonchalance, 'how is the vampire business going for you these days?'

Horst was uncharacteristically dumbstruck. Eventually he managed, 'By which you mean . . . ?'

'By which I mean that vampires, even those that were good men or women in their previous existences, are not pleasant company. There is a corruption of the spirit there, at least in the vast majority of cases. Have you felt within yourself any hints of such?'

Horst said nothing, but simply seemed uncomfortable and avoided eye contact.

'Oh, for heaven's sake,' said Cabal, 'we're talking about vampirism, not genital warts. I shall assume that you have been experiencing a desire to treat humanity as low and expendable.'

Horst swallowed. 'Yes,' he said in a shamed whisper. 'It's horrible.'

'Is it?' Cabal was honestly surprised. 'I was about to say I sympathise entirely. That has long been my relationship with my fellow humans. I can see it would be an unpleasant experience to you, though. There is, however, a simple enough solution, although one that requires mental effort and discipline on your part.' He indicated his eyes with a gesture of his index and middle fingers. 'Look at me.'

Horst did so, somewhat suspiciously. 'You're not going to try to hypnotise me, are you?'

'That's rather more your forte than mine,' said Cabal a little pointedly, as Horst realised that his mild manipulations of his brother's memories during the early stages of his convalescence had not gone as unnoticed as Horst had hoped. 'No, I simply want your full attention. Do I have it? Yes? Good. Then mark what I say and see in my face that there is no dissimulation or pettifogging.

'Horst, you are a good man. You have always been so, and your soul is an untrammelled thing indeed.'

Horst winced and interrupted. 'Ah. Well. Maybe not. There was that business with a lacrosse team . . .'

Now it was Cabal's turn to wince. 'Did anyone suffer?'

'Oh, no. Nothing like that.'

'Was everyone happy?'

'I flatter myself a little to think, yes. Everyone was very nice afterwards, anyway.'

'Then shut up. In a world as grimy and sin-ridden as ours, you're a paragon precisely because your intentions are always good.'

'Johannes, I killed a man.'

'Pffft.' Cabal expressed his opinion of that crime with pursed lips and sharp exhalation. 'A man who had just killed once before your very eyes and was about to murder at least three more unless you intervened. I mean, Horst . . . a *werebadger*.' He said it with leaden disdain. 'That was a mercy killing. You are a good man. I've seen evil. By many metrics, I *am* evil. I know what it looks like. You are not even similar. Remember that, brother. Let that be your bulwark against the impulses your condition imposes upon you.'

Horst sat, absorbing whatever wisdom he could draw from the words, or at least, most of the words. 'Bulwark?' he asked.

'Bulwark. Do you know what that is?'

'I can look it up later. But thanks. Thank you, Johannes.'

Johannes Cabal fluttered his hand, reinforcing the humanity of a vampire being child's play, apparently. 'Now, kindly continue. You were just in a circumstance by which your doom was assured.'

'It was pretty desperate,' said Horst, slightly miffed at his brother's lack of concern.

'But here you are, telling me the tale. Really, Horst, you undermine all the tension of the narrative by being the storyteller. I *know* you survive.'

'I can't help that,' said Horst, and continued.

Chapter 12

IN WHICH SACRIFICES ARE MADE

Horst imagined himself as a stilt walker, striding along on lengths of insensate wood, except in his case they were lengths of insensate flesh and blood that in happier times he would refer to as his legs. These were not happy times, however, and his legs—in addition to insensate—were not rigid. His first attempt to stilt walk upon his own legs ended in failure, as did the second and third. He only kept doing it because it was no slower than crawling and also because it raised him high so that perhaps Becky on the footplate might see him and stop the train.

And then the train *did* stop reversing out of the spur, but only for a moment while the gears were thrown into forward drive, and the train moved ponderously away from him. Behind, he could hear thuds, highly pitched screams emitted by no creatures that had ever walked the Earth before, and other noises that defied description exactly because their like had never been heard on Earth before. Also, they seemed to be growing closer.

Horst was forced to the conclusion that the jig was very likely up with him. Besides, even if the creatures didn't finish him, the cloud was still steadily thinning. He had only vague memories of how the sun had felt last time it sent him to leaves and ashes, but those memories were not joyful. He hated to die again, with things unfinished like this.

Beneath him, the ground purred with impacts and he rolled onto his back to see what was coming. His old friend, the giant carnivorous woodlouse or another very like it, was heading directly for him. He doubted he could depend on the statue creature intervening again, so resorted to feebly waving his hands at it and saying 'Shoo' in a aged whisper.

This only seemed to incense the creature. It reared high, spreading the edges of the ridges behind its head in the way a hooded cobra might, if it had lots of legs and was very ugly indeed. Horst wished he had a spear, or a sword, or a pointed stick, anything that might upset it as it stood before him, convinced of its victory and with its underbelly exposed. Admittedly, he wouldn't go so far as to call it a *soft* underbelly, coated as it was with chitinous plating. It was still an underbelly, however, and he wished he had something with which to aggressively poke it there. Even if he couldn't kill it, he could perhaps bruise it a little, causing it some discomfort later. He appreciated that his situation was so hopeless that causing the thing that killed him mild discomfort sometime after it had eaten him would be the closest thing to a Pyrrhic victory he could arrange. This was the limit of his dismay beyond the wish he could have seen things through and perhaps died a little less pathetically. He could barely think anymore. He stopped waving his hands at the monster and just wafted one dismissively at it as he lapsed back.

He stared up at the arcane cloud that had brought his doom and all its little pal dooms. 'Ah. Whatever,' he said, fully knowledgeable that they were poor last words. Last words weren't on his short list of final regrets, however, so he let them slide.

The woodlouse thing seemed upset by such inattention, however, and made a dreadful noise. It was a complicatedly dreadful noise, and Horst was unable to make out the nuances due to the mechanical chattering coming from the other direction. The chattering seemed vaguely familiar and probably something to do with the stream of bullets creasing the air above him. Ah, yes. Thompson sub-machine gun, .45 ACP. Now he remembered.

The creature was making so much fuss because, it transpired, its underbelly actually *was* quite soft when gunfire was hosed across it. It crashed back down to bring its heavier outer armour into play and then, either from surprise or prudence, rolled up once more into its great tyre-like form.

'On your feet, Cabal!' he heard somebody . . . Major Haskins, yes . . . shouting.

'I can't manage that,' he replied, slightly peevishly as if he'd been asked to do handsprings. 'I'm weak. Run out of . . . oomph.' This latter thing he said, because his sense of propriety cavilled at talking about blood in polite company.

'Oomph?' The major was closer now. 'Take the gun, take the gun!' he said to somebody else. Then Horst felt his collar gripped and he was suddenly being dragged up the small slope to the edge of the showground.

'This is very kind of you,' said Horst as he was unceremoniously rolled under the fence before being dragged again.

'Never leave a man behind,' said the major. 'Not if you can help it.'

'How does this thing work?' That was Professor Stone.

'It doesn't,' managed the major between heavy breaths. Horst *sans* oomph was turning out to be an awkward load. 'Out of ammo. Damn it, help me, man!'

Professor Stone contributed his spare hand and Horst found himself sliding backwards across the green swathe a little more rapidly. He was glad he'd already decided his current clothing was going for rags the first chance he had to change, as he shuddered to think how deeply the grass stains would run. It was the latest in a day of horrors.

'When you say *oomph*,' huffed the major through his exertions, 'do you mean to say . . .'

'Blood,' said the professor, also starting to breathe heavily. 'He means blood.'

Horst only raised a hand and waved a finger in the professor's direction. *Yes. That.*

'Right,' said the major, and dropped Horst. While the professor was still at the 'What the blazes?' stage, the major cut over him with 'We'll never make it to the rendezvous going like this. We're not even outrunning the zombies, never mind those other . . . *things*. Professor, take the gun and run ahead. We'll catch you up.'

'What hope have . . .' began the professor, then paused as he understood the plan. 'Major, that's not wise. He is starving. He may not be able to control his need for sustenance.'

Part of Horst's mind also understood now. Unfortunately, it was the part that rubbed its hands at the realisation, and said, *Good-oh.*

Hush, you, said Horst inwardly. *I told you to clear off. It was very dramatic. Don't go undermining me by coming back and spoiling everything.*

'We'll have to take that risk.'

'No,' whispered Horst, 'leave me. Don't risk yourselves.' But neither of them heard him.

There was little time for prevarication; a crash made the professor and major look to the town in time to see a creature of the proportions of a harvestman spider* expanded to a scale wherein

---

* At this point, Johannes Cabal interrupted the narrative to explain that the harvestman, known in North America as the 'daddy longlegs' (an obvious nonsense as 'daddy longlegs' is, of course, a colloquial name for the common crane fly), isn't a spider at all, but of the order *Opiliones*, which, while arachnid, are not actually closely related to spiders. He spoke on this theme for several minutes. It was fascinating.

its legs were as thick as any girder to be found in a Scottish ship-yard crash through the wall of the town's general store. Screaming locals were noticeable by their absence, and both men saw with relief that the impromptu evacuation had been as near total as they could have hoped for.

'Very well,' said the professor. 'Good luck. Both of you.'

As the professor ran from them, Major Haskins lifted Horst into a sitting position like a man with an impracticably large ventriloquist doll. 'Right, you can have a pint, and that's your lot,' he said.

'I . . . may not be able to control it,' whispered Horst.

The major looked him in the eye. 'Well, you better bloody had, Cabal. That's the long and short of it. Besides, I think you're a better man than to let whatever little voice bids you do evil call the shots for you.'

Wha . . . ? said Horst's evil little voice within him. *How did he know?*

Shut up, Horst said to it with his big inner voice. *I've told you. Clear off.*

I'll be back, said the little voice, and it seemed to mean it. In any case, it grew quiet.

'I'll control it,' Horst said out loud. 'I'm my own man. One pint, no more.'

'Righty-oh,' said the major without obvious enthusiasm. 'Let's get this over with before we attract any attention.' He jerked down the side of his collar to expose his jugular, his expression that of long-suffering impatience.

Horst felt his fangs extend, but felt he couldn't just bite without some preamble. 'This is terribly kind of you, Major—' he began.

'*Do* crack along,' the major interrupted him. 'I'm not inviting you to afternoon tea.'

'No,' admitted Horst. 'Quite.' And drove in his fangs.

'Ow!' said the major tersely, but otherwise maintained a dignified silence while Horst fed.

One pint only, Horst said to himself, although he wasn't quite sure how much that felt like. It had been a very long time since he had drunk a pint of beer, for example, or a pint of milk, and the experience of vampiric drinking was profoundly different anyway. Most people don't go around attaching themselves to kegs and udders by their canines, after all. Not *most* people.

Instead, Horst relied on the quantities he had learned to take that did not unduly inconvenience the donor during his year with the carnival. That situation had been different, though. He had been at liberty to feed frequently and lightly on patrons who would be expecting to come away from a carnival with a love bite or two in any case or they would regard it as a wasted evening. He had never starved before, but for the time he had endured several years in a crypt. Most of that time had been spent in a fog of inactivity when—day or night—he did not move for weeks on end, and had never had reason to exert himself. This whole fighting zombies, werewolves, and otherworldly creatures business was the most wearing thing he had ever done in his life and unlife, and so he had never before burnt his resources down to nothing.

'Is that . . . that *must* be a pint?' he heard someone say nearby, but he decided to ignore them, whoever they were. Or, at least, *part* of him decided to ignore it, and the rest went along with it for a moment because the sensation of returning strength was so pleasurable, and anything was better than being a weak, doddering mess. But with strength, there also returned clarity, and this detected in the part of him that said that nobody had spoken a certain smugness that he had taken it at its word. That was enough to break the spell.

Horst lifted his head and wiped the blood from his lips. 'Yes, Major Haskins,' he said, 'I'm sure it must be. Thank you.'

Horst stood easily, his weakness fading from his memory almost as quickly as his body. The major followed him while tentatively touching his wounded neck. 'Should I get some iodine on these?'

'You can if you like, but from what I understand, a vampire's bite is very clean. My brother theorised that it was because all the bacteria you normally get in a human mouth can't survive, so a vampire's mouth is sterile. Other plus points are fresh breath and no plaque.' He pointed towards the line where he hoped the train had stopped, just out of view beyond a small wood. 'We should get along, Major. They won't wait forever.'

He turned back just in time to see the major hit by the giant woodlouse thing. It smashed into him like a charging bull, jaws scissoring as it caught his arm and took it off in the middle of the biceps. Major Haskins cried out in startlement more than pain as he was borne down onto his back by the vast bulk of the creature. His cry was echoed distantly by Professor Stone, who was just climbing over the far fence when the disaster struck.

Horst did not hesitate, but flung himself at the louse, grabbing it under the near edge of the carapace and attempting to flip it. The louse really didn't care to be lifted, and a host of hook-ended feet thrust into the earth meant that usually it got its wish. The hook system, while efficient and effective, however, had never evolved to deal with the efforts of an impassioned vampire. With a grassy tear of ripping sod, the louse found itself on its back. It made a baying, chittering shriek at such indignity, which, while painful to the ear, didn't help it back onto its feet in the slightest. Instead it writhed on its back in the way known so well to its smaller, non-terrifying cousins.

Horst went to help Haskins, but hesitated when he saw the extent of his wounds. Not only had one arm been taken, but the creature's slicing mouthparts had done their work on his chest, too. The ribs were laid open, the broken ends of bone visible, and something pulsed in the cavity beyond that Horst feared was the major's exposed heart.

'Cabal . . .' The major wheezed the words though the agony of his wrecked ribcage must have made even breathing desperately painful. 'Cabal . . . take what . . . you need . . .'

'I'll get the professor,' said Horst hopelessly. He looked over at Professor Stone. He had the sub-machine gun under the crook of his right arm, and his left hand to his mouth in shock. It hardly surprised Horst. Even from over there, the extent of the major's injuries must have been appallingly apparent. 'I'll get help.'

Major Haskins managed a very exasperated sigh despite everything. 'Don't be a damn . . . damn fool, lad. I'm . . . done for . . . My blood . . .' He held up his hands and they were dripping red. 'Don't need it now. Be . . . be my guest.' He lolled back, his eyes dimming as he lapsed into shock.

Horst had a feeling, a sense of some bit of Miss Manners etiquette that he'd heard somewhere that it was rather discourteous to feed on people like that. On the other hand, he *had* been invited, and it would be rude to refuse. So he held Haskins close and reopened the so recently sealed wounds, all the while keeping an eye on the giant louse.

He was therefore looking in the right direction when a stream of grey-white fluid sprayed onto it from somewhere on high. The fluid behaved oddly, however; it had seemed liquid enough on impact, but now it flowed quickly and not entirely in the direction usually suggested by gravity. Instead it ran between body segments, and around legs, losing its wet gleam within moments to turn a dull matte. The louse certainly didn't like it. It squealed and flexed, scraping its legs in an effort to cast the stuff off, but only succeeding in gluing its legs together. Then, like a marionette whisked from the stage, it was gone, pulled into the air on the now very solid stream, up, up, into the waiting jaws of the great harvestman. It seemed the harvestman had more tricks up its many sleeves than merely being very big.

Horst stopped drinking and looked up awestruck as it looked down upon him, probably less awestruck. It watched him with the high disinterest of a hanging judge as it slowly crunched on the louse, bits of twitching chitin raining from its jaws, themselves devices of great complexity that dismantled as they manipulated as they chewed.

The louse lasted no time at all, and the harvestman's hunger was not assuaged. Before Horst could react, another jet of the grey web was arcing down from some gland mounted over the giant's jaws. Horst threw himself back, but he was not the target. The major was gone in a thrice, although a splash of the liquid settled upon Horst's ankles and might have drawn him up, too, but for the thinness of the strand connecting it to the main mass. Even so, his feet were off the floor before it snapped, dumping him on his back as the major, mercifully beyond sensation, met a swift end in the slashing mandibles of the harvestman.

Horst stared, horrified. The small voice that he usually ignored, however, was pointing out with increasing vigour that there is a lot less meat in a human than a giant woodlouse, and the harvestman had disposed of the latter in less than fifteen seconds. It would therefore take proportionately less time to deal with the major, at which point it would look for the next snack it could snag and masticate. As Horst was lying sprawled *right in front of it* this would not be a long search. Perhaps Horst might want to consider making life a little more problematical for the giant harvestman rather than just lying there like finger food?

Horst blurred into motion, and unblurred ten feet away in a spectacular forward roll that took him another fifteen. The resultant grass stains were *shocking*. The problem was his ankles were no longer quite as independent of one another as he—and they—were used to. The webbing, more like a great mass of pale grey rubber, had dried rapidly and was hobbling him as effectively as any pair of manacles. He tried tearing the stuff away, but it was flexible enough to require time he did not have to remove it and, worse still, the surface ruptured to reveal a still-wet web that his hand almost stuck to. Having two limbs glued was proving nuisance enough; if he ended up with a hand and both feet all joined together, it didn't entirely preclude the possibility of escape, but it certainly damned any hope of doing it with panache.

Instead, therefore, he tried hopping. This he could do neither efficiently nor stylishly. Instead, it only reminded him of the sack races he had competed in (and usually won) at primary school. It also had the effect of exciting the attention of the harvestman, which had started to make the odd head-bobbing movements that one associates with every predator from raptors through cats and so to mantises. These are movements that never presage well for the object of their attention, and Horst decided that a sack race without a sack was not the tactic that would save him. He tried bounding, instead, hands together, running as a dog might. A very slow dog.

'Run, you fool!' he managed to shout at the professor. It was bad enough that he was going to die not only haplessly, but without dignity, and he surely didn't need an audience for it. The professor, stirred into action, turned and ran. That, at least, was something, Horst thought.

The highlight of Miss Virginia Montgomery's Flying Circus display was to have been a lot of quite cheap fireworks made more spectacular by being dumped from altitude from the underside of Miss Virginia's own trusty Copperhead. For the usual collections of yokels they performed for, this was something new and astonishing. It was certainly new and astonishing to the harvestman when a buzzy flying thing suddenly appeared before it and—while the monster's quite simple brain was deciding whether to catch and eat it rather than the funny hoppy thing with no panache—dumped a load of flashy, burning, popping, explodey things in its face.

The harvestman had never been so insulted, or surprised, or terrified. It backed away rapidly, backpedalling across the showground and so into the ruin of the general store, where it crouched within the remaining walls, making a touchingly futile attempt to hide.

The *Spirit of '76* meanwhile performed a hard bank and decelerated hard to come to a hover directly before Horst. The rear pilot canopy slid back and Miss Virginia leaned over the side. 'Come on, for Christ's sake!' she shouted at him over the deep roar of the engine. 'That was all the fireworks I had!'

Horst hobbled to his feet and hopped to the side of the forward co-pilot and weaponeer's seat as the entomopter set down so gently that the landing gear barely depressed. There it stayed, ready to fly at a touch of the controls and as eager to be off as a dog in the traces. The forward part of the canopy was designed to slide forward, but he only managed to get it to slide forward six inches before it jammed. He looked back to tell Miss Virginia as much when he saw the great angular frame of the harvestman starting to rise up again, eyeing them through its several eyes with rapacious interest.

His expression told her all she needed to know. She shouted, 'Hang on!' He got halfway through saying, 'Why?' And then suddenly they were airborne.

Fortunately, Horst had been holding on before he had been asked to, and his enhanced strength combined with a healthy fear of hitting the ground from a height combined to anchor his hands to the inside edge of the forward cockpit with a tenacity that a crowbar would have found difficult to trouble.

The entomopter jigged sideways, neatly dodging a jet of web that would have caused havoc if it had got onto the wings. Miss Virginia put the nose down and shoved the throttle through the gate all the way to the maximum 'buster' setting. The engine howled with power and the wings momentarily started to accelerate harshly, but she changed their collective setting so they were biting harder, putting their newfound energy into shifting more air rather than just fluttering faster. The Copperhead tore along the edge of the showground, picking up speed rather than altitude.

Horst saw little of this, concentrating solely on making himself a fixture of the entomopter's side. As he clung there, however, an unpleasant thought occurred to him. Even without the thinning of the supernatural cloud, the aircraft's speed would soon take them out of the curious shielding effect it offered him as a vampire. As soon as they broke out from it altogether, he would become comatose after a few minutes and fall, assuming he wasn't burning before then. He would hate for that to happen; it would make a dreadful mess of the entomopter's beautiful paintwork.

Miss Virginia didn't want that, either, or perhaps she valued his continued existence. Whatever the reason, she hardened the manoeuvre to present the side of the fuselage as horizontal as she could manage. It was enough; he released one hand and used it to shove the canopy all the way open, and threw himself into the cockpit.

He pulled the forward canopy shut as she closed the rear,

cutting the engine sound to a level where they could manage a conversation in merely raised tones rather than bellowing. 'There's a blanket in there,' she told him. 'Use it to cover yourself. We'll be out from under the cloud in a minute.'

Gratefully, he looked around the cockpit floor and found a thick, folded Indian blanket stowed beneath the seat. It certainly looked opaque enough to do the job and he started to unfurl it as Miss Virginia stayed under cloud cover as long as she dared with an increasingly batey colossal harvestman-like monster trying to shoot her down. He glanced sideways from the cockpit, and froze.

'There's a man down there,' he said.

'It'll be a dead 'un,' she replied. 'Nothing livin'. Well, nothin' human and livin'.'

That's not what it looked like at all to Horst. He looked *hard*, enhancing his sight to the point where a kestrel would have requested binoculars.

It was a man, and a living man, he was sure. He was dressed properly, not decked out in rags or shroud, although 'properly' was a very relative term; Horst found little to approve of in the man's choice of wardrobe. He was also walking rather than shambling or staggering around. The zombies ignored him, he noted. Even when one of the strange statue creatures leapt out from the wheat at him, it fell short in a frantic windmilling of limbs as if it had changed its mind at the point of jumping. It *shied* away from the man, as if frightened by him, or at least cowed by his presence. It stepped back from him a little way, then jumped on a zombie instead.

'I know him,' said Horst slowly. 'I've seen him . . . where have I seen him? In pictures? Somewhere. Where have I . . . ? Oh. Oh, dear God.'

'What is it?'

'It can't be. It just can't be.' He looked as hard as his inhumanly sharp senses would allow. 'You . . .' he said beneath his breath. 'It's you. But . . . you're dead!'

A Short Interlude

Johannes Cabal had been leaning back on a small hill of plumped-up pillows, his eyes closed throughout the recitation. 'What?' Now they opened and he looked testily at his brother. '*What?*' He sat upright, any lingering weakness lost in a sense of effrontery. 'You mock me,' he said.

'I swear, Johannes. Those were my exact words. I would have laughed when you said much the same—'

'*Exactly* the same thing . . .'

'Much the same thing when you saw me. I didn't laugh, though. I didn't think you'd appreciate it.'

In this, Horst was correct.

Johannes Cabal settled back again, but hardly in the best of moods. He really was feeling much more like his old self.

Chapter 12 (Continued)

IN WHICH A FACE IS RECOGNISED

Horst knew the man. He had seen newspaper images, wanted posters of him. He had seen his corpse, for heaven's sake, brought into town of an evening when, bizarrely, his brother was proclaimed a hero for killing that very man.

The man looked up, shading his eyes, watching the *Spirit of '76* as it circled him. Then he waved. Horst had to fight the impulse to wave back.

'It can't be,' he shouted back to Miss Virginia. 'It simply can't be!'

'You know that feller?' she demanded. It was impossible to tell if her tone was curious or suspicious. Horst thought she had reasonable grounds for both.

'Yes! But it's impossible. That's Rufus Maleficarus!'

A Slightly Longer Interlude

Johannes Cabal was sitting bolt upright once more. 'What?' he snapped. *'What?'*

'Well, quite,' said Horst mildly. 'I was surprised, too. I thought you'd killed him. You did say you'd killed him, didn't you?'

'Of course I said it! I *did* kill him. I shot him. I shot him repeatedly. With a Webley .577. I shot him repeatedly with a Webley .577 until he was quite, quite dead.'

Horst regarded him a little too sincerely to be entirely sincere. 'You seem very emphatic about that.'

'Because I *killed* him very emphatically. It is impossible. He cannot be alive. His body was recovered. The town's people gibbeted him, by all that is holy and much that isn't. He *cannot* be alive. Are you *sure*?'

Horst considered. 'Well, I'm fairly sure. I saw his picture, and I saw his body.'

'This man on the showground. Describe him.'

'Not much to say, really. He just looked a lot like Rufus Maleficarus. Big man. Mad hair.'

Cabal sighed, just for once more from relief than exasperation. 'That could be anyone.'

Horst nodded, conceding the point. 'You could be right. Oh.' He raised a finger to indicate a remembered detail. 'He was wearing plus fours.'

The effect upon his brother was terrible. He blanched a horrible grey, reminiscent of unsatisfying pancake batter. *'Ach du lieber Gott!'* he managed in an awful whisper. 'It *is* him.'

Chapter 12 (Continued Further)

IN WHICH A STRATEGY IS ADVANCED

'Rufus *who?*' said Miss Virginia.

'Maleficarus. He was . . . well, *is* it seems, a wizard. His father was a stage magician, I think, rabbits out of hats and so on, but then he started dabbling with the real thing, and *fils* followed *père*.'

'How's it impossible to be him if you're so damn sure that it *is* him?'

'Because he's dead. My brother shot him to death, and believe me, when my brother puts his mind to something, he follows through. Maleficarus was threatening a town, and my brother stopped him.'

'Yeah? Your brother sounds okay.'

Horst decided not to expand on his brother's motives for protecting the town, which were less altruistic than they might seem. It had been less an heroic intervention and more the fighting of predators over a tasty scrap. Instead he said, 'He has his moments,' without actually saying that this had been one of them, for that would have been a lie. Still, Johannes *did* have his moments. 'If the *Ministerium* has somehow resurrected Rufus, then their power is enormous. This is too much for a handful of Dee Society agents to deal with.'

'I thought they were getting governments involved?'

'They're trying, but it will be too late. They need something very dangerous on their side to even their odds and they need it now.'

'More dangerous than a vampire?' Even over the engine noise, the amusement in her tone was obvious.

'Oh, but I'm lovely. And I'm really not much into the whole "Prince of Darkness" business. No, they need something . . . somebody . . . much more dangerous than me.' He swallowed. He could hardly believe he was going to suggest this. 'We need my brother, Johannes.'

A Quite Long Sort of Interlude

'Seriously?' said Johannes. Being irked was doing wonders for returning some small hints of colour to his face. 'You seriously posited me as some sort of weapon too dreadful to use? I don't know whether to be flattered or not. Ah, a resolution is coming to me. No. I'm not flattered.'

'Don't give me that,' scoffed Horst. 'You've been needled ever since I told you about the *Ministerium* needing a pet necromancer, and they didn't come to you.'

'I would have told them their project did not interest me.'

'Liar. A whole country where you could operate legally and in the open. You would have jumped at it. All you have to do is rustle up an army of zombies and—'

'I *abominate* zombies. Every one of them is by definition a failure. I haven't risen one deliberately since my first experiments.'

'I like the use of "deliberately" there . . .'

'They are a necromantic dead end, and don't dare think that pun was deliberate. The principles involved are simple and well understood. I could grind out those things until the cows came home, and were likely eaten alive by the zombies. If that is this Misericorde's limit, she is no necromancer. Merely a dabbler.'

'Hmmm.' Horst nodded in mock sympathy. 'Galling when some piker comes along and gets the job you should have had, isn't it?'

Cabal looked at Horst angrily. 'Mayhap being dead repeatedly has affected your hearing. I would not have accepted the role if all it entailed on my part was something as facile as getting a cemetery or two on the move.'

'Liar. Liar. Liar. Ends and means, Johannes. You'd have swallowed your pride for the time it took to put together an army of the dead for them, if it meant a free hand and unlimited resources for research afterwards.'

There was a tense silence, but Cabal's anger was abating. He chewed it and swallowed it with difficulty, for they both knew Horst was right.

'And the monsters,' asked Cabal at last, 'these pets of Maleficarus—what became of them?'

'I understand they . . . died. Just died. Fell over and passed away.'

'As the cloud dissipated?'

'Yes,' said Horst. 'When the cloud faded away. The last to die was the big harvestman spi . . . thing. Made an awful mess as it fell. Dea Boom and Daisy Hewlett circled the area to make sure everyone was out.'

'Very public-spirited of them,' said Cabal, his thoughts elsewhere.

'Daisy didn't come back.'

Cabal looked over at his brother to find Horst looking intently at him. Somewhat disquieted by this, he asked, 'What happened?'

'Boom lost sight of her. Some of the smaller monsters were still falling from the cloud. Smaller than the harvestman. Still massive. Then she saw fire on the ground.' He took a deep breath before he continued. 'It was the *Queen of the Desert*. There was a lot of debris, with one of those woodlouse things in the middle of it. Already dead by the look of it. Boom reckons it must have hit Daisy while she was looking for stragglers.'

Cabal tightened his jaw. 'She should have stayed out of the cloud's shadow.'

'That's where stragglers were in danger, Johannes. It's where Miss Virginia flew to save me. Daisy Hewlett died trying to help people.' Horst was looking intently at his brother. 'Can you say it was a foolish death?'

Cabal said nothing, then abruptly, 'So. What do you want from me? Assuming that your tale is done?'

Horst nodded. Once his brother would have called Daisy stupid, and discounted her life and death as a trifle. He decided not to draw attention to this observation.

'Pretty much done, yes. We joined up with the train, although I don't remember much about it. As soon as Ginny Montgomery was out from underneath the cloud, I passed out. Thank God for the blanket. Still, that night, we made plans, sorted out a schedule, decided on rendezvous points, and so on. It was all very military.' He sighed. 'Haskins would have approved. As for what we want from you: your experience and knowledge.'

'Well, it's lovely to be wanted,' said Cabal. 'The type of wanted that doesn't involve bounties, dead or alive. I should warn you, my last advisory role did not go very well.'

'I know. I was the one who found you dying, remember? Occupational hazard, though, surely?'

Cabal nodded, then fell into deep thought for a minute or two until his brother, slightly impatiently, said, 'Well?'

Cabal looked at him, mildly curious. 'Well what, pray?'

'Will you help us?'

Cabal frowned at such a stupid question. 'Of course I'll help you.'

'There's no "of course" about it, Johannes. Just because a great occult evil is rising on the Continent, just because the lives of millions are threatened with a dictatorship of the dead, just because your brother asks you nicely, none of these are enough for an "of course" from you. I know you too well. So . . . why?'

'You need to ask?'

Horst nodded. 'I do.'

'First and foremost, Rufus Maleficarus. I don't think you realise what a great threat he is.'

'You told me he was an idiot in big trousers.'

'He is a *powerful* idiot in big trousers, although the trousers represent only a small part of the threat. This is a man who used the Ereshkigal Working in an ill-considered revenge plot.'

'The what?'

Cabal grunted with irritation. 'Your ignorance appalls me.'

'Almost everything about me has appalled you sometime or another.'

'True. In fairness, there's no good reason why you should know of the Working. Briefly, it is a ritual that allows an animatory power into our world. Its subjects of choice are freshly dead humans. These rise and kill more, which rise and so on and so forth.'

'Is that what Lady Misericorde used?'

'Emphatically not. The Ereshkigal Working is a trap. The ritualist who summons this power has control over it, but that control fails permanently when they fail to exert it. By falling asleep, for example. The animating power then does whatever it likes, such as killing the ritualist and then carrying on as it sees fit.'

'More killing and raising undead?'

'Exactly so. The Ereshkigal Working is a cancer in which the corrupted cells are walking dead. Left to its own devices, it will continue to spread indefinitely. It has been used twice in antiquity, and was fought to a halt on both occasions, although at great cost. It has been used once in modernity, by a loud idiot in big trousers who couldn't be bothered reading the relevant texts to see how badly things worked out the last times it was used.'

'How did it fail this last time?'

'Oh.' Cabal sniffed dismissively. 'I was there. I dealt with it.'

'You were there?' Horst looked at him askance. 'That was quite a coincidence.'

'No coincidence at all. I was the subject of the half-baked revenge attempt whereby Maleficarus performed the ritual. Murder by apocalypse.' Cabal stretched and rested his hands behind his head. 'Oh, Horst, he is such a *Scheißkopf*, you wouldn't believe.'

'You haven't mentioned exactly why he wanted revenge on you in the first place. Professional jealousy?'

'Oh, he'd got the idea I'd killed his father from somewhere.'

'And . . . had you?'

'No. I destroyed his father, but he was already dead at the time.'

Horst raised his eyebrows, which he felt showed impressive self-control under the circumstances. 'You destroyed his father's corpse?'

'Yes,' said Cabal emphatically. 'The idiot had already killed himself, so there was no point in his son becoming so very upset over it.'

Horst shook his head. 'I feel I'm missing some important factor here. If Maleficarus Senior was already dead, why did you destroy his body?'

'Because he was trying to kill me at the time,' said Cabal, surprised at having to explain such an obvious thing.

'His son was trying to kill you, so you destroyed the father's body?'

Cabal looked at him as if realising his brother was actually a complete nincompoop. 'No,' he said. 'This was long before I even knew there *was* a son. The father tried to kill me.'

'Before he killed himself?'

'*After* he killed himself. Really, Horst, this isn't complicated.'

Horst grimaced. 'I would accuse you of having an unnecessarily convoluted lifestyle, but then I remember that I'm a vampire on the run from a huge supernatural conspiracy. Very well; so this all boils down to Rufus Maleficarus would be dangerous enough with a box of matches, never mind the keys of life and death? Is that it?'

'You have it. Conspiracy or not, Maleficarus is too dangerous to have running around, summoning monsters and wearing bad tweed. For that alone, I would join you.'

' "For that alone"?' Horst looked seriously at Cabal. 'You have other motivations?'

'They are legion. They somehow raised Maleficarus as a functional human being. Well, at least as functional as he was before I shot him. That is very interesting, and I intend to discover how they did it.'

'They raised me, too. Somehow,' said Horst.

Cabal looked at him and frowned. 'Yes. About that. I honestly had no idea that it was a possibility, Horst. You know that, don't you? I would have tried if I had but known.'

'I didn't die in an accident. Not the second time.' Horst's tone was cold. 'I wouldn't have thanked you.'

'No,' admitted Cabal. 'No, I doubt you would have.' He coughed, embarrassed. 'Although that is another major reason that I am offering my help. If the Dee Society had asked me, I would probably have agreed, despite my recent experiences of working with secret organisations. But I would have considered it at greater length than, in reality, I have, and would likely have asked for much in return. I am familiar with the Dee Society, Horst. Their archives are a tar pit for certain books and artefacts. Once the Dee people have their hands on something, it might as well have been destroyed for all the good it will do for certain enterprising individuals.' He saw how his brother was looking at him. 'Yes. Like myself.'

'You'd have made them pay for your help in possibly saving the Earth?'

'Don't overstate affairs.'

'The Ereshkigal Working, Johannes. Rufus Maleficarus still knows it, even if he may have learned not to use it.'

Cabal nodded. 'That is fair. But I would still have sought some advantage.'

Horst suddenly sat upright. 'My God. Johannes, are you saying that you're accepting this task because *I* asked you?'

Cabal did not reply. Instead he found a loose thread on the eiderdown and fiddled distractedly with it. Horst sat on the side of the bed, embraced his brother around the shoulders with one arm, and rubbed the top of his head with the knuckles of the other.

'Horst!' snapped Cabal. 'I am no longer eight years old!'

Horst kissed him on the top of the head. 'You'll always be my little brother, Johannes, even if you look older than me now.'

'Ah, yes. Only you could find the redeeming virtue of vampirism to be savings in male toiletries.'

Horst rose and looked at Cabal expectantly. 'You're with us, then?'

'I'm with *you*. The rest of the miscreants and ne'er-do-wells you have in your train are pure corollary.'

'Good enough.' Horst grinned. 'Well, look at us. The necromancer and the vampire against the forces of elemental evil. The Brothers Cabal ride again!'

'Yeehaw,' said Cabal evenly.

Chapter 13

IN WHICH THE BROTHERS CABAL RIDE AGAIN

'What are the transport arrangements?' demanded Johannes Cabal, a necromancer, of his brother, Horst, a vampire.

'What makes you think anything has been arranged?'

Cabal wrinkled his nose irritably. 'While I have never entirely seen eye to eye with the Dee Society, and while on the rare occasions our paths have crossed there has been some acrimony, harsh words, and a little shooting, I still respect their pedigree and their efficiency. By your own admission, you consulted with this Professor Stone and Fräulein Bartos before heading for England.' He paused. 'How exactly *did* you find me? You had little enough time to stop and ask *en route*.'

Horst was many things—dead, for example—but there were times when his natural glibness deserted him in the face of a direct question and traipsed out of the door, taking his ability to dissemble with it. This being one such occasion, he could only smile weakly.

'Ah,' said his brother, looking at him steadily. 'I sense the Dee Society at work again. They know where I live?'

'They had a very good idea. I'm sorry, Johannes; they have very nearly chapter and verse on you. The professor is something of an expert on the subject of Herr Cabal the Necromancer. Once he got talking about you, it was hard to shut him up. I think you impress him.'

'Yet they have never seen fit to visit. Perhaps for tea. More likely to kill me and burn the house down. Why would that be?'

'This isn't going to sound flattering, but let me finish before you lose your temper, yes?' Cabal's eyes merely narrowed, which didn't bode well. 'It's because you're not considered a threat.' He saw his brother's eyebrow loft and pressed on rapidly to forestall the storm. 'They *used* to. You're right, Johannes. They were going to get around to dealing with you and your researches at one point. Yes, when I say "dealing with", I mean killing you and burning this house down. Then they realised that you weren't the kind of necromancer they were used to "dealing with". More so since after I . . . after I took my sabbatical from reality.' He coughed, embarrassed. 'The professor tells me that you, well . . . that you saved the world.'

Cabal shrugged. 'Probably. I do a lot of things.'

Horst gave him a hard look. 'I mean, *saved the world*. You. You did.'

'Yes,' said Cabal innocently. 'I know. I heard you.' He looked at his brother, very faintly inquisitive. 'Which particular time was that?'

'Don't test me.'

'I'm not. I've saved the world on two occasions of which I am aware. You remember our little chat about the Ereshkigal Working? Well, that was once, although it was some time ago, and whatever I have done to unblot my copybook with the Dee Society is apparently more recent than that. A clue, please?'

Horst did not trust himself to say anything for a long moment. Then he said, 'Some sort of super wizard.'

'Well, it's very kind of them to say so, of course, but . . . Oh, you mean that was the occasion? Then that must be Umtak Ktharl, yes?'

Horst snapped his fingers. 'That was the name. Couldn't remember it. You mean it's true?'

'Well, of course it's true. It was very bad luck finding him in the first place, of course, but yes, I extemporised a little and brought things to a satisfactory conclusion. It was also necessary to brutalise an archbishop, thereby combining business with pleasure. Yes, at the risk of apparent conceit, that was a good day's work.'

'Since when have you cared about appearing conceited?'

The question took Cabal by the lee, and he was unable to answer immediately. 'I don't care. It's just a turn of phrase.'

Horst looked at the clock on the chest of drawers. 'To return to your original question, dawn is three hours away. In an hour or so, Miss Virginia Montgomery will be arriving in her entomopter. It will be the third time she's crossed Europe by air in the space of a week, and she will then embark on the fourth immediately. You will be in the co-pilot's seat, and I shall be wrapped in tarpaulin in the cargo space, because being a vampire is so glamorous. So . . .' He waved a hand around the room. 'You'd better get cracking.'

' "Cracking", he says. "Cracking",' muttered Cabal. 'Might I remind you that I am not at the peak of my physical powers at present. I shall have a bath and a shave, both less leisurely than I would have liked, and then put together some accoutrements that may prove useful. I would be obliged if you could pack a bag of the more mundane necessities for me.'

Horst folded his arms. 'I'm not your valet, Johannes.'

'No sensible person would tolerate you as a valet. I am merely asking you to help expedite matters.' He waved a finger at the wardrobe. 'Oooh, clothes. How exciting. You love clothes, Horst. Think how much fun you'll have sorting out some outfits for me.'

Horst did not unfold his arms and skip joyfully off to the

wardrobe. Instead he cocked his head to one side. 'All your suits, cravats, socks, and shoes are black. All your shirts and underwear are white.' He looked at the rug by the bed. 'And your slippers are red tartan. You don't have outfits, Johannes. You have a uniform.' He shook his head and went to the wardrobe anyway. 'Very well. Where's the suitcase?'

'Under the stairs, as was it ever. Ah, before you start on that, bottom drawer of the chest of drawers, please.'

Horst opened it. 'Socks,' he said, underwhelmed.

'Behind the socks, at the back of the drawer.'

Horst pulled the drawer most of the way out and paused. 'Oh. Of course. I forgot the other necessary part of your dress. Johannes, there are two guns here, both in their original packing.'

'There should be three.'

'What?' Horst picked up a bundle of soft cloth from the corner and unwrapped it. Within was a rolled-up shoulder holster, a semi-automatic pistol secured within it. 'Not a Webley?' he said in mock outrage. 'They'll be so upset when they hear that you've been seeing other gunsmiths.'

'Don't flaunt your ignorance, Horst. It *is* a Webley. It holds eight .38 rounds and, as the man in the shop assured me, has decent stopping power. I have decided to start carrying one as a matter of course.'

'What about that big fat revolver you normally use?'

'I shall, of course, continue to carry a Boxer .577 in my bag. Bring that, too. Oh, and the two boxes of ammunition, and the cleaning kit, please.'

'Johannes, there are two .577 revolvers here.'

'They're both the same. Just bring me one.'

'That's not what I mean. I mean, you're bulk buying handguns. What does that say about your lifestyle?'

'It says I'm prudent and farsighted.'

'That's not all it says.' Horst put one of the gun boxes on the chest of drawers, stacking a box of .577 and a box of .38 ACP ammunition on it, and then topped the pile with the automatic pistol and holster rewrapped in its cloth to form a convenient load. He picked them up together and turned to Cabal. 'May I ask what happened to your last revolver?'

'It turned into a sword.'

'Of course it did.'

'And then the ghouls probably stole it.' Cabal smiled with an expression so close to fondness that it made Horst stare. 'The naughty rapscallions.'

Johannes Cabal fairly creaked around the house as he performed his toilette and gathered his necessities. Both were routines he performed efficiently and as quickly as his slightly atrophied musculature would allow. But while the former was a necessity attended to grudgingly, the latter was something in which he took some pleasure.

The small suitcase, taken from the hallway cupboard beneath the stairs, was wiped down and divested of dust and dead spiders, before Horst set about filling it with assorted items of clothing in black and white (the slippers could stay in the house, he decided). Cabal, however, took himself up into the attic laboratory, recovered a retired but serviceable Gladstone bag from beneath his workbench, and started to fill it with the accoutrements of an ungentlemanly necromancer. A standardised notebook,* a roll of cloth containing pockets in which nestled assorted surgical instruments, a small padded box of about the dimensions required to hold a pair of opera glasses yet which actually contained several sealed test tubes in which liquids and powders of strange creation and composition flowed, the two boxes of ammunition now light-

---

* He lost them too easily for him to put much faith into holding on to a notebook indefinitely. Thus, he maintained a master list of useful information, ready to be copied into a new notebook as utility demanded. It took a few hours to accomplish—and he was considering the possibility of having them printed—resulting in a small black notebook, half filled in a tightly written shorthand of his own invention. The other half was to be used for notes he made as necessary during experiments, explorations, and larceny.

ened by several rounds, and—freshly emerged from its packaging, cleaned, and loaded—a Webley Boxer pistol of outrageous calibre.

In a little over an hour he was almost ready. He dropped a switchblade knife into his jacket pocket, took a cane topped with a silver skull from the umbrella stand in the hall, slid blue-glass spectacles equipped with side-baffles into his breast pocket, and took down a slouch-brimmed black hat from the cloak rack.

As he brushed the thin layer of dust that had settled upon it during his absence and his recuperation, he said to Horst, 'I wore this hat to Hell.' He held the hat up to his nose and inhaled. 'Still faintly redolent of brimstone. That smell gets everywhere.'

Horst, waiting by the door with the packed suitcase, said, 'When a normal person uses a phrase like they wore a hat to Hell, one naturally assumes they just wore it a lot.'

Cabal smiled slightly and donned the hat. 'Are you suggesting I'm not normal, O brother mine?'

'You'd be outraged if anyone ever called you normal, O odd sibling. Come on. Our ride should be along soon.'

They stepped outside into the last hour or so of darkness. Cabal closed, locked, double locked, and performed a small ritual upon the door. To human eyes, it was no more efficacious than saying 'Bless you' after a sneeze, but to Horst's senses, there was a feeling of tautness, as if the building had suddenly been wrapped in ethereal chains, drawn tight.

'Do you ever get the feeling you're not coming back?' Horst said, looking up into the old house's eaves.

'Every time,' said his brother as he drew on black kid leather gloves. 'Even when I go out to purchase groceries.'

'Your defences aren't as good as you think. I walked through them easily enough.'

'They are more than sufficient. They are also highly discerning. I made them thus.'

'Discerning? What, do you mean to say they *let* me through?'

Cabal did not answer. He hefted his Gladstone bag and walked down the garden path to the gate. Horst followed him, still talking.

'But you thought I was dead. Really dead. Properly dead. Why would you . . . ?'

'I created a ritual such that the house will defend against intruders, not those who are invited, and not those who call—or called—that house "home".' He opened the gate and walked through. 'It was once your home, too, Horst.'

Horst picked up the suitcase and followed him out. He watched as his brother closed the gate behind them. 'I think I feel quite flattered,' he said.

'As long as it doesn't overflow into a disgusting display of emotion, you're welcome,' said Cabal.

Then he turned to the garden and addressed it. 'I was unimpressed by my welcome when last I stood beyond this wall. The terms of our compact are clear.'

Within the garden, small things watched him with beady little eyes full of malice, guile, and severely limited intelligence.

'We didn't *actually* eat you,' said a tiny wheedling voice.

'I didn't *actually* give you the chance, but your duplicity was evident all the same. Allow me to refresh your obviously faulty memories. I allow you to stay within my front garden on the understanding that you defend the house against all intruders, except the ones I have described, on numerous occasions. Torch-bearing mobs?'

'Eat them!' chorused the criminally insane fey of Cabal's garden, a tribe whose stature was inversely proportional to their malevolence.

'Correct. The postman?'

'Eat him!' they cried joyfully.

'No!' snapped Cabal. 'You let the postman by!'

'Oops,' said the garden. There was some small shuffling while they hid a peaked cap behind a rosebush.

Cabal grunted angrily. 'Salesmen?'

'Eat them?' came the reply, only half the chorus being entirely sure.

'Yes.'

Horst leaned into Cabal's view and mouthed *Salesmen?* Cabal wafted him away impatiently. 'Do not worry. We don't get salesmen out here,' he said, before adding in an undertone, 'not anymore, anyway.' Horst's acute hearing caught the addendum, but he decided to let it pass for the time being.

Cabal turned his attention to the garden once more. 'Johannes Cabal?'

'Eaaaa . . .' The word drained away like a sinkful of embarrassing water. There was a heated discussion in the undergrowth. 'Don't eat Johannes Cabal,' they finally said, with none of the enthusiasm of their previous answers.

'And why don't you eat Johannes Cabal?'

More discussion. They seemed honestly nonplussed by this for a minute or so. Then one of the brighter ones had a revelation, communicated it to the others, and they took up the cry, 'The Compact! The Compact!'

'Correct. But not just the Compact between us. Can you think of another reason?'

Evidently, they could not, although they took a while to admit it. Cabal leaned over the wall and snarled, 'Remember the Skirtingboard People. You get one warning, and this is it.'

As Cabal straightened up, Horst asked, 'The *Skirtingboard* People? What are they?'

'Extinct,' said Cabal meaningfully and more for the benefit of the listening garden than for Horst.

Johannes and Horst Cabal sat on the wall at the end of the garden and waited. They waited mainly in silence, but for the small sound of Johannes Cabal occasionally drawing up his sleeve to read his wristwatch. Finally, he looked sideways at Horst and said, 'You seem remarkably calm about the approaching dawn.'

'I know when it's about to crest the horizon. If they're not here by dawn, I shall just have to retire to the snug little resting place I made myself in the cellar and we shall go at sundown instead.'

'The cellar . . .' said his brother.

'Of course the cellar. Where else could I be assured somewhere to rest where no ray of sunlight would fall on me?'

'Of course.' Cabal grew quiet, but his eyes betrayed his preoccupation.

Horst, who had no need of vampiric super-senses in most dealings with his brother, stroked his chin and added as an innocent afterthought, 'Funny. I remembered the cellar as being much larger than that.'

Cabal jumped to his feet and started walking back and forth distractedly, checking his watch yet again. 'Where is that entomopter?'

Horst smiled to himself, started to say something, but then the smile faded and he looked up at the starry night. 'They're coming.'

'They?'

'Miss Montgomery said she'd bring one of the others with her in case we needed to carry very much gear. Just as well; the cargo space in her Copperhead was pretty crowded with just me in there on the outward journey. The other 'mopter can take your case and bag. That cane will be awkward if you were planning to take it into the cockpit, too. I'd put it in there if I were you.'

'Extra cargo space . . .' Cabal was thinking rapidly. 'Just a moment.'

He hurdled the wall into the front garden, much to the dismay of the wee folk who scattered almost invisibly but with plenty of tiny screams and several foul curses delivered in tones like chiming fairy bells. Cabal had no time for their finer feelings; he was already at the front door, temporarily annulling its occult defences, unlocking it, and ducking inside. Horst was conflicted by his interest in this new development and keeping an eye out for the approaching aircraft. Both the entomopters appeared in the eastern horizon, outrunning the sun, at the same moment Cabal reappeared in the open doorway. He had slung across his back a long canvas bag, and over his shoulder a fishing bag. Horst ached with curiosity to know how fly-fishing was going to help matters, but contented himself with instead lighting the flares he had been supplied with to delineate a clear landing area; two greens to mark the entry side, two red to mark the far edge. As the *Spirit of '76* and the *Buzzbomb* decelerated and came in to land on 45-degree descents, his brother joined him to watch.

'Fascinating machines,' said Cabal.

'I thought your scientific interests were more biological?'

'Professionally, yes, but one cannot help but be impressed by the mechanical ingenuity of an entomopter.'

'So enthusiastic. You should take lessons.'

'I did. I can fly.'

Leaving his brother openmouthed in his wake for the second time in one night, Cabal approached the aircraft respectfully from the front, well clear of the blur of wings as they slowed to a halt.

When the wings were travelling at a visible speed and therefore unlikely to do more than break a limb if one were foolish enough to stand by them, the cockpits of both aircraft opened, the Copperhead's rear half canopy sliding back, and the Giaguaro's along hinges on its trailing edge. Cabal watched as two women climbed down, both exhibiting the unconscious awareness of where exactly the wings were that one would expect from highly experienced pilots so as not to inadvertently walk within their sweep and receive anything from a bone-shattering slap up to an impromptu amputation.

The woman from the Giaguaro was the first to reach Cabal. They eyed each other with a degree of suspicion in the flickering red and green light of the flares. To Dea Boom's eye, Johannes Cabal looked like a walking dead man, gaunt with illness, his paleness picking up the strange illumination making him look like a ghost in a cheap theatrical production. He stood resolute, yet the long bag on his back was clearly weighing on him, and for all his willpower he could not help wavering slightly beneath it. She did not know whether to respect him for that pride or despise him. For his part, he first noted the shoulder holster she wore, was aware of the weight of the Webley automatic snugged away in his own, and briefly felt a sense of comradeship in the Great International

League of Shoulder Holster Wearers. She took off her flying helmet and ruffled her fingers through the short blond hair therein, and he decided—instinctively and with a terrible irrationality that would have made him snort in derision only a year or two before—that she was all right and that they would probably get along nicely. After all, she had short blond hair, a pistol in a shoulder holster, and she flew an entomopter. That was three commonalities right there.

'You're the necromancer, right?' she said, and even over the sound of the engines winding down, he could make out the distinctive intonations of a Dutch accent. While many Germans find the Dutch accent inherently hilarious, Cabal's humours were balanced differently: strong in the choleric, and barely less so in the melancholic, a good showing for the phlegmatic, but the sanguine potters over the finishing line last and alone. Thus, as a practical linguist, he found nothing remarkable there, still less amusing. Then again, this was a man who had remained straight-faced while a medium—claiming to speak an obscure dialect of Enochian—had lowed at him like a cow in calf for ten minutes.

'I am Johannes Cabal,' said Cabal. 'I am not defined by my profession.'

She pursed her lips. 'And this profession that doesn't define you, that would be necromancy?'

Cabal belatedly realised that his rhetorical skills, never his strongest suit, had been blunted still further by his illness. 'Yes,' he replied, wisely cutting his losses.

'Right.'

By this point, the woman from the Copperhead had joined them. Cabal noted that she, too, wore a pistol in a shoulder holster. Her flying helmet, however, concealed shoulder-long auburn hair that had not enjoyed being forced under the leather of the helmet. She dropped her gloves into the helmet she held in one hand while she ran her fingers absently through her hair in an effort to separate the locks and make them flow, rather than sit unbecomingly in a mound on the crown of her head. Where the

Dutch woman was, he gauged, somewhere in her mid-twenties, the Copperhead pilot looked to be in her early thirties and comported herself with the confidence of a leader. Even if Cabal had not already identified her from her aircraft, her manner would have done the job just as well.

'That Horst's brother?' she asked of Dea.

'The necromancer,' confirmed Dea, never looking away from Cabal. 'Right.'

They both looked at him without further comment for a period that started to grow uncomfortable.

Are they judging *me?* thought Cabal, with a growing sense of umbrage.

'Ginny! Dea!' said Horst, joining them. He smiled, and they smiled back at him, dropping Cabal from their attention like an overripe haddock.

Thus was it ever, thought Cabal.

'This is my little brother, Johannes,' he said, and unwisely made to ruffle Cabal's hair before remembering why it would be unwise in much the same way that making to tickle a feral polecat under the chin may be considered unwise. 'He's the brains of my family.'

'While Horst laid claim to several other organs,' said Cabal. 'I'm delighted to make your acquaintances, Miss Montgomery, Mevrouw Boom.' He looked as delighted as a rabbi inheriting a pig farm.

They, however, had been warned of his icy demeanour, and took no offence, which he found unsettling. Causing offence at first acquaintance was his forte, and he considered himself more than commonly good at it.

'You must be shattered after all that flying,' said Horst. 'Do you need to rest?'

'We're okay,' said Virginia. 'We set down to refuel at a French aerofield just over the Channel. Grabbed some shut-eye while we had the chance. We're good for a few hours now.'

'I made you some coffee and sandwiches.' Horst produced a

calico shopping bag adorned with a floral pattern so unmercifully twee that Cabal was sure only the poor light saved him from blindness, specifically by clawing out his own eyes. From the depths of this radioactively pretty receptacle, emitting fast particles in the quaint spectrum, Horst took two packets of greaseproof paper and two metal cylinders.

'Those are dewar vessels,' said Cabal jealously, 'from *my* laboratory.'

'Are they? I thought they were thermos flasks. Well, never mind, I'm sure they'll do just as well.' Horst passed them to the pilots, who accepted them gratefully.

'You wouldn't be so keen on that coffee if you knew what had been in those vessels previously,' muttered Cabal, at pains to make it loud enough to be heard.

'Ignore him. I got them straight from their boxes in the store cupboard.'

'Is nothing sacrosanct?' muttered Cabal at the same muttering volume as previously.

'And I ran them through the autoclave just to be safe. Believe me, they're surgically clean.'

'You used my autoclave,' said Cabal, so outraged that he forgot to mutter, 'for *washing dishes?*'

'Yes,' replied Horst. He smiled, unabashed.

'Your brother's a lot of fun,' said Dea, addressing Horst but looking at Johannes.

'True,' replied Horst, the spirit of ingenuousness. 'Although some days he's in a bad mood.'

'I can see my brother has already inculcated you into his comedy troupe,' said Cabal. 'So, unless anyone has any other morsels of rollicking humour with which they wish to bless this gathering, perhaps we can get along, the sooner to kill Maleficarus.'

'Your brother doesn't beat around the bush none, does he, Horst?' said Virginia, showing a small sign of warming slightly to Cabal through the agency of a half smile. 'Calls a shovel a shovel.'

'Actually, I call it a "spade",' Cabal said.

She looked at him, and an eyebrow raised. The smile, however, remained infuriatingly only-sort-of there and only-sort-of not.

Cabal frowned suspiciously. 'Are you *flirting* with me?' he demanded.

Horst clapped his hands, startling them all. 'Right!' he said with forced bonhomie. 'Let's get our gear packed, I can take up residence in my luxurious stateroom, and we can get back to the saving of the good old world. Can't we?' He smiled a slightly desperate smile at them all. 'Get back to the good old train? In our good old entomopters?'

'Oh!' said Dea. 'I forgot to tell you, Ginny. There's a problem with the train.'

Virginia and Horst exchanged worried glances whose main function, it seemed to Cabal, was to make him feel still more supernumerary. 'Mechanical?' Virginia asked.

'Mechanic. Becky's exhausted. The footplate men from the freight train who helped her get the train away from the town left.' She shrugged. 'You can't blame them. They have families to go to. But it means Becky's doing everything—keeping the train and the 'mopters going and driving the train. She's running on coffee and willpower. She's going to start making mistakes, Ginny.'

Virginia did not argue the point, but nor was she happy. 'We can't just put an ad in the classifieds, "Train crew required for monster-battling expedition. No money, limited life expectancy".'

'Maybe Becky can stay driving the train and we find a good 'mopter mechanic somewhere?' suggested Dea.

'No! Hell, no. Would you trust somebody to fool with your 'mopter just like that? No. Becky's the best grease monkey I've ever seen. We can't just replace her, and it would break her heart if we even tried. Horst, you helped her drive once. Could you take over at the footplate?'

'Well, I suppose I could.' He did not sound at all certain. 'But . . . won't I be needed for the fighting? All the stuff with the strength and the fangs and suchlike? And my working hours are a bit limited anyway, remember?'

'It isn't a problem,' said Cabal. They all looked at him. 'Yes, I *am* still here.' He unslung his bags and handed them to Horst. 'Load those aboard, would you, Horst? I shall be back shortly.'

Horst hefted the longer of the two bags. 'This is really heavy for a fishing rod,' he said, a little ironically.

'It's an elephant gun,' replied Cabal blandly. 'And ammunition. You mentioned Maleficarus's pets tend to be on the big side.' He turned to go back to the house, paused for long enough to add, 'I suspect he's overcompensating for something,' and walked off.

They had just finished putting away Johannes Cabal's gear in the *Buzzbomb*'s cargo space and were discussing Horst's travelling arrangements, when Dea shouted 'Zombies!' and went to draw her pistol. Horst and Virginia whirled to see Cabal walking towards them, a coil of rope in one hand and apparently unaware of the two corpses that walked behind him.

'Zombies?' he said. 'Really? Where?' He turned and saw the two monsters barely a yard away from him. 'Oh, I see. Not technically zombies, but an easy mistake for the layman to make. Laywoman. Layperson.'

For the third time in one night, Horst was astonished. 'You're kidding, Johannes? You've still got them?'

'Waste not, want not.' He walked to them and stopped, and the dead men following him stopped, too. Close to, Virginia and Dea could see that these were not at all like the undead who had attacked the train and, later, the town. Where those things had been relatively fresh, fleshly, albeit discoloured, malodorous, and slightly drippy, these examples of the necromancer's art were dry, clearly not at all new, creaked slightly as they walked, and their flesh seemed to be coated with varnish over clown make-up. One stood tall and thin, and the other shorter and not so much stout as sagging where once it might have been fat. They wore filthy coveralls, and perched upon their heads were Casey Jones engineer hats, grimy and cobwebbed. With a horrible crunching noise as of a thousand ants eating a popadam next to a microphone, they smiled at the women. The women did not smile back.

'What,' said Virginia in a terrible whisper, 'the living hell are *those?*'

'Dennis and Denzil,' said Cabal, as if introducing old school friends. 'Despite appearances, they have their uses. Specifically, they can drive a train.' He looked at them and frowned. 'Possibly Denzil and Dennis. I forget which is which. It doesn't really matter.'

Dennis and Denzil nodded in agreement. They had long since come to understand that it mattered only to them and, even then, not always. They were currently just glorying in the sensation of not being in the shed at the bottom of Cabal's back garden where they had been sitting patiently waiting for him to remember them for a little over two years. In this time they had kept themselves amused with any number of little plans and shenanigans, some of which had taken them from the confines of the shed. This Cabal did not know, which was just as well. Still, they had always come back to sit and wait, while spiders made webs around them and millipedes processed across their boots.

This, however, was clearly a special occasion, as Johannes Cabal had remembered them and they were out of the shed and under an open sky at his prompting and with his blessing. There were also two women present, who, the dusty archives of their memories assured them, were attractive, although any reason why that should be relevant eluded them. They had just been introduced, so obviously they would be going out on a blind date with them. Things were certainly looking up for Dennis and Denzil.

Dawn found the *Spirit of '76* and *Buzzbomb* airborne and heading towards the Continent. Through the blue skies, barely marked by a few half-hearted nimbi rolling in from the southwest, they whirred in a mist of multiple wings and exhaust fumes. Their pilots squinted through sunglasses as the morning sun struck them, driving Horst Cabal into a deep sleep where he lay curled in the Copperhead's stowage. He no longer dreamt as he slept, but at least he knew why he had for a while, and why the dreams had all featured Johannes wandering around in a strange world of wonder and terror.

For his part, Johannes Cabal now only troubled the Dream-lands in his dreams, which was his current activity. Hat pulled down over his eyes, he sat slumbering in the front seat of the *Spirit of '76*, markedly unimpressed by the whole business of aerotravel. As he had climbed into the seat, he had said he much preferred entomopter travel to aeroship, a statement that to the average man on the street was as ridiculous as saying a pogo stick was a finer way to travel than cruise liner. It had won the kind regards of the pilots present, however, and all the more so because the sentiment was so plainly sincere; Johannes Cabal was evidently not a man given to dissimulation.

The *Buzzbomb* was bearing an unexpected cargo, but one well within its capabilities. On either side of the fuselage below the level of the cockpit and forward of the leading edges of the moving wings were two further short, stub-ended wings. Once, their main function had been to carry external armaments. Now, instead of bombs, rockets, or fuel pods, each wing bore a living dead man, tied firmly around their midriffs with lengths of rope. The slip-stream battered them, but they did not care; this was the most fun they had ever had, living or dead. With their engineer hats firmly joined to their heads with rusty staples, they looked to the dawn and greeted it with joyful hoots and groans.

Chapter 14

IN WHICH JOHANNES CABAL MEETS ALL SORTS OF PEOPLE WHO WOULD LOVE TO KILL HIM

The journey was uneventful, though tedious. The only great complication was that the flight required two halts for refuelling, both of which raised the question of what to do with two happy dead men, neither of whom were likely to be popular nor welcome at even the most cosmopolitan of aerofields. They devised a simple plan wherein Johannes Cabal, Dennis, and Denzil would be deposited in an out-of-the-way sort of place as near the aerofield as possible, and then the aircraft would refuel and pick them up again.

The first time this was attempted, Virginia and Dea returned to find Cabal asleep with his hat over his face and the two hideous corpses slowly fighting one another over some imagined slight. Virginia Montgomery awakened Cabal a little pettishly and admonished him for not keeping an eye on his charges. He said nothing.

The second time, they returned to find Cabal awake and watching the two hideous corpses slowly fighting one another over some imagined slight. Miss Virginia did not know what to say to that, so she kept her silence.

Sleep was at a premium; both aviatrices slept during refuelling and restocked their thermoses with coffee before leaving. They also took tablets of what they referred to as 'pilot's salt', and which Cabal quickly identified as some amphetamine or another. He was naturally appalled; he used *much* more efficacious drugs when he needed to stay awake and sharp for long periods. If he had but known, he would have brought some along. Naturally, extended use resulted in anything from temporary psychosis to catatonia, but sometimes it is necessary to take a few risks.

Europe is a decently sized continent, but entomopters fly fast, and just shy of eight hours after they had lifted from outside Cabal's house, they were almost at their destination. There was still light left in the sky as Virginia throttled back to fall abreast of the *Buzz-bomb*. Cabal looked over his shoulder with interest as the two pilots communicated in emphatic hand signals for a few seconds. Dea Boom gave a thumbs-up and peeled away. In seconds her entomopter was lost in the gathering gloom, Denzil, strapped to the nearer stump wing, waving at Cabal all the way.

'What is the plan, Miss Montgomery?' asked Cabal through the telephonic link between the fore and aft parts of the cockpit.

'I wouldn't do this if the sun was down, but we just have enough time to fly by the castle. I guess you should get an idea what we're up against.'

'Is that necessary?' he asked. 'I have seen castles before.'

'Lay of the land, Mr Cabal,' she replied. Cabal noticed that she'd called Horst by his forename; he had no idea whether to be insulted or honoured that she didn't do the same for him. 'Don't worry, I won't go in too close. Those people are way too good at causing trouble if you kick their hornets' nest. Maybe a mile away. By the time they hear our engine note, we'll already be gone.'

Cabal was going to insist that he wasn't worried exactly; more expressing a rational concern, but he'd had enough of such caveats recently. At Virginia's direction, he found a set of small but powerful ex-military field glasses in a holder built into the cockpit side, raised his tinted spectacles to his forehead, and looked in the direction that she indicated. It took a few seconds of tinkering with the focus and several more to allow for the movement of the aircraft, but he finally found the run-down little city in which the castle of the Red Queen nestled, and thence he found the castle itself.

'Do you see it, Mr Cabal?'

There was no reply.

She let the pause grow for a while, uncertain whether he had heard her or not. Just as she decided that he couldn't have and was about to ask again, he lowered the field glasses. He continued to look through the cockpit glass as if he could see something there that she could not, and for the first time she felt a mild shudder travel through her. That he was a necromancer had hitherto been an unpleasant piece of knowledge to have, but Horst seemed decent enough for a vampire, and had vouched for his brother, so she'd let it slide. The two dead guys were hideous, true enough, but they behaved like good-natured village idiots rather than ravening kill-ers from the grave, so Denzil and Dennis, too, she had let slide. Now, however, there was something about the stillness of the man that made her uncomfortable. She knew, Horst had told her as much, that Johannes Cabal was a man who had seen things few others had ever seen, and fewer still with their sanity intact. He had been to places that one simply wasn't supposed to walk away from, and yet he had. With the best will, however, she could not truly imagine what that meant. Now, she was beginning to have an inkling.

'Yes, thank you, Miss Montgomery. I saw it very well.' He put the field glasses back into their holder and took his own glasses from his forehead and slid them away into his jacket's breast pocket. He said no more for the remainder of the journey.

The *Spirit of '76* set down some twenty minutes later and forty miles away, Miss Montgomery not caring to push the entomopter too hard after its long cruise across Europe. 'There's a tone on port that I don't like,' she said to Cabal, although she might as well have been talking to herself. 'I'll have Becky check the wing roots. If there's a problem, she'll find it.'

Cabal didn't even grunt. He was looking out of the side of the cockpit at nothing in particular. She could see his distorted reflection in the canopy's bullet-resistant glass, his pale skin showing clearly against the darkening world outside. He was so deeply in thought he seemed entranced. She could almost smell the workings of a dangerous mind in the confined space of the cockpit. Not for the first time, Miss Montgomery wondered how she had got herself and her girls tangled up in such a mess. Then she thought of the alternative, and remembered.

The Copperhead found the train in a secluded spur line running into a wood. Cabal recognised it as the site of the abandoned mine that Horst had mentioned during his narrative. Of the train or, indeed, any sign of activity he could see none, but the sky was em-purpled with dusk in the west, and the shadows ran long and deep. Virginia brought the entomopter gently to a full halt over a clearing and descended below the treetops, coming to rest on the bumpy leaf mould beneath. Even as the engine was winding down, the shadows around them started to move.

Cabal reached for his pistol, but Miss Virginia said, 'Hey, easy on the trigger, there, Joe. They're on our side.'

It certainly seemed to be the case. A couple of women whom Cabal guessed to be Mink and Becky led a group of about six men equipped with a hook on a cable. This they connected to the nose of the Copperhead, and used it to pull the entomopter across the uneven surface until it was under the tree cover.

Cabal waited for the wings to slow to a halt before he released the catch on the front section of the cockpit and shoved it forward. He climbed out as Miss Virginia Montgomery was standing up behind him, and clambered with less dignity than he would have liked out of the entomopter, dropping the last bit of the distance and almost toppling over on the forest floor.

'Mr Cabal?' said an approaching man. 'Mr Johannes Cabal?'

Cabal gave him a swift appraisal and placed him immediately as an academic abroad. 'Professor Stone, I presume?' he said, stretching out the kinks in his neck and shoulder.

'Indeed so! Indeed so, sir!' Stone seemed delighted to see him. 'It's a delight to meet you.' He took Cabal's hand, despite him not proffering it, and pumped it enthusiastically.

Cabal looked at him more suspiciously than was his wont. 'It is?'

'Yes, indeed. I was so afraid that when we finally met, it would be to kill you. This is much more agreeable.' He considered. 'Perhaps that's the wrong term to use for an occult conspiracy raising an army of monsters. Still, it's an ill wind. At the very least, I shall have the pleasure of your acquaintance and, I hope, your cooperation, without the necessity of shooting you.' He smiled throughout this, and it was an honest, open smile, not the leer of somebody given to the more melodramatic end of the threats market.

'You have the better of me,' said Cabal.

'You're a necromancer, Mr Cabal. If the law found you—and by *law* I mean people who actually mean to uphold it rather than that tame police sergeant you have on your payroll—they would hang you. If they were to fail, we would probably take on the role of the entire judiciary, right up to the position of executioners.'

Cabal thought this was all remarkably menacing for a friendly chat. 'And what of the defence?'

'Alas, any defence is considered before we sally forth. Still, the practise seems to work. You're alive, aren't you?'

'Evidently,' said Cabal, although there had been circumstances in his history where 'alive' and 'evidently' would not have set well together. He raised an eyebrow. 'Yes, I have not been troubled by your society to any great degree. Why would that be, Professor?'

'The business with Maleficarus and the Ereshkigal Working

garnered you a great deal of tolerance, you know. Saving the world, no matter how selfish your motivations, will do that. Don't think the business with Umtak Ktharl went unnoticed, either. These, taken along with your general discreet profile and lack of the megalomania that so often distinguishes others of your profession, have made you a very low priority for us.'

'And if I'd had a higher "profile" . . . ?'

'We would have put you down like a dog, yes.' The professor was still smiling, all throughout, as if telling somebody that they weren't marked for death was the most considerate thing he'd done for days.

Horst appeared, very literally.

'Hullo,' he said to the professor and his brother, ignoring the small jump the professor had made at the unexpected materialisation. Horst ruffled his hair, rendered unruly by the trip. He looked back at the Copperhead, where a couple of the new people were quickly and efficiently rolling up the tarpaulin in which Horst had travelled. They put it neatly back into the cargo space and closed it up, under Miss Virginia's assiduous eye. Satisfied, she lit a cigarette and headed off to discuss developments with her crew.

'It's the only way to travel,' said Horst perhaps just a little absently. He watched Miss Virginia walking away for a second before turning back to Cabal and the professor. 'Unless there's almost any other way available, of course.' He sighed through his nose. 'I miss my coffin.'

'I gather all these people are your reinforcements,' said Cabal to the professor. 'I didn't think the Dee Society was so large.'

'It isn't,' said Stone. 'We've called upon every similar organisation that we dared. There are Templars, Yellow Inquisitors, Sisters of Medea, the Daughters of Hecate . . . are you all right, Mr Cabal?'

This he asked because Cabal's face had been growing more tight and ashen as the list was recited. 'I am better than I have been,' he said. 'I'm just a little dismayed, given that the last time I met representatives of those organisations, there was some friction.'

'They tried to kill you?'

'Quite.'

'All of them?'

'Four of them.'

'I only mentioned four.'

Cabal looked around. More than a few of the shadowy figures under the trees seemed to be watching him quite intently. 'All of them, then.'

The tension was, if not dissipated, at least ameliorated by the reappearance of Miss Virginia and her crew. 'Becky!' said Horst. 'You're limping! Are you all right?'

'Two zombies turned up on my footplate,' she replied. 'They came in one way, I fell out the other. A word of warning next time, if that's possible? I almost started shooting.'

'My mistake,' said Dea, smirking slightly.

'I gave Mr Cabal the four-bit tour,' said Virginia, cutting off any further badinage. 'Eyeballed the castle at a safe distance.'

While she said it, she was eyeballing Mr Cabal, too. For her efforts he looked sideways at her, and said, 'It used to be a motte and bailey about a thousand years ago, but that didn't last too long. Reduced three times, each subsequent design being of contemporary castle-building philosophy, and eventually rebuilt as an early example of a concentric castle. From then on it evolved. No longer necessary as a defensive position but simply a seat of power, each iteration of construction concentrated on making it grander rather than any more secure. It was, after all, by now an imperial residence rather than a military redoubt. Ballrooms, audience chambers, and several dining rooms, all of which sport long tables upon which one may conduct sword duels should that prove necessary.' He seemed exasperated and even a little desperate as he said it.

'Good Lord,' said Professor Stone. 'You could tell all that just by looking at it?'

Miss Virginia seemed more wary than astonished. 'And all from a mile away through binoculars.' She was watching him closely now.

'I have been here before,' said Johannes Cabal wearily. He seemed like a man run to ground. 'It's Harslaus Castle, isn't it? We're in Mirkarvia.'

'Mirkarvia, is it?' said Horst. 'I suppose I should have asked where I was at some point.'

Cabal could not bring himself to chide his brother, a man who cultivated wilful ignorance so as not to take all the surprises out of life. He was too busy berating himself inwardly for not making sure of the facts. Early on in Horst's narrative he had got the impression that Horst was talking about one of the Germanies— probably somewhere like Bavaria or the far east of Prussia—and he had clung to that notion without confirmation. This he put down to his recent illness dulling his faculties, rendering him unable to penetrate the caul of reluctance with which the subject of Mirkarvia was cloaked in his mind.

'You've been here before, you say, Mr Cabal?' asked Stone.

Dull Cabal's wits may have been before, but they were sharpening up again nicely now, and the professor's question—delivered with no detectable casuistic intent—furnished him with the reassuring revelation that the Dee Society did not know every single thing about him after all.

'Yes, briefly. That was before the revolt, of course.' This was technically true. That Cabal had been instrumental in provoking the revolt was something he decided not to burden the company with. He had done this for entirely self-serving purposes, specifically to cause a distraction while he saved his own neck, yet he had felt it was something that Mirkarvia both needed and deserved. It was a ridiculous little country with ridiculously grandiose dreams, and a nice revolution with a subsequent clearing-out of the calcified ranks of its vicious and inbred aristocracy was the perfect thing to give the place a dose of modern realities.

All this he had told himself as he left the country burning behind him. He had never troubled to open a newspaper subsequently to discover the current state of affairs there. Turning the place into a testing ground for some sort of absurd magocracy funded by foreign venture capitalists of the most despicable kind was a surprise, a very unpleasant surprise. Ever since recovering his soul, he suffered occasional prickles of mental pain that he had learned to characterise as his conscience making itself felt. Now he felt a spiritual sickening and he knew it was guilt. This was indirectly his fault, and the knowledge clung to him like clay.

Still, there was no need to go around telling people about it.

'You seem to know a lot about the castle for somebody who was just passing through,' said Miss Virginia Montgomery.

'I was here to secure a book that was not available elsewhere.'

'That's Johannesese for "I came to steal it",' explained Horst.

'Exactly so,' agreed Cabal. 'It did not quite go to plan and, subsequently, I was briefly a guest of Harslaus Castle.'

Horst started to translate that, too, but Virginia waved him to silence. 'It's okay, I know what he really means.'

'It appears that the revolution left a power vacuum that this *Ministerium Tenebrae* has sought to fill.'

Professor Stone shook his head. 'Not quite. Our information is that they were invited in.' He rubbed his hands together. 'It's getting chilly. We should retire to one of the carriages to continue this conversation. I think representatives of some of our allies would like to talk to you, too.'

'I came here to help,' said Cabal. 'I will not be interrogated.'

'Nor shall you,' said the professor quickly. 'Some of the others were a little . . . circumspect about you being upon the strength. Excluding them from discussions will only breed distrust.'

Cabal looked at Horst a little truculently. 'This would be politics, then?'

'I know, Johannes, I know.' Horst patted him on the shoulder. 'You came out here spoiling for a fight with arcane powers and things man was not meant to know, but before you get to the juicy stuff you have to sit on a committee. Life's cruel. I know.'

'Do shut up,' said Cabal.

* * *

The meeting was held in the train's guard van around an impromptu table constructed from crates and the seating consisting of a fine variety of chairs, none of which was a brother to another. Cabal took pains to choose a decent office chair of the swivelling type, and manoeuvred it to the head of the table before the other attendees arrived. If he were to be examined by the sort of reactionaries and Luddites that had dogged his steps for years, he would at least suffer it from a position of authority and in the nicest chair, distressed though the leather of its seat and back were.

Horst sat at his left and Professor Stone at his right as the table filled. It did not take great powers of deduction to place most of those present within their assorted secret societies. The Templars sent their regrets, but they were currently engaged in saving the world in North Africa where a great terrible evil had emerged from the sands. They were sure that, whatever the situation in Mirkarvia, the other societies would prove sufficient in dealing with it. The note was polite, elegant, and carried a beautifully crafted subtext that the terrible evil in North Africa was inestimably more dangerous and serious than anything likely to occur in Mirkarvia, but that such a kindergarten level of menace was within even the limited capabilities of the dim-witted bumblers of the Dee Society *et al.*

Professor Stone read out the decoded note, and it was greeted with a withering silence. The professor coughed and tossed the note into the open grate of the stove, an action met with unspoken appreciation by all those there gathered.

Thus, there were only four secret societies around the table. The languid man sitting opposite Cabal could have come from anywhere on the Mediterranean coast from the boot of Italy westwards to Gibraltar and thence around the Bay of Biscay, and gave the impression that his standard state of facial hair was an eternal five o'clock shadow. If he had been picking his teeth with a stiletto, he could hardly have looked more crooked. Cabal made an educated guess that he was likely to be a Yellow Inquisitor, a creature of one of the Vatican's less clever ideas for freelance counter-heresy operations of which they had lost control within a year of institution. Rather than admitting to fallibility, the Vatican simply cut them loose and, when pushed, made indistinct noises about rogue Jesuits before noticing something amusing out of the window. If one ever wants to have a cardinal suddenly become fascinated by a passing squirrel, one need only mention the Yellow Inquisition. Cabal had little personal experience of their operations, since he mainly confined his activities to the British Isles, and the Yellow Inquisitors preferred warmer climes.

Still, he had once visited a certain address in Marseilles to take certain texts from the private library of a certain necromancer who was a blockhead and did not, in Cabal's professional opinion, deserve them. He found the place unguarded and the air foul, for the certain necromancer was certainly dead, a parody of a papal bull attached to his chest by a steel stake driven clean through, nailing him to the floorboards. What little of the parchment Cabal could read (due to the blood staining) was in execrable Latin, but identified the Yellow Inquisition's involvement to his satisfaction. Much more to his satisfaction was that the killer had done a very cursory job of destroying the dead man's papers and missed the hidden cubbyhole that housed the rarest works altogether. Cabal was able to fill a suitcase with rare and useful books and manuscripts with neither let nor hindrance, which was delightful to him and well worth the stink and the flies. Thus, Cabal was kindly disposed to the Yellow Inquisition, brutal idiots though they were.

Two women took places directly opposite one another and were so icily polite to one another that Cabal gauged one of them to be a representative of the Daughters of Hecate and the other an agent of the Sisters of Medea, a splinter group. To the outsider, the groups were functionally identical, but Cabal had once been lectured at near unendurable length on the differences between the two. He had been taking cover behind a tumbledown wall of a ruined farmhouse at the time while the Medeans angled for a clear shot at him, and he had made the awful *faux pas* of mistaking them for Hecatians. Apparently the Hecatians were all ivory towers and theory, never getting anything done, while the Medeans were more militant. Interestingly, he had once found himself in possession of Hecatian documentation that said exactly the same but with the names swapped around. For what little it was worth, he found himself irrationally preferring the Daughters of Hecate, if only because he preferred Hecate to Medea. There was more to admire in a chthonian goddess than an infanticidal sorceress, he felt.

The presence at the table was completed by Professor Stone, Alisha Bartos, and Miss Virginia Montgomery, the later nursing yet more coffee and a febrile glint in her eye indicating that the 'pilot's salts' had not yet entirely run their course. Horst lurked in a corner, sitting upon a tea chest, and undermining any menace his vampiric presence might have brought to proceedings by reading an ancient copy of *Comic Cuts* that he had found somewhere.

'This will be brief,' said the professor, taking the role of chairman. 'Mr Cabal and especially Miss Montgomery have travelled a long way today and need to rest. Essentially, we are here to introduce ourselves to one another, and to avow our joint determinations to see this business through. While I appreciate that there may be some . . . tensions between parties, it's desperately important that we are united in this current endeavour.' There was neither a rumble of assent or dissent, just a stony silence. Almost everybody at the table seemed to be looking at Cabal.

The professor coughed, sensing the awkwardness of the gathering. The Yellow Inquisitor produced a stiletto and started picking his teeth with it, all the while looking intently at Cabal. 'Well, perhaps if I go around the table, we can all intro—'

'Johannes Cabal, necromancer,' said Cabal. He was about to expand on the point, specifically citing that there was hardly a one of them there who didn't want to kill him, and if they wanted a go, they should get it out of their system now (in this piece of bravado, he would be trusting primarily to the good offices of his brother to defend him rather than his own marksmanship).

'We know,' said the Medean agent, or possibly the Hecatian. 'Your infamy precedes you.' There was nodding around the table.

'Does it?' Cabal felt slightly disturbed by this. 'I was under the impression my infamy was some little thing.'

Horst laughed. 'You can't decide whether to be worried or flattered, can you?'

'Don't talk nonsense,' snapped Cabal, irked because it was true.

'Well, Mr Cabal seems to be known to the company. Anybody unfamiliar with . . . ? No?' Professor Stone looked around the table, but it was very clear that Johannes Cabal's presence was concentrating the minds of many of the other attendees wonderfully. 'No. Very well. Well, we shall move on, then. I am Professor Jeremy Stone—'

'And I'm Alisha Bartos,' interrupted Alisha Bartos. She looked around the table, giving them all looks not dissimilar to those they had been lavishing upon Cabal. 'We're here representing the Dee Society. First on the scene.'

'And first to put the *Ministerium* on their guard,' said Cabal to himself. He was feeling a little deaf at that exact moment, however, so everybody heard the comment.

One of the women smiled. The one who did not said, 'I am Atropos Straka, a sister of Medea. You and your brother are abominations, Cabal. When this is over, we shall seek you out.'

Cabal glowered, but Horst smiled brightly. 'You will?' he said with delight. 'Well, that's lovely! My brother doesn't get many visitors, and I'm always trying to socialise him a bit. If you come around, please call ahead and I'll lay in some Battenberg.'

Atropos wavered slightly. 'When I say we shall seek you out . . .'

Horst looked concerned. 'But what if you don't like Battenberg? Do you like Battenberg? I'd have thought everybody would, but I once met a man who hated almonds.' He spoke as if of a tragedy. 'Can you imagine? Nothing's certain in this world of ours, is it? If you don't like Battenberg, just say. We can always get some other sort of cake in. I suppose. Just tell me if you don't like Battenberg.' He visibly steeled himself for possibly harrowing news.

'I . . .' Atropos was aware of the rest looking at her. 'I don't know what "Battenberg" is.'

'You don't?' Horst was so astounded he almost leapt to his feet. His smile returned in full power. 'Then you have a treat waiting for you! It's wonderful! I mean, I remember it as being wonderful. I do not eat cake. Not now. Being a vampire and everything. You did know I'm a vampire, didn't you?' He suddenly seemed to remember that they were doing introductions and held up his hand. 'Horst Cabal, vampire. Didn't especially want to be, but there you go. I miss Battenberg. Hello, everyone!'

There was a baffled pause followed by a couple of desultory greetings, all but the Yellow Inquisitor, who grinned with pleasure and said, ''Allo, 'Orst!' in a broad French accent. Cabal, for his part, recognised it as a Marseilles accent, and had a short yet vivid remembrance of a dead man in an apartment that stank of decay. 'My name is Henri Palomer, representing *l'Inquisition Jaune*. Delighted to meet you all.' There was an easygoing mockery in his manner that was constructed in equal parts of charisma and provocation, a man who made one want to embrace him one moment, and punch him the next.

'Melkorka Olvirdóttir,' said the other woman, and she, too, smiled. Cabal couldn't help noticing it was directed at Horst. 'Daughter of Hecate.' Where Atropos had the appearance of a woman looking for a Greek tragedy to enact—something horrid with entrails and heavy irony, dark and dramatic, and terribly serious (both the simile's tragedy and her physical appearance)— Melkorka was blond and pink and smiley and—Cabal reminded himself—highly dangerous. Which wasn't to say Atropos wasn't, only that she looked it, too. Melkorka, on the other hand, was tantamount to a white bunny with a machete—sweet, winsome, and fully capable of taking one's hands off at the wrist should she so desire. The Hecatians and the Medeans were witches to a woman, and it did not pay to antagonise witches.

'Virginia Montgomery,' said Virginia Montgomery, 'and this is my damn train.' She looked around the table as if challenging somebody to fight her for it. There were no takers.

'Marvellous,' said Cabal. 'I feel I've known you all my life. Can I get some sleep now?' He cast a sideways glance at Miss Virginia Montgomery. 'And a sedative for this lady?'

'I am *fine*,' she said a little too abruptly.

'No. You're not. You are awash with amphetamines. You need liquids, and to run around a bit to metabolise it. Then you need a sedative to put you out.'

'You're a doctor,' said Alisha.

'I am not, and I would thank you not to say such an appalling thing to someone on first acquaintance. I am, however, a scientist who deals with biological functions and although amphetamines aren't something I tend to play with, I do understand their effects.' He looked around, feeling pleasantly belligerent. 'Any other comments? No? Then . . .'

'We'll be sure to tell the Red Queen you need your rest if she turns up tonight,' said Atropos Straka.

Cabal cocked his head. 'Is that likely? I mean to say, have you received any intelligence that she's on the move? I shall be frank, ladies and gentlemen. My interest here begins and ends with Rufus Maleficarus. Him, I shall deal with for you, and I shall be delighted and satisfied to do so. You can keep your *Ministeriums* and your Red Queens and . . .' He paused as a thought occurred to him. 'My brother's lurid but haphazard recounting of events skipped such trifling details as who this Red Queen is anyway. I assume you know who she is?'

'We don't,' said the professor ruefully. 'We know very little about her.'

'She's a bandit queen,' said Alisha. 'From the north, up in Katamenia. The story is that she led her forces straight through Senzan territory to reach Mirkarvia. The Senzans tried to stop her, but when they realised she was only interested in their territory for as long as it took her to lead her brigands through it and then into Mirkarvia, they stepped back and let them pass unchallenged.'

'Brigands,' said Cabal. 'How very picturesque. A bandit queen. I can envisage their campfire dances now. There are a lot of tambourines involved.' He looked around the council of war, such as it was. 'And what happened when this romantic creature reached Mirkarvia?'

'The government was on the edge of collapse anyway,' said Atropos Straka. 'The arrival of the barbarians caused its final dissolution. The Red Queen took over.'

'And nobody knows her real name?'

There was silence.

Cabal snorted contentiously. 'I am saddened. I truly am. All my professional career, I have been dogged by assorted societies, conspiracies, and interested parties such as yourselves. I feared for my life, and my work, and I took measures to protect both.' He looked at those there assembled. 'What a colossal waste of effort. You people are dolts.'

There was a general feeling of deepening threat from his audience, for which Cabal did not give a fig, nor even half a fig. 'All your vaunted investigative abilities, your sources, and your techniques, and you cannot find out that trifling fact?'

'She 'as covered 'er identity well,' said Palomer, shrugging. He seemed very magnanimous about his own defeat, which was very decent of him. 'My people could find no trace of 'er previous life in Katamenia.'

'Well, of course they couldn't,' said Cabal wearily. 'She isn't Katamenian. She's plainly Mirkarvian. She's highborn, which is why the establishment accepted her rule so easily, and she knows enough about the corridors of power here that she was able to immediately target and dispose of anyone who might cause any trouble.'

'That's quite a series of deductions, Mr Cabal,' said the professor. Cabal could see the cogs of his intellect were whirring and it pleased him to see at least one other person present was thinking. 'Unless, of course, they aren't deductions.'

Cabal smiled coldly at him. 'And what else could they possibly be?'

'They could be foreknowledge, just like your foreknowledge of Harslaus Castle.'

Cabal rose. '*Just* like my foreknowledge of Harslaus Castle.' He looked around the assembly. 'Your "Red Queen" is, with a high degree of probability, Lady Orfilia Ninuka, daughter of the late Count Marechal, arch-manipulator and professional bastard. That description applies to both father and daughter, by the way. I thought *she* was dead, too. Obviously killing Rufus Maleficarus isn't going to be enough, after all. I shall also have to kill Ninuka.' He sighed heavily. 'Chores just multiply, don't they? Well, I shall need my rest. Good night.'

So saying, Cabal turned his back on several semi-professional killers who loathed him, and went off to find a bed.

Chapter 15

IN WHICH THE RED QUEEN MAKES HER MOVE

Horst followed Cabal out. 'You never cease to astonish me, Johannes.' It was not clear from his tone whether this was a good or bad thing.

'How so, on this particular occasion?' said Cabal without turning.

'You just arrive and know everything. How do you *do* that?'

'I've had dealings in Mirkarvia before, as I think I mentioned earlier. Also Senza, and very briefly in Katamenia.'

'Who is this Orfilia Ninuka, anyway?'

'My description to the august gathering back there was essentially correct. Lady Ninuka is a spoilt brat, a sensualist, and utterly divorced from any moral scruples.' He suddenly halted. 'You're giving me a look, aren't you? I can almost feel the raised eyebrow.' He turned and found Horst was, indeed, standing there with arms crossed and eyebrow raised. 'Staggering as it may seem, Horst, I am not as single-minded—'

'Bloody-minded . . .'

'—as I was. On occasion I have been known to not do something despite it being logical, or done something despite it being somewhat irrational.'

'That is the most grudging description of a conscience I have ever heard.' Horst unfolded his arms and instead leaned against the corridor wall. 'So she's a spoilt brat. How did she get from having tantrums over dresses to bankrolling a supernatural empire of evil?'

Cabal looked out of the window into the darkness as he considered his answer. 'I can't say for a certainty, but I think she always had the capacity for such things, just not the opportunity. She understands how people think, and uses that to manipulate them, and I suspect she has always had great ambition. When the lines of succession were in place, I expect she had a plan to get herself the last few steps up the ladder into the topmost echelon, perhaps even the emperor's wife or mistress. Now all that structure has gone, she has used the chaos to her advantage. I would not be surprised if she envisions herself as Empress Orfilia the First. As far as I can make out, she already is the *de facto* ruler of Mirkarvia. "The Red Queen". I wonder how much blood was spilt to give her that name?'

'You might be wrong,' said Horst. 'You can't know for sure that it is Lady Ninuka.'

'I could be wrong,' admitted Cabal. 'It pains me to confess to fallibility, but Lady Ninuka may not be the Red Queen.' He rubbed the bridge of his nose, deep in thought. 'But it *is* her. I am sure of it.'

'Necromancer's intuition?'

'Would that there were such a thing. No, the ambition and the melodrama on show convince me. That, and the impatience of it. She does not merely wish to rule, she wishes to rule while she is yet still young. Risks have been taken in this enterprise that may have been avoided with a little more time. You were chosen too easily, Horst. Marechal once told me that Mirkarvia used to have a population of vampire—"*nosferatu*", he called them. Why go to the trouble of raising a vampire in England when they had their own home-grown examples?' The rhetorical question seemed to trouble him. 'Why indeed?' He shook his head. 'Insufficient data with which to postulate.'

Horst smiled indulgently. 'I'm glad you've got your soul back, and I'm very glad it seems to have come with a conscience but— really, Johannes—you're still a bit thick, aren't you?'

Cabal regarded him icily. 'Define "thick",' he said slowly.

'Do I have to? Look, work it out yourself. What was your relationship with this woman?'

'Relationship? There was none. We merely travelled on the same aeroship for a few days.'

'Oh, and there was no interaction between you at all?'

Cabal shrugged. 'Well, yes, but nothing extraordinary. Let me see. There was a murder, I investigated, she tried to seduce me, there was all sorts of unpleasantness, and then I thought she died.' There was no reply. Cabal looked at his brother to discover him thunderstruck. 'Did I say something?' asked Cabal.

'You said quite a lot. Attempted to seduce you?'

Cabal wrinkled his nose. 'Apparently. I didn't notice at the time. That must have been galling for her.'

'I can imagine. No. No, I can't. Why did she . . . ? No, it doesn't matter. So, you didn't part the best of friends?'

'No,' admitted Cabal. 'I think she holds me responsible for the death of her father.'

'The death of her . . . ? I am getting such a sense of *déjà vu*. May I ask why she thinks you're responsible?'

'I shot him.'

Horst took a moment to consider this. 'And . . . he died from his injuries?'

'I would hope so. I shot him in the head. He was shooting at me at the time, too, so don't imagine it was entirely cold-blooded.'

'Does Lady Ninuka know that?'

'Oh, yes. She was there at the time. It was all very aboveboard. Clear case of self-defence.'

'Johannes . . . please, I'm trying to get this straight. You shot her father dead . . . in front of her?'

'Yes.'

Horst slumped. 'My God.'

Cabal's brow furrowed, as if mentally working through a particularly ferocious piece of spherical geometry. 'Hold on. Are you suggesting that she might still be upset about that?' First Maleficarus and now Ninuka. It seemed disposing of people's fathers was more fraught with complications than he'd given it credit for.

'I'm bait,' said Horst weakly. 'I can't believe it. I'm bait.'

'What are you talking about?'

'All of this, all the trouble to seek out whatever was left of me, raising me, bringing me here. All this time, I've just been a puppet.' Horst looked Cabal in the face, and Cabal was surprised to see the depth of horrified realisation he found there. 'It was always about you, Johannes. She wanted you here.' He shook his head as if trying to disperse the growing anguish. 'The drawbridge. She destroyed it herself to stop them sending too many monsters after us. She helped us escape. She knew I'd think of bringing you here sooner or later. All of this was to do that. All because she wanted you here.'

Cabal frowned. 'She's not going to try to seduce me again, is she?'

'Oh, Johannes,' said Horst in a thin, weak voice that barely admitted any hope, and turned and left him there, astonished and uncomprehending.

To his credit, Johannes Cabal went looking for his brother. No one reported seeing him, however. Cabal gave up quickly; he knew that if his brother didn't want to be found, then he would *not* be found. Instead he located a camp bed in the corner of one of the train's nooks, knocked the previous occupant's belongings onto the floor, and lay down. He didn't much care what they might think when they came back to find him there; everybody hated him anyway, so it made few odds.

He kicked his shoes off, arranged himself upon the khaki-coloured canvas, looked at the discoloured ceiling, and decided to think himself to sleep.

So, Mirkarvia. A small country with a brief flicker of glorious empire a long time ago, and a subsequent history of trying to re-capture that moment. It hadn't even been a very good empire; blundered into opportunely and squandered by a ruling class that couldn't believe its luck. Even most of the neighbouring regions that had been conquered for what was history's equivalent of five minutes on a Sunday afternoon were faintly bemused when they happened to stumble across it in the textbooks. 'We were vassals of Mirkarvia?' they said, very slightly surprised. 'Really? Fancy.' And then they would forget about it again, usually not even being able to dredge the information up if challenged for it in a pub quiz.

Subsequent attempts to re-establish the empire had varied in ex-ecution from the brutal to the hilarious, but all had failed because it takes more to become an empire than just national pride. They re-quire a multitude of factors to be in accord, military, societal, and economic, and simply wishing for the essence of empire-building to fall upon them didn't make it so. Mirkarvia was a chocolate soldier, a social maelstrom, and a busted flush.

The populace had seemingly understood this before their splen-didly oblivious leadership, an ants' nest of petty nobles so busily playing politics that it had become an end unto itself. In truth, Cabal had not deliberately fomented a riot that became a revolt that became the death of the old order and the foundations of the rule of the Red Queen. It had been an accident. He had simply wished to create a little diversion to give himself an opportunity to escape. That the Mirkarvian public had grabbed this weak straw and brought about the current state of affairs was surprising to him. That the incipient madness of Mirkarvian politics had al-lowed some lunatic at the head of a band of Katamenian bandits—

a breed of whom even other bandits spoke disparagingly—to take control with so little resistance did not surprise Cabal at all. A shock force of a couple of hundred such cutthroats would be enough to take the capital city of Krenz, and the Red Queen's noble blood and inside knowledge would be enough to hold it.

This all assumed the Red Queen was Lady Ninuka, of course. But, *of course* the Red Queen was Lady Ninuka. There was nobody else who fitted the bill quite so well. He had no idea how she had survived their last encounter, but he had experience of such human cockroaches before. Their resilience was as breathtaking as it was irritating. Indeed, Rufus Maleficarus was of similar ilk; actual cockroaches would probably be in quiet awe of his uncanny ability to not be dead despite being very thoroughly squashed.

Cabal frowned. He was prepared to believe that the Red Queen was in reality Lady Ninuka purely on supposition. Maleficarus, however . . . could it really be him? He hadn't seen Ninuka die, and hadn't cared much one way or the other if she did in fact die. Rufus Maleficarus, by contrast, had been murdered by Cabal's very own hand. There had been no possibility that he had survived. His body had not tumbled into a foaming sea or into a clouded abyss from which he might later make an unexpected return through the good offices of kindly dolphins or giant eagles. Cabal had himself checked that all life was extinguished by searching for a pulse, looking for clouding on a mirror held to the corpse's mouth, and by kicking repeatedly. This latter was not scientific, but had served to alleviate Cabal's own tension and bile admirably. He had not liked or been impressed by Maleficarus in the slightest; if he counted as Cabal's arch-enemy, then clearly Cabal needed to do much better. One is often judged by the quality of one's enemies, and Maleficarus would not have made a strong enough nemesis for a crime-solving chimpanzee, never mind a necromancer of ambition.

Maleficarus's ego had always outrun his competence. Only a blithering incompetent would dream of using the Ereshkigal Working, and on their second encounter, Maleficarus had fallen back on using the creation of a more ingenious if, as it turned out, not infallible wizard in an attempt to doom Cabal. Yet here Cabal was, resolutely undoomed.

Rufus Maleficarus, therefore, was never going to trouble the list of the top ten wizards in any foreseeable future. Yet he had performed two impressive feats, neither of which Cabal would ever have expected from him. In the first place, he wasn't dead, despite having been murdered—indeed, very much a poster boy for the extremely murdered. In the second, he had somehow become a summoner of extra-dimensional entities. This was not a simple undertaking. Summoning involved not simply opening a way through to the selected otherly place, but an opening that induced through the specific creatures one wanted, and then imposing one's will upon them. It was a mare's nest of conflicting magical forces and presented a conundrum commensurate to any currently troubling minds in the fields of mathematics and physics, with which magic shares so much. Maleficarus, whom Cabal believed lacking the necessary cognitive capability to button up his waistcoat correctly on the first attempt, was so surely incapable of any such feat that it was laughable.

And yet . . . plus fours. Who else would consider plus fours suitable attire for unleashing eldritch horrors upon the Earth? Weren't eldritch horrors a bad enough thing to be unleashing without the addition of plus fours?

So Johannes Cabal passed into sleep thinking on the subject of trousers that are baggy around the thighs and their relationship with megalomania (the correlation with jodhpurs was naturally noted).

As he slept, matters were moving along elsewhere. Specifically in the great castle of Harslaus, overlooking the depressingly decrepit city of Krenz, capital of the depressingly decrepit country of Mirkarvia, of which the citizens were depressed by the decrepitude. Also by all the monsters that were roaming around all of a sudden. Mirkarvians as a breed were used to there being things wandering in the night that should be avoided by wise citizens. At one time it had been *nosferatu* and packs of wolves. Then, once the wolves and the *nosferatu* had been pushed to near extinction by hunters and tax collectors respectively, the citizenry found the night instead owned by rampaging nobles. Young, rich, and stupid, with vast reserves of entitlement, they haunted the taverns and byways, drunk and tumescent with poorly regulated lusts. These manifested physically in weak chins, soft skins, low alcohol thresholds, grating laughs, and jodhpurs among the younger examples, before transitioning seamlessly into long chins and noses, angular forms, silly little beards, intense gazes, beetling brows, and barking laughs among their elders. Riding crops were evident throughout this spectrum.

Just as the population was on the point of becoming blasé about neighing laughs, inexpert ravishments (the early 'Ha ha! My, but you're a feisty filly, aren't you, my girl?' procedures were carried out with hereditary élan, but subsequently most of the nobles had little idea what was supposed to occur and were reduced to sitting at the end of the bed, head in their hands, whispering to themselves about expectations and peer pressure until the sun came up), and riding boots on the dinner table, along came the monsters. None of the monsters evinced performance anxieties; they were all very good at what they did. Theirs was a limited repertoire, but one executed with vigour.

To the citizens of Mirkarvia in general, and those of Krenz in particular—for here the monsters were barracked and therefore concentrated—life continued as usual, i.e., they were constantly oppressed. At least, however, the new oppressors were consistent in their manner, and staying off the streets after dark was a good way to avoid their attentions. That was the shapechangers, at least. The zombies were rarely let out, and when they were they merely pottered about the place good-naturedly. When it transpired that brain-eating, contagious undead were of a greater rarity than the cinema might suggest, and that the variety raised by Lady Misericorde were of a more traditional ilk, the common folk of Mirkarvia grew almost fond of them. While the walking dead and the were-wolves, *kitsune*, and *rakshasa* that haunted the land may occasion-ally frighten or, in the case of the shapechangers, eat those caught on the highways and the byways when the moon hung high, at least they didn't have painful laughs or undeveloped senses of hu-mour, and nor did they run up bar bills that they had no intention of paying. The Mirkarvians preferred this arrangement.

Admittedly, the new sensation of unnatural clouds that dis-gorged assorted creatures patently not of this Earth was not met with such *sang-froid*. The clouds manifested over the city were few and small, but even so created unreasonable fuss. The much larger cloud that had unloaded great towering harvestmen and killer woodlice the size of bison, for example, had essentially destroyed the small settlement over which it had been deployed, and the worthies of that place, on returning to find the place shattered and littered with corpse pieces and shards of aliens, had written a sharp note to central government asking them not to do such a thing again.

The note formed part of the minutes of a meeting that evening by the *Ministerium Tenebrae*, who were now Mirkarvia's *de facto* government. The citizenry noticed little difference in adminis-tration except for the aforementioned substitution of nobles for better-behaved monsters. The man in the street was still down-trodden, disenfranchised, and disregarded. He was also—if not off the street much after sundown—eaten. The common folk found this tolerable.

The *Ministerium* met in the same great room where they had first been introduced to Horst Cabal, although none of the lords were present. They had little interest in the political minutiae of the land, and were happy to absent themselves. The table did have one notable addition, however; at its head sat a veiled woman in a dress the colour of poppies on a war memorial. The others, even the avowedly republican Mr Burton Collingwood, referred to her as 'your majesty'. She spoke little as they discussed policy and preparations for the re-creation of Mirkarvia into a land of shadow and base for expansion. This suited the men there present perfectly, not only because it meant that they could get on with the manly business of applying power, but because this woman, the Red Queen, frightened them, and they were not used to being frightened.

On the rare occasions when she did speak, her voice was a whisper that nonetheless silenced the company. There was something ophidian about it, which made them fear what lay behind the veil. By their own inquiries (and as wealthy businessmen, they appreciated the importance of reliable information), they had arrived at the same conclusion as Johannes Cabal; that she was almost certainly Lady Orfilia Ninuka. In which case, she had survived a terrible disaster, and who knew at what physical cost? She had once been considered beautiful, but now she veiled her face, and her voice betokened the huskiness of a damaged larynx. It was easy to imagine that Lady Ninuka had died, and the fire that had killed her had birthed this creature, this Red Queen.

She knew all the highways and byways of Mirkarvian politics, certainly. The surviving great families were in thrall to her, for she knew where the bodies were buried, both literally and figuratively, and through the offices of Lady Misericorde had set several of the former striding into the homes of the few recalcitrant families. She knew their secrets, she had the forces of darkness at her beck, and she still had a substantial shock force of Katamenian bandits as her loyal and eager imperial guard. These she had wisely billeted outside Krenz in a small town that was suffering badly under such a toxic privilege. She also had the keys to the Mirkarvian exchequer, and that wealth equalled their fortunes combined. Still, it was insufficient by itself for the future they envisioned and plotted for, and so they were bound together by money and ambition.

The demeanour of the three men suggested tension; they had no idea why the Red Queen had so abruptly and imperiously demanded a meeting, and both the suddenness and high-handedness of it had put them on edge. Despite being very nearly positive that they knew her true identity, that thin ribbon of doubt chafed. It is in human nature to expect the unlikely to be true, to build castles in Spain on the strength of a lottery ticket, and so they all harboured a tiny niggling suspicion that she was in reality some unknown quantity, and therefore unpredictable and potentially that much more dangerous. Human nature and human foolishness, for if they had delved beneath the 'poor little rich girl' patina of Orfilia Ninuka as presented in their reports, they would have appreciated that the only way that she could have been more dangerous would have been to have had nitroglycerine for blood, had sticks of dynamite for bones, and been fond of hopscotch.

Still, she was a lady, and they were gentlemen, so they rose when she entered the chamber, the more old-worldly of them offering at least a nod in deference as she took her place, and then sat. There was a silence of a minute or so while the servants filled wine glasses for the men, although not for her crimson majesty, of course—the veil mitigating against it.

'So,' said de Osma, as the pause threatened to become indecent. 'Why did you call this meeting, your majesty?'

The figure in red did not reply immediately, nor even move for a long moment. The stillness was unnerving in itself. Then she said, 'We have come to a pivotal moment in the campaign, gentlemen. We decided that this was some grounds for celebration.'

De Osma frowned. 'What pivotal moment? We . . . or at least, I was not aware of any new part of the plans to be put into operation this day.'

'Not everything is in our hands, Vizconde,' she said. Her voice was thin, barely more than a whisper, but it travelled well in that stone-walled room. 'Certain events must occur before we may proceed.'

'Certain events?' said Mr Burton Collingwood. He sipped from his goblet while he thought, then added, 'Have you been holding out on us, ma'am? I'm with de Osma on this; I didn't know of anything that we had to wait for.'

'True, Mr Collingwood, but our plans are subject to a form of astrology. If certain bodies are in certain places, then it is propitious. We are in receipt of intelligence that indicates that today is such a propitious day.' She said nothing for a moment, but despite the veil, there was a sense of great satisfaction, and that behind the veil, she was smiling. 'Cabal is here.'

'Here?' said von Ziegler, growing pale. 'Here in the castle?'

'Mr Cabal was nothing but a disappointment,' said Collingwood. 'I thought he had scooted, and good riddance.'

'No,' whispered the Red Queen. 'Not Horst. *Johannes* Cabal is in Mirkarvia.'

The three men looked at one another. De Osma spoke for them all when he said, 'Who?'

'The sponsor of our feast. Without him, Mirkarvia would not be the place it is today. We owe him so very much.'

De Osma glanced once again around the faces of his colleagues, but received nothing but blank looks, and slight shakes of the head. 'This . . . *Johannes* Cabal . . . he is an ally, then?'

'He is a necromancer.'

'We already have a necromancer, though. Do we need another?'

The Red Queen made a stifled noise that could as easily have been a laugh as a sob. 'We do not. My Lady Misericorde is all the necromancer we need.'

'Then . . .' De Osma looked at the others and shrugged, nonplussed.

'You may consider him superfluous to your concerns, gentlemen. You are primarily here to mark another important phase in our great undertaking. Specifically, that our financial advisors inform us that the monies that you promised are finally all in place and accounted for.'

Collingwood grunted impatiently. 'Are you serious, ma'am? You're cracking open a bottle because our cheques cleared?'

'Not at all,' she said. There was an amusement in her whispers that was icy enough to chill the air. 'We feel that what this signifies is, however, worthy of some celebration.'

'Which is . . . ?' said Collingwood, a little weary at the queen's circumlocutions.

'None of you could transfer capital directly for reasons of legality and discretion,' she said. 'All of you had to enact certain financial instruments to leak considerable monies to Mirkarvia.'

'Yes,' said de Osma slowly. 'We discussed all this months ago.'

'And now these instruments are active, and the flow of money is unhindered,' continued the queen.

'At *our* discretion,' said Collingwood firmly. 'We're not charities, ma'am, we are businessmen. No donations. Only investments.'

To punctuate his point, he crossed his arms, adopted an adamant expression, and fell unconscious. The servant behind his chair caught him before he could fall forward.

'My God! Collingwood!' cried von Ziegler, but his concern rapidly circled back onto his own affairs when he discovered he couldn't stand. De Osma wasn't even capable of that much effort. His eyes rolled up in his head and he slumped forward onto the table, knocking over his goblet. Where the last of the wine fell, an acute eye might have made out flat crystals among the dregs, quite different from the common potassium tartrate crystals amid which they nestled.

'Finally,' said the Red Queen as de Osma slumped insensibly back into his seat. 'We thought you were never going to succumb.'

'What . . .' Graf von Ziegler was the last of the *Ministerium* to remain conscious, having barely touched his wine beyond a sip to ascertain that he still didn't like Mirkarvian vintages. 'What have you done?'

'Ah, von Ziegler. We are so pleased that you are still with us. We particularly dislike you, and would wish you to be aware of what is to happen now.'

He squinted at her through tearing eyes. 'What have you done?' he mumbled.

'We have secured your fortunes. In creating the financial instruments we described, you have left your finances vulnerable. We have signatures, names, and the access numbers of Swiss bank accounts. Your various administrators have been habituated once to large outgoings; they will not cavil as we take all your wealth for Mirkarvia. It is a worthwhile goal, is it not?'

'No . . . no . . .' With an effort, von Ziegler summoned up some gall. 'You bitch. It won't work. Questions . . . there will be questions. You can't get rid of us . . . you *need* us.'

'We *needed* you,' corrected the Red Queen. 'And should it be necessary for one or another of you to personally explain why you are transferring so much money, you will do so. More correctly, you will appear to do so.' She signalled to the servants. One went to the double doors and opened them. With difficulty, von Ziegler turned to look. He gaped. The things waiting outside were humanoid, but could hardly be considered human. Doughy, unfinished, bland figures of flowing flesh and eyeless faces.

'My Lord Alsager's search for shapechangers produced some interesting examples,' said the Red Queen. 'You are familiar with the idea of doppelgängers?'

Von Ziegler croaked fearfully in the back of his throat. The figures moved into the room. There were three of them.

'Alsager tells us the legend is flawed. He says such as these should more accurately be called "shape-eaters".'

The figures moved to either side of the table until one stood behind each of the chairs occupied by the *Ministerium* members. Von Ziegler tried to rise, but a misshapen hand like that of a waxwork left in the sun slammed down on his wrist, holding him in his chair. He mewled in terror. 'Please . . . please, your majesty . . .'

'The *Ministerium Tenebrae* was always larger than you three, but you were not brought here as its representatives because of your ability. In your cases it was always because you were the richest. That you confused wealth for worth is now the least of your problems.'

Von Ziegler was weeping.

'Do not fear. You do not die alone, and you will live on, at least in appearance.'

Across the table, the creature leaned down towards de Osma's head as he lay slumped and insensible. The creature's mouth opened and opened and opened.

Von Ziegler tried to scream, but all that came out was a whimper. Then he saw the Red Queen reach up to her veil, and lift it that she might watch the proceedings more clearly. He saw her face, and even the whimper died away in his throat. He barely felt the doppelgänger's hands grip his head to hold it steady, or the drip of its salivating mouth upon his pate.

His last sight was of that face. That accursed face. And, when he saw it, he finally—if briefly—understood the depth of her evil.

Not so very far away, Johannes Cabal stirred discomforted in his sleep, a reaction analogous to that of a bacterium upon the stage of a microscope, monitored by another consciousness yet not entirely alive to it. He turned over and fell into a deeper sleep, sliding away from the layer of dream, which was likely just as well. Even dreams were no safe territory for him these days.

He awoke properly an hour before dawn and sought out Horst. He knew his brother's moods and knew that he would not stay away from others for too long. *He* was not the loner; that was the role of Johannes. He found Horst sitting on the edge of one of the entomopter transporters, swinging his legs and looking miserable.

'Buck up,' said Johannes Cabal. 'You're already dead. What else could happen?'

'When you're around, plenty.' His brother managed a smile. 'Sorry for going off like that. I just hadn't thought . . .' He stopped, unable to define such an alien concept.

'You hadn't thought it couldn't all be about you. I sympathise.'

'No, you don't.'

'Not for a second. Still, I appreciate it must be a shock to the system. When was the last time such a dreadfully unnatural event occurred?'

'More unnatural than becoming a vampire?'

Cabal grimaced. 'That process is entirely natural, just poorly understood. No, the heavens shake and the gears of the great engines of creation shudder and protest when Horst Cabal isn't the centre of attention. I understand there's going to be a symposium on the subject.'

The two brothers looked at one another for several seconds. Then, remarkably, they both smiled.

'You're right about the natural order of things being upset, Johannes,' said Horst. 'I'm finding myself liking you.'

'The end days are upon us.'

Horst looked down at his shoes. His smile faded. 'Still can't quite believe they'd go to all this trouble just to drag you into play.'

'By "trouble", I presume you refer to your own resurrection? It surprises me a little, too. That is no minor cantrip. Presumably the formula must have been happened upon during their researches and they saw an opportunity. That you were specifically chosen, however, is either enormously petty or worryingly cunning. I suspect both motivations were in play.'

'You must have made an impression on her.'

'I did. I simply did not realise how great an impression.' Cabal affected nonchalance. 'Not an experience unknown to you, I think.'

Horst laughed. 'Some hard looks, harsh words. Once was visited by a couple of really scary brothers.' He paused, and reconsidered his words. 'Not scary like us. Not a vampire and a necromancer.' He raised a level hand above his head height. '"Big" sort of scary. Anyway. None of them ever resurrected someone for the sole purpose of luring me to my death, though. That's . . . special.'

'I always was the special one.'

Horst did not argue with this. 'Do you have a plan?'

'I have two. The first is to infiltrate Harslaus, then locate and dispose of both Maleficarus and this "Red Queen" character, plus anyone else who looks like they need disposing of. That, however, was before I discovered that the Red Queen is probably the Lady Ninuka. She knows me personally and will likely have researched my background closely.'

'She knew about me,' agreed Horst. 'Damn it, Johannes, she even knew where to find me.'

'By divination, but practitioners good enough to be worth house space are few and far between, and their services are difficult to secure. Here we see the strange occult power of money at work once again.' He looked in the approximate direction of Krenz. 'I wonder if she intends to kill her backers once she has what she needs. She doesn't want their opinions, just their money. I digress. The second plan, which I have formulated in the last three minutes, is to launch an immediate attack on Harslaus Castle at the earliest possible opportunity with the express intention of drawing out their forces and destroying them in the field. Meanwhile, a small group of determined volunteers will infiltrate the castle to . . . Well, very much as the first plan, actually. All that disposal business.'

Horst blew out a breath. 'If you mean "us" by "determined volunteers", please say so, Johannes.'

'I certainly meant me. I don't want that bunch of half-wits from the freelance asylums they call "secret societies" running around, burning valuable papers in the name of their God, or their morals, or something else equally nebulous. If you'd like to accompany me, that would be nice.' He said *nice* as if it were a new concept to him and he found the word interesting and exotic.

Horst nodded. 'Fine. Count me in. The two of us.'

'The three of us,' said a voice from beneath them, causing even Horst to jump slightly. Alisha Bartos climbed out from beneath the flatbed and stood before them, fixing them with a steady stare as she brushed her hands off on her knees.

'You were spying on us!' said Horst in slightly amused outrage.

'Of course she was,' said Cabal, settling once more into his swamp of general misanthropy. 'She's a professional spy.'

'An ex-spy,' she said.

'Oh, don't bore me,' said Cabal. 'There's no "ex" about it, apart from the shift in your loyalties away from the Prussians. The Dee Society is no more a ragamuffin collection of concerned individuals facing down the unknown than I am a respected pillar of the community. The Dee Society has been a deniable asset of the

British security service under its myriad names since the days of Walsingham, and do not insult me by pretending otherwise.'

Alisha's smirk vanished like hope after an election, but she did not deny the accusation.

Horst did not know whether to be outraged or delighted, so settled for both. 'Oh! All your stuff about government contacts who could help . . . No wonder. Oh, that's rich. I think I like that.'

'Very well,' said Cabal. 'It would not make sense for the infiltration to consist of more than three, and it would be as well if those three have at least some knowledge of the castle.'

Horst looked at Cabal, eyebrows raised. 'No argument, Johannes? You're just going to say "yes" just like that?'

'Of course. A solo infiltration would provide no flexibility, you and I would have better odds, but still be limited, whereas having Fräulein Bartos along means that you can act as a scout using your . . . unusual capabilities, she will act as my bodyguard . . .' Alisha looked askance at this, but still kept her silence. 'And I shall direct the operation *in situ*.'

'You're not my boss,' said Alisha Bartos.

'While we're in that castle,' said Johannes Cabal, leaning forward to look her in the eyes, 'yes, I am.'

Chapter 16

IN WHICH A PRIEST IS DISMAYED AND BATTLE IS JOINED

'Three of you,' said Melkorka 'Korka' Olvirdóttir. 'Three of you to go into the enemy stronghold and decapitate their leadership.'

This was a less formal council of war, drawn up over a pre-dawn breakfast. The faction leaders were there, as were several other assorted lieutenants and adjutants. They chewed bacon, spooned porridge, and listened.

'I wasn't planning on decapitation exactly,' said Johannes Cabal, 'but if that's what it takes to put Maleficarus down and keep him down, I'm all for it.'

Korka looked at him stonily.

'I think Miss Olvirdóttir was speaking figuratively,' said the professor.

'Doesn't stop it being a good idea,' said Cabal.

'And while you are doing this we shall be dying outside,' said Atropos of the Sisters. 'I do not like this plan.'

'You dying is not actually a necessary part of the plan,' said Horst. 'You should avoid it if you can. The thing is, sooner or later the *Ministerium*'s forces will have to be faced. Now, even if they lose and are destroyed to the last werewolf and zombie, there are still the means to create more. Inside the castle are the people with those means. If the battle starts to turn against them, we can't expect them just to sit there politely and wait for us to get to them.'

'They will not escape,' said Atropos.

'Ah, Ma'amselle Straka, I do not share your optimism,' said Palomer, the inquisitor. 'The castle is large and ancient, its perimeter vast. We have good numbers gathered, but we cannot fight their army in the field and still have enough in reserve to surround Harslaus. Even if we did, there will be hidden ways out of the castle, and perhaps this "Lord of Powers" of theirs has magical methods of escape ready, too. I like this scheme of theirs.' He smiled at them. Specifically he smiled at Alisha. 'Sometimes a knife in the back is better than a thousand rifles on the battleground. They get my vote providing one detail can be explained to me. The timing of the assault.'

'The day, or the time?' asked Cabal.

'Both. Today, an hour before dusk. That is a lot to organise in a few hours, and just before dusk is not so very advantageous to us, hmmm?'

'It's true,' said Melkorka of the Hecatians. 'We should attack at dawn. The light of day is our ally.'

'Fascinating,' said Cabal, picking a disreputable piece of bacon from his sandwich and casting it aside. It was hard to tell whether the offending morsel or Melkorka's statement was the subject of the comment. 'You're all used to fighting monsters, lycanthropes, ghouls . . .'

'Necromancers . . .'

'Thank you, Horst. You're all used to fighting creatures that are inimical to daylight, and so your attraction to using it without further thought has become calcified. But consider. The *Ministerium*'s main force consists of zombies, which do not care especially what o'clock it is. Their primary support the last two outings have been non-terrestrial creatures that seem unconcerned by daylight, too. Even the majority of their shapechangers, apart from a few of the werewolves, can change as and when they desire, full moon or no. We, on the other hand, have the only vampire in play unless they've shown remarkable vigour in acquiring one of their home-grown *nosferatu*. This seems unlikely to me, not least because *nosferatu* are ugly in form, mind, and manner, and will probably attack rather than reason with whoever has to raise them from the dust. This in contrast to my brother, whose first demand on resurrection was . . .' He gestured to Horst.

'Trousers,' said Horst.

'Trousers. So, I feel sure we have the only vampire and, for all his undoubted blessings, he labours under one major disadvantage. Daylight. He is our ace in the hole, but we are limited in when he can be used. Thus, your attack is scheduled for one hour before dusk. When the enemy are fully engaged, then Horst will awaken, and he, Fräulein Bartos, and I shall infiltrate the fortress. Therein, we shall perform the necessary *decapitation* of the *Ministerium*. I, for one, am looking forward to it.'

'He's cold,' said Palomer to Straka. 'I like that.' She did not reply, but nor did she manifest her usual show of repugnance for the Yellow Inquisitor, so that passed for agreement.

'Strategically, the aim is to destroy the *Ministerium Tenebrae* in one night. How that will be achieved tactically is what we shall discuss now. I have,' said Cabal impressively, 'a flip chart.'

'Dawn's coming,' said Horst brightly. 'I had best be off to bed. Good luck with the planning, everyone!' He vanished before anyone could even reply.

Plans were laid. As the sky lightened, the train was already preparing to move, and operatives were spreading out across the countryside. Time was short, and there was so very much to do.

It took some gentle persuasion that actually *was* gentle persuasion and not a euphemism for horrible torture, but Henri Palomer managed to find Father Hornung of the church of St Francis in Halderberg, a small town some twenty miles from Krenz. He was not the only agent there; both Johannes Cabal and 'Korka' Olvirdóttir were also in town on errands of their own.

Palomer, however, was a Catholic born and bred, and even if the Vatican had decided that it could, and indeed should, do without the services of the Yellow Inquisition, he would not, and indeed could not, live without Mother Church. So, he sought out the father in humility and respect.

That he had to seek him out at all rather than just walking into the church was a demonstration of how the state of Mirkarvia was in transition from a nominal monarchy (but in reality a military oligarchy) into its interesting new form as a teratarchy, to use the exciting new term coined by Professor Stone. The new ruling class did not care much for churches and the like, places where the wrong god or gods were worshipped. When things had stabilised a little more and the Mirkarvian bureaucracy had adjusted to its new form, then the churches, synagogues, and the handful of temples and mosques to be found within its boundaries would be closed and, where necessary, deconsecrated. As it was, a rigorously enforced 'worship tax' was already in place, causing the closure of all but the most well-attended. The survivors served both to swell the Mirkarvian coffers while concentrating the more devout botherers of God into a few well-defined locations for ease of persecution.

Even while Palomer bemoaned such wickedness, Cabal could not help but enjoy the irony of major organised religions suffering a degree of the troubles they had visited so vigorously on others down the centuries. He had joined Palomer after securing a few minor requisites of his own, and now they sat on pew ends about the northern aisle of the church. This particular church was not open to worshippers by mandate of the Red Queen, and the priest had suffered visits from servants of the state to remind him of this. That these servants spoke with Katamenian accents and had emphasised their points with blows was no surprise in these difficult times.

'These are perilous times for followers of the faith,' said Father Hornung. He looked harried and tired, unshaved for at least a day, and a cut on his cheek still healing from the last time he'd been reminded that Mirkarvia's state religion was no longer Christianity or any of its near relations.

'Which faith is that?' asked Cabal. He looked around, affecting to have only just noticed the seven-hundred-year-old building in which he was sitting. 'Oh, *that* one. Pardon my interruption. Please, carry on.'

Hornung gave Cabal a hard look.

'Do not mind him,' said Palomer. 'He cannot help it.'

Hornung leaned close and whispered, 'Apostate?'

Palomer smiled and shook his head. 'Necromancer.'

Hornung was thunderstruck. 'Here? In the house of God? Impossible!'

'If you're going to have a whispered conversation,' said Cabal, 'you might do better than to hold it in a building with such excellent acoustics. Yes, Father, I am a necromancer. Yes, I am on consecrated ground but haven't burst into flames as you so clearly believe I should. Consider this: if you are wrong on a detail such as that, upon what else may you be mistaken?'

Cabal was, of course, being entirely disingenuous. Necromancers as a rule *do* catch fire on consecrated ground as an effect of being divested of their souls. Not all necromancers follow such a path, but most take the plunge in the early stages of their career. Johannes Cabal had done exactly that himself and, as a result, been forced to dance hotfoot across several stretches of church land in his time. Unlike most necromancers who make such a sacrifice, however, Cabal's interests in necromancy were analytical and not simply confined to littering the world with zombies and animated skeletons, the usual highly limited domain of the popular necromancer, which is to say, the highly *un*popular necromancer. To him, the lack of a soul had become a burden. Alas, not in any metaphysical or poetical sense, but simply because it was a nuisance and caused perturbations in his experiments. Thus, he had gone to some little trouble to recover it.

This he did not trouble to tell Father Hornung, both because it would have indicated that Hornung's belief in the ungodliness of necromancers was not entirely unfounded and also because the mechanism by which Cabal had recovered his own soul involved dealings with Satan himself and the offhand dooming of a lot of incidental *hoi polloi* to eternal damnation in the fiery pits of Hell. Cabal thought that this latter point would just have led to a lot of tedious moralising by the priest, so he kept it to himself.

Despite such a rhetorical nicety on the part of Cabal, however, Father Hornung did not instantly warm to him. Instead he pointedly ignored Cabal and spoke to Palomer as if there were no one else present.

'I have asked for instructions from the cardinal, but he no longer replies,' said Hornung. 'At first I thought the post was disrupted, just like everything else is in Mirkarvia these days, but now I hear Cardinal Etter was arrested. Nobody knows where he is. The Vatican has *demanded* the government explain its actions.'

Cabal's derisive snort echoed around the pillars and plaster saints. 'Sorry,' he said. 'I just found what you said enormously amusing. Don't mind me.'

Father Hornung paled beneath his stubble. 'You find the Vatican amusing, sir?'

'Oh, yes,' said Cabal. 'Very much so. Verging on hilarious at times.'

'*This* is the kind of man that your order is allying itself with?' Hornung demanded of Palomer. 'You're dining with a devil.'

'I have a *very* long spoon, Father,' said Palomer, measuring out a length of air between his index fingers to indicate a spoon of remarkable length.

Suddenly there was a crash from the roof almost overhead. Something dark flashed down by the window. Father Hornung leapt to his feet.

'The devils! They've come!'

'No, no, Father,' said Cabal in a tone that, if intended as soothing, only succeeded in seeming a little arch. 'That's our associate.'

The face of Korka Olvirdóttir smiled engagingly through a hole that had freshly appeared in the plaster of the roof. 'Sorry!' she called down. 'It got away from me.'

'How long until you're done?' asked Cabal.

'Soon. Already got most of what we'll need. Another ten minutes?'

'Thank you,' said Cabal.

'Who is that woman?' demanded the priest, pointing at the hole with a trembling finger. 'What is she doing up there?'

'Lead,' explained Cabal. 'We need some lead. Not very much. No more than a hundredweight, I should think. You've got tons of it up there, you'll never even notice that little bit's gone.' He looked at the hole and considered. 'Except when it rains.'

'How dare you!' Father Hornung looked like he might be moved to violence. 'How dare you defile this church without . . .'

Cabal rose to look the priest in the eye. 'As you seem to be under the impression that the Red Queen is just going to go away if you complain enough, let me disabuse you of that notion. She is not. To the contrary, she will consolidate her grip on this country, and she will expunge all religions except the dark ones in which she is currently comparison shopping.'

'You can't possibly know . . .'

'She is Lady Orfilia Ninuka, daughter of the late Count Marechal.'

The animosity left the priest's face in a moment, replaced by astonishment. 'The count's daughter? Didn't she die?'

'Alas, no.'

'But . . . No, you're mistaken. She cannot be the Red Queen. The Lady Ninuka was . . . *is* just a bit flighty.'

'No,' said Cabal. 'She's a sociopath with nothing to lose, who is also a bit flighty. We need the lead to stop her. Should we fail, you won't have a church within the space of a year. The forces she is bringing to Mirkarvia will not tolerate churches.' He perceived the unspoken question in Hornung's mind. 'Yes, those are exactly the forces I am talking about. Now, given the alternative, isn't that worth a few damp pews?'

Hornung seemed to make up his mind. 'I can get a tarpaulin to cover the hole.'

Cabal smiled, or at least he flexed his face in such a way that the corners of his mouth rose. 'Splendid. Pragmatism suits you, Father Hornung. Now, while you're in a cooperative mood, I have a tiny little request to make of you.'

'What?' said Hornung. He darted a glance at Palomer, who only shrugged. 'You want more? Such as?'

'Well, in the first instance, do you know where we might lay hands on several large barrels?'

'Barrels?'

Cabal nodded. 'Oh, and a carpenter. And a hearse.'

The attack came from the west. As the sentries on the ramparts of Harslaus Castle squinted into the setting sun, a force numbering a few hundred appeared around the bend in the river and advanced in skirmishing order on the fortress.

It didn't look much like a military operation, and that was entirely deliberate. Careful planning was to be found in the apparent disarray, meant to suggest yet another minor demonstration of the locals' anger at their new overlords. The common folk of Mirkarvia were used to tyrants, and took it as part of the social contract that they were permitted to mass and shout and string up a couple of magistrates, just so long as they then ran away into the night and settled themselves, ready to be downtrodden some more as and when the authorities found a gap in their appointments.

Their new masters, however, were of a different ilk altogether, and the Mirkarvian people—traditionalists all—weren't about to settle for all this newfangled 'republic of occult evils' nonsense without making their feelings felt. This was done every week or two on average, and had settled down into a routine that began with splendid indifference from the muck-mucks in the castle, and finished with a spirited game of 'Eat the Dissident' involving were-wolves. The Mirkarvian people, long inured to vigorous relations with their ruling class, sensed a tradition forming, and were begin-ning to think that perhaps the new regime were going to be okay after all.

This developing harmony between the suppressed and the sup-pressors was monitored and quantified by the militaristic minds of the Templars—a contingent of whom had belatedly arrived, the 'Great Evil' rising from the sands of North Africa having been discovered to be terribly evil, but not so very great—and so they were able to predict that the attack date that had been forced upon them was not such a bad one, as it fell quite neatly upon the sweet spot when the castle authorities would be expecting some trouble from the yokels, yet just before the yokels actually felt quite ag-grieved enough to provide it.

Into this window of unfulfilled expectation entered the com-bined forces of several of the world's more benign secret societies, where 'benign' is left open to a degree of interpretation. By and large they were unused to doing their skulking *en masse* but to their credit had adapted well. The Templars formed their heavy infantry, men (and a few women, for the order no longer cleaved quite so closely to many of the precepts under which the Templars were formed; the first to go had been the business about never shaving and generally keeping a poor toilette, this when it became understood that hairiness is not necessarily next to godliness, and God would prefer to stand upwind if that was all the same to them?) who dealt with the enemies in their manifold holy wars with vigour and certainty, or brutality and cruelty, depending on one's viewpoint.

They were flanked by the lighter skirmishers of the Dee Soci-ety on their right and the Yellow Inquisitors to the left. The Dee Society had already lost many of its best in the failed assault of a month before and, although reinforced by people who absolutely were *not*—perish the thought—mercenaries hired by the British government and detached British intelligence agents of splendid expendability, they were still under strength. Of Yellow Inquisitors, however, there was no shortage. After centuries of quietly doing the work of the Vatican, often to the great surprise of the Vatican, who had long since forgotten there had ever been a Yellow Inquisition, this was their grand chance to face evil personified, and they were much looking forward to sticking a stiletto in its ribs. In an orgy of dead-letter drops and secret handshakes, the Inquisitors had been roused from their secretive lives and they had answered with the cheerful satisfaction of professional torturers and assassins on a busman's holiday.

Backing the Dee Society and the Yellow Inquisition were the witches of the rival cults of Hecate and Medea respectively, carefully kept separate from one another to no complaints from anyone. The Inquisitors had actually asked to have the humourless Sisters at their back, possibly because their businesslike demeanour impressed the Inquisitors, but more likely because the Inquisitors found the tight lips and narrowed eyes of the witches inexpressibly amusing. Unlike the better-known inquisitions, the Yellow had found a sense of humour to make up for losing papal dispensations, and strolled through life as rapscallions and troubadours, songs in their hearts and thumbscrews in their pockets. There was pleasure to be found in the irony of witches, traditionally wanton and lascivious, and inquisitors, equally traditionally sombre and duty bound, swapping their stereotypes. Nor did the Yellow Inquisition mind having witches at their back; they had long since traded in cant and dogma for compromise and pragmatism. They judged by deeds, and the Sisters of Medea had done much good. Some evil here and there, it was true, but nothing on the scale of that which the *Ministerium Tenebrae* threatened.

Equally, the Dee Society were content to have their backs covered by the ever-practical Daughters of Hecate. To them, the great mystery of everything was wound up in their Witch Goddess, a grand dame of the ancient pantheons to whom even Nyarlathotep had been known to bow courteously and hold the door open, and a large part of that mystery could be expressed as 'It's all bigger than you can deal with, so why worry?' Thus, they carried on through life as agents of Hecate, adhering to principles that wavered between 'Do unto others as you would have them do unto you' and 'Do as thou wilt, and that shall be a fair bit of the law'. Managing to reconcile Christianity, Thelema, some woolly Earth Mother beliefs, and the worship of an ancient and unknowable goddess of powers who was also pretty good fun at parties, the Daughters of Hecate could afford to be patient and happy, because no matter who ended up winning the war of creation, it would somehow still be them. In the meantime, they asked themselves daily 'What would Hecate do?' and then went for the most enjoyable option. In their philosophy, 'enjoyable' did not necessarily mean 'safe', which was how a force of them came to be there unto the breach. They might die, but at least they'd do it pissing off the forces of seriousness.

Whenever a Templar happened to look at them, the Daughters of Hecate would grin back. The Templars always broke eye contact first.

That the witches were not in the vanguard was in no way any reflection of their combat worthiness or upon their sex. Rather it was in their forte, which was the remote bringing down of trouble upon the heads of their foes. They were roughly equivalent to the secret little army's artillery, and therefore kept back where they could do the most good without being distracted in close combat.

The castle sentries must have spotted them a good half mile away, but there was no hue and cry, no alarums and excursions. The sentries watched, drinking tea and eating sandwiches. There was no great hurry, after all; such events had the air of an overrehearsed local amateur dramatics performance that had long since lost any likelihood of surprising the audience. Finally somebody realised the coconut fancies had been left in the guardroom so they sent somebody down to fetch them who, in passing, remembered to sound the alert.

There was no longer the slightest intention of sending human soldiers out to deal with this latest *bijou* uprising; the guards instead busied themselves taking bets as to how long the attackers would last before routing. The few who did not gamble or were waiting on payday trailed off to ensure the castle's defences were tight, i.e., the windows were shut. Up on the battlements, they heard an ironic cheer as the newly repaired drawbridge rattled down. This could only mean that the sally was commencing.

In days of yore, this would have consisted of a bunch of knights, squires, and assorted varlets boiling out of a sally port like weevils from a biscuit to disrupt the besieging army, returning smartly before any real resistance could be organised. That was days of yore. Now, the main gate opened, the portcullis rose, and an uninterested horde of zombies staggered out into the early evening. They staggered, and they groaned, and they stuck their arms out in attitudes of deathly menace, but even they in the last dim glimmerings of their intellect were getting bored with this. Usually the irked Mirkarvians thought better of it and ran away at the first sight of the undead. Sometimes, they would actually engage, lose a few people, and *then* think better of it. More rarely still, they would engage, make a decent fist of it, but then the lycanthropes would turn up like the vainglorious windbags they were and steal the glory. One wouldn't have thought there were many fates worse than death, but for the zombies being dead *and* upstaged by a bunch of furry bastards fitted the bill precisely.

.The zombies moved out onto the road on the far side of the river and milled around for a minute, groaning threateningly at one another while they got themselves sorted out. Finally sighting their actual designated victims for the evening's wander, they set off westwards, following the riverbank as they closed on the attackers.

If they had been possessed of a little more tactical sense, they might have wondered why the opposing force was neither advancing nor retreating, but was instead consolidating their line. If the sentries on the battlements had actually been paying much attention, they might have wondered that, too, but they were currently preoccupied with getting their fair share of the coconut fancies.

The undead came on, arms waving, and only appreciated that something was different on this occasion when there was a solitary crack of a pistol going off in the rear of the besiegers and, a moment later, a green parachute flare floated slowly down, twinkling sickly in the dying light of the sun.

The zombies paused, first with confusion, and then to point and coo at this wonder, a small pretty thing in an afterlife less noteworthy than they had been led to believe.

Two miles away on a branch line that was now lucky to see a train a week, Denzil and Dennis stood on the footplate of the locomotive, pointing at the new green star in the sky, and making ghoulish hoots of happiness. Their afterlife was certainly looking more engaging these days. They'd experienced air travel, been given a new train to drive, and now there was a green star to hoot at. This was, indeed, paradise.

Three entomopters lined up on the dirt track running parallel to the track. Miss Virginia Montgomery checked her watch, made an unhappy face, and walked down the row of machines, their engines silent, their pilots standing by them.

'This is a hell of a thing we have got ourselves into,' she had said to them. 'A hell of a thing I have got us into. We've seen what the black hats have got lined up, we know they're playing hardball, we know there's going to be some empty seats tomorrow. You signed up with me as aerial performers. Not as thieves, not as warriors. Sure as hell not as martyrs. I . . .'

'If you're going to say we don't have to go, maybe you should've said it before we stole all these guns, bombs, and ammunition,' said Dea Boom. She nodded sideways to indicate the opened gunports with the tips of muzzle shrouds projecting from them, the gleaming rocket racks, the dull black ten-pounder bombs held below the stubby ordnance wings

'Maybe I should've,' admitted Miss Montgomery. 'But I'm telling you now. Anyone wants to stay, I don't blame you, and I won't hold it against you.'

There was silence.

Then Mink picked up her helmet from within the cockpit and started sorting out the chin strap. 'We done now? I want to blow up zombies.'

Horst awoke in a different place. Reaching around himself, he realised he was encased in some sort of metal box, about the size of a coffin. The air was close, and he was glad that he didn't have to breathe much these days except for a smidgeon for his metabolism, for speech, and for nostalgia, as he held a strong conviction that the box was hermetically sealed. He did not panic, however. He sensed the methodical hand of Johannes at work here and would trust to his brother's planning.

Nor was this trust ill founded. Some fifteen minutes later as he was working on anagrams of 'bored vampire', the upper edge of the box to the right of his head was penetrated by a curved steel blade that, after a moment or two's observation as it rocked back and forth cutting its way through the soft metal of his enclosure, he realised was essentially a large sort of can opener. The metal parted easily, confirming his suspicion that it was lead, and he helped push it open as the blade continued down the length of the box.

Horst sat up to discover he had been travelling in a lead-lined coffin. 'Very swish,' he commented to his brother. Cabal threw down the curved blade, and took up his jacket from where he'd thrown it over the tailgate of a horse-drawn hearse.

'Your definition of *swish* has changed over time, I see,' he said as he shrugged into the jacket.

Horst climbed from the coffin and joined his brother. They were in a gloomy, low-ceilinged vault of some kind. Open stalls ran down either side of the wide and oppressive space. 'Where are we?'

'The stable undercroft of Harslaus Castle. The guards are, as predicted, terrified of those they are nominally guarding.' He took down a black top hat, its crown circumscribed by a long black silk ribbon that trailed over the rear of the rim. He dusted some lint from it absent-mindedly. 'A delivery order signed by Lady Misericorde and countersigned by Vizconde Velasco de Osma was sufficient to cow them.'

Horst looked at the hearse, the top hat, and then Cabal. 'A delivery order?'

'For a three-week-old corpse. "Nice and ripe", as I characterised it to the guards. Required for m'lady's experiments.'

Horst looked at the buckled lining. 'Hence all the lead?'

'Both to discourage careful searches and to protect you from daylight should they decide to open the coffin. An unnecessary precaution as it turns out. A piece of paper with Lady Misericorde's name upon it was sufficient to put the fear of God upon them.' He sniffed. 'I swear, Horst, I've never heard of the woman.'

Horst smiled. No; in truth, he grinned. 'Oh, Johannes. Infamy envy.'

'Certainly not,' snapped Cabal. 'Simply stating a fact.' He made a show of looking around. 'Speaking of women, where has Fräulein Bartos got to? She said she was just going to perform a brief reconnoitre, but that was fifteen minutes ago.'

Horst was delving into the coffin to recover his brother's weapons. These comprised the compact automatic in its shoulder holster, and the Webley .577 in a gun belt supplied by the Dee Society. 'It rather puts a hole into any pretence of being stealthy if you're seen wandering about with a gun at your hip,' he said as he passed them over.

Cabal shrugged into the shoulder holster. 'You're a known enemy, Fräulein Bartos is much the same, and I am an unfamiliar face. I think we can forget about passing ourselves off. At some point the guards who let us in will start to worry if they've done the right thing and inform their superiors. They may already have done so. I think I shall be glad of the extra ammunition that I have brought along.'

He finished strapping on the big military-issue gun belt and was just pulling on his jacket when he became aware of Alisha Bartos at his side. He almost managed to hide a slight jump of surprise. Unhappily, only 'almost', so he had the twin humiliations of jumping and an ineffectual dissembling to live down. He dealt with both in his habitual way: applied testiness.

'If you could spend a little more of your time lurking up on the enemy rather than your allies, madam, perhaps we might stand some small chance of succeeding in this enterprise.' She just looked at him with her head tilted slightly to one side as if he were a competent but bland painting in a gallery. 'Those guards may wonder what happened to us,' he persisted. 'What have you done to find us a route out of here and into the castle proper?'

'They won't be calling anyone. They're dead drunk in the guardroom.'

Cabal looked at her suspiciously. 'Are we talking about the same guards? Katamenian fellows. Disreputable in many ways, but perfectly sober when we came through.'

'Not with a syringeful of scopolamine in a solution of ethyl alcohol delivered via the carotid artery, they're not.'

There was a momentary silence.

'There were three of them.'

'Yes,' agreed Alisha. 'I've only got one syringe left now.'

'I see,' said Cabal. He regarded her as one might a competent but unsettling picture in that same art gallery. 'I see. Very well. And the reconnaissance . . . ?'

'Herman and I mapped as much of the building as we could access. The *Ministerium* and its lords and lady had some areas we could not reach without causing suspicion. Otherwise, most of the castle is known to us.'

'Very efficient,' said Horst. Then to Johannes, 'Isn't she efficient?'

'Shut up,' said Cabal.

Two miles away, a flight of three entomopters took to the sky and headed towards Harslaus Castle, two CI-650 Giaguaros in echelon behind a J-55 Copperhead. Behind them they left a train, two mummified corpses dancing and waving at the rapidly diminishing aircraft, a tired and grim mechanic, and a carriage upon which a sign had once read:

MISS VIRGINIA MONTGOMERY'S
FLYING CIRCUS

Now the last two words had been painted over in white and in the new blankness a single word had taken their place. In a hasty but pleasing hand it read in proud black characters:

WARBIRDS

Chapter 17

IN WHICH FOREWARNED IS FOREARMED

They made their way out of the undercroft. Alisha moved from corner to corner using cover, gun drawn and ready. Horst stayed to the rear, his superhumanly acute senses honed and alert. Johannes Cabal walked in the middle with a poorly concealed air of impatience about him, like a father given charge of a pair of overactive children who had cleared out a sweet jar an hour before.

They encountered no one *en route*. 'They'll be on the battlements, enjoying the show by now,' said Alisha in a whisper as she crept along, pistol held in a two-handed grip.

'All of them?' said Cabal in a normal tone. Alisha narrowed her eyes at him. He was unabashed. 'That seems unlikely.'

Horst appeared at his side in a localised weather condition of stiff breezes, forcing Cabal to straighten his hair. 'Likely or not, there's nobody around. You suspect a trap?'

'I always suspect a trap. That, however, is not my point. They will not all be on the battlements. Life continues for the servants, if no one else. We should be cautious.' Alisha went back to leading the way quite pointedly, unamused by the suggestion that she was anything less than diligent. Cabal was rendered entirely unrepentant by her sharp looks as was his way, long exposure to sharp looks in general having lent him immunity.

'I,' he offered, 'am of the opinion that we should split our force. I can make a couple of decent guesses where you are likely to find the officers of the *Ministerium*, and I can make a damn good guess where Maleficarus is to be found.'

'No,' said Alisha. 'We stick together.'

'That does seem more sensible,' said Horst. 'Isn't being divided a good way to be conquered?'

'In the usual run of things, I would agree,' said Cabal, 'but we have time against us. We can be sure of the defenders' responses to the attack, and we know how they will climax. If it reaches that stage, our allies without shall shortly be fodder.'

'You mean Maleficarus,' said Alisha.

'Indeed so. If we stop him, the *Ministerium* will take the opportunity to rally their forces in a tight defensive shield about themselves, or run. Either way, they will survive the night, and this whole cycle will start again in a few months when they have replaced their losses.

'Alternatively, we exterminate the *Ministerium* . . .'

'That sounds a bit ruthless,' said Horst.

'You could stay outside while Fräulein Bartos and I do what is necessary. By the time we're done, the attacking force will probably already be dead at the tentacles, mandibles, or whatever other excesses Maleficarus's latest recruits happen to be sporting. In short, we need to deal with both Maleficarus *and* the *Ministerium* at one and the same time. Thus, we must split our force.'

'He's right,' said Alisha, very unwillingly.

'So who goes after who?' asked Horst.

'Maleficarus is mine,' said Cabal. 'You will probably find the *Ministerium* in either the hall where you dined the first night, or in the room where you eavesdropped upon them. I shall find Rufus Maleficarus in the most melodramatic location available, because that is the nature of the beast.'

He walked off, leaving Horst and Alisha behind without a second glance.

'So,' said Horst, in the awkward silence that followed. 'That's my brother. What do you think?'

The castle's defenders, which is to say the minimum-wage earners of sufficient amorality not to care greatly that they were working for demonstrably evil people, got their first inkling that all was not well when the 'undisciplined mob of disenfranchised Mirkarvians' (approaching across the very same area of scrubland from which the Dee Society had launched the previous attack on the building) not only failed to be dismayed at the approaching horde of the undead, but instead took positions and stood ready for the counter-assault. Then, at a range of fifty yards, they opened fire. This was no panicked fire of dismayed common folk, but a disciplined and well-placed volley. The castle guard, viewing the action from on high, clearly saw many of the front rank of the zombie horde drop as if their strings had been cut.

'They're shooting for the heads,' said one guard.

'Never mind that,' said the sergeant. 'They're shooting for the heads and *hitting* them. They've got marksmen down there. Where are my bloody field glasses?' Locating his binoculars (they were around his neck), the sergeant set to scanning the ranks of the attackers. 'There's something not right about this lot,' he said. 'There's something a bit . . . *professional* about all this. Hullo . . .' He peered off towards the edges of the common scrubland. 'Who are that lot? There's a bunch of women just standing around . . .'

One of the women was watching the engagement through her own pair of binoculars. She looked up towards the castle, and their gaze met through several sets of lenses and prisms. The sergeant had a faint premonition that this meeting did not bode well. The woman lowered her glasses and looked directly at him. She had a very intense look about her, and she seemed to be mouthing something. The sergeant was just noting that she was a very handsome woman, from somewhere in the eastern Mediterranean he would guess, when his eyes unexpectedly burst into flames. This distressed him, and he staggered around, blood-red fire erupting from the sockets, while he explained the degree of agony he was enduring and how much he would appreciate assistance of an unspecified form from those present. Then his head caught fire and his conversation became very scream orientated.

For their part, the other guardsmen looked on, crying much profanity and incoherent expressions of dismay and consternation. They did not help him, for they did not understand what was happening and they were filled with fear.

The sergeant fell with a final groan, and they stood and watched him burn down to dust.

Out in the ranks of the attackers, there was some dissent. Henri Palomer had made his way back to remonstrate with Atropos Straka of the Medeans.

'Ma'amselle Straka . . .' he said, a scoped rifle slung beneath his arm.

'Ms . . .' growled Ms Straka.

'Ms Straka, you have tipped our hand.' He gestured at the battlements. 'Now they know we are not just angry locals.'

'I think they were well on their way to seeing that when you started mowing down their zombies.'

'Ah, but that was a suspicion. Now it is a certainty. Why did you feel you had to break from the plan anyway?'

She nodded castle-wards. 'He was looking at me.'

Palomer set his jaw askew while he absorbed this. '*I* am looking at you,' he said, not unreasonably. There was a long moment during which they looked at one another. On this occasion, Ms Straka did not invoke the powers of Hades to immolate her observer, which was nice.

Palomer sighed. '*Alors*,' he said heavily, and returned to his place in the line.

* * *

In a window in one of the towers, Lady Misericorde, dressed in a fetching black shift, was joined by Devlin Alsager, dressed in nothing at all, which might also be regarded as fetching depending on one's disposition. She was not required for the deployment of the undead, having shared that responsibility with the captain of the guard. Thus, she had not been called upon when the zombies had been sent out to remonstrate with the attackers. Instead, she had stayed abed with Alsager in one of the more remote guest rooms, and it was from here that she watched her creations being mown down and one of the sergeants burning up.

Alsager stood behind her, his arms encircling her waist, and his desire tactilely very apparent against her bottom. He kissed her neck. 'Come back to bed, my lady. The guards can handle this.'

'Can they?' She smiled slightly, but her eyes were active and intelligent, taking in the activity below. 'I have my doubts.'

Below, another volley crackled out and still more of the zombies stumbled and fell. The muzzle flashes gave her some idea of the attackers' positions in the deepening gloom. There seemed to be three sections she could make out, the centre very defined, the flanks less so. And she could see movement further back still. A reserve, perhaps?

She bumped her hips back coquettishly into him. 'Get changed.'

Alsager frowned. 'For dinner? I didn't hear the gong.'

She turned and, drawing his face down to hers, kissed him deeply and thoroughly. When she broke the kiss, he blinked as if waking unexpectedly from sleep. 'Those shots were your gong,' she whispered, 'and your dinner waits outside the castle walls.'

He blinked stupidly once more and looked out of the window. 'Oh,' he said, comprehension dawning. '*That* sort of changing. You don't really think that rabble is such a great threat, do you?'

'They're not a rabble, and yes, I do.'

Alsager reluctantly let her go and walked, still naked, to the door. He was cut from a thoroughly heroic pattern physically, a model for saturnine bad boys throughout the world of romantic novels, and he knew it. That his heart throbbed with love primarily for himself and his soul was a shrivelled affair was neither here nor there. He looked wonderful and was prone to wandering the corridors of Harslaus in tight breeches, riding boots, and an open frilly shirt to prove it. Going naked was no great step from that. In any case, he would soon be suited in fur. Indeed, already his lupine nature was expressing in the lineaments of his face, and the hairiness of his buttocks above which the nub of a burgeoning tail was forming.

He paused at the door. Misericorde was standing by the window, her arms cradled across her stomach, hands to elbows, as she watched the developing battle. 'You're not how I imagined a necromancer to be,' he said. The words sounded rough and improperly fashioned, the fault of his palate extending and his larynx deforming.

She didn't trouble to look at him. 'Good.'

Alsager sensed an ineffable dismissal and, further, felt it wisest to comply. He left her, a dark form silhouetted against a dark sky.

The undead were not faring well. The usual sense of *ennui* at being sent out to do battle was becoming tempered with a new and distinct feeling that they had not previously experienced. It was a slow realisation, making its way through slow mental processes mired in decay and maggots, but the penny was very gently dropping that perhaps they were losing this one.

This hardly concerned them tactically; they had been given orders and it was beyond their ability to do aught but obey. Nor were they subject to such living frailties as failing morale. They were already dead. Further deadness was not something that bothered them unduly. There was, however, the remnants of the very human instinct towards curiosity, and they wondered in a nebulous sort of way how it was that their numbers were thinning so distinctly. Even deceased, the human mind searches for patterns and repetitions, and is sensitive to breaks in a sequence, to holes in the tapestry.

Then, usually, such strange and tenuous ghost trains of thought were smartly brought to the buffers by a bullet travelling through the brainpan of the philosophical zombie, and that was that. Of the survivors, there was a distant inkling of something about running away from danger. It was an interesting thought, and they considered it with cobwebbed ratiocinations as they continued on to the guns of the attackers.

Professor Stone watched them coming on, gauged their rate of attrition, and found it while impressive, insufficient. 'They'll be on us in a minute,' he said to one of the reinforcements London had sent.

The man paused to reload, thumbing rounds into his Winchester rifle. 'Should we give ground, Professor?' he asked. He seemed very cool and resolute under pressure, the professor noted. One of the skilled and experienced reservist combatants the Society's shadowy sponsors in Whitehall kept on call, no doubt.

'Not just yet. With any luck, we won't have to.'

Behind them, over the rattle of disciplined fire into the zombie ranks, a distant drone sounded. As it grew louder, the image it brought to mind was the largest, angriest dragonfly imaginable, something from the ancient days before dinosaurs were dinosaurs and not being aquatic still had novelty value. Soon, minor tonal variants in the droning gave the impression to the acute ear that perhaps there was more than one colossal, angry dragonfly on its way from the late Carboniferous period, and it might be an idea to hide.

Despite knowing the origin of the sound, and knowing it was allied to their cause, the attackers still hunched slightly as the drone became a roar. The zombies, showing the polite interest of a politician at a primary school, raised their heads to look into the glowing horizon.

What they saw there did not illuminate their ignorance at all. Three black spots against an Egyptian blue sky that grew and diverged slightly as they did so. Then suddenly the black spots resolved into entomopters and flew directly overhead. Several of the zombies tried to track them by looking up so keenly that they fell over, as boggled as any troupe of penguins overflown by an aircraft. The zombie advance halted in confusion and slapstick as the following ranks tripped over the freshly fallen or were knocked down like skittles.

From her high window, Lady Misericorde rolled her eyes with exasperation and went off to recover her dress from the chamber floor.

On every fuselage, navigation lights flared. While it might possibly make them a little easier to shoot down, that was better than colliding with another entomopter in the gathering dark. Miss Montgomery's Warbirds crisscrossed the sky over the zombies' heads, causing about as much dismay among their ranks as they had ever encountered post-mortem. Few people had much experience of being buzzed by low-flying aircraft, and the zombies had none. They were at a loss. Some wandered off in random directions, others waved wasted limbs in anger at their roaring tormentors, and many just fell over. The army of the dead that had left the castle now looked like an ill-starred attempt at the record for the world's largest rugby scrum. As in confusion they rolled around, one of the entomopters, *Striking Dragon*, performed a stall turn and headed directly for them.

But while the *Striking Dragon*, piloted by the redoubtable Mink Choi, bears down upon the horde, we have time for a short and illuminating digression.

There are several methods of imperfect resurrection, the poor bastardised ways of raising the dead with which Johannes Cabal held no truck. While he searched for the path by which the dead can be brought back to life perfect in body, mind, and soul, most if not all other necromancers contented themselves with ways by which the dead can be put back on their feet to do simple, repetitive tasks. Working on plantations, mobbing the houses of critics, or making unsolicited telephone calls to sell patios and double glazing, these were all examples to which necromancers of greater or lesser vindictiveness and commercial acumen had set their creations. Such resurrections were comparatively simple, but—as alluded to previously—there is more than one way to skin a cat and then bring it back to life, should one be so disposed.

Firstly, there was the classic Voodoo approach. This hinged on ancient magics from the primordial past, held in the rituals of a thousand generations in Africa, and then diluted unforgivably in the space of a handful of years by, of all things, Roman Catholicism. The rituals and necessities were relatively straightforward, if lengthy in commission, and, at the end of it all, one was the proud possessor of a quiet, diligent, albeit unimaginative and inflexible servant. There was the detail about never allowing the zombie to taste salt or it would realise it was dead and wander off in a huff before returning to the soil. Still, that was a small detail and easily attended to through a long needle, strong thread, and a few minutes spent sewing up the zombie's mouth. Practical, if aesthetically displeasing. Such creatures were rarely dangerous unless directly ordered to be so. Mass resurrections of the sort needed to raise an army were impossible. This, then, Johannes Cabal had concluded, was not the source of Lady Misericorde's powers.

Next we have the corrupted zombie, created by the agency of a parasite that usurps the body's architecture and uses the corpse as a vector by which to spread itself. These undead are, in essence, a virus writ large, subsuming humans to its cause of proliferation in the same way a virus does so with individual cells. No necromancer worth his or her salt—not even the underachieving ones—would stoop to such creations. Firstly, as a matter of pride. Secondly, as a matter of practicality. There is no controlling creatures such as these, no more than one may control a rabid dog.

Next there was, both to Cabal's knowledge and damnable experience, the form of undead raised by the infamous Ereshkigal Working, upon which we have already touched. These were animated by a supernatural force of an atavistic nature, its primary concern being reproduction. Reproduction for zombies is, aesthetically fortunately while practically unhappily, attained by killing. While the ritual keeps the lightest of leashes on the growing mob of undead it creates, this lasts until the caster falls asleep, at which point the leash is slipped, the foolish ritualist is added to his or her own army by being murdered while dreaming, and the horde grows geometrically unless halted using extreme measures.

Interestingly, these latter stages of the Ereshkigal Working are not mentioned in the rare parchments that survive. Most occultists guess that the very intelligence that animates the dead may well be the one that whispered the ritual into the minds of gullible Mesopotamian magicians all those millennia ago and skipped the bit about an inevitable zombie apocalypse following. Misericorde, however, had undoubtedly slept many times since creating her rotting regiment and had never once lost control. She, at least, had the sense to leave the Ereshkigal Working well alone.

The next category was a narrow and unusual one—machine zombies. Cabal had encountered their like precisely once and was not keen to repeat the experience. These poor wretches were a combination of flesh and metal, the former enforced and directed by the latter, and the spark of life kept burning through the agency of electricity. They were, however, very easy to identify thanks to all the metal bits melding into the flesh on limbs and head. This, he had been assured by those with direct experience of Misericorde's corps of cadavers, was certainly not the case here.

Thus, by a steady process of deduction, Cabal had arrived at the only remaining method by which he believed his counterpart within the *Ministerium* could have made her army.

In any event, Cabal was certain that Lady Misericorde had turned to good, old-school diabolism, her wonder to perform. She had contacted a demon—probably the long-suffering Lucifuge Rofocale*—sold her soul, and gained powers thereby. This was an

---

* Here, Cabal was wrong. The actual demon who was summoned was one Ragtag Slyboots. The negotiations for Lady Misericorde's boon had gone

eminently understandable route to take if one sought only direct influence by the technique of setting zombies on anyone who presented difficulties. In research terms it was an occult-de-sac, to coin a phrase, long since explored and abandoned by Cabal.

Still, he had an understanding of what faced the—for want of a better term, taking in secret societies, assassins, a necromancer, and a vampire—'good guys' far beyond that of the average man on the Clapham omnibus, who would be dismayed by zombies but fail to observe them analytically as they made their way up the spiral stairs to the top deck of the omnibus. Very dismayed.

This was the state of knowledge upon which plans had been enacted.

Just as the *Striking Dragon* was about to overfly the zombies, there was a metallic *clink* audible even over the sound of the engine and the wings, and a cloud started to form in the entomopter's wake. It was light and misty, and was whirled easily into complex curlicues by the turbulence of the aircraft's passage. Thence, it settled in a wide bloom, a ghostly ribbon that hung over the zombies until, with another *clink*, the ribbon was cut. That which had been laid fell slowly upon the creatures below, and so soft and fine was it, none of them noticed it. Not, at least, until it reached them. Then they certainly noticed it, yes, indeed.

For where it touched bare dead skin, each tiny droplet took offence at the devlish nature of these particular examples of the walking dead, and manifested that offence by burning with a bright blue ghostly flame of outraged purity. One tiny mote created one flare of azure about the size of a freshly struck match, and every zombie was hit with hundreds or thousands.

---

much along expected lines until the name 'Johannes Cabal' had come up as a potential enemy. Ragtag had peremptorily torn up the agreement they had just signed and told her that her soul was hers to enjoy for eternity, and that she might have the power she sought *gratis*, a freebie from the Pit. Thus, Cabal's penchant for making enemies in low places came back to torment him. It was hardly the first time.

With a great cry and a roar of supernatural combustion, Lady Misericorde's army burst into flames.

They staggered around, more so than usual, and when they staggered into one another, the flames combined and were magnified. Where there were stragglers, *Striking Dragon* sought them out and struck them down. Every pass laid down more clouds, and after every pass the flames grew less as the tainted flesh burned and the spirits of the dead were released to finish their journeys to wherever they were supposed to be going before the uncalled-for interruption of zombification.

At a balcony, Lady Misericorde watched the conflagration with tight lips. By her stood a bear of a man in tweed and an unconscionable beard.

'Holy water,' she muttered. 'How did they know?'

'Johannes Cabal,' said the man.

'Of course. I had hoped they might use more conventional means. More time-consuming means.'

'Cabal is a nuisance and a danger, my lady.'

'Precisely. That's what Her Majesty in Crimson was counting upon. Still . . .' She watched a burning zombie topple into the moat. It continued to burn as it sank, a diminishing blue glow coruscating beneath the surface. 'I doubt she was expecting him to be *quite* this efficient.'

Off to the south, a howl shuddered through the night. Lady Misericorde nodded and allowed herself a small smile. 'Ah, finally. Alsager has got his animals together. Perhaps things will go back onto schedule now.'

Alsager's menagerie of assorted metamorphic human/animals, animals that were actually humans, a few animals that sometimes pretended to be humans, and all shades in between came barrelling out of the castle like a mass escape from a zoological garden. They made a sweeping turn as they came out of the guard post building at the outer end of the drawbridge, and headed as a broad wave of claws and teeth towards the attacking force, tending their route over a little to avoid the powdery pile of former zombies and the few still animated examples that were floundering around as the holy fire devoured them.

'They really are terrifically predictable,' noted Professor Stone, and raised a Very pistol. A moment later, a white star shell was rising into the heavens.

The Warbirds barely needed the signal. They had already spotted the new threat and were responding to it as had been decided earlier in the day. *Striking Dragon* swung around the battlefield, while *Spirit of '76* and *Buzzbomb* formed up in echelon, Dea Boom's bird leading and to the north. As they got within two hundred yards of the lycanthropes, she put her entomopter's nose down and opened fire.

Contrary to popular expectation, machine-gun fire rarely causes great gouts of earth to plume up dramatically under the impact of a few grains of lead. Instead they usually insert themselves under the sod with little fuss but for perhaps a few bits of soil being tossed into the air, shook loose by the admittedly fierce transfer of energy from the decelerating bullet. On a hard surface, impacts may be seen, and on a baked earthy surface, perhaps you might get something like those little fountains of dust so beloved of the cinematicians.

Alsager's lycanthropes were offered no such aesthetically pleasing sight. The twin lines of fire stitched the ground towards them, and it was only the tracer rounds mixed into the guns' ammunition that made them think that perhaps they weren't standing in the ideal place. A *kitsune* was struck and fell wordlessly, for not all lycanthropes share the werewolves' resistance to non-silver munitions. Indeed, one of the wolfmen stopped and threw up his arms in contemptuous challenge.

'Your feeble bullets cannot harm me!' he cried in a voice half human bellow and half lupine howl. Unhappily, these were to be his last words, as the entomopter's guns bore an ammunition mix that included 10 percent silver rounds. Still, at least he found a sort of immortality as an amusing anecdote bandied around in the more esoteric circles.

Devlin Alsager roared at his troops, 'Get out of the way, you fools! Up against the riverbank!'

There was a surge in their ranks as they obeyed, although whether out of obedience or simply because it was away from the line of the strafing run is open to interpretation. They crowded in close, but continued to move towards the Templar line, the sooner to be out of the confined area and into the enemy ranks where the Warbirds dare not attack. So busy were they in this that none noticed the trailing Warbird sashay lazily north to bring itself on a run for their new position.

As it approached, valves clicked, and another haze of atomised liquid from the entomopter's crop-spraying nozzles started to drift down. The mist was thick this time, a product of the Copperhead's larger cargo capacity, and dense wreaths of spray fell upon the shapechangers.

Alsager shook his clawed fist as the aircraft passed over him, barely thirty feet above. 'Holy water?' he shouted derisively. 'What's this? You think we're like Misericorde's useless creatures? Or . . .' He laughed, a horrid barking noise. 'You're blessing us? How sweet! How thoughtful! How . . .'

It was then that the scent of the mist finally reached his nostrils. He had been aware of something almost immediately, but had dismissed it as part of the entomopter's exhaust. Now he knew differently.

The *Spirit of '76* was venting aviation fuel spirit.

He saw *Striking Dragon* and *Buzzbomb* bearing down on his troop, already committed to a strafing run.

'. . . shit,' he said, which was less amusing as last words go. 'Shitshitshitshitshitshi . . .'

Mink's guns blazed, their bullet streams blazed with tracers, and—when the bright rounds penetrated the bank of fuel vapour floating over the lycanthropes—the air blazed, too, albeit briefly. Cabal had explained that such a mist would not merely burn, but would explode. He had been exactly right. The timing of the attack run had been precise; the lead entomopter was already a quarter of a mile away with its throttles fully open to escape the blast, and the aircraft assigned to light the cloud had banked up and clear as soon as its short bursts of fire—dense with tracer rounds—was airborne.

The blast was perfunctory and brutal. Those directly beneath were crushed and burned, those to the edges thrown by the massive over-pressure wave. A *rakshasa*, screaming like a cat, was flung clean across the river moat, cartwheeling as it flew, to smash into the castle wall and fall silently to the ground. Those who were not burnt had their lungs exploded inside their chests, their eardrums shattered, their eyeballs crushed.

The violence of the concussion startled even the attacking force despite their expectation of it, and the firing from their ranks halted. The shapechangers lay mangled and more than dead. Here and there, there was movement—a maimed werebear here, a disembowelled werefox there clung pitifully to their lives. Ensuring their weapons were charged with silver, the attackers advanced to deal with the survivors.

The line faltered as, from the veil of smoke and steam boiled from flesh and grass, a huge figure emerged at a charge. Its hide burnt, and the tussock of coarse black hair between its shoulders alight, the werebull—Minotaur incarnate—bore down upon the shocked ranks of the secret societies.

There was a remarkably loud *bang*. The werebull carried on running for several more steps until its metabolism regretfully admitted that even its autonomic processes were having a few problems getting along now that the werebull's brain had been comprehensively liquefied, at which point the creature fell forward nervelessly to lie twitching on the sod. Slowly, it started to metamorphose into its human form, an accounts payable clerk from a stationery company in Basingstoke.

Atropos Straka patted the breach of the borrowed Holland & Holland .577 Nitro Express elephant gun appreciatively. The effect of the massive 750-grain bullet had been most gratifying. Her shoulder would be sorely bruised come the morning, she knew, but that was better than being gored by a werebull. The necromancer Cabal had offered the gun to her when he had decided that it was too bulky a weapon to be used during the infiltration and, in any case, the *Ministerium*'s heavy forces would be outside the castle if all went to plan. She nodded to those nearby, many of whom were twitching their heads in an effort to dissipate the ringing in their ears.

'I like this gun,' said Atropos Straka. 'It is a good gun.'

Professor Stone glanced back and saw Korka Olvirdóttir looking nervously ahead. She caught his glance and gave him a smile and thumbs-up, but her smile was wan. He could hardly blame her. Cabal had dissected the likely waves of the attack for them in his interminable, frequently supercilious, but—it transpired—very accurate briefing. He had dismissed the undead as almost beneath his notice, the lycanthropes as only slightly more problematical, and he had proposed ways of wiping them out quickly and effectively that had proved themselves most dramatically. Then he had given his view of what the third wave must be and told them, 'This is when you will likely die.' Johannes Cabal might have many positive attributes, thought the professor, but rousing pep talks did not feature anywhere among them.

Chapter 18

IN WHICH MASKS FALL AWAY

The big man in the plus fours and monumental beard stood upon the flat, circular roof that, not so very long before, had seen an aeroyacht disgorge a bemused vampire. He looked down upon the vista to the west of the castle. Across the river, the agents of mundanity were advancing past the twice-dead zombies and the freshly exploded lycanthropes. They moved with discipline and caution; they knew what was coming.

Once, Rufus Maleficarus would have gloried in this moment, the dramatic pause before he poured terror and damnation upon his enemies. His father had been a performer, a practitioner of magics both illusory and real, and Rufus had followed in his path. His father had also been, by most lights, evil and insane. Rufus had followed him there, as well. Rufus had thundered and he had raged, never spoke when he might declaim, never moved but that he might pose,

Yet now he was quiet and composed. He gestured once, twice, and reality ripped in the air above him. The night's sky glimmered as if the light reflected from a babbling brook had been magnified and placed there, floating in a scintillating rend through the dimensions. It only took a moment for the tear to be noticed by that which lay beyond, the light intensified, and a new monstrosity shouldered its way through.

Rufus Maleficarus watched it with bland disinterest; a glittering patch of spiky light that flickered and dazzled. It was most like a jellyfish, but not *that* alike. Yes, there was a head analogous to the dome of a jellyfish, but this was more acutely angled, more akin to the head of a pencil. Yes, there were things like tentacles, but these hung heavily like roots from an unearthed plant, bifurcating and rejoining with themselves and their neighbours to form an untidy mass of bedragglement. Hanging further than these, however, was one longer tentacle, discrete and distinct from the others, from the creature's central axis. Unlike its listless fellows, this appendage twitched and swayed as if sensing its surroundings. Yet the creature was strangely beautiful; it pulsed in brilliant colours forming ever-moving patterns in blurred ranks of shapes that seemed neither chaotic nor geometric. Nor, however, were they entirely comfortable viewing. There was a sense that there were other colours that existed outside human perception, but flickering, perhaps lapping, at the edge of it. Infra-violet, ultra-red, nowhere to be found on the electromagnetic spectrum as understood by any creature of Earth.* The patterns and the colours made the creature very hard to look at. Then, the observers realised to their rising dread, it also made them impossible to look away from.

---

* It bears noting that Johannes Cabal would never have referred to these colours thus, pointing out with agonising pedantry that infra-violet is simply indigo or, more likely, blue, while ultra-red is better known as 'orange'. This is why these stories are written in the third person.

With a wet sucking sound, a second creature appeared from the void, rimed with extra-dimensional menace, and then a third.

Maleficarus pointed at the attackers below and then, as the entities went down to do his bidding, stuck his hands in his pockets like a man watching an unexciting local football fixture on a damp afternoon.

'My, my,' said Johannes Cabal from behind him. 'How insouciant you have become, Rufus. Once upon a time, you would have found yourself a suitable merlon, clambered upon it, and delivered a speech about how puissant your magic and how encompassing your ambition are.' Cabal looked around. 'You didn't even bring an audience. This isn't like you at all.'

Rufus Maleficarus turned to face him, but said nothing.

'And that summoning. The elegance of it. Where is all your posturing, your imprecations to arcane forces, your very . . . *physical* stylings that seem to imply that a successful casting will also clear your constipation? I'm disappointed, Rufus. Just a casual wave of your hand to summon an extra-dimensional entity. Where's the drama in that?'

Still, Maleficarus remained silent. Cabal walked closer, stopping some ten feet from what passed for his arch-enemy.

'But, of course,' he continued, 'you're not really Rufus Maleficarus at all, are you?'

'Hullo, everyone,' said Horst Cabal.

'Everyone', in this context, consisted of the ministers of the *Ministerium Tenebrae* and Lady Misericorde. They turned to face him from the westerly windows as he pushed the double doors wide and entered. Alisha Bartos moved by him, a large semiautomatic pistol of German origin in her hand. She walked sideways, opening a cross fire between her own position and Horst's, providing he'd been carrying a gun, too, which he wasn't, which was a shame, but the thought was there.

Burton Collingwood walked straight up to him, ignoring

Alisha's pistol. 'Thank heavens you've come back to us, my boy!' he said. 'We need you desperately. I don't know who these people out there are, but they're cutting through our forces like wire through cheese!'

'Well, Mr Collingwood,' said Horst affably, 'I would but for two significant little problems. One, I'm actually *with* those attackers, so technically I suppose that makes me your enemy.' He shrugged and pulled a regretful face. 'Sorry. The other is . . . Well, since I became what I've become, my senses are really very, very good. That's important because, last time I met you, you had a very distinct scent combining cigar smoke, expensive soap, and cologne, and a hint in your sweat that you should cut down on your drinking a bit. Whereas now'—he looked very seriously at Collingwood—'you smell like a butcher's shop. Why do you suppose that is?'

Collingwood did not reply, at least not verbally. Instead he thrust both hands, which had become very sharp and spiny in the blink of an eye, straight through Horst's chest.

Horst hadn't felt pain commensurate with his mortal existence in a long time, but this experience filled in that vacancy nicely. He cried out in agony as the spines punched clean through him, emerging from the back of his jacket.

'Shapechangers!' shouted Alisha, opening fire on the others.

'Yes, thank you,' Horst managed, 'the business with the changing shape was a clue.' The spines flexed, turning into hooks at their tips to prevent him freeing himself. 'Help?'

The thing that was not Mr Burton Collingwood was just in the process of tearing Horst atwain when Alisha put a close group of three rounds in the back of its head. The shapechanger's flesh, already achieving unseemly levels of motility as it transformed, was ill prepared to resist such an intrusion, and it sloughed its face onto Horst's shirt.

'Oh,' said Horst unhappily. Then he slid from the creature's spines as they softened in death to be dumped on the floor, subject to mixed emotions and great pain. He was hardly aware of the other false *Ministerium* councillors charging Alisha, dropping their forms as easily as an Essexian drops an *H*. Horst heard her gun bark rapidly, then she cried out. With an effort he looked up.

They were killing her. One—he thought it might have been Vizconde de Osma until a moment before—had reached her despite being clipped by at least one bullet and had her speared clean through to the floor. The last one was heading towards Horst to finish what the Collingwood monster had begun.

Horst tried to raise himself but staggered and fell back to his knees. He'd lost too much blood in the first attack. What little he could spare he was burning to accelerate his own mind, to stretch objective seconds into a subjective minute. He reached out for plans, tactics, bright ideas, stupid ideas, it's-a-million-to-one-shot-but-it-might-just-work ideas, but all of them foundered on his injuries and weakness.

Well, well, well, said a small voice in his head. *So Mr Morality could do with a bit of help, could he?*

'Yes, actually,' thought Horst.

Not going to happen, mate, said the little voice, somewhat spitefully. *I think I'll just let this one play out.*

'That particular scenario finishes with me being torn to pieces,' pointed out Horst.

No skin off my nose.

'Look, I think you're forgetting something important here.'

Oh?

'You're not actually a separate entity,' thought Horst. 'You're just a convenient mental construction that I've created to allow me to compartmentalise the unacceptable urges of my vampirism.'

There was a pause.

I'm not sure what that means.

'If I die, you die, which is pretty much *all* the skin off your nose. Besides, you're missing another point which is of more immediate importance to you,' added Horst, ever the people person, even when the people was him. 'The shapechangers are human, despite appearances. If we're going to survive, they have to die. And they are *full* of blood.'

Another pause.

Still not quite following.

'They are full of blood, and they are all yours.'

Oh . . . said the little voice. *Well, why didn't you say so?*

For the doppelgänger charging him, there was a moment when it blinked, and in that instant Horst was suddenly right in front of it. 'Hello,' said Horst, and smiled a very unfriendly smile.

The doppelgänger never completed the thought that began, *What long fangs this fellow . . .*

Rufus Maleficarus smiled. 'When did you guess?'

Cabal winced. 'Guess? I'm a scientist. I study the evidence. The fact that I killed you very thoroughly was my starting point.'

'So? You're a necromancer. Is it so hard to believe that I rose again?'

'Yes. Yes, it is. As a zombie, I could have believed it. As a revenant, like your dear doubly departed father, this, too, I could believe. But look at you. You're in full ruddy health. I've spent years trying to perfect such a process. Years.' Cabal seemed momentarily distracted as he realised the weight of the word. He rallied his concentration and looked keenly at Maleficarus. 'Frankly, Rufus—you don't mind if I call you "Rufus", do you? Just for the sake of convenience?—you're not clever enough to produce such a miracle.'

'Yet here I am, me *and* my magic,' said Maleficarus. His smile had not flickered a millimetre. He nodded back at the parapet behind him, beyond which the sound of gunfire was clearly audible. An entomopter—the *Striking Dragon*—flashed by, guns blazing at the shining horrors Maleficarus had let slip into the mortal world.

'*And* your magic,' said Cabal with heavy emphasis. 'That's the thing, though. It's not really magic for you, is it? It's reflexive and natural. Always has been. No hocus pocus, incantations, and slaughtering goats for you, is there, Rufus?'

The smile still did not waver. 'My name is not Rufus.'

'I know, but I have no idea what your real name is or if you even have one. I am talking to the animating spirit within the so-called Ereshkigal Working, am I not?'

The smile flickered down half a candela before recovering.

'I see I am. I *knew* I killed Rufus properly. I know death, you see. You . . . he was very dead. There's "dead" and then there's "dead", though, so it seems.'

The *Buzzbomb* unleashed a rocket salvo at the alien entities. It missed, slamming into the tower wall thirty feet below. Fire and smoke arose behind Maleficarus.

Cabal raised a hand. 'Let me speculate. Something went . . . not exactly awry, but *differently* with the Ereshkigal Working when Rufus performed it? What was that, then? Did he make a mistake? I'm quite prepared to believe he made a mess of it.'

'No,' said the inexpressibly dangerous entity currently occupying the form of an obstreperous nincompoop. 'You did.'

Cabal blinked with surprise, and put his hand to his chest in an expression of injured innocence.

The silver rounds were doing no good. Nor were the holy ones, the explosive ones, the frangible ones, nor the armour-piercing ones. The shimmering beasts, if beasts they were and not expressions of a god's thought or some of reality's antibodies freed from the blood of creation, descended towards the ranks of the secret societies with not the smallest indication that having several pounds of lead thrown at them per second was making the slightest difference to their disposition or progress. It was noticeable that the bullets that went in came straight out of the other side. This was barely discernible for most of the shots fired at the entity, but the guns of the entomopters were larded with tracer rounds that scored white lines across the air, into the glistening, flashing creatures, and emerged unimpeded from the far side.

Uncertainty and perhaps even fear was starting to grow in the ranks of the society agents; they were employing every trick that they had ever learned against a veritable bestiary of creatures not to be found in the more commonplace natural history museums, but what were they to do against creatures that impolitely declined to be sufficiently substantial enough to hurt?

The one thing that mitigated against their invulnerability was that at least they had not attacked anyone, although the business with being visually fascinating to the point of compulsion was neither pleasant nor unthreatening. It was even impossible to raise hands to block out the sight, though the spectators' arms were not paralysed. It was all very disconcerting and rather disagreeable, but while there was a threat in the air—very literally—nothing actually dangerous about the creatures had yet materialised. After all, no one had died yet.

Then the central tentacle of the leading creature seemed to find one of the Templars in the front rank of interest. The lights along the length of the tentacle pulsed and throbbed up into the floating body above as if inhaling. The Templar made an involuntary step forward, started to cry out, and then died suddenly as his eyes, optic nerves, and the parts of the brain to which they were connected (specifically the lateral geniculate body, the superior colliculus, and—that old favourite—the suprachiasmatic nucleus) burst into fierce, brilliant flames that mirrored the intensity of the creatures' light. He fell without a further sound, his eyes guttering in their sockets like falling firework rockets. The onlookers who saw his fate in their peripheral vision redoubled their efforts to look away, or even to simply blink their tearing eyes, but they could not.

And, all the time, the things came on, implacable and scintillant.

Miss Virginia Montgomery was certainly finding it hard to look away from the creatures, but at least she had a mechanism at hand to force her to. With a shove of her entomopter's control yoke, she made the aircraft turn away. She found it impossible to prevent her head scanning sideways to keep the monsters in view, but then the edge of the cockpit intervened and both her line of sight and the spell were broken.

She breathed a sigh of relief and fought down the fear the last few moments had placed in her. She'd heard all about the stories of snakes hypnotising their prey, but knew them to be an exaggeration. This, on the other hand, was the real thing. The victim was not immobilised, true, but getting away became a great deal more difficult when you couldn't look to find your escape route. She was irked by this ability, but not unduly affrighted by it; she, after all, had not seen the fate of the Templar with the flammable eyes.

It is perhaps just as well that she did not know that these creatures were incendiary cousins of the Medusa, for that might have worried her enough to fog her thinking, and it was her clear mind that was responsible for subsequent events.

As the world teetered on the edge of apocalypse, Johannes Cabal was having a snit.

'Me? My fault? I think not. I had nothing to do with your . . . Rufus's failings, multitudinous as they are. How do you propose that all this is *my* fault?' He drew the Webley, perhaps rather belatedly, from its place at his hip, but did not raise it against Maleficarus. Rather, he let it dangle at his side, part threat, part convenience. 'I thought I'd killed you—twice—and came here to finish the job. Here, to Mirkarvia.' He said the name as if coughing up smoke from a burning skunk. 'But, yes, I now see that I succeeded the second time. Whatever you are, you are not Rufus Maleficarus. There may be a few shreds of his glittering personality left, you can still probably tell the difference between a soupspoon and a fish knife, assuming he could, but that startling ego married to a deep and frankly impressive stupidity . . . I don't see much evidence of that anymore. You've taken ownership of the rambling manse that once called itself "Rufus Maleficarus", and you haven't redirected his post.'

'You know me.'

'Yes, I know you. All too well. So, what's all this about?'

Maleficarus said nothing for long seconds, as if considering. Then: 'I have come to the Earth of men three times. Twice my will was thwarted in war and blood. Desperate were my enemies. With fire they burned my armies. With fear they denied me my reinforcements. I fell back into chaos to wait. Once. Twice.'

Cabal was glad of the weight of the pistol in his hand, even though he doubted it would be of much use. 'Rufus Maleficarus was the third time.'

'Rufus Maleficarus was the third time,' agreed Rufus Maleficarus in form if not in spirit, 'but I was denied my due that time by cunning and guile. I lost my armies, but he lived. That was . . . novel to me—the summoner had always been destroyed before. He lived, and through him I could still taste the world. The soul of Rufus Maleficarus was an improperly sealed portal. I bent my energies to ensuring that it never entirely closed.'

'Not even when I shot him? Not even when he died?'

'I was close. So close. But his limbs would not stir for me. His eyes would not open.'

'And then . . . the *Ministerium*?' Cabal took the silence for affirmation. 'They dug Rufus up, carried out some sort of half-witted, half-arsed ritual, no doubt, and were quite giddy with glee when you resurrected perfectly, the depredations of the grave worms and several large-calibre bullet holes—my own small contributions'—and here he waved his revolver demonstratively—'remarkably repaired, rejuvenated, and just as wonderful a human being as the day I shot you.'

Rufus Maleficarus continued smiling. Even when he spoke, his lips didn't move. Then again, his voice didn't sound entirely like his own. 'The *Ministerium* were most helpful.'

'I didn't think they could go any lower in my estimation, but that was before they kicked open the door you'd got your foot in.' He regarded Maleficarus as one might a man who *may* just be a great intellect, but who is far more likely simply to be the village idiot. 'That's a metaphor.'

'I am familiar with meta—'

'They kicked open that door and laid out a welcome to a banquet of humanity.'

'You speak without meaning.'

'Do I? Then perhaps you will understand this—you have invaded my world three times before and failed three times. You should brace yourself for further disappointment.'

The smile of Rufus Maleficarus was an unnerving thing to behold. For long minutes it had held without a twitch or a waver, not even while he was speaking, an unpleasant detail in itself. He did not speak immediately, but looked down from the parapet. 'Your allies will die soon. Then you will die. I shall possess your corpses. This time I will not be thwarted.'

'Oh,' said Cabal, 'that's not true. You *will* be thwarted. Now, in fact.'

For the first time, the smile altered. It grew stronger, creasing itself into a rictus. 'Your guns cannot harm me.'

'Guns?' Cabal looked at the pistol as if he'd forgotten about it. 'Oh, guns. Well, yes, they can blow holes through you, but that isn't what you're talking about, is it? You mean you are an incorporeal entity that is simply riding around in poor old Rufus, and I can damage his body, but not you? Quite. You're perfectly correct. I cannot hurt you. Not physically.' Cabal crossed his arms, the pistol pointing off at a jaunty angle. 'You must feel remarkably secure in your lack of corporeality. All the time you've existed, which is millennia to my certain knowledge and surely far beyond, and you've never felt pain. Just . . . frustration. Of course, that's a sort of pain in itself, isn't it?'

'Your guns cannot harm me. *You* cannot harm me.'

'Ah,' said Johannes Cabal. He slid the .577 revolver back into its holster. 'I cannot *kill* you. Harm, however, is a broader category.' He reached into an inside pocket and produced a handle rendered in steel, dark wood, and cheap ivory. With a *snik*, a blade snapped out into position.

The hideous smile did not waver. 'With that?'

'With this.'

'What makes you believe it will be any more efficacious than a bullet?'

'For much the same reason surgeons don't carry out operations with a pistol. I will be requiring precision in a minute.'

At last, the smile faded. 'You cannot hurt me.'

'*Hurt.* As if you even know what that really means. Allow me to demonstrate.'

He did not raise the knife or even approach Rufus Maleficarus. Instead, he started to recite in carefully moderated tones sentences that the world had only heard three times before. The language was strange, belonging to a race that was long since extinct and not especially human when it had lived.

The effect was immediate. Maleficarus staggered as if stricken by a sudden illness, his face paling, his expression frantic. 'Stop! What are you doing? What are you *doing?*'

Cabal finished a phrase, commented, 'Why, summoning you, of course. The ritual is pathetically simple, but that was always deliberate on your part, wasn't it?' and continued with the strange, alien, yet eminently pronounceable words of power.

'But . . . why? I am here! Right here!' Maleficarus fell to his knees. 'Why?'

Cabal paused. For that moment, Maleficarus rallied, but not enough. Cabal examined the blade in his hand, and flicked away some lint at the pivot. 'Because, as you so conceitedly noted, I cannot hurt you. I can, however, inconvenience you enormously.' He continued the ritual. With a groan, Maleficarus fell onto all fours.

Cabal watched him dispassionately. He had little enough sympathy for Rufus Maleficarus when he *was* Rufus Maleficarus. Now that he was merely a convenient vessel for a monstrous otherworldly energy dedicated to control and proliferation, Cabal regarded him with less compassion than one might regard the death of a bacterium within the blood of a recovering invalid. He felt the drag within his own spirit as it pulled the Ereshkigal animus towards him, tearing it from its anchorage in Maleficarus.

'Please . . . Cabal . . . don't do this . . .'

'Who's talking?' asked Cabal. 'Not that it matters. In either case, nobody and nothing that I respect.'

With a ripple in the air, the Ereshkigal animus lost its last fingerhold on the physical frame of Maleficarus. His eyes rolled up in his skull, and he died, yet again.

Cabal could feel the animus drawing close, but he could see it, too, an oily disturbance in the light as if something were being dragged along behind the canvas scenery it pleases us to call 'Reality'. Closer it came, and closer still, rendered eager to join with him by the terms of the ritual, yet reluctant, for it knew who and what he was. He said the words, the ancient words of power, and pulled it closer with every syllable.

And when it was one yard from him, he stopped, and smiled an unpleasant smile, and he said, 'Actually, I've changed my mind. I don't think I'll summon you at all.'

The distortion wavered.

'I don't suppose,' said Cabal conversationally, '*this* is something that's ever happened to you before, either. Previously you've always left this world by being evicted. Yet here you are, neither one thing nor another. That sounds like a very volatile state for something like you. Why, I shouldn't be at all surprised if you were just to'—he waved the fingers of his free hand—'boil away into nothing.'

The distortion slid like butter in a hot pan straight back towards the recently abandoned body of Rufus Maleficarus. He was very dead by this time, but the Ereshkigal Working was used to raising cold, rotting corpses as its puppets. Rufus's still warm carcass represented no sort of challenge to it. It would occupy him, murder Cabal, and work its way up from there. This time (it thought with less confidence than it had on similar occasions in the past), this time it *would* devour the Earth.

Rufus Maleficarus shook as he reanimated, the baleful energies coursing through the cooling fibres of the corpse. The eyes darkened with blood, he shook once more, then started to rise.

'Thank you so much,' said Cabal. While the entity had been otherwise distracted he had walked to the body and waited, knife in hand and a patient expression upon his face. He knelt, putting one knee between Rufus's shoulder blades, thereby pinning the freshly created revenant to the floor. 'Comfy in there? I hope so, for your sake.'

Cabal barely hesitated as he aimed his blade at the top of Rufus's neck. Then he drove the steel between the occipital lobe and the atlas vertebra with a surety that betokened distressing quantities of practise. Rufus Maleficarus shuddered and lay still.

No, that's not quite true. His eyes rolled and his eyelids flickered. His jaw worked angrily, and within the stolen mouth, the wet tongue could be seen to flex and extend. Then, summoning shreds of power, he spoke.

'What . . .' The voice was horrible, only faintly like the bluff conversational roar of Rufus Maleficarus. This came from somewhere else, a voice from beyond the ajar door into another reality. 'What have you done, Cabal?' It was breathy and reptilian, and the vowels were extended unforgivably. Despite the lack of sibilants in that short sentence, it was the kind of voice that assured the listener that when sibilants became available, the sibilance would be extreme.

'What have I done?' Cabal seemed honestly nonplussed. 'Why, I've forced you to occupy an unsuitable vessel as both animating spirit and animatee, and then broken the body in such a way that you are localised from the neck up. Surely that's obvious?' He looked around the rooftop as if seeking inspiration or, as it turned out, surgical instruments. 'Really, the first time in ages I come out without my bag and—wouldn't you know it?—that's the very evening a bone saw would be handy.' He rose and gave the corpse a friendly kick. 'I would guess that this is an entirely novel experience for you?'

'You have not won, Cabal.'

Cabal smiled, not kindly. 'Yes, I have.'

Miss Virginia Montgomery had set off enough pyrotechnics in her time to be very familiar with the way that smoke moved, and there was plenty of smoke hanging over the field of battle from guns, explosives, and burning werebeasts. As her gaze had been dragged around to break from the Medusae, she had noted the wreaths of smoke underlit by the fires started by the fuel explosion, and that it was making no effort to fill a particular volume of air that bore more than a passing resemblance to a great, flying jellyfish.

With the commendably clear thinking earlier alluded to, married to a greater appreciation of the unlikely creatures one might find falling out of purple clouds these days, she drew a conclusion and immediately decided to act upon it.

She reached into the cockpit's map compartment and slid out the aviator's sunglasses she kept stowed there. She wasn't fond of night flying at the best of times, and was not formally qualified for it, just as Becky had once told Horst. Low flying after dusk with sunglasses on seemed like a good way to hit something hard and unforgiving like the castle, or a hill, or just about anything, but she hoped the lenses would at least reduce the effect of the Medusan lights. She shook out the spectacles' arms and put them on, resting near the tip of her nose so she could look over them until she was ready.

Years of formation flying had given her a pretty good idea of where her aircraft was in relation to the battlefield and the castle, and she could only hope the few seconds of strange fascination she had endured had not disorientated her. She gave her instruments one last scrutiny, checked the 'Master Arm' switch for the *Spirit of '76*'s weapons was on, pushed the glasses up to cover her eyes, and brought the entomopter around to starboard to bear on the castle.

Whatever curious frequencies the creatures generated to snare the eye foundered badly when faced by polarised glass. There was certainly still some of the Lorelei about the glimmering colours, but their power was vastly reduced, allowing Miss Virginia to blink, although her eyes were still drawn back to the Medusae if she allowed them to do so.

But, there! Again that strange billow in the smoke. She side-swept a little further to starboard to line it up with the nearest of the three visible Medusae. Not, she suspected, that there was more than one. These creatures could apparently do very clever things with light, including letting it slide through them, and producing images elsewhere. The human weapons were not ineffective because the Medusae were somehow incorporeal, but because they were illusions.

The nearest apparent Medusa shimmered as if seen through oil, the puppeteer's invisibility being impressive, but not perfect. She placed the area of distortion squarely in the reflector sight, allowed for range, and opened fire.

This time the tracers did not sail harmlessly through the target. Instead, the glittering stream hit seemingly empty air and made it shudder. A terrible cry, like an injured whale, echoed around the battlefield. The rearmost Medusa flickered as if shadows were sliding rapidly across its skin and then it vanished like an extinguished candle.

Miss Virginia Montgomery came on, grim as a Fury, and her entomopter's rocket pods stuttered with vengeance. Rocket trails split the night sky, tearing lines of lights and smoke across the air like magical telegraph wires being drawn to the receiver of what was to be some very bad news. Most missed their marks, but two struck the void in the smoke and exploded violently. Both of the remaining Medusae vanished, and in their place a single new one appeared, dripping yellowish blood. Its attention was entirely focussed upon its tormentor, and lights swam across its surface with brilliant intensity.

'Good God! There! There!' cried Professor Stone. 'Fire upon it! Fire!' Given new heart, the ground troops focussed on the true enemy and poured lead into it.

This assistance, unhappily, was coming too late to help Miss Virginia. The Medusa's redoubled efforts to snare her seemed to be working. Even through the medium of her sunglasses, the light was working upon her. She couldn't blink, couldn't look away, could barely move, could barely breathe. Oddly, her eyes seemed to be growing hot in her skull. She had an intimation these would be her last moments, and she met them with a snarl.

'Fine,' she whispered. 'Me for you, you beautiful son of a bitch.'

With her last iota of will, she opened the throttle to full and thumbed the reburn control, dumping fuel into the hot rear exhaust. The *Spirit of '76* surged forward, accelerating hard.

The agents watched as the entomopter drove into the great bulk of the Medusa, not hitting it quite squarely but with the root of the port wings. They stopped moving quickly in a spray of yellow blood as they slid cleanly halfway through the glowing mass. The Medusa spun a quarter rotation to the clockwise, keening in agony. The entomopter's wreck slid from it, and yellow gore and entrails gushed from the great wound. Entomopter and otherworldly offal fell into the river.

The Medusa, its light failing, tried to retreat to the top of the castle tower, as if hoping to return to its home dimension to die, but there was no strength left in it. It wavered, tracking haphazardly across the far side of the river for a hundred feet, and then dropped lifeless to the grassy bank.

Many of the assorted secret agents and secret soldiers there gathered heaved sighs of relief and gave throat to cries of reprieve and triumph. Melkorka 'Korka' Olvirdóttir, however, was already throwing off her outer clothes and boots before diving into the river and swimming strongly to where one forlorn wingtip broke the surface.

Johannes Cabal found Horst some twenty minutes later. The room was a chaotic mess of wrecked furniture, torn-down tapestries, and paintings bespattered with blood. In the centre of it, amidst the ruined corpses of three things that had once passed for members of the *Ministerium Tenebrae*, knelt Horst Cabal by the body of Alisha Bartos.

Cabal paused in the doorway, a battle axe liberated from a wall display over his shoulder, a knotted tablecloth from a small occasional table dangling from the base of the axehead. The blade was smeared with blood, and more was soaking through the cloth, dripping slowly onto the stone floor. The overall effect was of a gentleman of the road who was not used to taking 'no' as an answer.

'She's dead.' Cabal could barely hear Horst's voice. 'I couldn't save her.'

Cabal dropped the axe and its bundle onto an overstuffed armchair near the door, irreparably staining the soft furnishings with gore. He was by Alisha in a few long strides.

'She's still warm,' he said, crouching by her and looking for a pulse in her throat. The cause of death was obvious enough; she was riddled with ragged puncture wounds, four that he could see and possibly more hidden amidst the blood. 'What happened?'

Horst waved his hand listlessly to take in the destroyed bodies of creatures with flesh like veal cooked in milk. 'The *Ministerium* . . . they were monsters. I mean *real* monsters. As in . . . not metaphorical monsters.' Cabal bit back the desire to say, yes, he understood what his brother meant. There was something in Horst's manner that disturbed him. It was a small surprise when he identified it; Horst was in shock and adrift. Part of him felt a glow of triumph—*at last the perfect Horst falters*—but it was an old part and he disregarded it as one might any artefact of one's callow youth.

'They attacked us,' said Horst. All this while, he hadn't looked away from the face of Alisha Bartos. There were bloody smudges on her eyelids that Cabal knew had been placed when Horst had closed her eyes, his fingers still red with the blood of her killers.

Cabal looked over at the nearest monstrous corpse, mentally subtracted the terrible injuries wrought upon it, presumably by Horst, added his arcane reading and experience and concluded, 'Doppelgängers. Specifically shape-eaters. The *Ministerium* men were devoured, and I think we can guess at whose behest.' He nodded at Alisha. 'It was too late by the time you reached her?'

Horst looked up at him, uncomprehending.

'To save her,' explained Cabal. 'To . . .' He tapped his own canines with the tips of his index and middle fingers, then gestured vaguely at Alisha's neck.

Horst shook his head. 'She said no. She didn't want to be like me. Even the horrible little voice in my head was silent, wasn't telling me to do it anyway. I think it's gone.' He looked down at Alisha's still face. 'I had to watch her die.'

The pause turned to a silence, and the silence drew out. Cabal drew in a breath and said slowly, 'There *are* other ways.'

Horst laughed humourlessly. 'You want me to end up like you, Johannes? Chasing smoke? Leaving misery?'

Cabal let the implied dismissal of his life's work slide over him. People had said worse. People had done worse. 'What else did you have planned? Another morning stroll in the sun?'

Horst rose and looked his brother in the eye. 'I'm not sure it's what she would want. Have wanted.'

'No. No, of course not,' said Johannes, looking down at the body. 'She really had her heart set on being murdered by doppelgängers.'

Horst wavered, then shook his head. 'It's not a decision I can make.'

'Well, somebody has to make it, and soon if she's to be preserved effectively.' Cabal looked at his brother and saw the torture within him. When he spoke again, his tone was softer. 'Horst, let me make the decision. I'm the real monster here. I'm used to people thinking the worst of me.'

'She's not some experiment, Johannes . . .'

'I know, I know.' He laid a hand upon Horst's shoulder. 'She's special to you, I can see that.' He looked down at her again, his jaw moving slowly from side to side as he cogitated. 'Only when the procedure is thoroughly understood and tested, yes?'

He looked sideways to find Horst looking at him warily. Johannes Cabal realised the one thing he could say to reassure him. 'Second. When it comes to it, I shall raise her second.'

Horst's eyebrows rose in consternation. '*After . . . ?*'

'Yes. After. Then will you be convinced of the procedure's safety?'

Horst's face showed his indecision. 'We can't just go around resurrecting people, Johannes. It's against nature.'

'Says the vampire. Truly, Horst, nature lets all sorts of awful things through on the nod. What I propose doesn't constitute *awful* in the pejorative sense to my mind.'

'What gives us the right . . . ?'

'I'm a necromancer. I claim the right.' He sighed. 'This is hardly the time for an ethical debate. I'm doing it. If she doesn't like it when I have her whole in body, mind, and spirit again, she can kill herself with my blessing and that will be the end of it. There; I'm making it her decision. Happy?'

Horst didn't look especially happy, but Cabal was no longer prepared to indulge his vacillations. 'Time is pressing. The *Ministerium*—or at least the members who were foolish enough to come here—are polymorph fodder, Alsager will have led out his troops and burned with them—assuming that all went to plan—and the troublesome thing that was steering Rufus Maleficarus is contained and thereby rendered harmless . . .'

'I shall be revenged upon you, Johannes Cabal . . .' hissed a voice from the bloodstained bundle.

'Oh, be quiet,' said Cabal with a peremptory wave of his hand.

'Is that . . . his head?' asked Horst.

'Indeed, now a vessel for the motivating spirit of the Ereshkigal Working. I shall have to find a box for it.'

Horst thought of the deep shelf beside the fireplace in Cabal's sitting room. Upon it were already two boxes, one containing the coldly burning skull of the hermit Ercusides and the other . . . well, he wasn't sure, but it whistled and sang nicely, and occasionally spoke, and the box was head-sized, so he presumed it contained another living head of some description.

'Are you *deliberately* collecting animated heads, Johannes?' he asked.

Cabal frowned, then accepted the point. 'Not deliberately. It just happens.' He frowned again. 'I was talking about something else, I think, before this business about heads. Ah, yes. Alsager, the *Ministerium*, Maleficarus—all dealt with.'

'Lady Misericorde,' said Horst. 'Where is she? She was here at the beginning of the fight.'

'You let her escape?'

Horst glared. 'I was busy being speared by three shapechanging monsters. I'm so sorry for the lapse.'

Cabal wrinkled his nose. 'She's not a hugely impressive necromancer in any case. I would just like to meet her.'

'That sounds very calm and professional of you.'

'I'm a very calm and professional person. I want to meet her and kill her, calmly and professionally.' He noted Horst's expression, which was much the same as it had been at the beginning of the sentence. 'You don't shock quite so easily anymore. I do hope you're not becoming jaded by all of this.'

'I'm not. I won't let you kill her.'

'Ah, it was fortitude and not acceptance. Well, we shall see. We have to find her before deciding what shall become of her. I would guess she would hie herself off to her chambers when she realised the jig was likely up, gather her materials, and thence into the cloak of night.'

'You would guess? You mean, it's what you would do.'

Cabal shrugged, and Horst—pausing to place Alisha onto a *chaise longue* and covering her with a tapestry—led the way to Misericorde's rooms.

They were empty, which surprised them not at all, and Horst knew the way to them without hesitation, which surprised Johannes Cabal not at all.

'She's gone,' said Horst, listlessly walking the room, flicking open books that lay on the desk and side tables as if she might be hiding within them. Cabal followed him, spending a little more time studying the books. As he walked, his brow furrowed and the furrows grew more profuse and deeper with every perusal.

'These books . . . they're odd.'

Horst paused to take up a volume. '*Hell's Antechamber: A Studie of the Works of Divers Nekromancie.* They're from a necromancer's library. Of course they're odd. Just because she's a woman doesn't mean she'd surround herself with light historical romances, Johannes.'

'No, no, no,' said Cabal. 'You don't understand. These books *are* light historical romances as far as a necromancer is concerned. They are about necromancers, but *not* necromancy. Nor are they accurate. Populist claptrap, by and large. If we want to hear lies and calumnies about us, we just wander into any tavern. We don't go out and buy books about it.'

Horst looked at the book in his hand, flicking through the pages. He started to develop his own frown as he read headings and the occasional sentence. 'This one *is* a bit sensationalist, now you mention it.' He dropped it on the chair where he'd found it. 'Maybe she finds them funny?'

'Perhaps one or two, but there must be twenty different titles here.' He looked at Horst. 'You say she has a laboratory?'

'In one of the lower levels. Not sure where; I never visited it.' He looked around the room. 'Oh.'

'Oh?'

'I hadn't noticed before. This chamber is a mirror image of the one they gave me. Over in the other wing.' He looked around, smiling slightly at the realisation. 'So odd how mirroring something can make it look so different.' He stopped and pointed at a wall. 'Except my room has an alcove there.'

They both looked at the panelled section of wall. 'Old building like this,' said Cabal. 'Different sections are bound to be renovated in different ways.'

'Hmmm,' said Horst.

Both of them continued to look at the wall.

'Although,' offered Horst, 'they are very fond of bare walls and tapestries in this place, I've noticed. No panelling at all.'

'Except here.'

'Except here.'

They walked quickly to the innocuous section of panelling and started searching. Perhaps surprisingly it was Horst, raised on a diet of thrilling adventure stories, rather than Cabal with his own slightly more practical experience of hidden mechanisms, that found the secret door. With a discreet *click*, the lock disengaged, and a section of wall one panel wide and two high swung inwards.

'Isn't this exciting?' said Horst, looking into the shadows beyond.

'Get on with it,' said Cabal, his gun already in his hand.

With Horst leading the way, his superior senses guiding him, they descended into the darkness. Cabal quickly lost sight of Horst and was obliged to lay a hand upon his brother's shoulder. Horst, for his part, whispered warnings about uneven steps and debris from the ancient walls. Down, down they crept in cool blackness to the point where Cabal grew bored, whereupon he tried to descend a step that wasn't there, and performed an awkward curtsey at what turned out to be their destination.

'I can't hear anything,' whispered Horst, then explained, 'There's a door here and I'm listening at it. Forgot you couldn't see. Sorry.'

Cabal pursed his lips with contained irritation. It was so dark that it made no difference if he had his eyes open or shut, although his eyeballs felt a little warmer with them shut. 'Is there a handle?'

'No, but there's a lever. Just a moment.'

With barely a sound, the door swung open. Cabal was momentarily blinded by the light that came forth, but quickly recovered for it was really quite subdued. Horst entered first, Cabal close on his heels.

'Well, this is all a bit *Phantom of the Opera*, isn't it?' said Horst.

He was not wrong in this assessment. The chamber into which they had entered was enough to send Poe skipping around, happily clapping. They were certainly below ground level, and the walls ran cold and veined with nitre. All about them, candles flickered in candelabras and torches bloomed orange flame in sconces. Ranged around the chamber, or possibly repurposed crypt, were freestanding bookshelves, tables, cupboards full of neatly labelled chemicals and insalubrious materials in jars and bottles. The focus of the room was upon, of all things, a dressing table, on which stood a very feminine admixture of make-up and papers, books and assorted tweezers of cosmetic purpose beyond the ken of mere men. While Cabal examined the books on the shelves, Horst stirred around amidst the items upon the dressing table, trying not to look in the mirror, for the state of his clothes perturbed him sadly.

'Oh,' he said suddenly.

Cabal turned and paused. Horst looked up to discover why his brother was taking so long to attend him and noticed his attitude. He followed Cabal's eyeline past his shoulder and saw, tucked into a small alcove across the way, another door similar to the one by which they had entered. 'Where do you suppose that goes?' he asked.

'I don't know,' said Cabal. 'I can only guess that it leads beyond the outer walls. Convenient escape routes are a necessity in the profession.' The nature of that guess was not immediately revealed, for instead he came to join Horst at the dressing table. 'What is it?'

Horst handed him a small tinted photograph in a frame that he had discovered. 'There she is,' he said.

'Indeed she is.' It was a while since Johannes Cabal had met the Lady Orfilia Ninuka, but he never forgot a face, especially when it belonged to somebody who meant him harm. Her little empire of the Red Queen might have taken a knock that night, but he would find her and attend to her and she would cease to be a concern. Heaven only knew where she was hiding, however. Their best chance was to find Misericorde and discover whatever she knew.

'Who's that with her?' asked Horst.

The picture had been taken in happier times for Lady Ninuka, which is to say, the days before she met Johannes Cabal. She stood, smiling archly beside an older man in military uniform. He wasn't smiling at all; indeed, he regarded the camera as if it was a piece of damn effrontery on its part to dare focus light onto emulsion that had once bounced from his countenance.

'Her father,' said Cabal slowly. Something about the exchange of information was bothering him. Hadn't he already told Horst about Count Marechal? He looked up from the picture at Horst. The recent business with doppelgängers suddenly made him wonder if Horst had been triumphant after all.

Horst frowned with exactly the tone of 'My puzzlement is great' that Cabal had known all his early life, and it did a lot to reassure him. It was true that shape-eaters absorbed much of their prey, but whether that included every foible and mannerism, he didn't know. Still, it seemed unlikely that a wily doppelgänger would deign to look quite so clueless.

'Is that a guess?' said Horst. 'You can't *know* it's her father. You said you'd never heard of her.'

Suddenly Cabal understood. He looked at the picture of the smiling Lady Ninuka and her very deceased father and felt cold. 'Horst. Tell me, who is in this picture?'

Horst looked baffled again and slightly suspicious. 'That's Misericorde,' he said. 'Lady Misericorde. The necromancer woman. Good grief, Johannes I've told you about her enough times.'

Cabal blanched, although a pale man growing paler in a dark room is a barely perceptible phenomenon.

Horst, however, saw. 'What's wrong, Johannes? You look awful.'

Cabal's mind was racing, trying to put pieces together and failing. 'She's played me for a fool,' he said, then shook his head. 'No. She's played *us* for fools, you and me, Horst. This is Orfilia Ninuka. The Red Queen. She's manipulated us. And . . . the *Ministerium*. They would never have agreed otherwise. They would never . . .' He looked around, a maniacal gleam in his eye. 'Why? What does she want?'

Horst had taken the picture from Cabal and was studying it. His air of bafflement was in no way lifting. 'The woman whose father you killed? Misericorde was the Red Queen all along . . . ? Well, revenge, I would have thought.'

'Revenge?' Cabal turned on him with a slightly hysterical laugh. 'Revenge? All this for revenge? Horst, wouldn't it have been cheaper and more direct to just hire some competent assassins and send them after me rather than, say, suborning your own country and declaring it an open house for all available monsters? Seeking the aid of a powerful secret society specifically for the purpose of having its senior members eaten? Calling down the wrath of a handful of assorted other secret societies who just don't agree with such tomfoolery?'

Horst thought about it. 'You may have a point,' he conceded finally.

Cabal was hardly listening. He was rifling the shelves in something like a bibliographical fury. 'I will *not* be manipulated,' he muttered under his breath.

Horst forbore to point out that, in fact, he *had* been manipulated, and instead asked, 'What are you looking for?'

'She's gone. Nothing is more certain, but we saw her off in a panic. That door over there undoubtedly leads into an escape tunnel. She couldn't have known about the Ereshkigal Working—that cannot have been part of her plan—but the doppelgängers were supposed to see us both off. I think. Probably. In any case, she may have left something she didn't mean to.'

He paused. 'Why does she have two copies of the same book?' He slid a handsomely bound volume from a series, and a much tattier and larger example from another shelf and placed them side by side on a reading table.

'They look nothing alike,' said Horst. 'The titles are different.'

'The individual volume was collated into a series of essays. It's the same book, albeit revised.' He flipped open the older book.

Inside, it was gutted. The heart of the book had been cut out to create a hiding place, and within it was a smaller book and a bundle of papers. Cabal barked a laugh of triumph and flicked quickly through the papers. As he did so, however, he slowed, a growing astonishment becoming apparent.

'What is it, Johannes?' asked Horst. 'What's in those?'

Wordlessly, Cabal passed him a slip of newspaper, cut from some archive somewhere, and watched his brother's face. The reaction was near instant. 'Father's obituary,' said Horst in a very small voice. 'Why would she have this? Why would she want it?'

Cabal didn't answer. Instead he laid out further cuttings and transcriptions from a dozen sources. A tragic drowning. A missing brother. A churchyard desecration. A disaster at a seaside town. Cabal unfolded a piece of parchment and read it slowly. Horst could see the document was old and could not even hazard a guess at the alphabet in which it was written. Finally, he could contain his curiosity no longer and demanded to know what it meant.

'It is a short treatise on the dangers of the Ereshkigal Working, emphasising the means and motives for the ritual existing at all.' He dropped the parchment to the table. 'She even knew about Rufus. She knew what he was. She didn't even care. She knew everything, Horst. Everything.' He drew up a chair and sat heavily. 'I feel so *used*. She's worse than Nyarlathotep.'

Horst decided he didn't need that comment explained, so distracted himself by picking out the smaller book where it nestled—matryoshka-like—within the larger volume. 'What's this?'

Cabal looked up with the smallest possible interest. 'Probably her notebook where she keeps a list of those she's made a bloody fool of. "Dear diary, today I manipulated Wall Street. Such fun".'

'It's not a diary. I'm not sure what it is. How good's your Latin?'

Wearily, Cabal gestured for Horst to hand it over. He opened it and noted the mark of the library of Krenz University on the inside cover. Beneath it was a 'Restricted Collection' stamp. He frowned, and turned the page. Then his eyes bulged.

'*Gott!*'

'Something saucy?' asked Horst.

Cabal wasn't listening. He'd risen to his feet and was looking at the book as if an angel of the Lord had come down, put the Holy Grail in his hand, said, 'Here you go,' pinched his cheek fondly, winked, and ascended once more.

'Presbyter Johannes,' he said in a dreadful voice.

'Lovely,' said Horst. 'Who's that, then?'

'*Being the One True Account of Presbyter Johannes by His Own Hand*. It exists?' Cabal's hand was visibly shaking. 'It exists and it was in Krenz bloody Library the whole time? I stole the *Principia Necromantica* from there, and I could have stolen *this* instead? Oh, gods. Oh, gods.' He slumped back into the chair.

'Hurray?' ventured Horst. 'It's . . . good, then?'

'Good?' Cabal looked up at him and Horst realised with a shock that his brother was crying. 'It's everything. It's everything I have ever worked towards. It is the key. The very *raison d'être* of . . .' His mouth worked noiselessly for a moment, his vocabulary insufficient to express his emotion. Instead, he fastened upon metaphor. Or, at least, what Horst took to be metaphor. 'You have surely heard of the Fountain of Youth? The Philosopher's Stone?'

'Yes?' said Horst, wondering at his brother's state of mind.

Cabal said nothing more, but simply held up the book and nodded slowly.

And he smiled, beatific and filled with joy.

Johannes Cabal smiled.

AUTHOR'S AFTERWORD

The reader is advised to stop reading now. Everything is lovely and there is nothing further to worry about. All Johannes Cabal's Christmases have come at once, and we're all very happy for him, I'm sure. Go back to your life. Fare you well.

Alternatively, you may wish to read an epilogue. There are two. One is pleasant enough. Read that one.

JLH

THE NICE EPILOGUE

They met the conquering heroes in the entrance hall. It was all very muted for a triumphal procession. The newcomers were weary mainly with the tension of a possible catastrophic reversal. They had done their part of the plan—simply to hold their position and let the enemy come on to them—and done it well, but it might have gone badly at any stage. Indeed, when Maleficarus had unleashed his monsters, there had been an unvoiced sentiment that the game that had endured zombies and werewolves was now up. That they had not died, by and large, remained an unexpected turn of events that they were still too surprised to appreciate fully.

There were a few faintly cheery noises coming from their ranks on entering through the shattered door, the drawbridge beyond having been left down after the ill-fated lycanthropic sortie, but even these few died away when they discovered Johannes Cabal, bearing a stolen briefcase and a muttering hatbox, and Horst Cabal, bearing the body of Alisha Bartos.

Professor Stone made a wordless cry of shock and ran to them. He looked at her, then at Horst, and Cabal noted there was no accusation in his face. He only demanded, 'Who did this?'

'The *Ministerium*,' said Horst. He didn't bother to mention that it had actually been the doing of a bunch of doppelgängers wearing the faces of the *Ministerium*. He could explain that later. Professor Stone looked closely at Horst and an unspoken question passed between them. 'No,' replied Horst. 'They won't be hurting anyone else again.'

Stone waved over a couple of his Dee Society associates to take Alisha away. Horst started to protest, but his brother coughed and the protestation died at the inhalation. Horst knew all too well why Johannes was being circumspect; demanding to keep Alisha's body at that juncture would cause trouble, and what was the point when Johannes was so adept at stealing corpses?

Despite her loss, however, the mood was perhaps surprisingly light. The attackers had always considered the possibility of being massacred unpleasantly high, yet few had died. The entomopters had exterminated the majority of the defenders, but several undead and a few lycanthropes had escaped the aerial strike and reached the ranks of the attackers, causing a handful of injuries and casualties. The toll was far lighter than they had had any right to expect, and relief and some slightly unprofessional triumphalism was apparent among them.

Cabal regarded the leaders of the factions arrayed before him with the special disdain he reserved for those that meant him harm.

'So,' he said. 'Ladies. Gentlemen. The immediate menace is defeated.'

'The immediate menace?' Atropos Straka regarded him suspiciously. 'What do you mean?'

Cabal shrugged as if discussing an unexpectedly heavy plumbing bill. 'I've done as you asked. The *Ministerium* is in retreat and in heavy disarray. Rufus Maleficarus is . . .' He glanced sideways at the hatbox he had requisitioned from the boudoir of Lady Misericorde. 'Dealt with. The problem has not been permanently resolved, however. Only three senior members of the *Ministerium* are dead; the rest of the organisation remains extant. And, most important, their sponsor, Orfilia Ninuka, also known as the Red Queen, also known as'—he paused for effect—'Lady Misericorde the Necromantrix . . .'

There were no gasps, but a few jaws dropped, which was good enough.

'. . . remains alive and at large. She is the greatest threat both to the world in general and specifically to each of your groups. I know from recent experience that she takes her revenge very seriously. You have all now opposed her and thereby aroused her opprobrium. You should guard yourselves carefully.'

'And what about us?' Miss Virginia Montgomery stepped forward, damply. She appeared have taken a bath while clothed. 'We lost Daisy, two 'mopters, and now you're telling us we have a witch with a grudge on our tails, too?'

Cabal winced. 'Necromancers are not witches . . .' he began.

'You lost another entomopter?' interrupted Horst. 'Which one was it?'

'Mine,' she said. 'The *Spirit of '76* had her last hurrah. It was a good one, though.'

'But you're all right?' said Horst, looking at her from head to foot searching for injuries.

'I'm fine. My bird's a wreck, though.'

'Well, perhaps this will help,' said Horst, and produced a box from his pocket.

Miss Virginia accepted it, a little suspiciously. She opened it to reveal a mass of small items of jewellery: earrings, brooches, rings, pendants. This solicited a gasp where the revelation that Lady Misericorde and Lady Ninuka were one and the same person had not, slightly to Cabal's irritation.

'I found them in Misericorde's . . . *Ninuka's* dressing table,' he said. 'They may be costume jewellery for all I know.'

'Lady Ninuka,' said Cabal pointedly, 'would sooner wear an inexpertly tattooed mandrill's arse on her person as costume jewellery. Those are real, I'm sure of it.'

'Will that be enough to buy you a new entomopter?' asked Horst.

'Oh, yeah.' Miss Virginia Montgomery closed the box and put it away. She smiled lopsidedly at Horst and nodded. 'Oh, yeah.'

'As for her revenge, you should remain alert, but I suspect she regards you as hirelings, and thereby beneath her attention,' said Cabal. He considered his words. 'I trust you take no offense at being referred to as "hirelings"?'

'If it keeps us out of that lunatic bitch's attention, we are entirely fine with it.'

'*Alors*,' said Henri Palomer, Yellow Inquisitor. 'Madame shows grace under pressure. Speaking of which, there will certainly be a counterattack to reclaim the castle, *mes amis*. We should scour the place for intelligence, and—why not?—any valuables that can fund our further activities, and be quick about it.'

'He's right,' said Atropos Straka. 'We don't have long.' She gave orders to her group and, without further consultation, they moved off into the body of the building.

Concerned that the Sisters of Medea might get all the good stuff, the other societies quickly followed, leaving the Brothers Cabal alone in the hall.

'Should we just steal Alisha's body now?' asked Horst. 'I'm a bit new to the whole body-snatching thing.'

'No,' said Cabal. 'I'll substitute a body in a winding sheet before dawn, if you'll help. One of the shapechangers is about the right build. They can burn it with my blessing.' He clapped Horst's arm reassuringly. 'Let them have their good-byes. Staying on the right side of secret societies is hard work at the best of times without provoking them. Besides, the chemicals I took from Ninuka's laboratory will keep Miss Bartos's body in a perfect state of preservation for a few weeks. I shall have plenty of time to prepare a longer-term solution without alienating our clandestine friends.'

Unconsciously, his hand drifted to the pocket in which he had secreted the book *Presbyter Johannes*.

'I have work to do,' he said. He looked at Horst a little furtively. '*We* have work to do. I can save them, Horst. I can save them both. And I think . . .' He looked at the floor. 'I'm not sure. I don't want to raise hopes.'

'Raise away, brother,' said Horst. 'I could do with a new pastime. Is saving the world always this tiring?'

'I once promised to try and reverse your condition.' He tapped his pocket. 'This may be the key to that.'

Horst did not smile. 'Perhaps,' he said slowly, 'I no longer wish to be just a man anymore. Perhaps I have grown used to my condition. Perhaps . . . I even *enjoy* my condition.'

Now Cabal looked him in the eye. 'Have you?'

Have you? said a small voice in Horst's mind.

Horst laughed, and answered them both. 'No!' He slapped Cabal on the shoulder hard enough to make him stagger. 'Come on, Johannes. You said it yourself; we have work to do. And the sun's not going to stay down forever.'

So, gathering up the few items they had looted from the apartments of Lady Ninuka, and the muttering hatbox, the Brothers Cabal left the confines of Harslaus Castle. There would be trials ahead, they knew. Danger, difficult decisions, horror, and despair awaited them, as they always had. But they had one another, the ingenuity and knowledge of Johannes, the personableness and supernatural powers of Horst, plus the purloined book that might be the key to all their hopes, plus a muttering hatbox to add to Johannes Cabal's growing collection of talking boxes.

Plus, Cabal inwardly admitted, he had swapped a very disappointing nemesis for one worthy of the title. One is often judged by the quality of one's enemies, after all. He was still troubled that Ninuka had gone to such extents to drag him into play for no better reason than revenge, but was beginning to see that he might have misunderstood the method of that revenge. No matter how nice they were in life, vampires are rarely the most moral creatures in death. That was her revenge right there; to bring Cabal's own brother back into the world as a monster. That was why she had gone to the trouble of recruiting Horst rather than one of their home-grown vampires. Of course. Cabal berated himself for ever thinking it might be anything more complicated than that.

She had misjudged Horst sorely, though, and that was all for the good. It might be necessary to deal with Ninuka in the future, but he expected she would be too busy reestablishing her grip on power for the moment to cause him any trouble for at least a couple of years. With the secret societies now very aware of her, he doubted she would be given that time.

All in all, things conceivably might have been better for a jobbing necromancer and his vampiric brother, but they could also have been a great deal worse, and that was grounds for optimism in itself.

Thus, they walked from Harslaus Castle, and entered upon the unknown adventure that awaited them with the pleasurable sense that the unreachable had become the attainable, that the road had an end, and that end was only just out of sight.

AUTHOR'S FURTHER AFTERWORD

There. Not quite as 'Happy ever after' as if you'd paid me any attention and stopped when I told you to, but still nice enough. Now stop. On no account read the final epilogue. Just leave well enough alone. Shoo.

JLH

THE NASTY EPILOGUE

Two thousand feet up, hidden in the scudding cloud, the aeroyacht *Catullus* held station above the action below. The castle had been taken and would be permitted to be left in the hands of the attackers for two hours only. Less, if they showed any sign of trying to burn the place down. Then the Katamenian bandits would counterattack, and the Dee Society et al would be suffered to beat a hasty retreat. After all, their mission was a success. Or so they thought.

In the observation room, Lady Misericorde and Lady Ninuka and the Red Queen all sat together in the same person and watched the fires guttering on the site of battle. She had abandoned the castle immediately after the fight between Horst Cabal and the shapechangers had begun, made her way out by diverse hidden means, and rendezvoused with her faithful lickspittle Encausse, who had taken her to the waiting *Catullus*. Now she watched and she considered matters.

Alsager was dead, which was to be expected, but the loss of almost all his lycanthropes was not. Still, such things happen in war. She would find some more from elsewhere. She had the reins of the *Ministerium* now and there were already agents en route to deal with any recalcitrant minor ministers. By tomorrow she'd have the interior decorators back into the castle, making good the ravages of battle. Using Maleficarus had been a calculated risk; there was always the chance that Cabal would fail and the Ereshkigal Working would be unleashed once more, probably finally and fatally for the world. Not that she cared. She no longer had any fear of death. Hadn't she died once already?

Does he have the book?

She looked at the ebony urn by her side, the coat of arms of Marechal upon it. She knew it didn't really speak. That would be absurd. No, she was insane. That made far more sense.

'I gave him long enough to find it,' she said distractedly.

You're a clever girl.

'Thank you, Daddy.'

ACKNOWLEDGEMENTS

The book you have just read is, of course, all my work and nobody else had a damn thing to do with it. More lily-livered authors might feel constrained to thank their editors (Peter Joseph, and copyeditor Bethany Reis), their agents (Sam Copeland of Rogers, Coleridge & White in the UK and Melissa Chinchillo of Fletcher & Company in the US), and artists (Michael J. Windsor for the cover and Linda "Snugbat" Smith for the chapter heads).

They might even feel some sort of necessity in my position to mention that I borrowed (with permission) the names "Mink Choi" and "Dea Boom" from real folk, because they are excellent names and I wanted to use them (I now return them, and apologies if they got scuffed at all. Thank you, Mink and Dea).

But not me, obviously. This book is entirely a product of my own incandescent genius.

Unless you didn't like it, in which case it's all their fault. Nothing to do with me. It was like that when I got here.

JLH